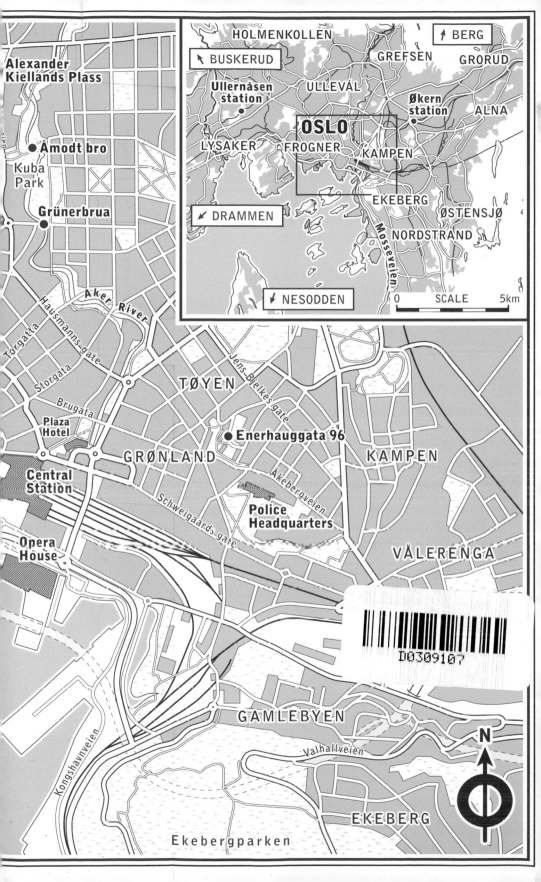

The Son

ALSO BY JO NESBO

The Harry Hole series

The Bat

Cockroaches

The Redbreast

Nemesis

The Devil's Star

The Redeemer

The Snowman

The Leopard

Phantom

Police

Headhunters

Jo Nesbo

THE SON

Translated from the Norwegian by Charlotte Barslund

Harvill *Secker*
LONDON

Published by Harvill Secker 2014

2 4 6 8 10 9 7 5 3 1

First published with the title *Sønnen* in 2014
by H. Aschehoug & Co. (W. Nygaard), Oslo

First published in Great Britain in 2014 by
HARVILL SECKER
Random House
20 Vauxhall Bridge Road
London SW1V 2SA

www.rbooks.co.uk

Addresses for companies within The Random House Group Limited
can be found at: www.randomhouse.co.uk/offices.htm

The Random House Group Limited Reg. No. 954009

A CIP catalogue record for this book is available from the British Library

ISBN 9781846557392 (hardback)
ISBN 9781846557408 (trade paperback)

The Random House Group Limited supports the Forest Stewardship Council® (FSC®),
the leading international forest-certification organisation. Our books carrying the FSC
label are printed on FSC®-certified paper. FSC is the only forest-certification scheme
supported by the leading environmental organisations, including Greenpeace.
Our paper procurement policy can be found at
www.randomhouse.co.uk/environment

Typeset in Scala by Palimpsest Book Production Limited, Falkirk, Stirlingshire

Printed and bound in Great Britain by Clays Ltd, St Ives plc

And he will come again to judge the living and the dead

PART ONE

1

ROVER KEPT HIS EYES ON the white-painted concrete floor in the eleven-square-metre prison cell. He bit down on the slightly too long gold front tooth in his lower jaw. He had reached the hardest part of his confession. The only sound in the cell was his nails scratching the madonna tattoo on his forearm. The boy sitting cross-legged on the bed opposite him had remained silent ever since Rover had entered. He had merely nodded and smiled his blissful Buddha smile, his gaze fixed at a point on Rover's forehead. People called the boy Sonny and said that he had killed two people as a teenager, that his father had been a corrupt police officer and that Sonny had healing hands. It was hard to see if the boy was listening, his green eyes and most of his face were hidden behind his long, matted hair, but that didn't matter. Rover just wanted his sins forgiven and to receive Sonny's distinctive blessing so that tomorrow he could walk out of Staten Maximum Security Prison with the feeling of being a truly cleansed man. Not that Rover was religious, but it could do no harm when he intended to change, to give going straight a real try. Rover took a deep breath.

'I think she was from Belarus. Minsk is in Belarus, innit?' Rover looked up quickly, but the boy made no reply. 'Nestor had nicknamed her Minsk,' Rover said. 'He told me to shoot her.'

The obvious advantage of confessing to someone whose brain was fried was that no name and incident would stick; it was like talking to yourself. This might explain why inmates at Staten preferred this guy to the chaplain or the psychologist.

'Nestor kept her and eight other girls in a cage down in Enerhaugen. East Europeans and Asians. Young. Teenagers. At least I hope they were as old as that. But Minsk was older. Stronger. She escaped. Got as far as Tøyen Park before Nestor's dog caught her. One of those Argentine mastiffs – know what I'm talking about?'

The boy's eyes never moved, but he raised his hand. Found his beard. He started to comb it slowly with his fingers. The sleeve of his filthy, oversized shirt slipped down and revealed scabs and needle marks. Rover went on.

'Bloody big albino dogs. Kills anything its owner points at. And quite a lot he doesn't. Banned in Norway, 'course. A guy out in Rælengen got some from the Czech Republic, breeds them and registers them as white boxers. Me and Nestor went there to buy one when it was a pup. It cost more than fifty grand in cash. The puppy was so cute you wouldn't ever think it . . .' Rover stopped. He knew he was only talking about the dog to put off the inevitable. 'Anyway . . .'

Anyway. Rover looked at the tattoo on his other forearm. A cathedral with two spires. One for each sentence he had served, neither of which had anything to do with today's confession. He used to supply guns to a biker gang and modify some of them in his workshop. He was good at it. Too good. So good that he couldn't remain below the radar forever and he was caught. And so good that, while serving his first sentence, Nestor had taken him under his wing. Nestor had made sure he owned him so that from then on only Nestor would get his hands on the best guns, rather than

4

the biker gang or any other rivals. He had paid him more for a few months' work than Rover could ever hope to earn in a lifetime in his workshop fixing motorbikes. But Nestor had demanded a lot in return. Too much.

'She was lying in the bushes, blood everywhere. She just lay there, dead still, staring up at us. The dog had taken a chunk out of her face – you could see straight to the teeth.' Rover grimaced. Get to the point. 'Nestor said it was time to teach them a lesson, show the other girls what would happen to them. And that Minsk was worthless to him now anyway, given the state of her face . . .' Rover swallowed. 'So he told me to do it. Finish her off. That's how I'd prove my loyalty, you see. I had an old Ruger MK II pistol that I'd done some work on. And I was going to do it. I really was. That wasn't the problem . . .'

Rover felt his throat tighten. He had thought about it so often, gone over those seconds during that night in Tøyen Park, seeing the girl over and over again. Nestor and himself taking the leading roles with the others as silent witnesses. Even the dog had been silent. He had thought about it perhaps a hundred times? A thousand? And yet it wasn't until now, when he said the words out loud for the first time, that he realised that it hadn't been a dream, that it really *had* happened. Or rather it was as if his body hadn't accepted it until now. That was why his stomach was churning. Rover breathed deeply through his nose to quell the nausea.

'But I couldn't do it. Even though I knew she was gonna die. They had the dog at the ready and I was thinking that me, I'd have preferred a bullet. But it was as if the trigger was locked in position. I just couldn't pull it.'

The young man seemed to be nodding faintly. Either in response to what Rover was telling him or to music only he could hear.

'Nestor said we didn't have all day, we were in a public park after all. So he took out a small, curved knife from a leg holster, stepped forward, grabbed her by the hair, pulled her up and just seemed to swing the knife in front of her throat. As if gutting a fish. Blood spurted out three, four times, then she was empty. But d'you know what I remember most of all? The dog. How it started howling at the sight of all that blood.'

Rover leaned forward in the chair with his elbows on his knees. He covered his ears with his hands and rocked back and forth.

'And I did nothing. I just stood there, looking on. I did sod all. While they wrapped her in a blanket and carried her to the car, I just watched. We drove her to the woods, to Østmarksetra. Lifted her out and rolled her down the slope towards Ulsrudsvannet. Lots of people take their dogs for walks there so she was found the next day. The point was, Nestor wanted her to be found, d'you get me? He wanted pictures in the papers of what had happened to her. So he could show them to the other girls.'

Rover removed his hands from his ears.

'I stopped sleeping; every time I closed my eyes I had nightmares. The girl with the missing cheek smiled at me and bared all her teeth. So I went to see Nestor and told him I wanted out. Said I'd had enough of filing down Uzis and Glocks, that I wanted to go back to fixing motorbikes. Live a quiet life, not worry about the cops the whole time. Nestor said that was OK, he'd probably sussed that I didn't have it in me to be a tough guy. But he made it very clear what would happen to me if I talked. I thought we were sorted. I turned down every job I was offered even though I still had some decent Uzis lying around. But I kept thinking that something was brewing. That I would be bumped off. So I was almost relieved when the cops came and I got put away. I thought I'd be safer in prison. They got me on an old case – I was only an accessory, but they had arrested two guys who both said that I had supplied them with weapons. I confessed to it on the spot.'

Rover laughed hard. He started to cough. He leaned back in his chair.

'In eighteen hours I'm getting out of this place. Haven't got a clue what's waiting for me on the outside. But I know that Nestor knows I'm coming out even though I'm being released four weeks early. He knows everything that goes on in here and with the police, I'm sure of it. He has eyes and ears everywhere. So what I'm thinking is, if he wanted me dead, he might as well have me killed in here rather than wait for me to get out. What do you think?'

Rover waited. Silence. The boy didn't look as if he thought anything at all.

'Whatever happens,' Rover said, 'a little blessing can't hurt, can it?'

It was as if a light came on in Sonny's eyes at the word 'blessing' and he raised his right hand to signal that Rover should come closer and kneel. Rover knelt on the prayer rug in front of the bed. Franck didn't let any of the other inmates have rugs on the floor in their cells – it was a part of the Swiss model they used at Staten: no superfluous items in the cells. The number of personal possessions was limited to twenty. If you wanted a pair of shoes, you would have to give up two pairs of underpants or two books. Rover looked up at Sonny's face. The boy moistened his dry, scaly lips with the tip of his tongue. His voice was surprisingly light even though the words came slowly, but his diction was perfectly clear.

'All earthly and heavenly gods have mercy on you and forgive your sins. You will die, but the soul of the penitent sinner shall be led to Paradise. Amen.'

Rover bowed his head. He felt the boy's hand on his shaved head. Sonny was left-handed, but in this case it didn't take a genius to work out that he had a shorter life expectancy than most right-handed people. The overdose could happen tomorrow or in ten years – who knew? But Rover didn't think for one minute that the boy's hand was healing like people said. Nor did he really believe this business with the blessing. So why was he here? Well, religion was like fire insurance; you never really thought you'd need it, so when people said that the boy was prepared to take your sins upon himself and didn't want anything in return, why not say yes to some peace of mind? What Rover did wonder was how someone like Sonny could have killed in cold blood. It made no sense to him. Perhaps it was like the old saying: The devil has many disguises.

'Salaam alaikum,' the voice said and the hand was lifted.

Rover stayed where he was with his head lowered. Probed the smooth backside of the gold tooth with his tongue. Was he ready now? Ready to meet his Maker if that was his fate? He raised his head.

'I know you never ask for anything in return, but . . .'

He looked at the boy's bare foot which he had tucked under. He saw the needle marks in the big vein on the instep. 'I did my last stretch in Botsen and getting hold of drugs in there was easy, no problem. Botsen isn't a maximum security prison, though. They say Franck has made it impossible to smuggle anything into Staten, but . . .' Rover stuck his hand in his pocket, '. . . but that's not quite true.'

He pulled something out. It was the size of a mobile phone, a gold-plated object shaped like a pistol. Rover pressed the trigger. A small flame shot out of the muzzle. 'Seen one of these before? Yeah, I bet you have. The officers who searched me when I came here certainly had. They told me they were selling smuggled cigarettes on the cheap if I was interested. So they let me keep the lighter. I don't suppose they'd read my rap sheet. No one bothers doing their job properly these days – makes you wonder how anything in this country ever gets done.'

Rover weighed the lighter in his hand.

'Eight years ago I made two of these. I ain't boasting if I tell you that nobody in Norway could have done a better job. I'd been contacted by a middleman who told me his client wanted a gun he would never have to hide, a gun that didn't look like a gun. So I came up with this. It's funny how people's minds work. At first they think it's a gun, obvs. But once you've shown them that you can use it as a lighter, they forget all about it being a gun. They still think it could also be a toothbrush or a screwdriver. But not a gun, no way. So . . .'

Rover turned a screw on the underside of the handle.

'It takes two 9mm bullets. I call it the Happy Couple Killer.' He aimed the barrel at the young man. 'One for you, sweetheart . . .' Then he pointed it at his own temple. 'And one for me . . .' Rover's laughter sounded strangely lonely in the small cell.

'Anyway. I was only supposed to make one; the client didn't want anyone else to know the secret behind my little invention. But I made another one. And I took it with me for protection, in case Nestor decided to try to kill me while I was inside. But as I'm getting out tomorrow and I won't need it any more, it's yours now. And here . . .'

Rover pulled out a packet of cigarettes from his other pocket. 'Because it'll look weird if you have a lighter, but no cigarettes, right?' He then took out a yellowed business card saying 'Rover's Motorcycle Workshop' and slipped it into the cigarette packet.

'Here's my address in case you ever have a motorbike that needs fixing. Or want to get yourself one hell of an Uzi. Like I said, I still have some lying—'

The door opened outwards and a voice thundered: 'Get out, Rover!'

Rover turned round. The trousers of the prison officer in the doorway were sagging due to the large bunch of keys that dangled from his belt, although this was partly obscured by his belly, which spilled over the lining like rising dough. 'His Holiness has a visitor.

9

A close relative, you could say.' He guffawed with laughter and turned to the man behind him. 'No offence, eh, Per?'

Rover slipped the gun and the cigarette packet under the duvet on the boy's bed and took one last look at him.

Then he left quickly.

The prison chaplain attempted a smile while he automatically straightened his ill-fitting dog collar. *A close relative. No offence.* He felt like spitting into the prison officer's fat, grinning face, but instead he nodded to the inmate emerging from the cell and pretended to recognise him. Glanced at the tattoos on his forearms. The madonna and a cathedral. But no, over the years the faces and the tattoos had become too numerous for him to distinguish between them.

The chaplain entered. He could smell incense. Or something that reminded him of incense. Like drugs being cooked.

'Hello, Sonny.'

The young man on the bed didn't look up, but he nodded slowly. Per Vollan took it to mean that his presence had been registered, acknowledged. Approved.

He sat down on the chair and experienced a slight discomfort when he felt the warmth from the previous occupant. He placed the Bible he had brought with him on the bed next to the boy.

'I put flowers on your parents' grave today,' he said. 'I know you haven't asked me to, but . . .'

Per Vollan tried to catch the boy's eye. He had two sons himself; both were grown up and had left the Vollan family home. As Vollan himself had. The difference was that his sons were always welcome back.

In court a witness for the defence, a teacher, had testified that Sonny had been a star pupil, a talented wrestler, popular, always helpful, indeed the boy had even expressed a desire to become a police officer like his father. But ever since his father had been found dead next to a suicide note in which he confessed to corruption Sonny hadn't been seen at school. The chaplain tried to imagine the shame of the fifteen-year-old boy. Tried to imagine his own sons' shame if they ever found out what their father had done. He straightened his dog collar again.

'Thank you,' Sonny said.

Per thought how strangely young Sonny seemed. Because he must be close to thirty by now. Yes. Sonny had served twelve years and he was eighteen when he was sent down. Perhaps it was the drugs that had preserved him, preventing him from ageing so that only his hair and beard grew while his innocent baby eyes continued to gaze at the world in wonder. A wicked world. God knows it was evil. Per Vollan had been a prison chaplain for over forty years and seen the world grow more and more sinful. Evil spread like cancer, it made healthy cells sick, poisoned them with its vampire bite and recruited them to do its work of corruption. And once bitten no one ever escaped. No one.

'How are you, Sonny? Did you enjoy being out on day release? Did you get to see the sea?'

No reply.

Per Vollan cleared his throat. 'The prison officer said you got to see the sea. You might have read in the papers that a woman was found murdered the next day, not far from where you were. She was found in bed, in her own home. Her head had been . . . well. All the details are in here . . .' He tapped his finger on the Bible. 'The officer has already filed a report saying you ran away while you were at the sea and that he found you by the road one hour later. That you refused to account for your whereabouts. It's important that you don't say anything that contradicts his statement, do you understand? As usual you'll say as little as possible. All right? Sonny?'

Per Vollan finally succeeded in making eye contact with the boy. His expression told Per little about what was going on inside his head, but he felt fairly certain that Sonny Lofthus would follow orders and not say anything unnecessary to the police or the public prosecutor. All he had to do was utter a light, soft 'Guilty' when he was asked how he pleaded. Though it sounded paradoxical, Vollan occasionally sensed a direction, a force of will, a survival instinct that distinguished this junkie from the others, from those who had always been in free fall, who had never had any other plans, who had been heading for the gutter all along. This willpower might express itself as a sudden flash of insight, a question that revealed he had paid attention all along and seen and heard everything. Or in the way he might suddenly stand up, with a coordination, balance and flexibility you didn't see in other habitual drug users. While at other times, like now, he seemed to register nothing at all.

Vollan squirmed in his chair.

'Of course this means no more trips on the outside for you for quite a while. But you don't like the outside anyway, do you? And you did get to see the sea.'

'It was a river. Did the husband do it?'

The chaplain jumped. As when something unexpected breaks through black water right in front of you. 'I don't know. Is that important?'

No reply. Vollan sighed. He felt nauseous again. Recently it seemed to come and go. Perhaps he should make a doctor's appointment and get it checked out.

'Don't you worry about that, Sonny. Just remember that on the outside people like you have to scavenge all day to get their next fix. While in here everything is taken care of. And don't forget that time passes. Once you finish serving out your old sentences, you'll be no use to them, but with this murder you can extend your detention.'

'So it was the husband. Is he rich?'

Vollan pointed to the Bible. 'In here you'll find a description of the house you entered. It's big and well furnished. But the alarm that was supposed to guard all this wealth wasn't turned on; the front door wasn't even locked. The family's name is Morsand. The ship-owner with the eyepatch. Seen him in the papers, have you?'

'Yes.'

'Have you? I didn't think that you—'

'Yes, I killed her. Yes, I'll read up on how I did it.'

Per Vollan exhaled. 'Good. There are certain details about how she was killed which you ought to memorise.'

'Right.'

'She was . . . the top of her head was severed. You used a saw. Do you understand?'

The words were followed by a long silence which Per Vollan considered filling with vomit. Throwing up was preferable to exploiting the boy. He looked at him. What determined the outcome of a life? A series of random events you had no control over or did some cosmic gravity pull everything in the direction it was predestined to go? He loosened his strangely uncomfortable dog collar, suppressed his nausea and steeled himself. Remembered what was at stake.

He got up. 'If you need to get in touch with me I'm currently staying at the Ila Centre on Alexander Kiellands Plass.'

He saw the boy's quizzical look.

'Just for the time being, you understand.' He laughed quickly. 'My wife threw me out and as I know the people who run the centre, they—'

He stopped abruptly. Suddenly he realised why so many of the inmates went to the young man to talk. It was the silence. The beckoning vacuum of someone who simply listens without reaction or judgement. Who extracts your words and your secrets from you without doing anything at all. He had striven for that ability as a chaplain all his life, but it was as if the inmates sensed that he had an agenda. They didn't know what it was, only that there was something he wanted by knowing their secrets. Access to their souls and later a possible recruitment prize in heaven.

The chaplain saw that the boy had opened the Bible. It was such a simple trick, it was comical; the cut-outs in the pages created a compartment. Inside were folded papers with the information Sonny needed in order to confess. And three small bags of heroin.

2

ARILD FRANCK BARKED A BRIEF 'Enter!' without taking his eyes off the document on his desk.

He heard the door open. Ina, his secretary in the front office, had already announced his visitor and, for a split second, Arild Franck considered asking her to tell the chaplain that he was busy. It wouldn't even be a lie; he had a meeting with the Commissioner at Politihuset, Oslo Police's headquarters, in half an hour. But recently Per Vollan hadn't been as stable as they needed him to be and there was no harm in double-checking that he could still hold it together. There was no room for screw-ups in this case, not for any of them.

'Don't bother sitting down,' Arild Franck said, signing the document and getting up. 'We'll have to walk and talk.'

He headed for the door, took his uniform cap from the coat stand and heard the chaplain's shuffling feet behind him. Arild Franck told Ina that he would be back in an hour and a half and pressed his index finger against the sensor at the door to the stairwell. The prison was on two floors and there was no lift. Lifts equalled shafts which equalled any number of escape routes and had to be closed off in the event of fire. And a fire and its ensuing evacuation chaos was just one of many methods ingenious inmates had used to break out of other prisons. For the same reason, all electric cables, fuse boxes and water pipes had been laid so they were inaccessible to the inmates, either outside the building itself or cemented into the walls. Here nothing had been left to chance. *He* had left nothing to chance. He had sat with the architects and international prison experts when they drew up the blueprint for Staten. Admittedly the Lenzburg Prison in the Aargau canton in Switzerland had provided the inspiration: hypermodern, but simple and with an emphasis on security and efficiency rather than comfort. But it was him, Arild Franck, who was responsible for its creation. Staten was Arild Franck and vice versa. So why had the board, in their infinite wisdom, damn them all to hell, made him only assistant prison governor and appointed that moron from Haldern Prison as governor? Yes, Franck was something of a rough diamond and, no, he wasn't the kind of guy who would suck up to politicians by jumping for joy at every bright new idea about how to reform the prison system while the previous reforms had yet to be implemented. But he knew how to do his job – keeping people locked up without them getting ill, dying or becoming noticeably worse human beings as a result. He was loyal to those who deserved his loyalty and he looked after his own. That was more than could be said for his superiors in this rotten-to-the-core, politically motivated hierarchy. Before he was deliberately overlooked for the post of governor, Arild Franck had hoped for a small bust as a memorial in the foyer when he retired – though his wife had expressed the opinion that his bull neck, bulldog face and straggly comb-over wouldn't suit a bust. But if people failed to reward your achievements, his view on the matter was you just had to help yourself.

'I can't keep doing this, Arild,' Per Vollan said behind him as they walked down the corridor.

'Doing what?'

'I'm a chaplain. What we're doing to the boy – making him take the fall for something he didn't do. Serve time for a husband who—'

'Hush.'

Outside the door to the control room, or 'the bridge' as Franck liked to call it, they passed an old man who paused his swabbing of the floor and gave a friendly nod to Franck. Johannes was the oldest man in the prison and an inmate after Franck's own heart, a gentle soul who sometime in the previous century had been picked up – almost by chance – for drug smuggling, had never hurt a fly since and over the years had become so institutionalised, conditioned and pacified that the only thing he dreaded was the day he was released. Sadly, inmates like him didn't represent a challenge for a prison like Staten.

'Is your conscience troubling you, Vollan?'

'Yes, yes, it is, Arild.'

Franck couldn't remember exactly when his staff had started addressing their superiors by their first names, or when prison governors started wearing plain clothes rather than uniforms. In some jails the prison officers wore plain clothes as well. During a riot at the Francisco de Mar Prison in São Paulo, officers had shot at their own colleagues in the tear-gas smoke because they couldn't tell staff from inmates.

'I want out,' the chaplain implored him.

'Is that right?' Franck was jogging down the stairs. He was in good shape for a man less than ten years away from retirement, because he worked out. A forgotten virtue in an industry where obesity was the rule rather than the exception. And hadn't he coached the local swimming team when his daughter used to compete? Done his bit for the community in his spare time, given something back to this country which had given so much to so many? So how dare they overlook him. 'And how is your conscience when it comes

to those young boys we've evidence you've been abusing, Vollan?'
Franck pressed his index finger against the sensor at the next door;
this took them to a corridor which to the west led to the cells, and
to the east, the staff changing rooms and the exit to the car park.

'I suggest you think of it as Sonny Lofthus atoning for your sins
as well, Vollan.'

Another door, another sensor. Franck pressed his finger against
it. He loved this invention which he had copied from the Obihiro
Prison in Kushiro, Japan. Instead of issuing keys that could be lost,
copied or misused, the fingerprints of everyone who was authorised
to pass through the doors were entered into a database. Not only
had they eliminated the risk of careless handling of the keys, they
also maintained a record of who had passed through which door
and when. They had installed surveillance cameras as well, of course,
but faces could be concealed. Not so with fingerprints. The door
opened with a sigh and they entered a lock, a small room with a
barred metal door at either end where one door had to be closed
before the other would open.

'I'm saying that I can't do it any more, Arild.'

Franck raised a finger to his lips. In addition to the surveillance
cameras which covered practically the entire prison, the locks had
been fitted with a two-way communication system so that you
could contact the control room if, for some reason, you got stuck.
They exited the lock and continued towards the changing rooms
where there were showers and a locker for clothing and personal
property for each staff member. The fact that the assistant prison
governor had a master key that opened every locker was something
Franck had decided his staff didn't need to know. Quite the opposite
in fact.

'I thought you knew who you were dealing with here,' Franck
said. 'You can't just quit. For these people loyalty is a matter of life
and death.'

'I know,' Per Vollan said; his breathing had acquired an ugly rasping. 'But I'm talking about eternal life and death.'

Franck stopped in front of the exit door and glanced quickly at the lockers to his left to make sure that they were alone.

'You know the risk?'

'As God is my witness, I won't breathe a word to anyone. I want you to use those exact words, Arild. Tell them I'll be as silent as the grave. I just want out. Please, help me?'

Franck looked down. At the sensor. Out. There were only two ways out. This one, the back way, and the other through reception at the front entrance. No ventilation shafts, no fire exits, no sewer pipes with dimensions just wide enough to allow a human body to squeeze through.

'Maybe,' he said and placed his finger on the sensor. A small red light at the top of the door handle flashed to indicate the database was being searched. It went off and a small green light appeared in its place. He pushed open the door. They were blinded by the bright sunlight and put on their sunglasses as they crossed the large car park. 'I'll tell them you want out,' Franck said and took out his car keys while he peered at the security booth. It was staffed with two armed guards 24/7 and both the roads in and out had steel barriers which even Franck's new Porsche Cayenne could not force. Possibly one could do it with a Hummer H1 which he had quite fancied buying, but that car would have been too wide since they had made the entrance narrow precisely to stop larger vehicles. It was also with large vehicles in mind that he had placed steel barricades within the six-metre-high fence which surrounded the entire prison. Franck had asked to have it electrified, but the planning authorities had turned down his application on the grounds that Staten was located in central Oslo and innocent civilians might hurt themselves. Innocent, ha – if anyone wanted to touch the fence from the street, they would first have to scale a five-metre-high wall with barbed wire on top.

'Where are you going, by the way?'

'Alexander Kiellands Plass,' Per Vollan said hopefully.

'Sorry,' Arild said. 'It's not on my way.'

'Not a problem, the bus stops right outside.'

'Good. I'll be in touch.'

The assistant prison governor got into his car and drove up to the security booth. The rules stated that all vehicles, including his own, must be stopped and the occupants checked. Only now, when the guards had seen him exit the prison building and get into the car, did they raise the barrier and let him pass. Franck returned the guards' salute. He stopped at the traffic lights by the main road. He glanced up at his beloved Staten in the rear-view mirror. It wasn't perfect, but it came close. He blamed the planning committee, the new, inane regulations from the ministry and the semi-corrupt human resources for any shortcomings. All he had ever wanted was the best for everyone, for all of Oslo's hard-working, honest citizens who deserved a safe existence and a certain standard of living. So, OK, things could have been different. He didn't like having to go about things this way. But like he always said to the learners in the pool: you sink or swim, no one is going to do you any favours. Then his thoughts returned to what lay ahead. He had a message to deliver. And he had no doubt as to the outcome.

The lights changed to green and he pressed the accelerator.

3

PER VOLLAN WALKED THROUGH THE park by Alexander Kiellands Plass. It had been a soaking wet and unseasonably cold July, but now the sun was back and the park was just as intensely green as on a spring day. Summer had returned, people around him sat with upturned faces and closed eyes soaking up the sunshine as if it was about to run out; there was a rumbling of skateboards and a clunking of six-packs of beers on their way to barbecues in the city's green spaces and balconies. There were, however, some who were even more delighted that the temperature had risen. People who looked as if the traffic around the park had coated them in fumes: shabby figures huddled up on benches or around the fountain, who called out to him in hoarse, happy voices that sounded like seagulls screeching. He waited for the green light at the junction of Uelandsgate and Waldemar Thranes gate while trucks and buses swept past him. He looked at the facades on the other side of the street as they flashed in front of him through the gaps in the traffic. Plastic sheeting covered the windows of the notorious pub, Tranen, which had quenched the thirst of the city's most parched residents since its construction in 1921 – the last thirty years accompanied by

Arnie 'Skiffle Joe' Norse who dressed in a cowboy costume and rode a unicycle while he played guitar and sang accompanied by his band consisting of an old, blind organist and a Thai woman on tambourine and car horn. Per Vollan's eyes shifted to the front of a building where cast-iron letters spelling out 'Ila Pensjonat' had been cemented into the facade. During the war the building had housed unmarried mothers. Now it was a residential facility for the city's most vulnerable addicts. Those who didn't want to get clean. Last stop before the end.

Per Vollan crossed the street, stopped outside the entrance to the centre, rang the bell and looked into the eye of the camera. He heard the door buzz open and he entered. For old times' sake the centre had offered him a room for two weeks. That was a month ago.

'Hi, Per,' said the young, brown-eyed woman who came down to open the barred gate to the stairs. Someone had damaged the lock so that the keys no longer worked from the outside. 'The cafe is shut now, but you're in time for dinner if you go in right away.'

'Thanks, Martha, but I'm not hungry.'

'You look tired.'

'I walked all the way from Staten.'

'Oh? I thought there was a bus?'

She had started climbing back up the stairs and he shuffled along after her.

'I had some thinking to do,' he said.

'Someone came by earlier asking for you.'

Per froze. 'Who?'

'Didn't ask. Could have been the police.'

'What makes you think that?'

'They seemed very keen to get hold of you, so I thought it might be about an inmate you know. Something like that.'

Already, Per thought, they've come for me already.

'Do you believe in anything, Martha?'

She turned on the stairs. Smiled. Per thought that a young man might fall deeply in love with that smile.

'Like God and Jesus?' Martha asked, pushing open the door into reception which was a hatch in a wall with an office behind it.

'Like fate. Like chance versus cosmic gravity.'

'I believe in Mad Greta,' Martha muttered as she leafed through some papers.

'Ghosts aren't—'

'Inger said she heard a baby cry yesterday.'

'Inger is highly strung, Martha.'

She stuck her head out of the hatch. 'We need to have a talk, Per . . .'

He sighed. 'I know. You're full and—'

'The centre in Sporveisgata called today to say the fire means they'll be closed for another two months at least. More than forty of our own residents are currently in shared rooms. We can't go on like this. They steal from each other and then they start fighting. It's only a matter of time before someone gets hurt.'

'It's all right; I won't be here very much longer.'

Martha tilted her head to one side and looked at him quizzically. 'Why won't she let you sleep in the house? How many years have you been married? Forty, is it?'

'Thirty-eight. She owns the house and it's . . . complicated.' Per smiled wearily.

He left her and walked down the corridor. Music was pounding behind two of the doors. Amphetamine. It was Monday, the benefits office was open after the weekend and trouble was brewing everywhere. He unlocked his door. The tiny, shabby room with a single bed and a wardrobe cost 6,000 kroner per month. You could rent a whole flat outside Oslo for that kind of money.

He sat down on the bed and stared out of the dusty window.

The traffic hummed sleepily outside. The sun shone through the flimsy curtains. A fly was fighting for its life on the windowsill. It would die soon. That was life. Not death, but life. Death was nothing. How many years was it since he had come to that conclusion? That everything apart from death, everything he preached about, was nothing but a defence people had created against their fear of death. And yet none of what he used to believe meant anything at all. What we humans think we know is nothing compared to what we need to believe to numb the fear and pain. Then he came full circle. He regained his faith in a forgiving God and life after death. He believed it now, more than ever. He took out a pad from under a newspaper and started writing.

Per Vollan didn't have much to write. A few sentences on a single sheet of paper, that was all. He crossed out his own name on an envelope which had contained a letter from Alma's lawyer briefly stating what share of the matrimonial property they thought Per was entitled to. Which wasn't much.

The chaplain looked in the mirror, adjusted his dog collar, put on his long coat and left.

Martha wasn't at reception. Inger took the envelope and promised to deliver it.

The sun was lower in the sky now; the day was retreating. He walked through the park while out of the corner of his eye he registered how everything and everyone played their parts without obvious errors. No one rose from a bench a little too quickly as he passed, no cars pulled out discreetly from the kerb when he changed his mind and decided to walk along Sannergata towards the river. But they were there. Behind a window which reflected a peaceful summer evening, in the casual glance of a passer-by, in the chill in the shadows that crept out from the eastside of the houses and banished the sunlight as they gained territory. And Per Vollan thought that his whole life had been like this; a constant, pointless, vacillating struggle between the darkness and the light, which never seemed to result in victory for either side. Or had it? With every day the darkness encroached a little more. They were heading for the long night.

He increased his speed.

4

SIMON KEFAS RAISED THE COFFEE cup to his mouth. From the kitchen table he could look out at the small garden in front of their house in Fagerliveien in Disen. It had rained overnight and the grass was still glistening in the morning sunlight. He thought he could actually see it grow. It meant another outing with the lawn-mower. A noisy, manual, sweat- and swear-inducing activity, but that was all good. Else had asked him why he didn't get an electric lawnmower like all their neighbours. His answer was simple: money. It was an answer which had ended most discussions when he was growing up in this house, as well as in the neighbourhood. But that was back when ordinary people lived here: teachers, hairdressers, taxi drivers, public sector workers. Or police officers, like him. Not that the current residents were anything special, but they worked in advertising or IT, they were journalists, doctors, had agencies for faddy products or had inherited enough money to buy one of the small, idyllic houses, pushing up the prices and moving the neigh-bourhood up the social ladder.

'What are you thinking about?' asked Else, who was standing behind his chair, stroking his hair. It was thinning noticeably; lit from above you could make out his scalp. But she claimed to like it. Liked that he looked what he was: a police officer close to retirement. Liked that she, too, would grow old one day. Even though he had twenty years' head start on her. One of their new neighbours, a moderately famous film producer, had mistaken her for Simon's daughter. That was all right with him.

'I'm thinking about how lucky I am,' he said. 'Because I have you. Because I have this.'

She kissed him on the top of his head. He could feel her lips right against his skin. Last night he had dreamed that he could give up his sight for her. And when he had woken up and not been able to see, he had – for a second before he realised that it was due to the eye mask he wore to block out the early-morning sun in summer – been a happy man.

The doorbell rang.

'That'll be Edith,' Else said. 'I'll go and change.'

She opened the door to her sister and disappeared upstairs.

'Hi, Uncle Simon!'

'Well, look who it is,' Simon said as he gazed at the boy's beaming face.

Edith came into the kitchen. 'Sorry, Simon, he kept pestering me to get here early so he would have time to try on your cap.'

'Of course,' Simon said. 'But why aren't you at school today, Mats?'

'Teacher-training day,' Edith sighed. 'Schools don't know what a nightmare it is for single mums.'

'Then it's especially kind of you to offer to drive Else.'

'Not at all. He's only in Oslo today and tomorrow, as far as I understand.'

'Who is?' Mats asked as he pulled and tugged at his uncle's arm to get him to move from his chair.

'An American doctor who is brilliant at eye operations,' Simon said, pretending to be even stiffer than he really was as he allowed himself be pulled to his feet. 'Come on, let's go and see if we can find that police cap. Help yourself to some coffee, Edith.'

Simon and Mats went out into the hallway and the boy squealed with delight when he saw the black-and-white police cap which his uncle took down from the wardrobe shelf. But he grew silent and reverent when Simon placed the cap on his head. They stood in front of the mirror. The boy pointed to the reflection of his uncle and made shooting noises.

'Who are you shooting at?' his uncle asked him.

'Villains,' the boy spluttered. 'Bang! Bang!'

'Let's call it target practice,' Simon said. 'Even the police can't shoot villains without permission.'

'Yes, you can! Bang! Bang!'

'If we do that, Mats, we go to jail.'

'We do?' The boy stopped and gave his uncle a baffled look. 'Why? We're the police.'

'Because if we shoot someone we could otherwise have arrested that makes us the bad guys.'

'But . . . when we've caught them, then we can shoot them, can't we?'

Simon laughed. 'No. Then it's up to the judge to decide how long they'll go to prison.'

'I thought you decided that, Uncle Simon.'

Simon could see the disappointment in the boy's eyes. 'Let me tell you something, Mats. I'm glad I don't have to decide that. I'm glad that all I have to do is catch criminals. Because that's the fun part of the job.'

Mats narrowed one eye and the cap tipped backwards. 'Uncle Simon . . .'

'Yes?'

'Why don't you and Auntie Else have any kids?'

Simon stepped behind Mats, placed his hands on the boy's shoulders and smiled at him in the mirror.

'We don't need kids, we've got you. Haven't we?'

Mats looked pensively at his uncle for a couple of seconds. Then his face lit up. 'Yeah!'

Simon stuck his hand in his pocket to answer his mobile which had started to buzz.

It was a colleague. Simon listened.

'Where by Aker River?' he asked.

'Past Kuba, by the art college. There's a pedestrian bridge—'

'I know where it is. I'll be there in thirty minutes.'

He put on his shoes, tied the laces and pulled on his jacket.

'Else!' he called out.

'Yes?' Her face appeared at the top of the stairs. It struck him once again how beautiful she was. Her long hair flowing like a red river around her petite face. The freckles on and around her small nose. And it occurred to him that those freckles would almost certainly still be there when he was gone. His next thought, which he tried to suppress, followed swiftly: who would take care of her then? He knew that she was unlikely to be able to see him from where she was standing, she was only pretending. He cleared his throat.

'I've got to go, sweetheart. Will you give me a call and tell me what the doctor said?'

'Yes. Drive carefully.'

Two middle-aged men walked through the park popularly known as Kuba. Most people thought the name had something to do with Cuba, possibly because political rallies were often held here and because Grünerløkka was once regarded as a working-class neighbourhood. You had to have lived there for many years to know that there used to be a large gas holder here and that it had had a framework shaped like a cube. The men crossed the pedestrian bridge which led to the old factory that was now an art college. Lovers had attached padlocks with dates and initials to the bars of the railings of the bridge. Simon stopped and looked at one of them. He had loved Else for ten years, every single day of the over three and a half thousand they had been together. There would never be another woman in his life and he didn't need a symbolic padlock to know that. And neither did she; hopefully she would outlive him for so many years that there would be time for new men in her life. And that was all good.

From where they were standing he could see Åmodt Bro, a modest little bridge that crossed a modest little river which divided this modest little capital into east and west. Once upon a time, a long time ago, when he was young and foolish, he had dived from this very bridge into the river. A drunken troika of three lads, two of them with an unshakeable faith in themselves and their prospects. Two of them convinced that they alone were the best of the three. The third one, Simon, had realised long ago that he couldn't compete with his friends when it came to intelligence, strength, social skills or appeal to women. But he was the bravest. Or, to put it another way, the most willing to take risks. And diving into polluted water didn't require intellect or physical skill, only recklessness. Simon Kefas had often thought that it was pessimism that had prompted him to gamble with a future he didn't value very much, an innate knowledge that he had less to lose than other people. He had balanced on the railings while his friends had screamed for him not to do it, that he was mad. And then he had jumped. From the bridge, out of life, into the wonderful, spinning roulette wheel which is fate. He had plunged through the water which had no surface, only white foam and, under that, an icy embrace. And in that embrace there was silence, solicitude and peace. When he resurfaced, unharmed, they had cheered. Simon, too. Even though he

30

had felt a vague disappointment at being back. It was amazing what a broken heart could drive a young man to do.

Simon shook off the memories and focused on the waterfall between the two bridges. More specifically on the figure that had been left there like a photograph, frozen in mid-fall.

'We think he floated downstream,' said the crime scene officer who was standing next to him. 'And then his clothes got caught on something sticking out of the water. The river is usually so shallow there that you can wade across it.'

'All right,' Simon said, sucking the tobacco in his mouth and cocking his head. The figure hung straight down with its arms out to the sides and the cascading water formed a white halo around the head and body. It reminded him of Else's hair. The other CSOs had finally got their boat into the water and were working on freeing the body.

'A beer says it's suicide.'

'I think you're wrong, Elias,' Simon said and hooked a finger under his upper lip to extract the *snus*. He was about to drop it into the water below, but he stopped himself. Different times. He looked around for a bin.

'So you won't bet a beer?'

'No, Elias, I won't.'

'Oh, sorry, I forgot . . .' The CSO looked embarrassed.

'That's all right,' Simon said and left. He nodded in passing to a tall, blonde woman in a black skirt and a short jacket. If it hadn't been for the police warrant card dangling around her neck he would have taken her to be a bank clerk. He chucked the *snus* into the green rubbish bin at the end of the bridge and walked down to the riverbank, scanning the ground with his eyes as he did.

'Chief Inspector Kefas?'

Elias looked up. The woman who had addressed him was the

archetypal Scandinavian female as imagined by foreigners. He suspected she thought she was too tall, which was why she stooped slightly and wore flat shoes.

'No, that's not me. Who are you?'

'Kari Adel.' She held up a warrant card around her neck. 'I've just joined the Homicide Squad. They told me I would find him here.'

'Welcome. What do you want with Simon?'

'He's supposed to mentor me.'

'Lucky you,' Elias said and pointed to the man walking along the river. 'That's him over there.'

'What's he looking for?'

'Evidence.'

'But surely the evidence will be in the river where the body is and not downstream.'

'Yes, so he's assuming we've already searched that area. And we have.'

'The other CSOs say it looks like a suicide.'

'Yes, I made the mistake of trying to bet a beer with him on it.'

'Mistake?'

'He has a problem,' Elias said. 'Had a problem.' He noticed the woman's raised eyebrows. 'It's no secret. And it's best that you know if you're going to work together.'

'No one told me I would be working with an alcoholic.'

'Not an alcoholic,' Elias said. 'A gambling addict.'

She brushed her blonde hair behind one ear and squinted against the sun. 'What kind of gambling?'

'The losing kind, as far as I understand. But if you're his new partner, you can ask him yourself. Where are you from?'

'Drug Squad.'

'Well, then you'll know all about the river.'

'Yes.' She narrowed her eyes and looked up at the body. 'It could have been a drug hit, of course, but the location is all wrong. They don't deal hard drugs this far up the river, for that you have to go down to Schous Plass and Nybrua. And people don't usually kill for cannabis.'

'Oh, good,' Elias said, nodding towards the boat. 'They've finally managed to get him down. If he has any ID on him, we'll soon know who—'

'I know who he is,' Kari Adel said. 'It's Per Vollan, the prison chaplain.'

Elias looked her up and down. He guessed she would soon give up dressing in smart clothes like the female detectives she had seen in American TV series. But apart from that she looked as if she had something about her. Perhaps she was one of those who would go the distance. Perhaps she belonged to that rare breed. But he had thought that about others before.

5

THE INTERVIEW ROOM WAS DECORATED in pale colours; the furniture was pine. Red curtains covered the window which faced the control room. Inspector Henrik Westad from Buskerud Police thought it was a nice room. He had made the trip from Drammen into Oslo before and sat in this very room. They had interviewed children in a sexual assault case and there had been anatomical dolls here. This time it was a murder inquiry. He studied the long-haired man with the beard sitting across the table. Sonny Lofthus. He looked younger than the age stated in the file. He didn't look as if he was drugged up, either; his pupils were normal-sized. But then people with a high drug tolerance rarely did. Westad cleared his throat.

'So you tied her up, used an ordinary hacksaw on her and then you left?'

'Yes,' the man said. He had declined his right to a lawyer, but answered practically every question with monosyllables. In the end Westad had resorted to asking him yes and no questions. Which seemed to work. Of course it bloody worked; they were getting a confession out of it. But it felt wrong. Westad looked at the photos in front of him. The top of the woman's head and her skull had nearly been sawn off and flipped aside so that they were attached only by the skin. The surface of the brain was left exposed. He had long since abandoned the idea that one could tell from looking at people what evil they were capable of. But this man, he . . . he didn't exude any of the iciness, the aggression or simply the imbecility Westad thought he had detected in other cold-blooded killers.

Westad leaned back in his chair. 'Why are you confessing to this?'

The man shrugged. 'DNA at the crime scene.'

'How do you know we found some?'

The man touched his long, thick hair which the prison management could have ordered to be cut if they wanted to. 'My hair falls out. It's a side effect of long-term drug abuse. Can I go now?'

Westad sighed. A confession. Technical evidence at the crime scene. So why did he still have doubts?

He leaned towards the microphone standing between them. 'Interview with suspect Sonny Lofthus stopped at 13.04.'

He saw the red light go out and knew that the officer outside had switched off the recording device. He got up and opened the door so that the prison officers could enter, unlock Lofthus's handcuffs and take him back to Staten.

'What do you think?' the officer asked as Westad came into the control room.

'Think?' Westad put on his jacket and zipped it up with a hard, irritated movement. 'He doesn't give me anything *to* think about.'

'And what about the interview earlier today?'

Westad shrugged. A friend of the victim had come forward. She had reported that the victim had told her that her husband, Yngve Morsand, had accused her of having an affair and threatened to kill her. That Kjersti Morsand had been scared. Not least because the husband had good grounds for his suspicion – she *had* met someone

35

and was thinking of leaving him. It was hard to think of a more classic motive for murder. But what about the boy's motive? The woman hadn't been raped, nothing in the house had been stolen. The medicine cupboard in the bathroom had been broken into and the husband claimed that some sleeping tablets were missing. But why would a man who, judging from his needle marks, had easy access to hard drugs bother with a few measly sleeping pills?

The next question presented itself immediately: Why would an investigator with a signed confession care about little things like that?

Johannes Halden was pushing the mop across the floor by the cells in A Wing when he saw two prison officers approach with the boy between them.

The boy smiled; he looked as if he was walking with two friends going somewhere nice, the handcuffs notwithstanding. Johannes stopped and raised his right arm. 'Look, Sonny! My shoulder is better. Thanks to you.'

The boy had to lift both hands to give the old man a thumbs up. The officers stopped in front of one of the cell doors and unlocked the handcuffs. They didn't need to unlock the door as well since all cell doors were opened automatically every morning at eight o'clock and were left open until ten o'clock at night. The staff up in the control room had shown Johannes how they could lock and unlock all the doors with a single keystroke. He liked the control room. That was why he always took his time washing the floor in there. It was a bit like steering a supertanker. A little like being where he should have ended up.

Before 'the incident' he had worked as an able seaman and studied nautical science. The plan had been to become a deck officer. Followed by mate, first mate and then captain. And eventually join his wife and daughter in the house outside Farsund and get himself a job as a pilot at the port. So why had he done it? Why had he ruined everything? What had made him agree to smuggle two big sacks out of the Port of Songkhla in Thailand? It wasn't that he didn't know they contained heroin. And it wasn't that he didn't know the penal code and the hysterical Norwegian legal system which at that time equated drug smuggling with murder. It wasn't even that he needed the huge amount of money he had been offered to deliver the sacks to an address in Oslo. So what was it? The thrill? Or the hope of seeing her again; the beautiful Thai girl in her silk dress with her long, shiny black hair, of looking into her almond eyes, hearing her soft voice whisper the difficult English words with sweet cherry lips, telling him he had to do it for her, for her family in Chiang Rai, that it was the only way he could save them. He had never believed her story, but he had believed in her kiss. And that kiss took him across oceans, through customs, into the remand cell, into the courtroom, into the visitors' room where his almost grown-up daughter had sat down and told him that the family wanted nothing more to do with him, through the divorce and into the cell in Ila Prison. That kiss was all he had wanted and the promise of that kiss was all he had left.

When he was released there had been no one waiting for him on the outside. His family had disowned him, his friends grown apart and he would never get work on a ship again. So he sought out the only people willing to accept him. Criminals. And resumed his old ways. Tramp shipping. Nestor, the Ukrainian, recruited him. Heroin from northern Thailand was smuggled in trucks using the old drug route via Turkey and the Balkans. In Germany the cargo was distributed to the Scandinavian countries and Johannes's job was to drive the last stretch. Later he became a confidential informant.

There hadn't been a good reason for that, either. Only a police officer who appealed to something inside him, something he didn't even know he had. And though that prospect – a clear conscience – had seemed worth less than the kiss of a beautiful woman, he had really believed in that police officer. There had been something about his eyes. Johannes might have gone straight, changed his ways, who knows? But then one autumn evening the police officer was killed. And for the first and only time Johannes heard the name, heard it whispered with a mixture of fear and awe. The Twin.

From then on it was only a matter of time before Johannes was pulled back in again. He took bigger and bigger risks, moved bigger and bigger loads. Dammit, he wanted to get caught. Atone for what he had done. So he was relieved when customs officers pulled him over at the Swedish border. The furniture in the back of his lorry was stuffed full of heroin. The judge had reminded the jury both of the large quantity involved and that it wasn't Johannes's first offence. That was ten years ago. He had been at Staten for the last four years, since the prison opened. He had seen inmates come and go, seen prison officers come and go too, and he had treated them all with the respect they deserved. And, in return, he got the respect he deserved. That is to say, he enjoyed the respect the old-timer gets. The guy who is no longer a threat. Because none of them knew his secret. The betrayal he was guilty of. The reason he inflicted this punishment on himself. And he had given up all hope of finally getting the only things that mattered. The kiss he had been promised by a forgotten woman. The clear conscience he had been promised by a dead police officer. Until he had been transferred to A Wing and had met the boy they said could heal you. Johannes had been startled when he heard the surname, but he hadn't said anything. He had just carried on mopping the floors, keeping his head down, smiling, doing and receiving the little favours that made life bearable in a place like this. The days, the weeks, the months and the years had flown by and turned into a life which would soon end. Cancer. Lung cancer. Small cell, the doctor had said. The aggressive kind which is the worst unless it is caught early.

It hadn't been caught early.

There was nothing anyone could do. Certainly not Sonny. He hadn't even come close to guessing what was wrong when Johannes had asked; the lad himself had suggested the groin, nudge nudge, wink wink. And his shoulder had got better of its own accord, if truth be told, not from Sonny's hand which definitely didn't have a higher temperature than the usual 37°C, was far colder in fact. But he was a good lad, he really was, and Johannes had no desire to disillusion him if he thought he had healing hands.

So Johannes had kept it to himself, both his illness and his betrayal. But he knew that time was running out. That he couldn't take this secret with him to the grave. Not if he wanted to rest in peace rather than the horror of waking up like a zombie, worm-eaten and trapped, doomed to eternal torment. He had no religious beliefs about who would be condemned to everlasting suffering or why, but he had been wrong about so many things in his life.

'So many things . . .' Johannes Halden muttered to himself.

Then he put the mop aside, walked over to Sonny's cell and knocked on the door. No reply. He knocked again.

Waited.

Then he opened the door.

Sonny sat with a rubber strap tied around his forearm below the elbow, the end of the strap between his teeth. He held a syringe just above a bulging vein. The angle was the prescribed thirty degrees for optimum insertion.

Sonny calmly looked up and smiled. 'Yes?'

'Sorry, I . . . it can wait.'

'Are you sure?'

'Yes, it's . . . there's no hurry.' Johannes laughed. 'It can wait another hour.'

'Can it wait four hours?'

'Four hours is fine.'

The old man saw the needle sink into the vein. The boy pressed the plunger. Silence and darkness seemed to fill the room like black water. Johannes withdrew quietly and closed the door.

6

SIMON HAD HIS MOBILE PRESSED to his ear and his feet on the desk while he rocked back on the chair. It was an act the troika had perfected to such an extent that when they had challenged each other, the winner was whoever could be bothered to balance the longest.

'So the American doctor didn't want to give you his opinion?' he said in a low voice, partly because he saw no reason to involve other members of the Homicide Squad in his personal life, and partly because this was how he and his wife always spoke on the phone. Softly, intimately. As if they were in bed, holding each other.

'Oh, he does,' Else said. 'But not yet. He wants to look at the test results and the scans first. I'll know more tomorrow.'

'OK. How are you feeling?'

'Fine.'

'How fine?'

She laughed. 'Don't worry so much, darling. I'll see you at dinner.'

'All right. Your sister, is she . . . ?'

'Yes, she's still here and she'll give me a lift home. Now stop fussing and hang up, you're at work!'

He ended the call reluctantly. Thought about his dream in which he gave her his sight.

'Chief Inspector Kefas?'

He looked up. And up. The woman standing in front of his desk was tall. Very tall. And skinny. Legs as thin of those of a daddy-long-legs stuck out from under a smart skirt.

'I'm Kari Adel. I've been told to assist you. I tried to find you at the crime scene, but you disappeared.'

And she was young. Very young. She looked more like an ambitious bank clerk than a police officer. Simon rocked the chair even further back. 'What crime scene?'

'Kuba.'

'And how do you know it's a crime scene?'

He saw her shift her weight. Look for a way out. But there wasn't one.

'Possible crime scene,' she then said.

'And who says I need help?'

She jerked her thumb behind her to indicate where the order had come from. 'But I think I'm the one in need of help. I'm new here.'

'Fresh out of training?'

'Eighteen months with the Drug Squad.'

'Fresh, then. And you've already made it to Homicide? Congratulations, Adel. You're either really lucky, well connected or . . .' He leaned back horizontally in the chair and wiggled out a tin of *snus* from his jeans pocket.

'A woman?' she suggested.

'I was going to say clever.'

She blushed and he could see the discomfort in her eyes.

'Are you clever?' Simon asked, pushing a piece of *snus* under his upper lip.

'I came second in my year.'

'And how long are you planning on staying with Homicide?'

'What do you mean?'

'If drugs didn't appeal to you, why would murder?'

She shifted her weight again. Simon saw that he had been right. She was one of those people who would make a brief guest appearance before disappearing up the building to the higher floors and up the ranks. Clever. Probably leave the police force altogether. Like the smart buggers at the Serious Fraud Office had done. Taken all their skills with them and left Simon in the lurch. The police force wasn't a place you stayed if you were bright, talented, ambitious and wanted a life.

'I left the crime scene because there was nothing to be found there,' Simon said. 'So tell me, where would you start?'

'I would talk to his next of kin,' Kari Adel said, looking around for a chair. 'Map his movements before he ended up in the river.'

Her accent suggested she was from the eastern part of west Oslo where people were terrified that the wrong accent might stigmatise them.

'Good, Adel. And his next of kin—'

'—is his wife. His soon-to-be ex-wife. She threw him out recently. I've spoken to her. He was staying at the Ila Centre for drug addicts. Is it OK if I sit down . . . ?'

Clever. Definitely clever.

'You won't need to now,' Simon said, getting up. He estimated her to be at least fifteen centimetres taller than him. Even so, she had to take two steps to one of his. Tight skirt. That was all good, but he suspected she would soon be wearing something else. Crimes were solved in jeans.

'You know you're not allowed in here.'

Martha blocked the access to the Ila Centre's front door as she looked at the two people. She thought she had seen the woman before. Her height and thinness made her hard to forget. Drug Squad? She had blonde, lifeless hair, wore hardly any make-up and had a slightly pained facial expression that made her look like the cowed daughter of a rich man.

The man was her direct opposite. Roughly 1.70 metres tall, somewhere in his sixties. Wrinkles in his face. But also laughter lines. Thinning grey hair above a pair of eyes in which she read 'kind', 'humorous' and 'stubborn'. Reading people was something she did automatically when she held the obligatory introduction interview with new residents to establish what kind of behaviour and trouble the staff could expect. Sometimes she was wrong. But not often.

'We don't need to come inside,' said the man who had introduced himself as Chief Inspector Kefas. 'We're from Homicide. It's about Per Vollan. He lived here—'

'Lived?'

'Yes, he's dead.'

Martha gasped. It was her initial reaction when she was told that yet another man had died. She wondered if it was to reassure herself that she was still alive. Surprise came next. Or rather, the fact that she wasn't surprised. But Per hadn't been a drug addict, he hadn't sat in death's waiting room with the rest of them. Or had he? And had she seen it, known it subconsciously? Was that why the usual gasp was followed by the equally routine mental reaction: of course. No, it wasn't that. It was the other thing.

'He was found in the Aker River.' The man did the talking. The woman had TRAINEE written on her forehead.

'Right,' Martha said.

'You don't sound surprised?'

'No. No, perhaps not. It's always a shock, of course, but . . .'

'. . . but it's par for the course in our line of work, yes?' The man gestured at the windows in the building next door. 'I didn't know Tranen had shut.'

44

'It's going to be an upmarket patisserie,' Martha said, hugging herself as if she were cold. 'For the latte-drinking yummy mummies.'

'So they've arrived here, too. How about that.' He nodded to one of the old-timers who shuffled past on trembling junkie knees and got a measured nod in return. 'There are many familiar faces here. Vollan, however, was a prison chaplain. The post-mortem report isn't ready yet, but we found no needle marks on him.'

'He wasn't staying here because he was using. He helped us out when we had trouble with ex-offenders who were living here. They trusted him. So when he had to move out of his home, we offered him temporary accommodation.'

'We know. What I'm asking is why you're not surprised he's dead when you know he wasn't using. His death could have been an accident.'

'Was it?'

Simon looked at the tall, thin woman. She hesitated until he gave her a nod. Then she finally opened her mouth. 'We haven't found any signs of violence, but the area around the river is a notorious criminal hot spot.'

Martha noticed her accent and concluded a strict mother had corrected her daughter's language at the dinner table. A mother who had told her she would never find a decent husband if she spoke like a shop girl.

The Chief Inspector tilted his head. 'What do you think, Martha?'

She liked him. He looked like someone who cared.

'I think he knew he was going to die.'

He raised an eyebrow. 'Why?'

'Because he wrote me a letter.'

Martha walked around the table in the meeting room which lay opposite the reception area on the first floor. They had managed to retain the Gothic style and it was easily the most beautiful room in the building. Not that there was much competition. She poured a cup of coffee for the Chief Inspector who sat down while he read the letter that Per Vollan had left for her at reception. His partner perched on the edge of a chair next to him, texting on her mobile. She had politely declined Martha's offer of coffee, tea and water as if she suspected even the tap water here to be contaminated with undesirable microbes. Kefas pushed the letter across to her. 'It says here he leaves everything he owns to the hostel.'

His colleague sent her text message and cleared her throat. The Chief Inspector turned to her. 'Yes, Adel?'

'You're not allowed to say a hostel any more; it's called a residential centre.'

Kefas looked genuinely surprised. 'Why?'

'Because we have social workers and a sickbay here,' Martha explained. 'That makes it more than just a hostel. Of course the real reason is that the word "hostel" now has unfortunate connotations. Drinking, brawling and squalid living conditions. So they slap some paint on the rust by renaming it.'

'But even so . . .' the Chief Inspector said. 'Was Vollan really going to leave everything he owned to this place?'

Martha shrugged. 'I doubt he had much to leave. Did you notice the date under his signature?'

'He wrote the letter yesterday. And you think he did that because he knew he was going to die? Are you saying he killed himself?'

Martha thought about it. 'I don't know.'

The tall, thin woman cleared her throat again. 'Marital breakdown is not, as far as I know, an uncommon reason for suicide in men over forty.'

Martha got the feeling that the quiet woman more than just knew it; she had the exact statistics at her fingertips.

'Did he seem depressed?' Simon asked.

'More low than depressed, I'd say.'

46

'It's not uncommon for a suicidal person to kill themselves as they come out of their depression,' the woman said and sounded as if she was reading from a book. The other two looked at her. 'The depression itself is often characterised by apathy and it takes a certain amount of initiative to commit suicide.' A beep indicated that she had received a text message.

Kefas turned to Martha. 'A middle-aged man is thrown out by his wife and writes something that could be seen as a farewell note to you. So why isn't it suicide?'

'I didn't say that it wasn't.'

'But?'

'He seemed scared.'

'Scared of what?'

Martha shrugged. She wondered if she was creating unnecessary trouble for herself.

'Per was a man with a dark side. He was very open about it. He said he became a chaplain because he needed forgiveness more than most.'

'You're saying he had done things not everyone would forgive him for?'

'Things that *no one* would forgive him for.'

'I see. Are we talking about the type of sins where the clergy seems to be over-represented?'

Martha didn't reply.

'Is that why his wife threw him out?'

Martha hesitated. This man was sharper than the other police officers she had met. But could she trust him?

'In my job you learn the art of forgiving the unforgivable, Chief Inspector. Of course it's possible that Per ultimately couldn't forgive himself and that's why he chose this way out. But it's also possible that—'

'—someone, let's say the father of a child who had been abused, wanted to avoid pressing charges that would also stigmatise the victim. And, besides, the someone couldn't be sure that Per Vollan would be punished and, in any case, whatever sentence he got wouldn't be enough. So the someone decided to be judge, jury and executioner.'

Martha nodded. 'It's only human if someone hurts your child, I guess. Haven't you ever come across cases in your work where the law is inadequate?'

Simon Kefas shook his head. 'If police officers gave in to that kind of temptation, the law would be pointless. And I actually believe in the rule of law. Justice must be blind. Do you suspect anyone in particular?'

'No.'

'Drug debt?' Kari Adel asked.

Martha shook her head. 'I would have known if he was using.'

'I'm asking because I've just texted an officer from the Drug Squad about Per Vollan. And he replied . . .' She took her mobile out of her tight jacket pocket and there was a clunk when a marble came out with it, hit the floor and started rolling eastwards. '*Seen him talking to one of Nestor's dealers sometimes,*' she read out loud while she rose and started looking for the marble. '*Seen him buy a wrap, but not pay.*' Kari Adel put the phone back in her pocket and caught the marble before it reached the wall.

'And what do you make of that?' Simon asked.

'That this building slopes towards Alexander Kiellands Plass. Probably more blue clay and less granite on that side.'

Martha chuckled.

The tall, thin woman smiled briefly. 'And that Vollan owed money to someone. A wrap of heroin costs three hundred kroner. And that's not even a full wrap, that's just 0.2 gram. Two bags a day—'

'Not so fast,' Simon interrupted her. 'Junkies don't get credit, do they?'

'Not usually, no. Perhaps he was doing favours for someone and was paid in heroin.'

Martha threw up her hands. 'He wasn't using, I keep telling you! Half my job is knowing if people are clean, OK?'

'You're right, of course, Miss Lian,' Simon said, rubbing his chin. 'Perhaps the heroin wasn't for him.' He got up. 'Anyway, we'll have to wait and see what the medical examiner says.'

'Good idea of yours to text the Drug Squad,' Simon said as he drove them down Uelandsgate towards the city centre.

'Thank you,' Kari said.

'Nice girl, that Martha Lian. Have you come across her before?'

'No, but I wouldn't have kicked her out of bed if I had.'

'What?'

'Sorry, bad joke. You meant if I knew her from my time with the Drug Squad. I do. She's lovely and I've always wondered why she works at the Ila Centre.'

'Because she's pretty?'

'It's a well-known fact that good looks improve the career prospects of people with only average intelligence and ability. Working at the Ila Centre isn't a springboard for anything as far as I can see.'

'Perhaps she thinks it's a worthwhile job.'

'Worthwhile? Have you any idea what they pay—'

'Worth doing. Police work doesn't pay very well, either.'

'True.'

'But it's a good place to start your career if you combine it with a law degree,' Simon said. 'When will you finish the second level?'

Again he detected a hint of reddening on Kari's neck and knew he had touched a nerve.

'Right,' Simon said. 'Nice to have the use of your services. I expect you'll be my boss soon. Or you'll get a job in the private sector where salaries are on average one and a half times more for people with skills like ours.'

'Perhaps,' Kari said. 'But I don't think I'll ever be your boss. You're due to retire next March.'

Simon didn't know whether to laugh or cry. He turned left at Grønlandsleiret, towards Police HQ.

'One and a half times your salary would come in very handy if you're doing up a property. Flat or house?'

'House,' Kari said. 'We plan on having two children and we need more room. Given the cost per square metre in central Oslo, you have to buy a place that needs doing up unless you inherit money. Both mine and Sam's parents are alive and well; and besides, Sam and I agree that subsidy corrupts.'

'Corrupts? Really?'

'Yes.'

Simon looked at the Pakistani shop owners who had left their overheated shops and come out into the street where they chatted, smoked cigarettes and watched the traffic.

'Aren't you curious how I knew that you're house-hunting?'

'The marble,' Kari said. 'Adults with no children only have one of those in their pocket if they're viewing old houses or flats and want to check if the floors are sloping due to subsidence so badly they'll have to be taken up.'

She really was clever.

'Just bear this in mind,' Simon said. 'If a house has been standing for 120 years, the floors should be a little crooked.'

'Perhaps so,' Kari said, leaning forward to look at the spire of Grønland Church. 'But I like it when the floors are level.'

Simon started to laugh. He might grow to like this girl. He liked the floors level, too.

7

'I KNEW YOUR FATHER,' Johannes Halden said.

It was raining outside. It had been a warm, sunny day; the clouds had built up on the horizon and the light summer drizzle fell across the city. Johannes remembered what it felt like before he was banged up. How the little drops of rain warmed up the moment they hit your sun-kissed skin. How it made the smell of dust rise from the tarmac. The scent of flowers, grass and leaves would make him wild, dizzy and frisky. Ah, to be young again.

'I was his confidential informant,' Johannes said.

Sonny sat in darkness close to the wall and it was impossible to see his face. Johannes didn't have very much time; the cells would soon be locked up for the night. He took a deep breath. Here it came. The sentence he needed to say, but dreaded the consequences. Uttering the words that had sat in his chest for so long he was afraid that they had taken root.

'It's not true that he shot himself, Sonny.'

There. He had finally told him.

Silence.

'You're not asleep, are you, Sonny?'

Johannes could see the body shift in the shadow.

'I know what it must have been like for you and your mother. Finding your father dead. Reading the note where he claimed he was the mole in the police who had helped drug dealers and traffickers. That he had told them about raids, evidence, suspects . . .'

He saw the white in a pair of blinking eyes.

'But it was the other way round, Sonny. Your father suspected who the mole was. I overheard Nestor talk on the phone to his boss about how they had to get rid of a policeman called Lofthus before he ruined everything for them. I told your father about that conversation, that he was in danger, that the police had to move quickly. But your father said that he couldn't involve other people, that he had to go it alone because he knew there were other police officers in hock to Nestor. So he got me to swear to keep my mouth shut and never breathe a word of it to a living soul. And I've kept that promise right up until now.'

Had Sonny understood? Possibly not, but the most important thing wasn't that Sonny had listened or the consequences, but that Johannes had got it off his chest. Finally told him. Delivered the message to its rightful owner.

'Your father was alone that weekend; you and your mother were at a wrestling competition out of town. He knew they were coming for him so he barricaded himself inside that yellow house of yours up in Berg.'

Johannes thought he could feel something in the darkness. A change in pulse and breathing.

'Even so, Nestor and his people still managed to get in. They didn't want the fallout that would come from shooting a police officer so they forced your father to write that suicide note.' Johannes swallowed. 'In return for a promise to spare you and your mother. Afterwards they shot him point-blank with his own gun.'

Johannes closed his eyes. It was very quiet and yet it felt as if someone was shouting into his ear. And there was a tightness in his chest and throat that he hadn't felt for many, many years. Dear God, when did he last cry? When his daughter was born? But he couldn't stop now; he had to finish what he had started.

'I guess you're wondering how Nestor got into the house?'

Johannes held his breath. It sounded as if the boy had also stopped breathing; all he could hear was the roar of blood in his ears.

'Someone had seen me talk to your father, and Nestor thought the police had been a little too lucky with the trucks they had stopped recently. I denied that it was me, said that I knew your father a bit and that he was trying to get information from me. So Nestor said that if your father believed I might become his confidential informant, I would be able to walk up to the front door and make him open it. That way I could prove where my loyalties lay, he said . . .'

Johannes could hear that the other had started breathing again. Quickly. Hard.

'Your father opened the door. Because you trust your informant, don't you?'

He sensed movement, but he didn't hear or see anything before the punch hit him. And while he lay on the floor tasting the metallic blood, feeling the tooth glide down his throat, hearing the boy scream and scream, the cell door opening, the officers' shouting and then the boy being restrained and handcuffed, he thought about the astonishing physical speed, accuracy and force in the blow from this junkie. And about forgiveness. The forgiveness which he hadn't got. And about time. About the passing seconds. About the approaching night.

8

WHAT ARILD FRANCK LIKED MOST about his Porsche Cayenne was the sound. Or rather the absence of sound. The hum of the 4.8-litre V8 engine reminded him of his mother's sewing machine when he was growing up in Stange outside of Hamar. That, too, had been the sound of silence. Of silence, calm and concentration.

The door on the passenger side opened and Einar Harnes got in. Franck didn't know where young lawyers in Oslo bought their suits; he just knew it wasn't the same shops he frequented. Nor had he ever seen the point of buying light-coloured suits. Suits were dark. And cost less than five thousand kroner. The difference in price between his suits and Harnes's ought to be paid into a savings account for future generations who had families of their own to support and who would continue the work of building Norway. Or fund an early and comfortable retirement. Or a Porsche Cayenne.

'I hear he's in solitary,' Harnes said as the car pulled away from the kerb outside the graffitied entrance to the law offices of Harnes & Fallbakken.

'He beat up a fellow inmate,' Franck said.

Harnes raised a well-groomed eyebrow. 'Gandhi pulled a punch?'

'You never can tell what junkies are capable of. But he's had four days of cold turkey so I imagine he's very cooperative by now.'

'Yes, it runs in the family – or so I've heard.'

'What have you heard?' Franck honked the horn at a slow Corolla.

'Only what everybody knows. Is there anything else?'

'No.'

Arild Franck steered the car in front of a Mercedes convertible. He had visited the isolation cell yesterday. Staff had just finished cleaning up vomit and the boy sat huddled up under a woollen blanket in the corner.

Franck had never met Ab Lofthus, but he knew that the son had followed in his father's footsteps. That he had been a wrestler like his father and showed such promise at the age of fifteen that the newspaper *Aftenposten* had predicted a national league career. Now he sat in a stinking cell, shaking like a leaf and sobbing like a little girl. In withdrawal everyone is equal.

They stopped in front of the security booth, Einar Harnes produced his ID and the steel barrier was raised. Franck parked the Cayenne in its allocated space and he and Harnes walked up to the main entrance where Harnes's visit was logged. Usually Franck let Harnes in through the back door by the staff changing rooms to avoid signing him in. He didn't want to give anyone cause to speculate what a lawyer with Harnes's reputation was doing visiting Staten so often.

Any inmate suspected of involvement in a new criminal case was usually questioned at Police HQ, but Franck had asked if this interview could take place at Staten, given that Sonny Lofthus was currently in solitary confinement.

A vacant cell had been cleared and made ready for this purpose. A policeman and a policewoman in plain clothes sat on one side of the table. Franck had seen them before, but couldn't remember their names. The figure on the other side of the table was so pale that he seemed to blend in with the milky-white wall. His head was bowed and his hands gripped the edge of the table tightly as if the room was spinning.

'So, Sonny,' Harnes said brightly, putting his hand on the boy's shoulder, 'are you ready?'

The policewoman cleared her throat. 'The question should rather be is he finished.'

Harnes smiled thinly at her and raised his eyebrows. 'What do you mean? I hope you haven't started questioning my client without his lawyer present.'

'He said he didn't need to wait for you,' the policeman replied.

Franck looked at the boy. He sensed trouble.

'So he's confessed already?' Harnes sighed, opened his briefcase and pulled out three sheets of paper stapled together. 'If you want it in writing then—'

'On the contrary,' the policewoman said. 'He's just denied having anything to do with the murder.'

The room fell so silent that Franck could hear the birds singing outside.

'He did what?' Harnes's eyebrows reached his hairline now. Franck didn't know what made him angrier, the lawyer's plucked eyebrows or his slowness to appreciate the catastrophe that was unfurling.

'Did he say anything else?' Franck asked.

The policewoman looked at the assistant prison governor, then at the lawyer.

'It's quite all right,' Harnes said. 'He's here at my request in case you needed more information about Lofthus's day release.'

'I granted it personally,' Franck said. 'And there was nothing to indicate that it would have such tragic consequences.'

'And we don't know that it has yet,' the policewoman said. 'Given that we don't have a confession.'

'But the evidence—' Arild Franck exclaimed, but then stopped himself.

'What do you know about the evidence?' the policeman asked him.

'I just presumed that you had some,' Franck said. 'Since Lofthus is a suspect. Isn't that right, Mr . . . ?'

'Detective Inspector Henrik Westad,' the policeman said. 'I was the first person to interview Lofthus, but now he's changed his statement. He even says he has an alibi for the time of the murder. A witness.'

'He does have a witness,' Harnes said, looking down at his silent client. 'The prison officer who accompanied him on his day release. And he has said that Lofthus disappeared for—'

'Another witness,' Westad said.

'And who might that be?' Franck scoffed.

'Lofthus says he met a man called Leif.'

'Leif what?'

Everyone stared at the long-haired prisoner who looked like he was very far away and entirely oblivious to their presence.

'He doesn't know,' Westad said. 'He says they chatted briefly at a lay by. He says the witness drove a blue Volvo with an "I ♥ Drammen" sticker and he thinks the witness might have been ill or had heart trouble.'

Franck barked with laughter.

'I think,' Einar Harnes said with forced composure as he returned the papers to his briefcase, 'that we should end it here so I can speak to my client to take his instructions.'

Franck had a habit of grinning when he got angry. And now the rage bubbled in his head like a boiling kettle and he had to pull himself together not to laugh out loud again. He glared at Harnes's so-called client. Sonny Lofthus must be mad. First his attack on old Halden and now this. The heroin must finally have corroded his brain. But Sonny wouldn't be allowed to upset this, it was much too big. Franck took a deep breath and heard an imaginary click

57

like a boiling kettle switching itself off. It was just a question of keeping cool, giving it time. Giving withdrawal a little more time.

Simon was standing on Sannerbrua looking down at the water which flowed eight metres below them. It was six o'clock in the evening and Kari Adel had just asked about the rules for overtime in the Homicide Squad.

'No idea,' Simon said. 'Talk to Human Resources.'

'Can you see anything down there?'

Simon shook his head. Behind the foliage on the east side of the river he could make out the towpath which followed the water all the way down to the new Opera House by Oslo Fjord. A man was sitting on the bench feeding the pigeons. He's retired, Simon thought. That's what you do when you retire. On the west side was a modern apartment block with windows and balconies offering a view of both the river and the bridge.

'So what are we doing here?' Kari said, kicking the tarmac impatiently.

'Is there somewhere you need to be?' Simon said and looked around. A car drove past at a leisurely pace, a smiling beggar asked if they had change for a 200-kronor note, a couple in designer sunglasses with a disposable barbecue in the bottom tray of their pram laughed at something as they strolled by. He loved Oslo in the summer holidays when the city emptied of people and became his once more. When it returned to being the slightly overgrown village of his childhood where nothing much ever happened and anything that did happen meant something. A city he understood.

'Some friends have invited Sam and me over for dinner.'

Friends, Simon thought. He used to have friends. What happened to them? Perhaps they were asking exactly the same question. What happened to him? He didn't know if he could give them a proper answer.

The river couldn't be more than a metre and a half deep. In some places rocks protruded from the water. The post-mortem report mentioned injuries consistent with a fall from a certain height, something which could fit with the broken neck which was the actual cause of death.

'We're here because we've walked up and down Aker River and this is the only place where the bridge is high enough and the water shallow enough for him to hit the rocks that hard. Besides, it's the nearest bridge to the hostel.'

'Residential centre,' Kari corrected him.

'Would you try to kill yourself here?'

'No.'

'I mean if you were going to kill yourself.'

Kari stopped shuffling her feet. Looked over the railing. 'I suppose I would have chosen somewhere higher. Too great a risk of surviving. Too big a risk of ending up in a wheelchair . . .'

'But you wouldn't push someone off this bridge, either, if you were trying to kill them, would you?'

'No, maybe not,' she yawned.

'So we're looking for someone who broke Per Vollan's neck and then threw him into the river from here.'

'That's what you call a theory, I suppose.'

'No, that's what *we* call a theory. That dinner . . .'

'Yes?'

'Ring your other half and say it's off.'

'Oh?'

'We're starting door-to-door inquiries for potential witnesses. You can begin by ringing the doorbell of anyone whose balcony overlooks the river. Next we need to go through the archives with a fine-tooth comb for potential neck-breakers.' Simon closed his eyes and inhaled the air. 'Don't you just love Oslo in the summer?'

9

EINAR HARNES NEVER HAD ANY ambition to save the world. Just a small part of it. More specifically his part. So he studied law. Just a small part of it. More precisely the part he needed to pass the exam. He got a job with a firm of lawyers operating decidedly at the bottom of Oslo's legal system, worked for them just long enough to get his licence, started his own firm with Erik Fallbakken, an ageing, borderline alcoholic, and together they had set a new low for dregs. They had taken on the most hopeless cases and lost every one of them, but in the process had earned themselves a reputation as the defenders of the lowest in society. The nature of their clients meant the legal partnership of Harnes & Fallbakken mostly had its invoices paid – if indeed they ever were – on the same dates that people collected their benefits. Einar Harnes had soon realised that he wasn't in the business of providing justice, he merely offered a marginally more expensive alternative to debt collectors, social services and fortune-tellers. He threatened the people he was paid to threaten with lawsuits, employed the city's most useless individuals on minimum wage and promised potential clients victory in court without exception. However, he had one client who was the real reason Harnes was still in business. This client had no record in the filing system – if you could call the total chaos that reigned in the filing cabinets, managed by a secretary who was more or less permanently on sick leave, a system. This client always paid his bills, usually in cash, and rarely asked for an invoice. Nor was this client likely to ask for one for the hours Harnes was about to run up, either.

Sonny Lofthus sat cross-legged on the bed with white desperation radiating from his eyes. It was six days since the notorious interview and the boy was having a rough time, but he had lasted longer than they had expected. The reports from the other inmates Harnes was in contact with were remarkable. Sonny hadn't tried to score drugs; on the contrary, he had turned down offers of speed and cannabis. He had been seen in the gym where he had run on the treadmill for two hours without stopping and then lifted weights for another two. Screams had been heard coming from Sonny's cell at night. But he was holding out. A guy who had been a hard-core H user for twelve years. The only people Harnes had heard of who had managed that before were people who had replaced drugs with something equally addictive, which could stimulate and motivate them just as much as the high from a hit. And it was a short list. They might find God, fall in love or have a child. That was it. In short, they finally found something which gave their lives a new and different purpose. Or was it only a drowning man's last trip to the surface before he finally went under? All Einar Harnes knew for certain was that his paymaster wanted an answer. No. Not an answer. Results.

'They have DNA evidence so you'll be convicted whether or not you confess. Why prolong the agony for no reason?'

No reply.

Harnes ran his hand so hard over his slicked-back hair that the roots stung. 'I could have a bag of Superboy here in an hour, so what's the problem? All I need is your signature here.' He tapped his finger on the three A4 sheets on his briefcase which was resting on his thighs.

The boy tried to moisten his dry, cracked lips with a tongue that was so white that Harnes wondered if it might be producing salt.

'Thank you. I'll consider it.'

Thank you? I'll consider it? He was offering drugs to a pathetic junkie in withdrawal! Had the boy repealed the laws of gravity?

'Listen, Sonny—'

'And thank you for your visit.'

Harnes shook his head and got up. The boy wouldn't last. Harnes would just have to wait another day. Until the age of miracles had passed.

When a prison officer had accompanied the lawyer through all the doors and locks and he was back at reception where he asked them to call him a taxi, he thought about what his client would say. Or rather what his client would do if Harnes didn't save the world.

His part of the world, that is.

Geir Goldsrud leaned forward in his chair and stared at the monitor.

'What the hell is he up to?'

'Looks like he's trying to get someone's attention,' said another prison officer in the control room.

Goldsrud looked at the boy. The long beard reached down to his bare chest. He was standing on a chair in front of one of the surveillance cameras, tapping the lens with the knuckle of his index finger while mouthing incomprehensible words.

'Finstad, come with me,' Goldsrud said, getting up.

They passed Johannes who was mopping the floor in the corridor. The sight vaguely reminded Goldsrud of something from a movie. They walked downstairs to the ground floor, let themselves in, passed the communal kitchen and walked further down the corridor where they found Sonny sitting on the chair he had just been standing on.

Goldsrud could see from his upper body and arms that the boy had recently worked out, the muscles and veins were clearly outlined under his skin. He had heard that some of the most hardened intravenous drug users would do biceps curls in the gym before shooting up. Amphetamine and all sorts of pills were in circulation, but Staten was one of the few prisons in Norway – quite possibly the only one – where they actually had some limited control over the importation of heroin. Even so, it didn't appear as if Sonny had ever had problems getting hold of it. Until now. Goldsrud could tell from the shaking that the boy hadn't had a fix for several days. No wonder he was desperate.

'Help me,' Sonny pleaded when he saw them approach.

'Sure,' Goldsrud said, winking at Finstad. 'A wrap will cost you two thousand.'

He meant it as a joke, but he could see that Finstad hadn't been quite sure.

The boy shook his head. His muscles were bulging even in his neck and throat. Goldsrud had heard a rumour that the boy had once been a promising wrestler. Perhaps it was true what they said, that any muscles you build up before you're twelve, you can regain in a matter of weeks as an adult.

'Lock me up.'

'We don't lock you up until ten o'clock, Lofthus.'

'Please.'

Goldsrud was puzzled. It happened that inmates asked to be locked in their cells because they were scared of someone. Sometimes, but not always, they had cause to be. Fear was a common by-product of a life of crime. Or vice versa. But Sonny was probably the only inmate in Staten who didn't have a single enemy among the other prisoners. On the contrary, they treated him like a sacred cow. And the lad had never shown any signs of fear and he clearly had the physique and mental stamina to handle addiction better than most. So why . . . ?

The boy picked at a scab from a needle mark on his forearm and it was then Goldsrud realised there were scabs on *all* the marks. He had no fresh ones. The boy had quit. That was why he wanted to be locked up. He was in withdrawal and all too aware that he would take anything he was offered, no matter what it was.

'Come on,' Goldsrud said.

'Lift your legs, will you, Simon?'

Simon looked up. The old cleaner was so small and bent double that she barely reached over the cleaning cart. She had worked at Police HQ since before Simon had started there himself sometime in the previous millennium. She was a woman with strong opinions, and always referred to herself – and to her colleagues regardless of gender – as a cleaning 'lady'.

'Hi, Sissel, is it that time again?' Simon looked at his watch. Past four o'clock. The official end of the working day in Norway. Indeed, employment law practically prescribed that you had to leave on the dot for king and country. In the past he couldn't have cared less about leaving on time, but that was then. He knew that Else was waiting for him, that she had started cooking dinner several hours ago and that when he came home she would pretend the meal was something she had just thrown together in a hurry and hope that he wouldn't see the mess, the spills and the other signs that revealed her sight had deteriorated a little more.

'Long time since you and I last had a fag together, Simon.'

'I use *snus* now.'

'I bet it's that young wife of yours who made you quit. Still no kids?'

'Still not retired, Sissel?'

'I think you already have a kid somewhere, that's why you don't want another one.'

Simon smiled, looked at her as she ran the mop under his legs and wondered, not for the first time, how it had been possible for Sissel Thou's tiny body to squeeze out such a huge offspring. Rosemary's Baby. He cleared away his papers. The Vollan case had been shelved. None of the residents in the Sannerbrua flats had seen anything and no other witnesses had come forward. Until they found evidence to suggest that a crime had been committed, the case would be downgraded, said his boss, and told Simon to spend the next couple of days fattening up reports on two solved murder cases where they had been given a bollocking by the public prosecutor who had described them as 'on the thin side'. She hadn't found any actual errors; she only wanted to see 'a certain raising of the level of detail'.

Simon switched off his computer, put on his jacket and headed for the door. It was still summer which meant that many of the staff who were not on holiday had left at three o'clock and in the open-plan office that smelled of glue from the old partition walls warmed by the sun he heard only scattered keystrokes. He spotted Kari behind one of the partitions. She had put her feet on the desk and was reading a book. He popped his head round.

'So no dinner with friends tonight?'

She automatically slammed the book shut and looked up at him with a mixture of irritation and guilt. He glanced at the title of the book: Company Law. He knew that she knew that she had no reason to feel bad for studying during work hours since no one had given her anything to do. It was par for the course in Homicide; no murders equalled no work. So Simon concluded from her blushes that she knew her law degree would eventually take her away from the department and it felt like a kind of treachery. And irritation, because though she had convinced herself that it must be accept-able to use her time like this, her instinctive reaction when he appeared had been to shut the book.

'Sam is surfing in Vestlandet this weekend. I thought I would read here rather than at home.'

Simon nodded. 'Police work can be dull. Even in Homicide.'

She looked at him.

He shrugged. 'Especially in Homicide.'

'So why did you become a homicide investigator?'

She had kicked off her shoes and pulled up her bare feet on the edge of the chair. As if she was hoping for a longer reply, Simon concluded. She was probably one of those people who prefer any company to solitude, who would rather sit in a near-deserted open-plan office with the chance of company than in their own living room where they were guaranteed peace and quiet.

'You may not believe it, but it was an act of protest,' he said, perching on the edge of the desk. 'My father was a watchmaker and wanted me to take over his business. I didn't want to be a bad copy of my father.'

Kari wrapped her arms around her long, insect-like legs. 'Any regrets?'

Simon looked towards the window. The heat made the air outside quiver.

'People have made money selling clocks.'

'Not my father,' Simon said. 'And he didn't like fakes, either. He refused to follow the trend and make cheap copies and plastic digital watches. He thought it was the path of least resistance. He went bankrupt in style.'

'Well, that explains why you didn't want to be a watchmaker.'

'No, I ended up a watchmaker all the same.'

'How?'

'Crime scene technician. Ballistics expert. Bullet trajectories and all that. It's almost the same as tinkering with watches. We're probably more like our parents than we'd like to believe.'

'So what happened?' she smiled. 'Did you go bankrupt?'

'Well.' He looked at his watch. 'I guess I became more interested in the why rather than the how. I don't know if it was the right decision to become a tactical investigator. Projectiles and bullet wounds are more predictable than the human brain.'

'So that's when you went to work for the Serious Fraud Office?'

'You've read my CV.'

'I always read up on people I'm going to work with. Had you had enough of blood and guts?'

'No, but I was scared Else, my wife, might have. When I got married, I promised her more regular working hours and no more shifts. I liked the Serious Fraud Office; it was a little like working with watches again. Talking of my wife . . .' He got up from the desk.

'Why did you leave the Serious Fraud Office if you enjoyed it so much?'

Simon smiled a tired smile. No, his CV wouldn't tell her that, would it?

'Lasagne. I think she's cooking lasagne. See you tomorrow.'

'Incidentally, I got a call from an old colleague. He told me he had seen a junkie wandering around wearing a dog collar.'

'A dog collar?'

'Like the one Per Vollan used to wear.'

'What did you do with the information?'

Kari opened her book again. 'Nothing. I told him the case had been shelved.'

'Downgraded. Until new evidence is found. What's the name of the junkie and where can we find him?'

'Gilberg. At the hostel.'

'The residential centre. Fancy a break from reading?'

Kari sighed and closed her book. 'What about the lasagne?'

Simon shrugged. 'All good. I'll call Else, she'll understand. And lasagne tastes better when it's reheated.'

10

JOHANNES TIPPED THE DIRTY WATER down the sink and put the bucket and the mop in the broom cupboard. He had washed every corridor on the first floor and in the control room and was looking forward to the book waiting for him back in his cell. *The Snows of Kilimanjaro*. It was a collection of short stories, but he read only the one story over and over again. It was about a man with gangrene in his foot who knows he is going to die. About how this knowledge doesn't make him a better or worse person, just more insightful, more honest, less patient. Johannes had never been much of a reader, the book had been recommended to him by the prison librarian, and since Johannes had been interested in Africa ever since he had sailed to Liberia and the Ivory Coast, he had read the first few pages about this apparently innocent, dying man in a tent on the savannah. The first time he had only skimmed through it, now he read slowly, one word at a time, looking for something even though he didn't even know what it was.

'Hi.'

Johannes turned round.

Sonny's 'hi' had been almost a whisper and the hollow-cheeked, wild-eyed figure standing in front of him was so pale it was almost transparent. Like an angel, Johannes thought.

'Hello, Sonny. I heard they put you in solitary. How are you doing now?'

Sonny shrugged.

'You've a good left hook, lad.' Johannes grinned and pointed to the gap where his front tooth used to be.

'I hope you can forgive me.'

Johannes gulped. 'I'm the one who needs forgiving, Sonny.'

The two of them looked at each other. Johannes saw Sonny glance up and down the corridor. There was a pause.

'Would you break out of prison for me, Johannes?'

Johannes took his time and tried shuffling the words to see if that made them make more sense before he asked: 'What do you mean? I don't want to escape. Besides, I've nowhere to go. I'll be found and brought back immediately.'

Sonny didn't reply, but his eyes radiated black desperation and Johannes understood.

'You want . . . you want me to break out so I can score some Superboy for you.'

Sonny still didn't reply, but continued to fix the old man's gaze with his own manic, intense stare. Poor lad, Johannes thought. Sodding heroin.

'Why me?'

'Because you're the only one with access to the control room so only you can do it.'

'Wrong. I'm the only one with access to the control room and that's why I know it can't be done. The doors can only be opened with fingerprints stored in the database. And I'm not in it, my friend. Nor can I be added without submitting four copies of an application which would need to be approved on high. I've seen them—'

'All the doors can be locked and unlocked from the control room.'

Johannes shook his head and looked around to make sure they were still alone in the corridor. 'Even if you make it outside, there are guards in the security booth in the car park. They check the ID of everyone coming or going.'

'Everyone?'

'Yes. Except during shift changes when they let out recognised cars and familiar faces.'

'Would that include people in a prison officer's uniform, by any chance?'

'Definitely.'

'So you would need to get yourself a uniform and break out when the officers change shift?'

Johannes placed his forefinger and thumb under his chin. His jaw still hurt.

'How would I get hold of the uniform?'

'From Sørensen's locker in the changing room. You'll have to force it open with a screwdriver.'

Sørensen was a prison officer who had been on sick leave for almost two months now. Nervous breakdown. Johannes knew they called it something else these days, but it was the same thing, a bloody great big mess of feelings. He had been there.

Johannes shook his head again. 'The changing room is full of prison officers during a shift change. Someone will recognise me.'

'Change your appearance.'

Johannes laughed. 'Right. And let's say I get hold of a uniform, now how would I go about threatening a group of prison officers so that they'll let me out?'

Sonny lifted up his long white shirt and produced a packet of cigarettes from his trouser pocket. Stuck a cigarette in between his dry lips and lit it with a lighter shaped like a pistol. Johannes nodded slowly.

70

'This isn't about drugs. There's something you want me to do on the outside, isn't there?'

Sonny sucked the flame from the lighter into the cigarette and exhaled the smoke. He narrowed his eyes.

'Will you do it?' His voice was warm and soft.

'Will you give me absolution from my sins?' Johannes asked.

Arild Franck spotted them as he came round the corner. Sonny Lofthus had placed his hand on the forehead of Johannes who was standing with his head bowed and his eyes closed. They looked like a pair of queers to him. He had seen them on the monitor in the control room; they had been talking for a while. From time to time he regretted not fitting every camera with a microphone because he could tell from the men's wary, sideways glances that they weren't discussing the next football pools coupon. Then Sonny had taken something out of his pocket. The boy had been standing with his back to the camera so it was impossible to make out what is was until they saw cigarette smoke rise above his head.

'Hey! You know you're only allowed to smoke in the designated areas.'

Johannes's grey-haired head slumped and Sonny let his hand drop.

Franck walked up to them. Gestured with his thumb over his shoulder. 'Go mop floors somewhere else, Johannes.' Franck waited until the old man had shuffled out of earshot. 'What were you talking about?'

Sonny shrugged.

'No, don't tell me, the sanctity of the confession is inviolable,' Arild Franck guffawed. The sound bounced between the bare corridor walls. 'So, Sonny, have you had time to think about it?'

The boy stubbed out the cigarette on the packet, put it in his pocket and scratched his armpit.

'Itchy?'

The boy said nothing.

'I imagine there are worse things than an itch. Worse even than cold turkey. Did you hear about the guy in 317? They think he hanged himself from the light fitting. But that he changed his mind after he had kicked the chair away from underneath him. That's why he clawed his own neck to pieces. What was his name again? Gomez? Diaz? He used to work for Nestor. There was some concern that he might start talking. No evidence, just a worry. That was all it took. Funny, isn't it, when you lie in your bed at night and you're in a prison and what scares you most is that the door to your cell might *not* be locked? That someone in the control room could give a prison full of killers access to you at the touch of a button?'

The boy had lowered his head, but Franck could see the beads of sweat on his forehead. The boy would come to his senses. He certainly ought to. Franck didn't like prisoners dying in their cells in his prison; eyebrows were inevitably raised no matter how plausible it looked.

'Yes.'

It came out so softly that Franck automatically leaned forward. 'Yes?' he echoed.

'Tomorrow. You'll get the confession tomorrow.'

Franck folded his arms across his chest and rocked back on his heels. 'Good. Then I'll bring Mr Harnes with me early tomorrow morning. And no funny business this time. When you lie in your bed tonight, I suggest you take another look at the light fitting in the ceiling. Understand?'

The boy raised his head and looked the assistant prison governor in the eye. Franck had long since dismissed the notion that the eyes mirrored the soul; he had stared into too many inmates' baby-blue eyes while they lied through their teeth. Besides, it was a strange expression. Mirror of the soul. Logically it meant that you saw your own soul in someone else's eyes. Was that why it was so uncomfortable to look into the boy's? Franck turned away. It was a question of staying focused. And not allowing yourself to get sidetracked by thoughts that led nowhere.

'It's haunted, innit?'

Lars Gilberg raised a thin roll-up to his lips with fingers the colour of charcoal and squinted up at the two police officers who were standing over him.

Simon and Kari had spent three hours looking for Gilberg and finally tracked him down under Grünerbrua. They had started their search at the Ila Centre where no one had seen him for over a week, continued via Bymisjonen's cafe in Skippergata, Plata by Oslo Central Station which still served as a marketplace for drugs, and finally the Salvation Army's hostel in Urtegata where information had taken them in the direction of the river to Elgen, a statue which marked the border between speed and heroin.

Along the way Kari had explained to Simon that the Albanians and the North Africans were currently in charge of the sale of amphetamine and methamphetamine along the river south of Elgen and down to Vaterland Bridge. Four Somalis were hanging around a bench, kicking their heels, their hoods pulled low down over their faces in the evening sun. One of them nodded when he saw the photo that Kari held up, pointed them north towards heroin country and winked at them as he asked if they fancied a gram of crystals for the journey. Their laughter had followed Simon and Kari as they plodded up the path towards Grünerbrua.

'You're saying you don't want to stay at the Ila Centre any more because you think it's haunted?' Simon asked him.

'It's not something I think, man. It's something I know. No one can get to sleep in a room there, it's already occupied, you feel a presence the moment you go in. I'd wake up in the middle of the night and there would be no one there, obviously, but it felt as if someone had been breathing on my face. And it wasn't just my room, you ask anyone there.' Gilberg looked at the finished cigarette with disapproval.

'So you prefer to sleep rough?' Simon asked, offering him his own tin of tobacco.

'Ghosts or no ghosts, to tell you the truth I can't handle small spaces, I feel trapped. And this place . . .' Gilberg gestured towards his bed of newspapers and the scruffy sleeping bag next to him. 'It's a top holiday destination, innit?' He pointed to the bridge. 'A roof that won't leak. A sea view. No expenses, easy access to public transport and local amenities. What more could you want?' He took three pieces of *snus* from Simon's tin and stuck one under his upper lip and the other two in his pocket.

'A job as a chaplain?' Kari suggested.

Gilberg tilted his head to one side and peered up at Simon.

'That dog collar you're wearing,' Simon said. 'You may have read in those newspapers of yours that a chaplain was found dead in the river just up from here.'

'I wouldn't know anything about that.' Gilberg took the two pieces of tobacco from his pocket, put them back in the tin and handed it to Simon.

'It'll take Forensics twenty minutes to prove that dog collar belonged to the chaplain, Lars. And it'll take you twenty years to serve out your sentence for his murder.'

'Murder? There was nothing about—'

'So you do read the crime section? He was dead before he was thrown in the river. We can tell from the bruises on his skin. He hit some rocks and bruises show up differently if you're already dead. Do you follow?'

'No.'

74

'Do you want me to spell it out to you? Or would you rather I tell you just how claustrophobic being in a prison cell really is?'

'But I haven't—'

'Even as a suspect you should expect to be remanded in custody for several weeks. And remand cells are much smaller.'

Gilberg looked pensive and sucked hard on the *snus* a couple of times.

'What d'you want?'

Simon squatted down in front of Gilberg. The homeless man's breath didn't just smell, it had a taste. The sweet, rotten taste of fallen fruit and death.

'We want you to tell us what happened.'

'I dunno know anything, I just told you.'

'You've told us nothing, Lars. But it sounds as if it's important to you. Not telling us, I mean. Why?'

'It was just this collar. It floated ashore and—'

Simon got up and grabbed Gilberg by the arm. 'Come on, off we go.'

'Wait!'

Simon released him.

Gilberg bowed his head. He heaved a sigh. 'They were Nestor's men. But I can't . . . you know what Nestor does to people who . . .'

'Yes, I know. But you also know that he'll hear about it if your name appears in the interview logs at Police HQ. So I suggest you tell us what you know right now and then I'll decide if we can leave it at that.'

Gilberg shook his head slowly.

'Now, Lars!'

'I was sitting on the bench under the trees where the path leads down to Sannerbrua. I was only ten metres away so I could see them up on the bridge, but I don't think they saw me, I was hidden among the leaves, you know what I mean? There were two of them and one was holding the chaplain while the other put his arm around his forehead. I was so close that I could see the white of the chaplain's eyes. They were completely white, by the way, it was like the eyeballs had rolled back into his head, you know what I mean? But he didn't make a sound. As if he knew there was no point. Then the second guy snapped his head backwards like a bloody chiropractor. I heard it break, I'm not kidding, it sounded like someone stepping on a twig in the forest.' Gilberg pressed his forefinger against his upper lip, blinked twice and stared into the distance. 'They took a look around. Christ, they've just killed a guy in the middle of Sannerbrua and they're completely cool. Then again Oslo can be strangely deserted in the middle of the summer, you know what I mean? So they threw him over the brick wall where the railing stops.'

'That fits with where the rocks stick up,' Kari said.

'He lay on the rocks for a little while before the current got hold of him and carried him off. I didn't move an inch. If those guys knew that I'd seen them . . .'

'But you had,' Simon said. 'And you were so close that you would be able to recognise them again.'

Gilberg shook his head. 'No chance. I've already forgotten them. That's the trouble when you get high on anything you can lay your hands on, you know what I mean? Messes with your head.'

'I think you mean that's the plus side,' Simon said, rubbing his face.

'But how did you know they worked for Nestor?' Kari shifted her weight restlessly.

'Their suits,' Gilberg said. 'The men looked identical, as if they had nicked a shipment of black two-piece suits destined for the Norwegian Undertakers' Association.' He manoeuvred the *snus* with his tongue. 'You know what I mean?'

*   *   *

'We're prioritising the case,' Simon said to Kari in the car on their way back to Police HQ. 'I want you to review Vollan's movements for the forty-eight hours before he was killed and get me a list of everyone, and I mean everyone, he came into contact with.'

'Fine,' Kari said.

They passed Blå and stopped for a flow of young pedestrians. Hipsters on their way to a concert, Simon thought and looked over at Kuba. He saw a big screen that had been erected on the outdoor stage while Kari called her father and said she wouldn't be coming for dinner. They were showing a black-and-white film. Images of Oslo. It looked like the fifties. A time Simon remembered from his own childhood. For the hipsters it was probably just a curiosity, something from the past, all innocent and possibly charming. He could hear laughter.

'I've been wondering about something,' Kari began. 'You said that Nestor would know if we brought Gilberg in for an interview. Were you serious?'

'What do you think?' Simon said and accelerated towards Hausmannsgate.

'I don't know, but it sounded like you meant it.'

'I don't know what I meant. It's a long story. For years there were rumours of a mole in the police force who leaked information to the person who ran most of the drugs and sex trafficking in Oslo. But it's a long time ago and though there was a lot of talk at the time no one ever produced any evidence to prove that this mole or that person actually existed.'

'What person?'

Simon looked out of the window. 'We called him the Twin.'

'Ah, the Twin,' Kari said. 'They talked about him in the Drug Squad, a bit like Gilberg's ghosts at the Ila Centre. Was he real?'

'Oh, the Twin is real.'

'And what about the mole?'

'Well. A man called Ab Lofthus left behind a suicide note in which he claimed to be the mole.'

'Wasn't that sufficient evidence?'

'Not in my book.'

'Why not?'

'Because Ab Lofthus was the least corrupt officer ever to work for Oslo Police.'

'How do you know?'

Simon stopped for a red light at Storgata. The darkness seemed to flow out of the buildings around them and with the darkness came the creatures of the night. They walked with shuffling footsteps, or slumped against walls in doorways where music pounded, or sat in cars with their elbows hanging out of the side window. Searching, hungry looks. Hunters.

'Because he was my best friend.'

Johannes checked the time. Ten minutes past ten. Ten minutes past lockdown. The others were locked in their cells by now; he would be manually locked in his once he had finished his final cleaning round at eleven o'clock. It was a strange thing. When you had been in prison for a long time the days started to fade away as quickly as minutes and the calendar girls on the wall in your cell couldn't keep up with the passing months. But this last hour had felt as long as a year. A long, horrible year.

He entered the control room.

There were three people on duty, one fewer than during the day. The springs in the chair creaked as one of them turned away from the monitors.

'Evening, Johannes.'

It was Geir Goldsrud. He pushed the rubbish bin out from under the desk with his foot. It was an automatic response. The young shift supervisor helping the old cleaner with the stiff back. Johannes had always liked Geir Goldsrud. He pulled the pistol out of his pocket and aimed it at Goldsrud's face.

'Cool. Where did you get that?' said one of the other officers, a blond man who played third-division football for Hasle-Løren.

Johannes didn't reply, he just kept his gaze and his aim fixed firmly at a point between Goldsrud's eyes.

'Light this for me, would you?' The third officer had stuck an unlit cigarette in between his lips.

'Put it away, Johannes.' Goldsrud spoke quietly without blinking and Johannes could see that he had understood. That this wasn't a novelty lighter.

'Proper James Bond gadget, mate. How much do you want for it?' The football player had got up and was coming towards Johannes to take a closer look.

Johannes aimed the small pistol at one of the monitors up under the ceiling and pulled the trigger. He didn't know quite what to expect and was just as startled as the others when there was a bang, the screen exploded and glass shattered.

The football player stood rooted to the spot.

'Get down on the floor!' Johannes was blessed with a booming baritone, but now his voice was high-pitched and squealing like a near-hysterical old woman. But it worked. The knowledge that a desperate man is standing in front of you with a lethal weapon has a greater impact than any authoritative voice. All three men now knelt down and put their hands behind their heads as if this was a drill, as if being threatened at gunpoint was something they had practised. And perhaps they had. Learned that total surrender is the only appropriate response. And probably the only acceptable one at their pay grade.

'All the way down. Down on the floor!'

They did as they were told. It was almost like magic.

He looked at the control board in front of him. Found the button that opened and shut the doors to the cells. Then the one that operated the locks and both entrances. Finally the big, red universal button, the one which opened every single door, to be used only in the event of fire. He pressed it. A long, howling tone indicated that the prison was now open. And a funny thought crossed his mind. That this was where he had always wanted to be. The skipper on the bridge of his ship.

'Keep your eyes on the floor,' he said. His voice was already growing stronger. 'If any of you try to stop me, me and my mates will come after you and your families. Remember that I know everything about you, boys. Trine, Valborg . . .' He reeled off the names of their wives and children, the schools they went to, their hobbies, where in Oslo they lived, information accumulated over the years, while he continued to look at the monitors. When he had finished, he left them. He went out of the door and then he started to run. He ran along the corridor, then downstairs to the floor below. He pulled the first door. It opened. He continued down the next corridor. His heart was already pounding, he hadn't worked out as much as he ought to, he hadn't kept in shape. He intended to start now. The second door opened as well. His legs protested at having to move so fast. Perhaps it was the cancer, perhaps it had reached his muscles and was weakening him. The third door led to the lock. He waited while the first door sealed behind him with a low hum, counting the seconds. He looked down the corridor towards the staff changing room. When he finally heard the door close, he grabbed the handle of the door in front of him. Pressed it down and pulled it.

Locked.

Damn! He pulled it again. The door refused to budge.

He looked at the white sensor plate by the door. Pressed his index finger against it. An indicator glowed yellow for a couple of seconds before it went out and another lit up red. Johannes knew it meant his fingerprint hadn't been recognised, but he tried to open the door anyway. Trapped. Defeated. He slumped to his knees in front of the door.

At the same time he heard Geir Goldsrud's voice:

'Sorry, Johannes.'

The voice was coming from a loudspeaker at the top of the wall and it sounded calm, almost comforting.

'We're just doing our job, Johannes. If we had to down tools every time someone threatens our families, there wouldn't be a single prison officer left in Norway. Relax, we'll come and get you. Do you want to slide the pistol out through the bars, or do you want us to gas you first?'

Johannes looked up at the camera. Could they see the despair in his face? Or the relief? His relief that his escape had ended here and that life would carry on as before. More or less. He could probably forget about mopping the floors upstairs.

He pushed the gold-plated pistol out through the bars. Then he lay down on the floor, put his hands behind his head and curled up like a bee that had just delivered its one and only sting. But when he closed his eyes he didn't hear hyenas and he wasn't on board a plane heading for the summit of Mount Kilimanjaro. He was still nowhere and alive. He was here.

11

IT HAD JUST GONE SEVEN THIRTY and the morning rain was falling on Staten's car park.

'It was only a matter of time,' Arild Franck said and held open the door to the back entrance. 'All addicts are essentially weak characters. I know it's not fashionable to say so, but believe me, I know what they're like.'

'As long as he signs that confession, that's all I care about.' Einar Harnes was about to enter, but had to step aside for three prison officers on their way out. 'I'm thinking of celebrating with a few glasses of bubbly myself tonight.'

'Ah, they pay you that well?'

'When I saw your car, I realised I had to raise my fees.' He grinned as he nodded towards the Porsche Cayenne in the car park. 'I put it down as an additional charge for antisocial work and Nestor said—'

'Shh!' Franck stuck his arm out in front of Harnes to let some more prison officers leave first. Most of the men had changed into civilian clothes, but some were clearly so keen to get home from the night shift that they practically ran to their cars still dressed in Staten's green uniforms. Harnes received a sharp glance from a man who wore a long coat loosely over his uniform. He knew he had seen his face before. But while he couldn't put a name to the face, he was fairly certain that the man could put a name to his: the shady lawyer who popped up in the papers in connection with equally shady cases. Perhaps this man and others like him were starting to wonder what Harnes was doing at Staten's back entrance. It would hardly improve his image if they overheard him mentioning Nestor . . .

Franck let himself and Harnes in through several doors until they reached the stairs leading to the first floor.

Nestor had made it clear that they had to get a signed confession today. Unless the investigation into Yngve Morsand could be wound up immediately, the police might uncover new evidence which would make Sonny's confession less credible. Harnes didn't know how Nestor had got this information and nor did he want to.

The prison governor had the biggest office, of course, but the office of the assistant prison governor had a view of the mosque and Ekebergåsen. It lay at the end of the corridor and was decorated with hideous paintings by a young female artist who specialised in painting flowers and discussing her libido with the tabloid press.

Franck pressed a button on the intercom and asked for the inmate in cell 317 to be brought to his office.

'That car cost me 1.2 million kroner,' Franck said.

'I bet half of that was for the Porsche insignia on the bonnet,' Harnes said.

'Yep, and the other half went to the government in taxes.' Franck sighed and flopped into the unusual, high-backed office chair. It looked like a throne, Harnes thought.

There was a knock on the door.

'Enter,' Franck called out.

A prison officer appeared. He had his cap tucked under his arm and made a half-hearted salute. From time to time Harnes wondered how Franck got his staff to accept military greeting rituals in a modern workplace. And what other rules they had to swallow.

'Yes, Goldsrud?'

'I'm off now, but before I go I just wanted to know if you have any questions about last night's shift report.'

'I haven't had a chance to look at it yet. Is there anything I should know about, seeing as you're here?'

'Nothing major except for an attempted breakout; I suppose you could call it that.'

Franck pressed his palms together and smiled. 'I'm delighted to hear that our inmates show such initiative and enterprise. Who and how?'

'Johannes Halden in cell 2—'

'238. The old man? Really?'

'He got hold of a pistol somehow. I think it was a spur-of-the-moment thing. I just stopped by to tell you that the whole incident was much less dramatic than it might come across in the report. If you want my opinion, mild repercussions should suffice. The man has done a good job for us for many years and—'

'Gaining someone's trust is a smart move if you wish to ambush them. Because I imagine that's what he did?'

'Well, you see . . .'

'Are you telling me that you allowed yourself to be outwitted, Goldsrud? How far did he get?'

Harnes felt some sympathy with the prison officer who ran his forefinger over a sweaty upper lip. He always empathised with those whose case was weak. He could easily imagine being in their shoes.

'As far as the lock. But there was never any real danger that he would get past the guards even if he had got outside. The security booth has bulletproof glass and gun slits and—'

'Thanks for telling me, but I practically designed this prison,

Goldsrud. And I think you have a soft spot for this guy you've been fraternising with a little too much. I'll refrain from saying anything further until I've read the report, but your entire shift should prepare themselves for some hard questions. As for Johannes, we can't be soft on him; we have a clientele that will exploit every sign of weakness. Understood?'

'Understood.'

The telephone rang.

'Dismissed,' Franck said, picking up the handset.

Harnes was expecting another salute, an about-turn and march, but Goldsrud left the room civilian-style. The lawyer watched him, but jumped as Arild Franck screamed: 'What the hell do you mean "gone"?'

Franck stared at the made-up bed in cell 317. In front of the bed stood a pair of sandals. On the bedside table lay a Bible, on the desk a disposable syringe still in its plastic wrapper and on a chair a white shirt. That was all. Even so, the prison officer behind Franck stated the obvious:

'He's not here.'

Franck glanced at his watch. The cell doors wouldn't be opened for another fourteen minutes so the missing prisoner couldn't be in any of the common rooms.

'He must have left his cell when Johannes opened all the doors from the control room last night.' Goldsrud was standing in the doorway.

'Dear Lord,' Harnes whispered and out of habit pressed his finger against the bridge of his nose where his glasses used to sit until he had paid 15,000 kroner cash last year for laser surgery in Thailand. 'If he has absconded—'

'Shut up,' Franck hissed. 'He can't have made it past the guards. He's still in here somewhere. Goldsrud, raise the alarm. Lock every door – no one gets in or out.'

'But I need to take my kids to—'

'Including you.'

'What about the police?' one of the prison officers said. 'Shouldn't they be informed?'

'No!' Franck yelled. 'Lofthus is still inside Staten, I tell you! Not a word to anyone.'

Arild Franck glowered at the old man. He had locked the door behind him and made sure that there were no prison officers standing outside it.

'Where is Sonny?'

Johannes lay in his bed, rubbing sleep out of his eyes. 'Isn't he in his cell?'

'You know damn well he isn't.'

'Then he must have escaped.'

Franck bent down, grabbed the old man's T-shirt by the neck and pulled him towards him.

'Wipe that grin off your face, Johannes. I know that the security guards outside haven't seen anything so he has to be in here. And if you don't tell me where he is, you can wave goodbye to your cancer treatment.' Franck saw the look of astonishment on the old man's face. 'Oh, you can forget about doctor–patient confidentiality, I've eyes and ears everywhere. So what's it to be?' He released his hold on Johannes, whose head fell back on the pillow.

The old man smoothed his thinning hair and folded his hands behind his head. He cleared his throat. 'Do you know something, Governor? I think I've lived long enough. There's no one waiting for me on the outside. And my sins have been forgiven, so for the first time I might just have a chance to get in upstairs. Perhaps I should take that chance while I still have it. What do you think?'

Arild Franck clenched his teeth so hard it felt as if his fillings might crack.

'What I think will happen, Johannes, is that you'll discover that not a single one of your sins has been forgiven. Because in here I am God and I can guarantee you a slow and painful death from cancer. I'll make sure that you stay here in your cell while the cancer eats you up without ever seeing as much as a glimpse of pain relief. And you wouldn't be the first, let me tell you.'

'Rather that than whatever hell you're going to, Governor.'

Franck wasn't sure if the gurgling noises coming from the old man's throat were death throes or laughter.

On his way back to cell 317 Franck checked his walkie-talkie again. Still no trace of Sonny Lofthus. He knew they would soon be forced to issue a wanted bulletin.

He went in to cell 317, landed heavily on the bed and scanned the floor, walls and ceiling with his eyes. He couldn't bloody believe it. He grabbed the Bible on the bedside table and hurled it against the wall. It fell open on the floor. He knew that Vollan had used the Bible to smuggle in heroin and he glanced at the mangled pages. Damaged creeds and broken sentences with no meaning.

He swore and threw the pillow against the wall.

He watched it land on the floor. Stared at the hair that spilled out. Reddish hair that looked like tufts of beard and some long strands. He kicked the pillow. More matted, dirty blond hair drifted out.

Short-haired. Newly shaven.

And it was at that moment it finally dawned on him.

'Night shift!' he screamed into the walkie-talkie. 'Check all the officers who left at the end of the night shift!'

Franck looked at his watch. 8.10 a.m. He knew what had happened now. And he knew that it was too late to do anything about it. He got up and kicked the chair which smashed into the shatter-proof mirror by the door.

* * *

The bus driver looked at the prison officer who was staring nonplussed at the ticket and the fifty kroner he had been given as change for his hundred-krone note. He could tell that the man was a prison officer because he was wearing a uniform under his long coat and had an ID card saying 'Sørensen' with a photo that looked nothing like him.

'Been a while since you last caught the bus, has it?' the driver asked.

The man with the bad haircut nodded.

'It's only twenty-six kroner if you buy a travel card in advance,' the driver said, but he could tell from the passenger's expression that he thought even this price was a rip-off. It was a common reaction in anyone who hadn't travelled by bus in Oslo for a few years.

'Thanks for your help,' the man said.

The bus driver pulled out from the kerb while he followed the back of the prison officer in his rear-view mirror. He didn't really know why, perhaps it was because of his voice. So warm and sincere as if he really thanked him with all his heart. He saw him sit down and gaze in wonder out of the window like one of those foreign tourists who strayed onto the bus from time to time. Saw him pull a set of keys out of his coat pocket and study them as if he hadn't seen them before. Take a packet of chewing gum from his other coat pocket.

Then he had to concentrate on the traffic in front of him.

PART TWO

12

ARILD FRANCK WAS STANDING AT the window in his office. He looked at his watch. Most escaped prisoners were brought back in the first twelve hours. He had told the press it was the first twenty-four hours so that he could call it a fast result, should it take longer than twelve. But it was coming up for twenty-five hours now, and they still had no leads to go on.

He had just been to the prison governor's large office. The one with no view. And there the man with no view had demanded an explanation. The prison governor was in a foul mood because he had been forced to return early from the annual Nordic prison conference in Reykjavik. On the telephone from Iceland yesterday he had said that he would contact the press. He liked talking to the media, did his boss. Franck had asked for twenty-four hours' media blackout to find Lofthus, but his boss had dismissed this out of hand and said that this wasn't something they could keep under wraps. Firstly, Sonny Lofthus was a killer so the public was entitled to be warned. Secondly, they needed to circulate his picture to the media to help find him.

And, thirdly, you want your own picture in the papers, Franck thought. So your political cronies can see that you're working rather than floating around a blue lagoon drinking Svartadaudir schnapps.

Franck had tried explaining to the governor that circulating pictures was unlikely to be very effective; any photos they had of Sonny Lofthus were from when he was jailed twelve years ago and even then he had had long hair and a beard. And the images from the CCTV cameras after he had cut off his hair were so grainy as to be unusable. And still the governor had insisted on dragging the name of Staten through the mud.

'The police are looking for him, Arild, so surely you know it's only a matter of time before I get a phone call from a reporter wondering why the breakout hasn't been made public and asking if Staten has covered up breakouts before. I prefer to control the story, Arild.'

The prison governor had gone on to ask which procedures Franck thought needed tightening up. And Franck knew why: so that the governor could go to his government friends and pass off the assistant prison governor's ideas as his own. Ideas from a man with a view. And yet he had shared his thoughts with the idiot. Voice recognition to replace fingerprints and electronic tagging with indestructible GPS chips. Ultimately there were things Franck valued higher than himself and Staten Prison was one of them.

Arild Franck looked at Ekebergåsen as it lay bathed in morning sunshine. Once it had been the sunny side of a working-class neighbourhood. Once he had dreamed of buying himself a little house there. Now he owned a bigger house in a more expensive part of Oslo. But he still dreamed about the little house.

Though Nestor appeared to have reacted to the news of the breakout with equanimity, it wasn't the loss of composure in Nestor and his ilk that worried Franck. On the contrary, he suspected they were at their most unruffled when making decisions which were so horrifying they made his blood run cold. On the other hand, they operated with a simple, clear and practical logic that Arild Franck couldn't help but admire.

'Find him,' Nestor had said. 'Or make sure that no one does.'

If they found Lofthus, they could persuade him to confess to the murder of Mrs Morsand before anyone else got to him. They had their methods. If they killed Lofthus, they could stop him from explaining away the technical evidence against him at the Morsand crime scene, but then they wouldn't be able to use him in future cases. That was how it was. Pros and cons. Ultimately, though, it was a matter of hard logic.

'There's a Simon Kefas on the phone for you.' It was Ina's voice on the intercom.

Arild Franck snorted automatically.

Simon Kefas.

Talk about a man who always looked out for number one. A spineless loser who had walked over more than one dead body in his gambling addiction. They said he had changed since he met the woman he was with now. But no one knew better than an assistant prison governor that people don't change; Franck had all the insight he needed into Simon Kefas.

'Tell him I'm not here.'

'He wants to meet with you later today. It's about Per Vollan.'

Vollan? Franck thought the police had declared Vollan's death to be a suicide. He heaved a sigh and looked down at the newspaper on his desk. The breakout was reported further in, but at least it wasn't on the front page. Presumably because the news desk didn't have a good photograph of the escaped prisoner. The vultures probably preferred to wait until they got an E-FIT drawing of the killer where, ideally, he would look like a fiend. In which case they would be disappointed.

'Arild?'

They had an unspoken agreement that she could address him by his first name when no one else was present.

'Find some space in my diary, Ina. Don't give him more than thirty minutes.'

Franck peered at the mosque. Soon it would be twenty-five hours.

Lars Gilberg moved a step closer.

The boy was lying on a flattened piece of cardboard and had covered himself with a long coat. He had arrived the day before and had found a spot to hide behind the bushes that grew along the path and the buildings behind. He had sat there, silent and motionless, as if playing hide-and-seek. Two uniformed police officers had stopped by, looked alternately at Gilberg and a photo they held up before moving on. Gilberg had said nothing. Later that evening when it started to rain, the boy had emerged and lain down under the bridge. Without asking for permission. It wasn't that permission wouldn't be granted, but he hadn't even asked to begin with. And then there was the other thing. He was wearing a uniform. Lars Gilberg wasn't sure what kind of uniform – he had been rejected by the army before he had time to see anything other than the recruiting officer's green one. 'Unsuitable' had been the somewhat vague reason given. From time to time Lars Gilberg wondered if there was anything he was suitable for. And, if so, would he ever find out what that was? Perhaps it was this: getting money for drugs and living under a bridge.

Like now.

The boy was asleep and his breathing was steady. Lars Gilberg took another step. There was something about the way the boy had moved and his skin colour that told Gilberg that he was a junkie. In which case he might still have some drugs on him.

Gilberg was now so close that he could see the boy's eyelids twitch as if the eyeballs underneath were spinning and moving. He squatted down on his haunches and carefully lifted the coat. Extended his fingers towards the breast pocket of the uniform jacket.

It happened so fast that Lars didn't even see it. The boy's hand locked around his wrist and Lars found himself on his knees with his face pressed into the wet soil and his arm twisted behind his back.

A voice whispered into his ear:

'What do you want?'

The voice didn't sound angry or aggressive, not even scared. More polite, rather, as if the boy genuinely wanted to know how he could help him. Lars Gilberg did what he always did when he realised he had been defeated. Cut his losses.

'Steal your stash. Or if you haven't got any, then your money.'

The boy had got him in the standard hold: his wrist bent into his forearm and with pressure applied to the back of his elbow. Police hold. But Gilberg knew how cops walked, talked, looked and smelled, and this boy wasn't one of them.

'What's your poison?'

'Morphine,' Gilberg groaned.

'How much can you get for fifty kroner?'

'A little. Not much.'

The hold was eased and Gilberg quickly snatched back his arm.

He looked up at the boy. Blinked at the banknote he was holding up to him. 'Sorry, it's all I've got.'

'I haven't got anything to sell, mate.'

'The money is for you. I've quit.'

Gilberg narrowed one eye. What was it they said? When something sounded too good to be true, it usually was. But then again, the guy might just be a regular nut job.

He snatched the fifty-krone note and stuffed it into his pocket.

'That's rent for letting you sleep here.'

'I saw the police walk by yesterday,' the boy said. 'Do they come round here a lot?'

'Now and then, but recently we've been overrun with them.'

'Do you happen to know a place they don't overrun?'

Gilberg tilted his head and studied the boy.

'If you wanna avoid the cops altogether, you need to get yourself a room in a hostel. Try the Ila Centre. They don't let cops in there.'

The boy looked pensively at the river, then he nodded slowly. 'Thanks for your help, my friend.'

'Don't mention it,' muttered an astonished Gilberg. Definitely a nut job.

And, as if to confirm his suspicions, the boy started to undress. To be on the safe side Gilberg moved back a couple of steps. When the boy was wearing just his underpants, he wrapped the uniform around the shoes. Gilberg handed him a plastic bag which the boy asked if he could have and into which he put the bundled-up clothes and shoes. He placed the bag under a rock between the bushes where he had spent yesterday.

'I'll make sure no one finds it,' Gilberg said.

'Thank you, I trust you.' Smiling, the boy buttoned his coat, all the way up so that his bare chest couldn't be seen.

Then he started walking down the path. Gilberg looked after him; saw the naked soles of his feet splash water from the puddles onto the tarmac.

I trust you?

Stark staring raving mad.

Martha stood in reception looking at the computer screen with CCTV images from the Ila Centre. More specifically at a man who was staring into the camera outside the entrance door. He hadn't rung the bell yet, hadn't discovered the little hole in the Plexiglas that covered the bell. They had had to install the Plexiglas as bashing in the bell was a common reaction when someone was denied access. Martha pressed the microphone button.

'Can I help you?'

The boy didn't reply. Martha had already established that he wasn't one of their seventy-six current residents. Though the centre had had a turnover of a hundred residents in the last four months, she remembered every single face. But she had concluded that he belonged to Ila's 'target client group' as it was known: drug addicts. Not that he looked high, because he didn't; it was his gaunt face. The lines around his mouth. The dreadful haircut. She sighed.

'Do you need a room?'

The boy nodded and she turned the key in the switch which opened the door lock downstairs. She called out to Stine, who was in the kitchen making sandwiches for one of the residents, to watch reception in her absence. Then she jogged down the stairs and past the iron gate used to bar access to the reception in case intruders forced their way through the entrance door. The boy was standing inside the door, looking around.

His coat was buttoned all the way up to his neck and reached down almost to his ankles. He was barefoot and she could see blood in one wet footprint by the entrance door. But Martha had seen most things by now so what caught her attention was first and foremost his eyes. The way he looked at her. She couldn't explain it any other way. His eyes were focused on her and in them she could see that he was processing the visual impression which she made. It might not be much, but it was more than she was used to at the Ila Centre. And, for a brief moment, it crossed her mind that he might not be using after all, but she dismissed the thought just as quickly.

'Hello. Come with me.'

He followed her up to the first floor and into the meeting room via reception. As usual she left the door open so Stine and the others could see them, asked him to take a seat and took out the forms for the obligatory introduction interview.

'Name?' she asked.

He hesitated.

'I need to put a name on this form,' she said, giving him the opening which many of the people who came here needed.

'Stig,' he said tentatively.

'Stig is fine,' she said. 'Anything else?'

'Berger?'

'Then that's what we'll write here. Date of birth?'

He stated a date and a year and she calculated that he had turned thirty. He looked much younger. That was the strange thing with addicts, it was easy to misjudge their age in either direction.

'Did anyone refer you here?'

He shook his head.

'Where did you sleep last night?'

'Under a bridge.'

'So I presume you're of no fixed abode and don't know which Social Services office you come under; therefore I'll pick the number eleven which is your birthday and that gives us . . .' She checked her list. 'Alna Social Services, which, in its infinite mercy, will hopefully decide to fund you. What kind of drugs are you on?'

Her pen was hovering, but he made no reply.

'Just mention your favourite poison.'

'I've quit.'

She put down her pen. 'The Ila Centre is a place for active drug users. I can make a call to the centre in Sporveisgata and see if they have a room for you. It's much nicer than here.'

'Are you saying . . . ?'

'Yes, I'm saying you need to get high on a regular basis to qualify.' She flashed him a tired smile.

'And if I were to say that I lied because I thought it would be easier to get a room here if I said I was clean?'

'Then you have also answered that question correctly, but you've no more lifelines left, my friend.'

'Heroin,' he said.

'And?'

'Just heroin.'

She ticked the box on the form, but doubted if it was true. There was hardly a single pure heroin user left in Oslo; everyone was a mixed-substance user these days for the simple reason that if you combined the already mixed heroin with a benzodiazepine such as Rohypnol, for example, you got a bigger bang for your buck in terms of both the intensity and length of the fix.

'Why have you come here?'

He shrugged. 'To get a roof over my head.'

'Any illnesses or essential medication?'

'No.'

'Do you have any plans for the future?'

He looked at her. Martha's father used to say that a person's past was written in their eyes and it was worth learning how to read it. But that their future couldn't be found there. The future was unknown. Even so, Martha would later look back at this moment and ask herself if she could, if she should have been able to read anything about the future plans of the man who called himself Stig Berger.

He shook his head and gave the same reaction to her questions about work, education, previous overdoses, somatic illnesses, blood infections and mental health issues. At the end she explained that the centre had a policy of total confidentiality and they wouldn't tell anyone that he was a resident, but should he wish to, he could complete a consent form naming anyone who could be given information, should they contact the centre.

'So that your parents, friends or girlfriend can get in touch with you, for example.'

He smiled wistfully. 'I've none of those.'

Martha Lian had heard this reply many times before. So many times it no longer made an impression on her. Her therapist called it compassion fatigue and had explained that it affected most people in her profession at some point. What worried Martha was that it didn't seem to get any better. Of course she understood that there is a limit to how cynical a person who worries about their own cynicism can be, but she had always been fuelled by empathy. Compassion. Love. And she was close to running on empty. So she was startled when she heard the words *I've none of those* touch something, like a needle causing an atrophied muscle to twitch.

She gathered up the papers and put them in a folder which she left at reception and took the new resident down to a small storeroom on the ground floor.

'I hope you're not the paranoid type who can't handle wearing second-hand clothing,' she said and turned her back while he took off his coat and put on the clothes and trainers she had selected for him.

She waited till he coughed. She turned round. Somehow he looked taller and straighter in the pale blue jumper and the jeans. Nor was he as skinny as he had looked in the coat. He glanced down at his plain blue trainers.

'Yes,' she said. 'The shoe of choice for the homeless.'

Large quantities of blue trainers had been donated to various deserving organisations in the 1980s by the Norwegian Army's surplus depot and they had become synonymous with drug addicts and the homeless.

'Thank you,' he said quietly.

Martha had initially started seeing her therapist because of a resident who failed to thank her. It had only been one more 'non-thank-you' in a long line of other 'non-thank-yous' from the self-destructive individuals who still enjoyed some sort of existence thanks to the welfare state and the various social organ-isations the same junkies spent the majority of their waking hours ranting at. She had lost her temper. Told him to go to hell if he didn't like the size of the disposable syringe he got for free so he could go to his room – for which Social Services paid six thousand kroner a month – to get high on drugs he had financed by stealing bicycles in the neighbourhood. Along with his complaint, the resident had filed a four-page-long hard-luck story. She had been forced to apologise.

'Let me take you to your room,' she said.

On the way up to the second floor she showed him where the bathrooms and lavatories were. Men walked past them with brisk footsteps and stoned eyes.

'Welcome to Oslo's best drugs shopping centre,' Martha said.

'In here?' the boy asked. 'You allow dealing?'

'Not according to the rules, but if you're using, you'll obviously have drugs in your possession. And I'm telling you this because it's useful for you to know, we don't check if that's one gram or one kilo. We've no control over what's being bought and sold in the rooms. We'll only enter if we suspect you of keeping weapons.'

'People do that?'

She gave him a sideways glance. 'Why do you ask?'

'I just want to know how dangerous staying here is going to be.'

'All the dealers here have runners who act as enforcers and they use everything from baseball bats to regular firearms to collect debts from the other residents. Last week I raided a room and found a harpoon gun under the bed.'

'A harpoon gun?'

'Yep. A loaded Sting 65.'

She surprised herself by laughing and he smiled back. He had a nice smile. So many of them did.

She knocked before unlocking the door to room 323.

'We've had to close off several rooms due to fire damage, so people are having to share until the damage has been made good. Your room-mate is called Johnny, the others call him Johnny Puma. He has ME and spends most of the day in bed. But he's a nice, quiet guy so I don't expect you'll have any trouble with him.'

She opened the door. The curtains were closed and it was dark inside. She turned on the light. The fluorescent tubes in the ceiling flashed a couple of times before they came on.

'How nice,' the boy said.

Martha looked around the room. She had never heard anyone describe the rooms at the Ila Centre as nice unless they were being sarcastic. But somehow he was right. Yes, the lino was worn and the sky-blue walls full of dents and graffiti which not even lye could wash off, but it was clean and light. The furniture consisted of a bunk bed, a chest of drawers and a scratched low table with peeling paint, but it was all intact and in working order. The air smelled of the man asleep in the bottom bunk. The boy had stated he had never overdosed, so she had allocated him the top bunk. They prioritised bottom bunks to residents most likely to overdose since it was much easier to move them from a bottom bunk and onto a stretcher.

'Here you are,' Martha said, handing him the key ring with the key. 'I'll be your primary contact which means you come to me if there's anything you need. OK?'

'Thank you,' he said, taking the blue plastic tag and looking at it. 'Thank you so much.'

13

'HE'S ON HIS WAY DOWN,' the receptionist called out to Simon and Kari, who were sitting on a leather sofa beneath a gigantic painting of something which might be a sunrise.

'That's what she said ten minutes ago,' Kari whispered.

'In heaven God decides what time it is,' Simon said and slipped a piece of *snus* under his upper lip. 'What do you think a painting like that costs? And why pick that one?'

'The acquisition of public art, as it's known, is nothing but a hidden subsidy for our country's mediocre artists,' Kari said. 'The buyers couldn't care less about what's on their walls as long as it matches the furniture and their budget.'

Simon glanced at her sideways. 'Has anyone ever told you that you sometimes sound as if you're reeling off quotes you've learned by rote?'

Kari smiled wryly. 'And *snus* is a poor substitute for smoking. Bad for your health. I presume your wife made you switch because the smell of cigarettes lingered on her clothes?'

Simon chuckled and shook his head. It must be what passed for humour among the young these days. 'Nice try, but you're wrong.

She asked me to stop because she wants me around for as long as possible. And she doesn't know I suck tobacco. I keep it at the office.'

'Let them in, Anne,' a voice bellowed.

Simon looked at the lock where a man in uniform and a cap that would have found favour with a Belarus president drummed his fingers on the metal bars.

Simon rose.

'We'll decide if we're going to let them out again later,' Arild Franck said.

Simon could tell from the receptionist's almost imperceptible rolling of the eyes that the joke was a very old one.

'So, what's it like to be back in the gutter?' Franck asked as he escorted them through the lock and over to the staircase. 'You're in the Serious Fraud Office now, I believe. Oh, I'm so sorry, I'm going senile, I completely forgot that they kicked you out.'

Simon made no attempt to laugh at the deliberate insult.

'We're here because of Per Vollan,'

'I heard. I thought the case had been closed?'

'We don't close a case until it's solved.'

'Is that a new thing?'

Simon mimed a smile by pressing his lips against his teeth. 'Per Vollan came here to visit inmates on the day he died, is that right?'

Franck opened the door to his office. 'Vollan was a prison chaplain so I assume he was doing his job. I can check the visitors' log, if you like.'

'Yes, please. And if you could give us a list of anyone he spoke to as well?'

'I'm afraid I wouldn't know the names of everybody he came into contact with while he was here.'

'We know of at least one person he saw that day,' Kari said.

'Oh?' Franck said, taking a seat behind the desk which had

followed him his entire career. 'Young lady, if you're planning on staying, please fetch the coffee cups from the cupboard over there while I check the visitors' log.'

'Thanks, but I don't drink caffeine,' Kari said. 'His name is Sonny Lofthus.'

Franck looked at her with a blank expression.

'We were wondering if it might be possible to visit him?' Simon said. He had taken a seat without being offered one. He looked up at Franck's already reddening face. 'Oh, I'm so sorry, I'm going senile. He's just escaped.'

Simon could see Franck composing an answer, but beat him to it.

'We're interested in him because the coincidence between Vollan's visit and Lofthus's escape makes Vollan's death even more suspicious.'

Franck tugged at his shirt collar. 'How do you know that they met?'

'All police interviews are stored in a shared database,' said Kari who had remained standing. 'When I looked up Per Vollan, I saw that his name was mentioned in an interview in connection with Lofthus's escape. By an inmate named Gustav Rover.'

'Rover has just been released. He was interviewed because he spoke to Sonny Lofthus shortly before he absconded. We wanted to know if Lofthus had said anything which might give us an idea of what he was up to.'

'We? Us?' Simon raised a grey eyebrow. 'Strictly speaking it's the police's job – and only ours – to catch escaped prisoners, not yours.'

'Lofthus is my prisoner, Kefas.'

'Rover doesn't appear to have been able to help you,' Simon said. 'But he mentioned when questioned that just as he was leaving the cell, Per Vollan arrived to talk to Lofthus.'

Franck shrugged his shoulders. 'What about it?'

'So we're wondering what the two of them talked about. And why one of them is killed shortly afterwards and the other one breaks out.'

'Might be a coincidence.'

'Of course. Do you know a man called Hugo Nestor, Franck? Also known as the Ukrainian?'

'I've heard the name.'

'So that's a yes. Is there anything to suggest that Nestor might be involved with the breakout?'

'How do you mean?'

'Did he help Lofthus escape or did he threaten Lofthus in prison, thus precipitating the escape?'

Franck drummed a pen against the desk. He looked as if he was deep in thought.

Out of the corner of his eye Simon saw Kari check her text messages.

'I know how badly you need a result, but you're not going to catch any big fish here,' Franck said. 'Sonny Lofthus absconded entirely on his own initiative.'

'Wow,' Simon said, leaning back in his chair and pressing his fingertips together. 'A young drug addict, a mere amateur, absconds from Staten, of all prisons, entirely unaided?'

Franck smiled. 'Do you want to bet on the amateur bit, Kefas?' And his grin spread when Simon failed to respond. 'So senile of me, you're no longer a betting man. So let me show you your amateur.'

'These are the recordings from the surveillance cameras,' Franck said, gesturing towards the twenty-four-inch computer screen. 'At this point all the officers in the control room are lying face down on the floor and Johannes has unlocked all the doors in the prison.'

The screen was split into sixteen windows, one for each camera, showing various sections of the prison. At the bottom of the screen was a clock.

'There he comes,' Franck said, pointing to a window showing one of the prison corridors.

Simon and Kari saw a young man coming out of a cell and running stiffly towards the camera. He was dressed in a white shirt that reached almost to his knees and Simon concluded that the man's barber must be even worse than his own; his hair looked as if it had been kicked off his head.

The young man disappeared out of the picture. And reappeared in one of the others.

'This is Lofthus going through the lock,' Franck said. 'And while he's there, Johannes is busy giving a speech about what he's going to do to the officers' families if anyone tries to stop him. The interesting part is what happens in the staff changing room.'

They saw Lofthus run into a room with lockers, but instead of continuing straight to the exit, he turned left and disappeared out of the picture behind the last row of lockers. Franck hit one of the keys angrily with his index finger and the clock at the bottom of the screen stopped running.

Franck moved the cursor over the clock and entered the time 07:20. Then he started playing the recording at four times the normal speed. Uniformed men appeared in a window on the screen. They walked in and out of the changing room and the door was constantly opening and closing. It was impossible to tell them apart until Franck froze the screen with another keystroke.

'There he is,' Kari said. 'He's wearing a uniform and a coat now.'

'Sørensen's uniform and coat,' Franck said. 'He must have switched clothes and waited in the changing room. Sat on the bench, kept his head down, pretending to be tying his shoelaces or something while the others came and went. We have such a high staff turnover here that no one would look twice at a new guy who was a bit slow getting changed. He waited until the morning rush peaked and left with the others. No one recognised Sonny without his beard and long hair, which he had cut off in his cell and stuffed into his pillow. Not even me . . .'

With another keystroke he restarted playback, this time at normal speed. The screen showed a young man in a coat and uniform leaving through the back entrance while Arild Franck and a man with swept-back hair and a grey suit were on their way in.

'And the guards outside never stopped him?'

Franck pointed to the image in the bottom right-hand corner of the screen.

'This is taken from the security booth. As you can see, we let cars and people leave without checking their ID. It would create a bottleneck if we had to go through full security procedures at every shift change. But from now on we will also check them out at shift changes.'

'Yes, I don't suppose anyone is queuing up to get in,' Simon joked.

In the silence that followed they could hear Kari suppress a yawn at Simon's spin on Franck's welcoming joke.

'So there's your amateur,' Franck said.

Simon Kefas made no reply, he just studied the back of the figure strolling past the security guards. For some reason he started to smile. He realised it was the way Lofthus walked. He recognised that walk.

Martha was standing with her arms folded across her chest, sizing up the two men in front of her. They couldn't be Drug Squad; she thought she knew most of the officers on the Drug Squad and she had never seen these two before.

'We're looking for . . .' one of them began, but the rest of his sentence was drowned out by the howling siren of an ambulance passing behind them in Waldemar Thranes gate.

'What?' Martha shouted. She wondered where she had seen black suits like that. In an advert?

'Sonny Lofthus?' the smaller of them repeated. He had blond hair and looked as if his nose had been broken several times. Martha saw noses like that every day, but she thought this one was the result of contact sport.

'We never give out the names of our residents,' she informed them.

The other, a tall yet compact man with black curls arranged in a strange semicircle around his head, showed her a photograph.

'He's escaped from Staten Prison and is considered dangerous.' Another ambulance approached and he leaned over her, shouting into her face: 'So if he's a resident here and you fail to tell us, it's on your head if anything happens. Do you understand?'

So not the Drug Squad; at least that explained why she hadn't seen them before. She nodded while she studied the photograph. Looked up at them again. Opened her mouth to say something when a gust of wind blew her dark fringe into her face. She was about to try again when she heard shouting behind her. It was Toy on the stairs.

'Oi, Martha, Burre has gone and cut himself. I dunno what to do. He's back in the cafe.'

'People come and go in the summer,' she said. 'It's a time when many of our residents prefer to sleep rough in the parks, and this in turn makes room for new arrivals. It's hard to remember every single face—'

'Like I said, his name is Sonny Lofthus.'

'—and not everybody wants to register under their real name. We don't expect our clients to have a passport or other forms of ID so we accept whatever name they give us.'

'But don't Social Services need to know who they are?' the blond one asked.

Martha bit her lower lip.

'Hey, Martha, Burre is, like, literally bleeding all over the place!'

The man with the curly halo placed a large, hairy hand on Martha's bare upper arm. 'Why don't you just let us have a look around and we'll see if we can find him?' He noticed the look in her eyes and withdrew his hand.

'Talking about ID,' she said. 'Perhaps I should ask to see yours?'

She saw something darken in the eyes of the blond man. And there was the hand of the curly-haired man again. Not on her upper arm this time, but around it.

'Burre is almost out of blood.' Toy had come over to where they were; he swayed and fixed the two men with his swimming eyes. 'What's going on here?'

Martha wriggled to free herself and put her hand on Toy's shoulder. 'Then we had better go and save his life. Gentleman, if you would care to wait.'

Martha and Toy walked across to the cafe. Another ambulance rushed past. Three ambulances. She shuddered involuntarily.

When she reached the door to the cafe, she turned round.

The two men were gone.

'So you and Harnes *saw* Sonny close up?' Simon asked as Franck escorted him and Kari back down to the ground floor.

Franck glanced at his watch. 'What we saw was a young, clean-shaven man with short hair in a uniform. The Sonny we knew wore a filthy shirt, had matted long hair and a beard.'

'So you're saying it'll be difficult to find him given how he now looks?' Kari asked.

'The pictures from the surveillance cameras are of poor quality, as you'd expect.' Arild Franck turned round and fixed her with his eyes. 'But we'll find him.'

'It's a shame it wasn't possible for us to talk to this Halden,' Simon remarked.

'Yes, as I said his illness has taken a turn for the worse,' Franck replied as he led them back to reception. 'I'll let you know when he's well enough for visitors.'

'And you've no idea what Lofthus might have been talking to Per Vollan about?'

Franck shook his head. 'The usual unburdening and spiritual guidance, I presume. Though Sonny Lofthus was himself a confidant.'

'Was he?'

'Lofthus kept himself apart from the other inmates. He was neutral, didn't belong to any of the factions you find in every prison. And he never talked. That's the definition of a good listener, isn't it? He had become a kind of confessor to the other inmates, someone they could trust with anything. Who would he tell? He had no allies and he was going to stay in prison for the foreseeable future.'

'What kind of murders was he in for?' Kari asked.

'Human murders,' Franck remarked drily.

'I mean—'

'Murders of the most brutal kind. He shot an Asian girl and strangled a Kosovo Albanian.' Franck held the exit door open for them.

'And to think that such a dangerous criminal is now at large,' Simon said, knowing he was twisting the knife now. Not that he was a sadist, but he was prepared to make an exception when it came to Arild Franck. Not because Franck was someone who was hard to like, in fact his personality was a mitigating circumstance. Nor because the man didn't do his job – everyone at Police HQ knew that Franck was the real boss at Staten, rather than the man who held the title of prison governor. No, it was the other matter, these apparent coincidences which combined to create a suspicion that had been gnawing away at Simon and was approaching the most frustrating kind of knowledge, the one you can't prove. That Arild Franck was on the take.

'I give him forty-eight hours, Chief Inspector,' Franck said. 'He has no money, no relatives or friends. He's a loner who has been in prison since he was eighteen years old. That's twelve years ago. He knows nothing about the world outside, he has nowhere to go, no places to hide.'

While Kari hurried to keep up with Simon on their way to the car, Simon thought about the forty-eight hours and was tempted by the bet. Because he had recognised something about the boy. He didn't know quite what it was; perhaps it was just the way he moved. Or perhaps he had inherited more than that.

14

JOHNNY PUMA TURNED OVER IN his bed and sized up his new room-mate. He didn't know who had invented the term room-mate, only that at the Ila Centre it was about as much of a misnomer as you could get. Room enemy would have been more appropriate. He had yet to share a room with anyone who didn't try to rob him blind. Or someone he hadn't tried to rob blind himself. So he kept all his valuables, which comprised a waterproof wallet containing three thousand kroner and a double plastic bag with three grams of amphetamine, taped to a thigh so hairy that any attempt to remove it would rouse him even from the deepest sleep.

This was what Johnny Puma's life had been about these last twenty years: amphetamines and sleep. He had been given most of the diagnoses they handed out in the seventies and onwards to explain why a young man would rather party than work, would rather fight and screw around than buy a house and start a family, get high rather than get clean and live a deadly boring life. But the last diagnosis had stuck. ME. Myalgic encephalomyelitis. Chronic exhaustion. Johnny Puma exhausted? Anyone who heard it simply laughed. Johnny Puma, the weightlifter, the life and soul of the party, Lillesand's most popular removal man who could shift a piano single-handed. It had started with a painful hip, painkillers that didn't work, followed by painkillers that worked only too well, and he was hooked. Now his life consisted of long days resting in bed, interspersed by intense periods of activity where he had to channel all his energy into getting drugs. Or find money to pay off his already alarmingly large debt to the centre's drug baron, a Lithuanian transsexual halfway through a sex change who called herself Coco.

Johnny could tell at a glance that the young man standing by the window needed to score. The constant, frantic search. The compulsion. The struggle.

'Please would you close the curtains, mate?'

The other obeyed and the room became pleasantly dark once more.

'What are you using, mate?'

'Heroin.'

Heroin? Here at the centre people said dope when they meant heroin. Shit, scag, horse or dust. Or boy. Or Superboy when it came to the new wonder drug you could buy down at Nybrua from a guy who looked like Sleepy from *Snow White*. Heroin was what people called it in prison. Or if they were rookies, of course. Though if you were a proper rookie, you could use expressions such as China White, Mexican Mud or any of the other nonsense terms you picked up from the movies.

'I can get you good, cheap heroin. You don't need to go out.'

Johnny saw something happen to the figure in the darkness. He had seen how junkies who were really desperate could get high at the mere promise of drugs; he believed tests had registered changes in the brain's pleasure centre in the several seconds before the fix. With a forty per cent gross margin on the drugs he could buy from Høvdingen in room 36, Johnny could buy three or four bags of speed for himself. It was preferable to robbing the neighbourhood again.

'No thanks. I can leave if you want to sleep.'

The voice coming from the window was so soft and low that Johnny couldn't understand how it managed to cut through Ila's constant noise of partying, screaming, music, arguing and traffic. So the guy wanted to know if Johnny was about to go to sleep, eh? So he could search him. Maybe find the wrap that Johnny had taped to his thigh.

'I never sleep, I just shut my eyes. You get me, mate?'

The young man nodded. 'I'm going out now.'

When the door had closed behind his new room enemy, Johnny Puma got out of bed. It took him only two minutes to search the guy's wardrobe and the top bunk. Nothing. De nada. His room enemy couldn't be as green as he looked; he carried everything with him.

Markus Engseth was frightened.

'Are you scared now?' said the bigger of the two boys blocking his path.

Markus shook his head and gulped.

'Yes, you're so scared you're sweating, you fat pig. Hey, can you smell that?'

'Look, he's going to cry,' the other boy laughed.

They were fifteen years old, possibly sixteen. Or even seventeen. Markus didn't know, he knew only that they were much bigger and older than him.

'We just want to borrow it,' said the bigger boy and grabbed hold of the handlebars of Markus's bicycle. 'We'll give it back to you.'

'Eventually,' the other laughed again.

Markus looked up at the windows of the houses in the quiet street. Black, blind, glass surfaces. Normally he didn't like people watching him. He liked being invisible so that he could sneak past the garden gate and up to the abandoned yellow house. But right now he hoped that a window would open up somewhere, that a grown-up voice would shout at the big boys to clear off. Back to Tåsen or Nydalen, or some other neighbourhood where thugs like them belonged. But it remained completely silent. Summer silence. It was the holidays and the other children in the street had gone off to cabins, beaches or foreign cities. It made no difference as far as playing was concerned, Markus always played on his own. But being small was riskier when you weren't one in a crowd.

The big boy yanked the bicycle out of Markus's hands and he realised that he didn't have the strength to blink away the tears any more. The bicycle his mum had bought him with money they could otherwise have spent going away somewhere this summer.

'My dad is home,' he said, pointing across the street towards their red house that lay opposite the empty yellow one he had just been inside.

'So why haven't you called for him?' The boy sat on Markus's bicycle to try it out; it wobbled and he seemed cross that there wasn't enough air in the tyres.

'Dad!' Markus called out, but could instantly hear how half-hearted and false it sounded.

The older boys howled with laughter. The other one had sat down on the parcel rack and Markus saw how the rubber tyres began twisting off the rim.

'I don't think you have a dad,' said the boy and spat on the ground. 'Come on, Herman, ride!'

'I'm trying, but you're stopping me.'

'No, I'm not.'

The three boys turned round.

A man was standing behind the bicycle holding onto the rack. He lifted the back of the bicycle so it started freewheeling and both boys fell forward. They stumbled off and glared at the man.

'What the hell do you think you're doing?' the older boy snarled.

The man made no reply, he just looked at him. Markus noticed his strange haircut, the Salvation Army logo on his T-shirt and the scars on his forearms. It was so quiet that Markus thought he could hear every bird in Berg singing. And now it looked like the two older boys had also noticed the man's scars.

'We were only going to borrow it.' The bigger boy's voice had taken on a different tone; it was croaky and small.

'But you can have it if you want,' the other one added quickly.

The man just carried on staring at them. He gestured to Markus to take the bicycle. The two boys started to back away.

'Where do you live?'

'Tåsen. Are . . . are you his dad?'

'Might be. Next stop Tåsen, OK?'

The boys nodded in unison. They turned round as if on command and marched off.

Markus looked up at the man who was smiling down at him. Behind them he heard one of the boys say to the other: 'His dad's a druggy – did you see his arms?'

'What's your name?' the man said.

'Markus,' he replied.

'Have a nice summer, Markus,' the man said, gave him back his bicycle and walked across to the gate to the yellow house. Markus held his breath. It was a house like every other house in the street; square like a box, not particularly large and surrounded by a small garden. But this house and its garden were in need of a lick of paint and a session with the lawnmower. Still, it was *The House*. The man headed straight for the basement stairs. Not the front door like Markus had seen salesmen or Jehovah's Witnesses do. Did he know about the key which was hidden on the beam above the basement door and which Markus was careful always to put back?

He got his answer when he heard the basement door open and close again.

Markus's jaw dropped. No one had been inside that house for as long as he could remember. Admittedly, he could only remember back as far as when he was five, which was seven years ago, but somehow it seemed right that the house was empty. Who would want to live in a house where someone had killed themselves?

Well, there was one person who turned up at least twice a year. Markus had only seen him once and guessed that he must be the one who turned the heating on low before the winter and turned it off again in the spring. He must be paying the bills. His mum had said that without power the house would have been so damaged by now that it would have been uninhabitable, but she didn't know who the man was, either. But he had looked nothing like the man who was inside the house now, Markus was convinced of it.

Markus could see the face of the new arrival in the kitchen window. There were no curtains in the house so whenever Markus went inside, he would stay well clear of the windows to avoid being seen. The man didn't look like he was there to turn on the heating, so what was he doing in there? How could Markus . . . then he remembered the telescope.

Markus pushed his bicycle through the gate to the red house and ran upstairs to his bedroom. His telescope – which was really just an ordinary pair of binoculars on a stand – was the only thing his dad hadn't taken with him when he left. Or so his mum said. Markus pointed the binoculars towards the yellow house and zoomed in. The man had gone. He moved the circular field of view across the wall of the house, from window to window. And there he was. In the boy's bedroom. Where the druggy had lived. Markus had explored the house and knew every nook and cranny. Including the secret hiding place under the loose floorboard in the master bedroom. But even if no one had killed themselves there, he would never want to live in the yellow house. Before it was abandoned for good, the son of the dead man had lived there. The son was a drug addict and had made a terrible mess and never cleaned up. He hadn't carried out any repairs, either, so the water leaked through the roof whenever it rained. The son had disappeared shortly after Markus was born. He went to prison, Markus's mum had said. For killing someone. And Markus had wondered if the house put an evil spell on those who lived in it so that they killed themselves or others. Markus shuddered. Even though it was his favourite thing about the house – that it was a bit sinister, that he could make up stories about what went on inside it. Only today he didn't have to make anything up, today something was going on inside it all by itself.

The man had opened the bedroom window – no wonder, the place needed airing. Even so, Markus liked this room best, though the bed linen was filthy and there were needles on the floor. The man was standing with his back to the window, looking at the pictures that Markus liked so much. The family photo where all three of them were smiling and looking happy. The one with the boy in the wrestling suit next to his father in a tracksuit holding up a sports trophy together. The picture of the father in his police uniform.

The man opened the wardrobe, took out the grey hoodie and the red sports bag with *Oslo Wrestling Club* in white letters. He put a couple of things into the bag, but Markus couldn't see what. Then he left the bedroom and disappeared. And reappeared again in the study, a small room with a desk pushed up against the window. His mum said that was where they had found the dead body. The man was looking for something near the window. Markus knew what he was looking for, but unless he knew his way around, he would never find it. Then the man appeared to be opening the desk drawer, but he had set down the sports bag on top of the desk so Markus could no longer see properly.

The man must have either found what he was looking for or given up because he took the sports bag and left. Then he went to the master bedroom before going downstairs and Markus lost sight of him.

Ten minutes later the basement door opened and the man came up the steps. He had put on the hoodie, pulled the hood up over his head and thrown the bag over his shoulder. He walked out of the gate and down the road the way he had come.

Markus jumped down and ran outside. He saw the back of the hoodie, jumped over the fence to the yellow house, raced across the lawn and down the basement steps. Trembling and out of breath he felt with his fingers along the beam. The key had been put back! He breathed a sigh of relief and let himself in. He wasn't scared, not really, in a way this was his house. It was the stranger who was the intruder. Unless . . .

He ran up to the study. Headed straight for the well-stacked bookshelves. Second shelf between *Lord of the Flies* and *They Burn the Thistles*. Stuck his fingers in. The key to the desk drawer was there. But had it been found and used? He looked at the desk while he inserted the key into the keyhole and turned it. There was a dark stain on the wood. It might be a greasy spot caused by years of use, but in Markus's mind there was no doubt that it was the imprint of the head which had lain in that very spot, in a pool of blood and with a blood spatter across the wall, just like he had seen in the movies.

Markus stared into the drawer. He gasped. It had gone! It must have been him. The son. He had come back. No one else could possibly know where the key to the desk drawer was kept. And he had had needle marks on his arms.

Markus went into the boy's bedroom. His room. He glanced around and immediately realised what was missing. The photo of the father in his police uniform. The Discman. And one of the four

CDs. He looked at the other three. The one which wasn't there was Depeche Mode, *Violator*. Markus had listened to it, but hadn't thought much of it.

He sat down in the middle of the room to be sure he couldn't be seen from the street. He listened to the summer silence outside. The son had returned. Markus had invented a whole life for the boy in the photo. But he had forgotten that people age. And now he had come back. To fetch the thing in the desk drawer.

Then Markus heard a car engine break the silence.

'Are you sure the numbering doesn't go the other way?' Kari asked as she peered out at the modest wooden houses, hoping to spot a house number for guidance. 'Perhaps we should ask that guy over there.'

She nodded towards the kerb where a guy in a hoodie with the hood up, his head down and a red bag over his shoulder was walking towards them.

'The house is just over the hill,' Simon said and accelerated. 'Trust me.'

'So you knew his father?'

'Yes. What did you find out about the boy?'

'Anyone at Staten who was prepared to talk to me said that he was quiet and didn't say much, but that he was well liked. He had no real friends and kept mainly to himself. I haven't been able to track down any relatives. This is his last known address.'

'Do you have keys to the house?'

'They were with his belongings that were being stored in the prison. I didn't need a new warrant – a search warrant had already been issued in connection with his escape.'

'So an officer has already visited?'

'Only to check if Sonny had gone home. Though no one really thought he would be that stupid.'

'No friends, no relatives, no money. That doesn't leave him with a lot of options. You'll soon learn that prisoners, as a rule, are remarkably stupid.'

'I know, but that breakout wasn't the work of an idiot.'

'Perhaps not,' Simon admitted.

'No,' Kari said firmly. 'Sonny Lofthus was an A-grade student. He was one of Norway's best wrestlers in his age group. Not because he was the strongest, but because he was a clever tactician.'

'You've done your homework.'

'No,' she said. 'I just googled his name, looked at PDFs of old newspapers, made a few phone calls. It's not rocket science.'

'There's the house,' he said.

Simon parked the car, they got out and Kari opened the garden gate.

'How dilapidated it looks now,' he remarked.

Simon took out his police issue revolver and checked the safety catch was off before Kari unlocked the front door.

Simon entered first with his weapon raised. He stopped in the hallway and listened. He flicked on the light switch. A wall lamp lit up.

'Oops,' he whispered. 'Unusual for an uninhabited house to have power. Looks like someone has recently—'

'No, Kari said. 'I've checked it. Ever since Lofthus went to prison the utility bills have been paid from a Cayman Islands account that's impossible to trace back to an individual. The amounts aren't huge, but it's—'

'—mysterious,' Simon said. 'That's all good, we detectives just love a good mystery, don't we?'

He led the way down the hallway and into the kitchen. He opened the fridge. He discovered that it wasn't plugged in even though there was a solitary carton of milk inside it. He nodded to Kari who gave him a puzzled look before she understood. She sniffed the open milk carton. No smell. Then she shook the carton and they heard the rattling of lumps that had once been milk. She followed Simon through the living room. Up the stairs to the first floor. They checked all the rooms and ended up in what was clearly the boy's bedroom. Simon sniffed the air.

'His family,' Kari said, pointing to one of the photographs on the wall.

'Yes,' Simon said.

'His mother – she looks like a singer or an actress, doesn't she?'

Simon made no reply; he was looking at the other photograph. The one that was missing. More precisely, he looked at the faded rectangle on the wallpaper where the photograph used to be. He sniffed the air again.

'I managed to speak to one of Sonny's old teachers,' Kari said. 'He said that Sonny wanted to be a police officer like his father, but that he went off the rails when his father died. Got into trouble at school, pushed people away, deliberately isolated himself and became self-destructive. His mother, too, fell apart after the suicide, she—'

'Helene,' Simon said.

'Pardon?'

'Her name was Helene. An overdose of sleeping pills.' Simon scanned the room. His gaze stopped at the dusty bedside table while Kari's voice intoned in the background:

'When Sonny was eighteen years old, he confessed to two murders and was sent to prison.'

There was a line in the dust.

'Up until then the police investigations had pointed in completely different directions.'

Simon took two brisk steps towards the window. The afternoon sunshine fell on the bicycle that was lying on the ground in front of the red house. He looked down the road they had come up. There was no one there now.

'Things aren't always how they appear,' he said.

'What do you mean?'

Simon closed his eyes. Did he have the energy? All over again? He took a deep breath.

'Everyone in the police thought that Ab Lofthus must have been the mole. When Ab died, the mole's activities ceased, no more strangely failed raids, or evidence, witnesses or suspects suddenly disappearing. They took that as proof.'

'But?'

Simon shrugged. 'Ab was a man who was proud of his work and the police force. He didn't care about getting rich, all he cared about was his family. But there is no doubt that there was a mole.'

'So?'

'So someone still has to find out who that mole was.'

Simon sniffed again. Sweat. He could smell sweat. Someone had been here recently.

'And who might that be?' she asked.

'Someone young and resourceful.' Simon looked at Kari. Over her shoulder. At the wardrobe door. Sweat. Fear.

'There's no one here,' Simon said loudly. 'All good. Let's go downstairs.'

Simon stopped halfway down the stairs and signalled to Kari to carry on walking. He remained where he was and waited. He listened out as he gripped the handle of his pistol tightly.

Silence.

Then he followed Kari.

He returned to the kitchen, found a pen and wrote something on a pad of yellow Post-it notes.

Kari cleared her throat. 'What exactly did Franck mean when he said you were kicked out of the Serious Fraud Office?'

'I'd rather not talk about it,' Simon said, tore off the Post-it note and stuck it on the fridge door.

'Did it have anything to do with gambling?'

Simon looked at her sharply. Then he left.

She read the note.

I knew your father. He was a good man and I think he would have said the same about me. Contact me and I promise you that I'll bring you in in a safe and proper manner.

Simon Kefas, tel. 550106573, simon.kefas@oslopol.no

Then she rushed after him.

Markus Engseth heard the car start and breathed a sigh of relief. He was squatting under the clothes on the hangers with his back pressed against the back of the wardrobe. He had never been so scared in his whole life; he could smell his T-shirt which was so wet with sweat that it was sticking to his body. And yet it had also been exhilarating. Like when he was in free fall from the ten-metre board at Frognerbadet's diving pool, thinking that the worst that could happen was that he might die. And that it wouldn't be that terrible, really.

15

'AND HOW MAY I HELP Sir today?' Tor Jonasson said.

It was how he usually addressed his customers. Tor was twenty years old, the average age of his customers twenty-five and the goods in the shop less than five. And that was why the archaic form of address was funny, in Tor Jonasson's opinion. However, it looked like his humour had gone way over his customer's head – though it was hard to tell since the guy's hood was pulled so far down that his face was basically in the shade. Words emerged from the land of shadows.

'I want one of those mobiles where you can't trace the caller.'

A drug dealer. Of course. They were the only customers who ever asked for such a phone.

'On this iPhone you can block the sender details,' Tor said and picked up a white phone from a shelf in the small shop. 'Your number won't show up on the display of the person you're calling. It's a great contract.'

The potential customer shifted his weight. Adjusted the strap of the red sports bag on his shoulder. Tor decided not to take his eyes off him until he was well outside the shop.

'No, I don't want a contract phone,' the guy said. 'I want one that can't be traced. Not even by the provider.'

Or the police, Tor Jonasson thought. 'You're thinking of a burner phone. Like they use in *The Wire*,' he said out loud.

'Sorry?'

'*The Wire*. The TV series. So the Drug Squad can't trace the phone back to its owner.'

Tor realised that his customer had no idea what he was talking about. God Almighty. A drug dealer who said sorry and who had never seen *The Wire*.

'That's in the US; we don't have those in Norway. Since 2005 you need to show ID even if you buy a phone with a prepaid SIM card. It needs to be registered to someone.'

'Someone?'

'Yes, it needs to be registered in your name. Or your parents' name if, say, you were getting them a phone.'

'OK,' the man said. 'Give me the cheapest phone you have. With a prepaid SIM card.'

'Certainly,' the shop assistant said, leaving out the Sir, putting the iPhone back and taking down a smaller mobile. 'This isn't the very, very cheapest, but it has Internet access. It's 1,200 kroner with the SIM card.'

'Internet access?'

Tor looked at the man again. He couldn't be much older than him, but he seemed genuinely confused. With two fingers Tor pushed his shoulder-length hair behind his ear. It was a mannerism he had adopted after watching Season One of *Sons of Anarchy*.

'The SIM card lets you surf the Net on your mobile.'

'Can't I do that in an Internet cafe?'

Tor Jonasson laughed. Perhaps they did share a sense of humour after all. 'My boss was just telling me that this shop used to be an Internet cafe a few years ago. Probably the last one in Oslo . . .'

The man appeared to be in two minds. Then he nodded. 'I'll take it.' He put a pile of banknotes on the counter.

Tor picked them up. The banknotes were stiff and dusty as if they had been stored somewhere for a long time. 'Like I said, I need to see some ID.'

The man produced an ID card from his pocket and handed it over. Tor looked at it and realised that he had been wrong. Completely wrong. There was no way this man was a drug dealer; quite the opposite. He entered the name into his computer. Helge Sørensen. Found the address. Returned the card with the change to the man he now knew was a prison officer.

'Do you sell batteries for this?' the man said, holding up a silver-coloured device.

'What is it?' Tor asked.

'It's a Discman,' the man replied. 'I can see that you sell headphones for it.'

Tor stared blankly at the display of headsets and earphones above the iPods. 'Do I?'

Tor opened the back of the museum piece and took out the old batteries. He found two rechargeable Sanyo AA batteries which he inserted and pressed *play*. A shrill hum could be heard coming from the headphones.

'These batteries are rechargeable.'

'So they won't die like the old ones?'

'Oh yes, but they'll rise again from the dead.'

Tor thought he saw a smile in the shadows. Then the man pushed back his hood and put on the earphones.

'Depeche Mode,' he said with a broad smile and paid for the batteries.

Then he turned round and left the shop.

It struck Tor Jonasson that he was surprised by the appealing face under the hood. He walked up to a new customer and asked how he could help Sir today. It wasn't until his lunch break that

Tor realised why the face had struck a chord with him. It wasn't because it was appealing. It was because it looked nothing like the photo on the ID card.

Just what made a face appealing? Martha asked herself as she looked at the young man behind the reception hatch. Perhaps it was simply the words he had uttered. Most people came to reception for a sandwich, a cup of coffee or a chat about their real or imagined problems. And if it wasn't that, then they would turn up with a container full of used syringes which they had to hand over in exchange for sterile ones. But this new resident had just told her that he had been pondering her question from their introductory talk: Did he have any plans for the future? And, yes, now he did. He was going to look for a job. But in order to do that he needed a professional appearance, a suit. And he had seen some in the clothing storeroom. Could he possibly borrow—

'Of course,' Martha said, getting up and leading the way. Her footsteps felt lighter than they had for a long time. True, it might be just a whim, a project he would abandon at the first hurdle, but at least it was something, it was hope, a temporary break from the relentless one-way traffic to rock bottom.

She sat on a chair by the door to the narrow storeroom and watched as he put on the suit trousers in front of a mirror leaning against the wall. This was the third suit he was trying on. Once a group of politicians from the City Council had visited the centre. They were there to reassure themselves that living standards in Oslo's residential facilities were more than just adequate. In the storeroom one of them had questioned why the centre had so many suits in stock, suggesting that this type of garment was surely inappropriate for its clientele. The politicians had exercised themselves about this until a smiling Martha replied: 'Because our residents attend many more funerals than you do.'

The young man was skinny, but not as frail as she had first thought. She saw muscles ripple under his skin when he raised his arms to put on one of the shirts she had found. He had no tattoos, but his pale skin was riddled with needle marks. On the back of his knees, his inner thighs, on his lower legs, on the side of his neck.

He put on the jacket and looked at himself before turning to her. It was a pinstriped suit whose previous owner had barely worn it before fashion changed and he – out of the kindness of his heart and good taste – had donated it to the centre together with the rest of last year's wardrobe. It was only slightly too big for the young man.

'Perfect,' she laughed and clapped her hands.

He smiled. And when the smile reached his eyes, it was as if an electric heater had been turned on. It was the kind of smile that softened stiff muscles and soothed hurt feelings. A smile someone suffering from compassion fatigue was sorely in need of. But – and the thought hadn't occurred to her until now – could not allow herself. She broke away from his gaze and looked him up and down.

'It's a shame I haven't got any smart shoes for you.'

'These are fine.' He tapped the floor with the heel of his blue trainer.

She smiled, but without looking up this time. 'And you need a haircut. Come on.'

She followed him up the stairs and back to reception, sat him down on a chair, covered him with two towels and found a pair of kitchen scissors. She wet his hair with water from the kitchen tap and combed his hair with her own comb. And while the other girls at reception commented and offered suggestions, tufts of hair fell to the floor. A couple of residents stopped outside the reception hatch and complained that they had never been offered a haircut, so why was the newcomer getting special treatment?

Martha waved them away and concentrated on the job in hand.

'Where will you try to get work?' she said and looked at the fine white hairs at the back of his neck. She needed an electric shaver for them. Or a disposable razor.

'I have some contacts, but I don't know where they live so I thought I would look them up in the phone book.'

'The phone book?' one of the girls snorted. 'You can just look them up on the Net.'

'I can do that?' the young man said.

'Are you for real?!' she laughed. A little too loud. And her eyes sparkled, Martha noticed.

'I've bought a mobile with Internet,' he said. 'But I don't know how you—'

'I'll show you!' The girl walked up to him and held out her hand.

He took out his mobile and handed it to her. She pressed the keys with easy familiarity. 'You just google them. What's the name?'

'The name?'

'Yes. Their name. My name is Maria, for example.'

Martha sent her a gentle warning look. The girl was young and had just started working with them. She had studied social science, but had little practical experience. The kind of experience that means you know exactly where the invisible line between professional concern and socialising with the residents is drawn.

'Iversen,' he said.

'That's going to result in too many hits. Do you know their first name?'

'Just show me how to search and I'll do the rest myself,' the young man said.

'OK.' Maria pressed some buttons and handed him the mobile. 'Just type in their name there.'

'Thank you so much.'

Martha had finished, only the fine hairs on his neck remained and she had just remembered that she had found a razor blade stuck to a window in a room she had cleared out earlier today. She had put the razor blade – which had undoubtedly been used to chop coke for sniffing – on the kitchen counter in order to dispose of it safely in the next syringe container that came in. She lit a match and held the razor blade over the flame for a few seconds. Then she rinsed it under the tap and pinched it between her thumb and index finger.

'You need to sit very still now,' she said.

'Mm,' said the young man who was busy pressing buttons on his mobile.

She shuddered as she watched the thin steel blade glide across the soft skin on his neck. She watched as the hairs were cut and fell. The thought announced itself spontaneously: How little it took. How little separated life from death. Happiness from tragedy. The meaningful from the meaningless. She finished and looked over his shoulder. Saw the name he had entered, the white tails of the searching symbol spinning.

'Done,' she said.

He leaned his head backwards and looked up at her.

'Thank you.'

She took the towels and walked quickly to the laundry room so as not to scatter loose hairs everywhere.

Johnny Puma was lying in the darkness with his face to the wall when he heard his room enemy come in and close the door silently behind him. Tiptoe across the floor. But Johnny was on his guard. The guy would get a taste of Puma's iron fist if he tried to nick his stash.

His room enemy, however, made no attempt to approach him; instead Johnny heard the wardrobe door open.

He turned over in his bed. It was his room enemy's wardrobe.

That was all right; Johnny assumed that the guy must already have searched Johnny's own wardrobe while he was asleep and discovered that nothing of value was stored there.

A beam of sunlight fell in between the curtains and on the young man. Puma flinched.

The boy had taken something out of a red sports bag and now Johnny could see what it was. The boy slipped the object into the empty box from the trainers which was then placed on the top shelf.

When he closed the wardrobe and turned round, Johnny quickly shut his eyes.

Bloody hell, he thought. And made sure to keep his eyes shut. But he knew he wouldn't be able to sleep.

Markus yawned. He pressed his eyes against the binoculars and studied the moon that hung above the yellow house. Then he aimed the binoculars at the house itself. It was completely still now. Nothing more had happened. But would the son return? Markus hoped so. Perhaps he would find out what he wanted to do with it, the old 'thing' that had been lying in the drawer, gleaming, smelling of oil and metal, and might be the one that the father had used when he . . .

Markus yawned again. It had been an eventful day. He knew he would sleep like a log tonight.

16

AGNETE IVERSEN WAS FORTY-NINE YEARS old, but if you judged her by her smooth skin, bright eyes and slim figure, she looked thirty-five. Most people, however, took her to be older than she was due to her greying hair, the conservative, classic and timeless way she dressed and her educated speech which bordered on the dated. And, of course, the life the Iversen family lived high up on Holmenkollåsen. They seemed to belong to a different, an older generation, with Agnete as the stay-at-home wife with two domestics who helped her manage the house and garden as well as service every need of Agnete herself, her husband Iver and their son Iver Junior.

Even compared to the other imposing houses in the neighbour-hood, the Iversen home was impressive. Nevertheless, the domestic tasks were still suitably manageable so that the help (or 'the staff' as Iver Junior liked to refer to them with a hint of sarcasm since he had finished his final school exams and developed a new and more social democratic frame of reference) didn't start work until twelve noon. This meant that Agnete Iversen could be the first person to rise, go for a little early-morning walk in the forest which bordered their property and pick a bouquet of ox-eye daisies before making breakfast for her two men. She sat with her teacup as she watched them consume the healthy and nutritious meal she had prepared for them as the start to a long and demanding day at the office. When they had finished eating and Iver Junior had thanked her for the meal with a handshake as had been the tradition in the Iversen household for several generations, she wiped the table and dried her hands on a white apron she would shortly drop into the laundry basket. Then she followed them out onto the front steps, gave them each a peck on the cheek and watched them get into the elderly, well-maintained Mercedes in the double garage and drive out into the bright sunshine. Iver Junior spent his school holidays at the family's property company in the hope that it would teach him the meaning of hard work, that nothing is for free, and to appreciate that controlling a family fortune entails as many obligations as privileges.

The gravel on the drive crunched as father and son drove up to the road while she waved to them from the steps. And if anyone had told her that the whole scene looked like a 1950s commercial, she would have laughed, agreed with them and then given the matter very little thought. Because Agnete Iversen lived the life she wanted. She spent her days taking care of the two men she loved so they in turn could manage assets in the best interests of the family and society – what could possibly be more rewarding?

From the radio in the kitchen she could just about make out the newsreader's voice say something about a spike in the number of fatal drugs overdoses in Oslo, a rise in prostitution and an escaped prisoner who had been at large for the last two days. There was so much unpleasantness in the world down below her. So many things which didn't work, which lacked the balance and the order one should always strive for. And while she stood there contemplating the perfect harmony of her own life – her family, her household, this day – she became aware that the side gate in the neatly trimmed, two-metre-tall hedge, which was used mostly by the domestic staff, had opened.

She raised her hand to shield her eyes from the sun.

The boy walking down the narrow flagstone path looked like he might be the same age as Iver Junior and her initial thought was that he must be a friend of his. She smoothed her apron. But as he came closer, she realised that he was probably some years older than her son and wearing clothes that neither Iver Junior nor any of his friends would ever wear: an unfashionable, brown pinstriped suit and a pair of blue trainers. He had a red sports bag slung over his shoulder and Agnete Iversen wondered if he was from the Jehovah's Witnesses before she remembered that they always came in pairs. Nor did he look like a door-to-door salesman. He had reached the foot of the steps.

'How can I help you?' she said obligingly.

'Is this where the Iversen family lives?'

'It is. But if you want to talk to Iver Junior or my husband then you've just missed them.' She pointed across the garden in the direction of the road.

The boy nodded, stuck his left hand into the sports bag and pulled something out. He aimed it at her while he took a small step to the left. Agnete had never experienced anything like it, not in real life. But there was nothing wrong with her eyesight, never had been, all the family had perfect sight. So she didn't doubt her eyes for one moment, just gasped for air and automatically retreated one step to the open door behind her.

It was a handgun.

She continued her retreat while she looked at the boy, but she couldn't catch his eye behind the weapon.

There was a bang and she felt as if someone had punched her, shoved her hard in the chest and she continued to move, stumbling backwards through the door, numb and with no control of her limbs and yet she stayed on her feet through the hallway; she flung out her arms in an attempt to regain her balance and felt her hand strike one of the pictures on the wall. She didn't fall until she crashed through the doorway to the kitchen and barely noticed that she banged her head against the kitchen counter and took with her a glass vase which was standing there. But when she lay on the floor with her head pressed up against the bottom drawer and her neck bowed so that she was looking down at herself, she saw the flowers. The ox-eye daisies lying amid the broken glass. And something that looked like a red rose growing on her white apron. She looked towards the front door. Saw the silhouette of the boy's head outside, saw him turn towards the maples to the left of the flagstone path. Then he bent down and was gone. And she prayed to God that he was.

She tried to get up, but she couldn't move; it was as if her body had been disconnected from her brain. She closed her eyes and felt the pain, a kind of pain she hadn't felt before. It flooded all of her body as if she was about to be torn in half, but at the same time it was numb, almost distant. The news had ended, they played classical music again. Schubert. 'Abends unter der Linde'.

She heard the sound of soft footsteps.

Trainers on the stone floor.

She opened her eyes.

The boy was coming towards her, but his gaze was focused on something pinched between his fingers. A cartridge shell; she had seen them when the family went hunting in the autumn at their cabin in Hardangervidda. He dropped it into the red bag, took out a pair of yellow washing-up gloves and a facecloth. He sat down on his haunches, put on the gloves and wiped something off the floor. Blood. Her blood. Then he rubbed the soles of his shoes with the cloth. Agnete realised that he was removing his footprints and cleaning his trainers. Like a professional killer would have done. Someone who didn't want to leave behind any evidence. Or any witnesses. She should feel afraid. But she didn't, she felt nothing – or she was capable only of observing, registering, reasoning.

He stepped over her and went back to the hallway, to the bathroom and bedrooms. He left the door open. Agnete managed to turn her head. The boy had opened her handbag which she had left on the bed – she was planning on going into town to buy a skirt from Ferner Jacobsen. He opened her purse, took out her money and discarded everything else. He went over to the chest of drawers, pulled out first the top drawer and then the second where she knew he would find her jewellery box. The beautiful and priceless pearl earrings she had inherited from her grandmother. Well, strictly speaking they weren't priceless; her husband had had them valued at 280,000 kroner.

She heard the jewellery rattle into the sports bag.

He disappeared into the family bathroom. He emerged again holding their toothbrushes, hers, Iver's and Iver Junior's. He must be either terribly poor or terribly disturbed, or both. He came over to her and bent down. He put his hand on her shoulder.

'Does it hurt?'

She managed to shake her head. She wasn't going to give him the satisfaction.

He moved his hand and she felt the rubber glove on her neck. His thumb and index finger pressed against her artery. Was he about to strangle her? No, he didn't press very hard.

'Your heart will stop beating shortly,' he said.

Then he got up and walked back to the front door. He wiped down the door handle with the facecloth. Closed the door behind him. Next she heard the garden gate close. Then Agnete Iversen felt it coming. The chill. It started in her feet and her hands. It spread to her head, the top of her scalp. Ate its way towards her heart from all sides. And darkness followed.

Sara looked at the man who had got on the metro at Holmenkollen Station. He sat down in the other carriage, the one she had just moved from when three youths with back-to-front baseball caps had got on at Voksenlia. During the summer holidays there were few people on the trains immediately following the morning rush hour so she had been the only passenger. And now they were starting to harass him, too. She heard the smallest of them – who was clearly the leader – call the man a loser, laugh at his trainers, tell him to get out of their carriage, saw him spit on the floor in front of him. Stupid gangsta-wannabes. Now one of them, a handsome blond lad, probably a neglected posh boy, pulled out a flick knife. Dear God, were they really going to . . . ? He jerked his hand in front of the man. Sara almost screamed. Howling laughter erupted in the other carriage. He had plunged the knife into the seat between the man's knees. The leader said something, gave the man five seconds to get out. The man rose. For a moment it looked as if he was thinking about fighting back. Yes, it actually did. But then he pulled the red sports bag closer to his body and moved to her carriage.

'Fucking coward!' they shouted out after him in their MTV Norwegian. Then they roared with laughter.

There was just her and him and the three youths on the train. In the door which connected the two carriages the man stopped and balanced for a few seconds and their eyes met. And though she couldn't exactly see the fear in his eyes, she knew it was there. The fear of the weak and the degenerate who always defer, slink away and yield territory to anyone who bares their teeth and threatens physical violence. Sara despised him. She despised his weakness. And the well-intentioned goodness he undoubtedly surrounded himself with. In some way she wished they *had* beaten him up.

Taught him to hate a little. And she hoped that he saw the contempt in her eyes. And that he would squirm, wriggle on the hook.

But instead he smiled to her, muttered a modest 'hello', sat down two rows away and looked dreamily out of the window as if nothing had happened. Good God, what kind of people have we become? A bunch of pathetic old women who don't even have the decency to be ashamed of ourselves. She was sorely tempted to spit on the floor herself.

17

'AND THEY SAY NORWAY DOESN'T have an upper class,' Simon Kefas remarked as he held up the white-and-orange police tape so that Kari Adel could duck under it.

A panting, uniformed police officer whose forehead glistened with sweat stopped them in front of the double garage. They showed him their warrant cards; he checked the photographs and asked Simon to remove his sunglasses.

'Who found her?' Simon asked, squinting against the sharp sunlight.

'The cleaners,' the policeman said. 'They turned up for work at twelve noon and called the emergency services.'

'Any witnesses who saw or heard anything?'

'No one saw anything,' the policeman said. 'But we've spoken to a neighbour who says that she heard a loud bang. At first she thought it might have been an exploding tyre. They wouldn't recognise gunshots in a neighbourhood like this.'

'Thank you,' Simon said, put his sunglasses back on and walked up the steps ahead of Kari to where a CSO in white overalls was examining the front door old-school style with a small, black-haired brush. Little flags marked the path the CSOs had already cleared and it led right to the body which was lying on the kitchen floor. A ray of sunlight fell through the window, stretched across the stone floor and sparkled in the puddles of water and the broken glass around the ox-eye daisies. A man dressed in a suit was squatting beside the body and conferring with a medical examiner whom Simon recognised.

'Excuse me,' Simon said and the man in the suit looked up. His hair, glistening with several different products, and his carefully combed, narrow sideburns made Simon wonder if he was Italian. 'Who are you?'

'I could ask you the same question,' the man said, making no attempt to get up. Simon guessed him to be in his early thirties.

'Chief Inspector Kefas, Homicide.'

'Pleased to meet you. Åsmund Bjørnstad, I'm a DI with Kripos. You don't look like you've been told that we're taking over this case.'

'Says who?'

'Your own boss, as it happens.'

'The Chief Superintendent?'

The suit shook his head and pointed at the ceiling. Simon noticed Bjørnstad's nails. They had to be manicured, surely.

'The Commissioner?'

Bjørnstad nodded. 'He contacted Kripos and told us we might as well come over right away.'

'Why?'

'I guess he thought you'd end up asking us for assistance sooner or later.'

'When you would have waltzed in like you have now and taken charge?'

Åsmund Bjørnstad smiled briefly. 'Listen, it wasn't my decision. But whenever Kripos is asked to assist in a murder inquiry, we always make it a condition that we're given overall responsibility for the investigation, tactical as well as technical.'

Simon nodded. He was well aware of it; it wasn't the first time that Oslo Police's Homicide Squad and the National Criminal Investigation Service, Kripos, were stepping on each other's toes. And he knew that what he ought to do was say thank you and be grateful for one less case to deal with, go back to his office and focus on the Vollan investigation instead.

'Well, as we're here, we might as well take a look around,' Simon said.

'Why?' Bjørnstad made no attempt to hide his irritation.

'I'm sure you have everything under control, Bjørnstad, but I have a newly qualified investigator with me; she would benefit from seeing how we examine a real-life crime scene. How about it?'

The Kripos investigator looked reluctantly at Kari. Then he shrugged.

'Great,' Simon said and squatted down.

It wasn't until now that he looked at the body. He had deliberately avoided it and waited until he could give it his full attention. You only get one chance at first impressions. The almost symmetrical circle of blood in the middle of the white apron briefly reminded him of the national flag of Japan. Apart from the fact that the sun had gone down and not up for the woman who stared at the ceiling with that dead look he had never grown used to. Simon had concluded the look was a combination of a human body and the totally dehumanised expression, the absence of vitality, a human being reduced to an object. He had been told that the victim's name was Agnete Iversen. What he knew for sure was that she had been shot in the chest. A single shot, or so it would appear. He looked at her hands. None of her nails were broken and her hands showed no sign of a struggle. The nail polish on the middle finger of her left hand was chipped, but that could have happened when she fell.

'Any sign of a break-in?' Simon asked and signalled to the medical examiner to turn over the body.

Bjørnstad shook his head. 'The door might have been left unlocked – the victim's husband and son had just left for work. We didn't find any fingerprints on the door handle, either.'

'Not one?' Simon let his gaze glide along the edge of the worktop.

'No. As you can see, she's very house-proud.'

Simon studied the exit wound on the victim's back. 'Straight through. The bullet appears to have gone through soft tissue only.'

The medical examiner pressed his lips together and pushed them out while he shrugged, a gesture that told Simon his conjecture wasn't unreasonable.

'And the bullet?' Simon asked, glancing up at the wall above the worktop.

Reluctantly Åsmund Bjørnstad pointed higher up.

'Thank you,' Simon said. 'And the shell?'

'Not found yet,' the investigator said and took out a mobile with a gold-coloured casing.

'I see. And what is Kripos's preliminary theory as to what happened here?'

'Theory?' Bjørnstad smiled, pressing the mobile to his ear. 'Surely that's obvious. The burglar entered, shot the victim in here, took whatever valuables he could find and fled the scene. A planned robbery that ended up with a unplanned killing, I think. Perhaps she put up a fight or started to scream.'

'And how do you think—'

Bjørnstad held up a hand to indicate his call had been answered. 'Hello, it's me. Can you get me a list of anyone currently around with convictions for violent robbery? Do a quick check to see if there's anyone in Oslo. Prioritise those who used guns. Thank you.' He dropped the mobile into his jacket pocket. 'Listen, old boy, we've quite a lot of work to do here, so I'm afraid I'll have to ask you to—'

'All good,' Simon said, proffering his broadest smile. 'But if we promise not to get in your way, perhaps we could take a look around first?'

The Kripos investigator looked at his older colleague with suspicion.

'And we promise not to step inside the flags.'

Bjørnstad granted his request with gracious benevolence.

'He found what he was looking for,' Kari observed when they stood in front of the bed on the thick wall-to-wall carpet in the master bedroom. On the bedspread lay a handbag, an open, emptied purse and a jewellery box lined with red velvet, also empty.

'Perhaps,' Simon said, ignoring the flag and squatting down beside the bed.

'He would have been standing roughly here when he tipped out the handbag and the jewellery box, don't you agree?'

'Yes, as everything is lying on the bed.'

Simon studied the carpet. He was about to get up again when he stopped mid-motion and bent down.

'What is it?'

'Blood,' Simon said.

'He bled on the carpet?'

'Unlikely. It's a rectangular mark so it's probably a shoeprint. Imagine you're burgling a house in a wealthy area like this: where do you think the safe is?'

Kari pointed to the wardrobe.

'Exactly,' Simon said, got up and opened the wardrobe door.

The safe was located in the middle of the wall and was the size of a microwave oven. Simon pressed the handle down. Locked.

'Unless the burglar took the time to lock the safe afterwards

– something which would seem odd given that he discarded the jewellery box and the purse – he didn't touch it,' Simon said. 'Let's see if they've finished with the body.'

On the way back to the kitchen, Simon went into the bathroom. He reappeared, frowning.

'What is it?' Kari asked.

'Did you know that in France they have one toothbrush per forty inhabitants?'

'That's a myth and those statistics are old,' she said.

'But then I'm an old man,' Simon said. 'Either way, the Iversen family doesn't have a single toothbrush between them.'

They returned to the kitchen where the body of Agnete Iversen had been temporarily abandoned and Simon could examine her unhindered. He looked at her hands, studying closely the angle of the entry and exit wounds. He got up and asked Kari to stand right in front of the victim's feet with her back to the worktop.

'I apologise in advance,' he said, walked up beside her, pressed one finger between her small breasts in the same spot as the bullet had entered Agnete Iversen and another in between her shoulder blades in a place which corresponded to the victim's exit wound. He studied the angle between the two points before he let his gaze travel up to the bullet hole on the wall. Then he bent down and picked up one of the ox-eye daisies, rested one knee on the worktop, stretched up and popped the flower into the bullet hole.

'Come on,' he said, sliding off the worktop and walking down the hallway towards the front door. He stopped at a picture which was hanging crooked, leaned closer and pointed at something red on the edge of the picture frame.

'Blood?' Kari asked.

'Nail polish,' Simon said and placed the back of his left hand against the picture and looked over his shoulder at the body. Then he continued towards the door. Stopped and squatted down by the threshold. Crouched over a lump of soil which had been marked with a flag.

'Don't you dare touch that!' said a voice behind them.

They looked up.

'Oh, it's you, Simon,' said the man in white and ran a finger over his wet lips in the depths of his ginger beard.

'Hi, Nils. Long time no see. Are they treating you properly in Kripos?'

The man shrugged. 'Oh, they are. But that's probably because I'm so old and over the hill that they feel sorry for me.'

'And are you?'

'Oh yes,' the crime scene technician sighed. 'It's all about DNA these days, Simon. DNA and computer models people like us don't understand. It's not like back in our day.'

'I don't think we're quite over the hill yet,' Simon said, studying the catch lock in the front door. 'Give my best to your wife, Nils.'

The bearded man remained standing. 'I still don't have a—'

'To your dog, then.'

'My dog's dead, Simon.'

'Then we'll have to skip the pleasantries, Nils,' Simon said and went outside. 'Kari, count to three and then scream as loud as you can. Afterwards come outside on the steps and stay there. OK?'

She nodded and he closed the door.

Kari looked at Nils, who shook his head before he walked away. Then she screamed at the top of her lungs. She yelled the word 'fore!' which was what she had been taught to shout to warn anyone on the rare occasions she hooked or sliced a golf stroke.

Then she opened the door.

Simon was aiming his index finger at her from the foot of the steps.

'Now move,' he said.

She did as she was told and saw him shift slightly to the left and narrow one eye.

'He must have been standing here,' Simon said, still aiming his index finger at her. She turned and saw the white ox-eye daisy on the kitchen wall.

Simon looked to the right. Went over to the maples. Spread them. Kari realised what he was looking for. The shell.

'Aha,' he muttered to himself, took out his mobile, held it up to his eye and she heard the digitally simulated sound of a camera shutter. He pinched some soil from the ground between his thumb and forefinger and scattered it. Then he returned to the steps to show her the picture he had taken.

'A shoeprint,' she said.

'The killer's,' he said.

'Oh?'

'Right, I think school's out, Kefas.'

They turned round. It was Bjørnstad. He looked angry. Three CSOs were standing alongside him, including Nils with the ginger beard.

'Almost done,' Simon said and tried to get back inside. 'I thought we would just—'

'I think we're done,' Bjørnstad said, legs akimbo and blocking the path as he folded his arms across his chest. 'I've found a flower in my bullet hole, and that's a step too far. That'll be all for today.'

Simon shrugged. 'Fine, we've seen enough anyway to draw our own conclusions. Good luck finding your assassin, folks.'

Bjørnstad scoffed. 'So you're trying to impress your young student here by calling it an assassination?' He turned to Kari. 'I'm sorry that real life isn't quite as exciting as the old boy here would like it to be. It's just a bog-standard murder.'

'You're wrong,' Simon said.

Bjørnstad rested his hand on his hip. 'My parents taught me to respect my elders. I'm giving you ten seconds of respect, and then I want you gone.' One of the CSOs tittered.

'What nice parents,' Simon said.

'Nine seconds.'

'The neighbour said she heard a shot.'

'What about it?'

'The properties here are large and there's plenty of room between them. And the houses are well insulated. The neighbour wouldn't have been able to hear something she could identify as a bang coming from inside the house. Outside, however . . .'

Bjørnstad leaned his head back as if to study Simon from another angle. 'What's your point?'

'Mrs Iversen was about as tall as Kari here. And the only angle that fits with her standing up when she was shot and her entry wound being here –' he pointed to Kari's chest – 'and her exit wound being on her back here, while the bullet ends up in the wall where I put the ox-eye daisy, is that the shooter was on a lower level than her, but that they both stood quite a long way from the kitchen wall. In other words, the victim was standing where we're standing now, while the shooter was standing at the bottom of the steps, on the flagstones. That was how the neighbour heard the shot. However, the neighbour didn't hear any screaming or noises preceding the shot, nothing to indicate commotion or resistance, so my guess is it happened quickly.'

Bjørnstad couldn't help glancing back at his colleagues. He shifted his weight. 'And then he dragged her inside, is that what you're saying?'

Simon shook his head. 'No, I think she stumbled backwards.'

'And what makes you think that?'

'You're right that Mrs Iversen was house-proud. The only thing in this house hanging crooked is that picture there.' The others turned to look where Simon was pointing. 'Besides, there's nail polish on the side of the picture frame closest to the door. It means she struck it as she staggered back inside; it fits with the chipped nail polish on her left middle finger.'

Bjørnstad shook his head. 'If she was shot in the doorway and walked backwards, there would have been bloodstains from the exit wound along the hallway.'

'And there were,' Simon said, 'but the killer cleaned them up. Like you said yourself, there were no fingerprints on the door handle. Not even the family's. Not because Agnete Iversen started spring-cleaning seconds after her husband and son had touched the handle on their way out, but because the killer didn't want to leave us any evidence. And I'm quite sure that the reason he mopped up the blood on the floor was that he had stepped in it and didn't want to leave shoeprints. So he also wiped down the soles of his shoes.'

'Is that right?' Bjørnstad said, still leaning his head backwards, but no longer grinning quite so broadly. 'And you surmise all this out of thin air?'

'When you dry the soles of your shoes, you don't remove the blood in between the ridges in the pattern of the sole,' Simon said, looking at his watch. 'But that blood will come out if, for example, you stand on a thick rug whose fibres get into the sole pattern and soak up the blood. In the bedroom you'll find a rectangular blood-stain in the carpet. I think your blood technician will agree with me, Bjørnstad.'

In the silence that followed, Kari heard the sound of a car being stopped by police officers further up the road. There were agitated voices, one of them belonging to a young man. The victim's husband and son.

'Whatever,' Bjørnstad said with forced indifference. 'Ultimately, it doesn't matter where the victim was shot, this is a burglary gone wrong, not an assassination. And it sounds as if someone will be here shortly who can confirm that jewellery is missing from the jewellery box.'

'Jewellery is all well and good,' Simon said, 'but if I'd been the burglar, I would have taken Agnete Iversen inside and forced her to show me where the real valuables are kept. Made her give me the combination to the safe which every idiot burglar knows a house like this will have. But instead he shoots her right here where the neighbours can hear. Not because he panics – the way he removed evidence shows how callous he is. No, he does it because he knows he won't be spending very long in the house, that he'll be long gone by the time the police arrive. Because he's not there to steal very much, is he? Just enough so that an inexperienced investigator with nice parents will swiftly conclude that it's a burglary gone wrong and not look too closely for the real motive.'

Simon had to admit that he enjoyed the silence and the sudden colour in Bjørnstad's face. Deep down Simon Kefas was a simple soul, but he wasn't vindictive. Though he was sorely tempted, he spared his young colleague his parting shot: *school's out, Bjørnstad.*

Given time and experience it was always possible that Åsmund Bjørnstad might one day make a good investigator. Humility was also something good investigators had to learn.

'Very enjoyable theory, Kefas,' Bjørnstad said. 'I'll keep it in mind. But time is passing and . . .' Short smile. '. . . perhaps you should be on your way?'

'Why didn't you tell him everything?' Kari asked while Simon carefully manoeuvred the car around the sharp bends coming down from Holmenkollåsen.

'Everything?' Simon said, feigning innocence. Kari had to laugh. Simon was doing his eccentric old-man act.

'You knew that the shell had landed somewhere in that flower bed. You didn't find a shell, but you did find a shoeprint. Which you photographed. And the soil there matched the soil in the hallway?'

'Yes.'

'So why not give him that information?'

'Because he's an ambitious investigator whose ego is bigger than his team spirit, so it's better if he discovers it himself. He'll be more motivated if he feels that it's his evidence and not mine they're following up when they start looking for a man who takes size 8½ shoes and who picked up an empty shell in that rose bed.'

They stopped for a red light at Stasjonsveien. Kari strangled a yawn. 'And how did you gain such insight into how an investigator like Bjørnstad thinks?'

Simon laughed. 'Easy. I was young and ambitious once.'

'But ambition fades in time?'

'Some of it does, yes.' Simon smiled. A wistful smile, Kari thought.

'Is that why you stopped working for the Serious Fraud Office?'

'What makes you say that?'

'You were management. Chief Inspector in charge of a large team. They've let you keep your title in Homicide, but the only person you're in charge of is me.'

'Yep,' Simon said, crossing the junction and continuing towards Smestad. 'Overpaid, overqualified, left over. Or just over.'

'So what happened?'

'You don't want to—'

'Yes, I do.'

They drove on in a silence which Kari deemed to be to her advantage so she kept her mouth shut. Even so, they had almost reached Majorstua before Simon began.

'I had uncovered a money laundering operation. We're talking serious money. People in high places. My fellow senior officers thought that my investigation and I represented a big risk. That I didn't have enough evidence, that we would be hung out to dry if we pursued the inquiry but failed to secure a conviction. We're not talking your usual common criminal, the suspects were powerful people, people who'll fight back using the very same system the police use. My colleagues were afraid that, even if we won, we would pay for it later, there would be a backlash.'

Another silence. Which lasted till they reached Frogner Park where Kari finally lost patience.

'So they kicked you out just because you'd launched a controversial inquiry?'

Simon shook his head. 'I had a problem. Gambling. Or, to use the technical expression, ludomania. I bought and sold shares. Not many. But when you work for the Serious Fraud Office . . .'

'. . . then you have access to inside information.'

'I never traded in shares I had information about, but I still broke the rules. And they worked that for all it was worth.'

Kari nodded. They weaved their way towards the city centre and the Ibsen Tunnel. 'And then?'

'I no longer gamble. Nor do I bother anyone.' Again this sad, resigned smile.

Kari thought about her plans for this evening. Go to the gym. Dinner with her in-laws. A viewing in Fagerborg. And heard herself ask the question which must have come from another, almost subconscious part of her brain: 'Why did the killer take the shell with him?'

'Every shell has a serial number, but it rarely leads us to the killer,' Simon said. 'He might have been scared that the shell would have his prints on it, but I think that this killer would have already thought of that, that he would have worn gloves when he loaded the gun. I think we can conclude that his gun is relatively recent, produced in the last few years.'

'Oh?'

'For ten years now it has been mandatory for handgun manufacturers to engrave a serial number on the weapon's firing pin so that it leaves a kind of unique fingerprint when it hits the cap on the shell. It means all we need to identify the owner is an empty shell and the Firearms Register.'

Kari struck out her lower lip and nodded slowly. 'OK, I get that. What I don't get is why he wanted it to look like a robbery.'

'Just like he's scared of the evidence on the shell, he's scared that if we know the real motive, it would lead us to him.'

'Well, then it's straightforward,' Kari said, but she was really thinking about the Fagerborg property ad. It had stated that the flat had two balconies, one east-facing, one west-facing.

'Oh?' Simon said.

'The husband,' Kari said. 'Every husband knows that he'll be the prime suspect unless he can make it look as if his wife was killed for another reason. A burglary, for instance.'

'Another reason apart from?'

'Apart from jealousy. Love. Hate. Is there anything else?'

'No,' Simon said. 'There isn't.'

18

EARLY THAT AFTERNOON A SHOWER of rain washed over Oslo without noticeably cooling down the city. And when the sun scorched its way through the layer of clouds, it was as if it wanted to make up for lost time by baking the capital in a white light which caused steam to rise from the roofs and streets.

Louis woke up when the sun was so low in the sky that the beams hit his eyes. He peered at the world. At the people and the cars going to and fro in front of him and his begging bowl. It had been a reasonably lucrative business until some years ago when Romanian gypsies started coming to Norway. A few had turned into many. Which in turn had become a swarm. A stealing, begging and swindling swarm of locusts. And like all vermin they must be fought with every possible means. It was Louis's simple opinion on the matter, that Norwegian beggars – just like Norwegian shipping companies – were entitled to government protection against foreign competition. As things were now, he was having to rely on stealing; something which was not only exhausting, but frankly beneath his dignity.

He heaved a sigh and prodded his begging bowl with a filthy

finger. Heard there was something in the bowl. Not coins. Banknotes? In which case he had better pocket them before one of the gypsies nicked them. He looked down in the bowl. Blinked twice. Then he picked it up. It was a watch. A lady's watch, it would seem. A Rolex. It was fake, obviously. But heavy. Very heavy. Did people really enjoy wearing such heavy objects around their wrists? He had heard that watches like that were water-resistant to a depth of fifty metres, something which was sure to come in handy if you went swimming while wearing a watch like this. Could it be . . . ? There were some weirdos around, no doubt about it. Louis looked up and down the street. He knew the watchmaker on the corner of Stortingsgata; they had been at school together. Perhaps he should . . .

Louis staggered to his feet.

Kine was standing next to her shopping trolley, smoking a cigarette. But when the green man lit up and the other pedestrians around her started walking, she stayed put. She had changed her mind. She wasn't going to cross the street today. She stayed where she was, finishing her cigarette. She had nicked the trolley from IKEA a long, long time ago. Simply rolled it out of the store and into the van in the car park. Driven that and a Hemnes bed, a Hemnes table and some Billy bookcases to a place she thought was their future. Her future. He had fixed the furniture before preparing a fix for both of them. He was dead now, she wasn't. And she was no longer a junkie. She was all right. But it was a long time since she last slept in the Hemnes bed. She trod on the cigarette and grabbed the handle of the IKEA trolley. She noticed that someone – probably one of the other pedestrians – had left a plastic bag on top of the filthy woollen blanket in her trolley. Irritated, she snatched the bag; it wasn't the first time people had mistaken the trolley with all her earthly possessions for a common bin. She turned round; she could tell the location of every rubbish bin in Oslo with her eyes shut and knew there was one right behind her. But then she stopped. The weight of the plastic bag stirred her curiosity. She opened it. Plunged her hand in and brought its contents up into the afternoon sunshine. It glittered and sparkled. Jewellery. Necklaces and a ring. The pendants were diamonds and the ring was solid gold. Real gold, real diamonds. Kine was almost certain; she had seen gold and diamonds before. After all, the furniture in her childhood home hadn't been self-assembly.

Johnny Puma widened his eyes, felt the terror creep up on him and turned over in the bed. He hadn't heard anyone come in, but now he could hear heavy breathing and moaning. Was Coco in the room? No, this panting sounded more like someone screwing than someone collecting a debt. A couple had been allowed to stay at the centre once; the management must have thought that the two of them needed each other so much that they had made an exception to the men-only rule. It was certainly true that the man had needed the woman – she had financed their heroin addiction by screwing her way from room to room until the management said enough was enough and threw her out.

It was the new arrival. He was lying on the floor, facing away from Johnny, and Johnny could faintly hear a synthetic, rhythmic track and a robotic, monotonous voice coming from the earphones he was wearing. The boy was doing push-ups. In his heyday Johnny could have done a hundred, using just the one arm. The boy was strong, no doubt about it, but he was struggling with stamina, his back was sagging already. In the light that seeped in between the curtains and hit the wall, he saw a photo which the boy must have pinned up. A man in a police uniform. And he saw something else, on the windowsill. A pair of earrings. They looked expensive; he wondered where the boy had stolen them.

If they were as expensive as they looked, they might just solve

Johnny's problem. Rumour had it Coco was moving out of the hostel tomorrow and that his runners were busy collecting any debts he was owed. It left Johnny with only a few hours to scrape some money together. He had considered burgling one of the apartments in Bislett as many people were away on holiday. Ring the doorbell and see where there was no answer. He just had to summon up the energy first. But this was simpler and safer.

He wondered if he could sneak out of bed and snap up the earrings without getting noticed, but dropped the idea. Stamina or no stamina, he risked a beating. The very idea was laughable. But he could always try to distract the newcomer, make up an excuse to get him out of the room and then strike. Suddenly Johnny found himself looking into the boy's eyes. He had turned round and was doing sit-ups. He smiled.

Johnny gestured that he wanted to say something and the boy pulled the earphones out. Johnny heard the lyrics '. . . *now I'm clean*' before he started to talk.

'Would you help me down to the cafe, mate? You'll need something to eat yourself after that workout. If the body can't burn fat or carbohydrates, it'll start eating muscle, you know. And all your hard work will have been for nothing.'

'Thanks for the tip, Johnny. I just need to shower first, but you get yourself ready.' The boy stood up. Slipped the earrings into his pocket and headed out of the door in the direction of the communal showers.

Damn! Johnny closed his eyes. Did he have the energy? Yes, he had to. Only two minutes. He counted the seconds. Then he sat up on the edge of the bed. Pushed off. Stood up. Grabbed his trousers from the chair. He was putting them on when there was a knock on the door. The boy must have forgotten his keys. Johnny limped over to the door and opened it. 'How many times do I have to—'

A clenched fist wearing knuckledusters landed right in Johnny Puma's forehead and he fell backwards.

The door opened fully and Coco and two of his boys entered. The boys grabbed his arms and Coco headbutted Johnny so the back of his head slammed into the top bunk. When he looked up again, he was staring right into Coco's ugly, heavily mascaraed eyes and the gleaming point of a stiletto.

'I'm busy man, Johnny,' Coco said in broken Norwegian. 'The others have money, but still they don't pay. You have no money, I know that, so you will be example.'

'E-example?'

'I'm reasonable man, Johnny. You keep one eye.'

'But . . . Please, Coco . . .'

'Don't move or eye will be damaged when I take it out. I show it to the other scumbags so they know is real eye, OK?'

Johnny started screaming, but was quickly stopped by a hand placed over his mouth.

'Easy, Johnny. Not many nerves in eye, little pain, I promise.'

Johnny knew that his fear was supposed to give him the strength to fight back, but it felt as if it had withered away. Johnny Puma, who had once lifted cars, stared apathetically at the point of the stiletto as it moved closer.

'How much?'

The voice sounded soft, almost like a whisper. They turned to the door. No one had heard him come in. His hair was wet and he was dressed only in his jeans.

'Get out!' Coco hissed.

The boy stayed put. 'How much does he owe?'

'Now! You want to taste my knife?'

The new arrival still didn't move. The gofer who was covering Johnny's mouth let go and walked up to him.

'He . . . he nicked my earrings,' Johnny said. 'It's true! They're in his pocket. I was going to pay you with them, Coco. Search him and you'll see! Please, please, Coco!' Johnny heard the sobbing in his own voice, but he didn't care. Besides, Coco didn't appear to hear him, he was staring at the boy. Probably liked what he saw, the sick pig. Coco called off the gofer with a gesture and chuckled to himself.

'Is Johnny boy telling the truth, handsome?'

'You could try finding out,' the boy said. 'But if I were you, I would say how much he owes you and there'll be less trouble. And less mess.'

'Twelve thousand,' Coco said. 'Why—'

He broke off when the boy stuffed his hand in his pocket, produced a small wad of notes and started counting out loud from the top. When he reached twelve, he handed them to Coco and stuffed the remaining notes back in his pocket.

Coco hesitated. As if there had to be something wrong with the money. Then he laughed. Opened his mouth and revealed the gold teeth he had had fitted to replace perfectly healthy white ones.

'I'll be damned. I'll be damned.'

Then he counted the notes again. Looked up.

'So are we done?' the boy asked, and not with the stony face of a young drug dealer who had seen too many movies. On the contrary, he smiled. Like waiters used to smile at Johnny back in the days when he dined in fine restaurants and they would ask him if everything was OK with the meal.

'We're good,' Coco grinned.

Johnny lay down on the bed and closed his eyes. He could hear Coco laughing long after he and his gofers had closed the door and disappeared down the corridor.

'Don't worry about it,' the boy said. Johnny could hear him even though he tried to shut out his voice. 'I'd have done the same if I'd been you.'

But you're not me, Johnny thought and felt how the tears were still there, somewhere between his throat and chest. You haven't been Johnny Puma. And then stopped being him.

'Why don't we go down to the cafe, Johnny?'

The glare from the computer screen was the only light in the study. Any noise came from outside the door which Simon had left ajar. It was the sound of a radio at low volume in the kitchen downstairs and of Else pottering about. She came from farming stock; there was always something that needed clearing up, washing, sorting, moving, planting, sewing, baking. The work was never-ending. No matter how much you did today, tomorrow would be another full day. It meant working at a steady pace and not rushing so that you broke your back doing it. It was the soothing hum of someone who finds joy and purpose in their chores, the sound of a steady pulse and contentment. To some extent he envied her. But he was also listening out for other sounds; stumbling footsteps or things falling to the floor. If it happened, he would wait. Wait to hear if she had things under control. And if he could hear that she was OK, he wouldn't ask about it later, but let her think that he hadn't noticed.

He had logged on to the Homicide Squad's intranet and read the reports on Per Vollan. Kari had written an impressive amount, she was a hard worker. And yet when he read them, they seemed to be lacking something. Even the most bureaucratic, procedural police report couldn't hide the passion of an enthusiastic investigator. Kari's reports were a textbook example of how a police report should sound: objective and factual. No tendentious assertions or prejudices on behalf of the author. Lifeless and cold. He read the witness statements to see if any interesting names cropped up among the people Vollan had been in contact with. Nothing. He stared at the wall. Thought about two words. Nestor. Shelved. Then he googled Agnete Iversen.

Headlines about the murder popped up.

'WELL-KNOWN PROPERTY INVESTOR BRUTALLY SLAIN.'

'SHOT AND ROBBED IN HER OWN HOME.'

He clicked on one of the headlines. Inspector Åsmund Bjørnstad was quoted from the Kripos press conference in Bryn. 'Kripos's investigation team has discovered that even though Agnete Iversen was found in the kitchen, she was probably shot on the doorstep.' And further down. 'Several pieces of evidence suggest that this is a robbery, but we can't rule out other motives for the time being.'

Simon scrolled down to some older newspaper articles. They came almost exclusively from the financial papers. Agnete Iversen was the daughter of one of Oslo's biggest property owners, she had an MBA in Economics from Wharton in Philadelphia and had at a relatively young age taken over the management of the family's property portfolio. However, after marrying Iver Iversen, a fellow economist, she had retired. One of the financial journalists had described her as the administrator, the refiner, someone who had managed the portfolio in an effective and profitable manner. Her husband, by contrast, had pursued a more aggressive strategy, frequently buying and selling, which involved greater risk, but also greater gain. Another article, two years old, had a photo of their son, Iver Junior, under the headline 'MILLIONAIRE HEIR LIVES JET-SET LIFE ON IBIZA'. Tanned, laughing, flashing a dazzling smile and red-eyed from the camera flash, sweaty after dancing with a champagne bottle in one hand and an equally sweaty blonde in the other. Three years ago, a page from the financial section, Iver Senior shaking hands with Oslo City Council's Head of Finance when it was announced that Iversen Property had spent 1 billion kroner buying up council properties.

Simon heard the door to his study being pushed open. A cup of steaming tea was set down in front of him.

'Don't you need some more light in here?' Else said, putting her hands on his shoulders. To massage him. Or to support herself.

'I'm still waiting for the next instalment,' Simon said.

'The next instalment of what?'

'Of what the doctor said.'

'But I called to tell you – are you getting forgetful, darling?' she chuckled and pressed her lips against his head. Her soft lips on his scalp. He suspected that she loved him.

'You said there wasn't much he could do,' Simon replied.

'Yes.'

'But?'

'But what?'

'I know you, Else. That wasn't all he said.'

She pulled away, leaving only one hand on his shoulder. He waited.

'He said there's a new kind of surgery in the US. It'll help those who come after me.'

'After?'

'When the surgery and the equipment become standard procedure. But that could take years. Right now it's a complicated operation that costs a fortune.'

Simon spun round so quickly on the swivel chair that she had to take a step back. He clasped her hands. 'But that's brilliant news! How much?'

'More than a woman on disability benefit and a man on a police salary can afford.'

'Else, listen. We've no children. We own the house, we don't spend money on anything else. We're frugal—'

'Stop it, Simon. You know very well we haven't got any money. And the house is mortgaged to the hilt.'

Simon swallowed. She hadn't called it by its true name – his gambling debt. As always she had been too tactful to remind him that they were still paying off his past sins. He squeezed her hands.

'I'll think of something. I have friends who will lend us the money. Trust me. How much?'

'You *had* friends, Simon. But you never speak to them these days. I keep telling you, you need to keep in touch or you'll drift apart.'

Simon sighed. He shrugged his shoulders. 'I have you.'

She shook her head. 'I'm not enough, Simon.'

'Yes, you are.'

'I don't want to be enough.' She bent down and kissed him on the forehead. 'I'm tired, I'll go and lie down.'

'OK, but how much does it cost . . . ?'

She had already left.

Simon looked after her. Then he switched off the computer and took out his mobile. Scrolled down his contacts list. Old friends. Old enemies. Some of them useful, most of them not. He pressed the number of one of the latter. An enemy. But useful.

Fredrik Ansgar was surprised to hear from him as Simon knew he would be, but feigned delight and agreed to meet; he didn't even pretend to be busy. When he had ended the call, Simon sat in the darkness, staring at his phone. Thought about his dream. His sight. He would give her his eyes. Then he realised what he was looking at on the mobile. It was the photo of the shoeprint in the rose bed.

'Good grub,' Johnny said, wiping his mouth. 'Aren't you gonna eat something?'

The boy smiled and shook his head.

Johnny looked around. The cafe was a room with an open kitchen, serving counters, a self-service section and tables which were all fully occupied. The cafe usually closed after lunch, but since the Meeting Place, Bymisjonen's cafe for drug addicts in Skippergata, was being renovated, they had extended their opening hours which meant that not everyone here was a resident. But most people had been at sometime or other, so Johnny recognised every face.

He took another slurp of his coffee as he watched the scowling addicts. It was the usual, constant paranoia and prowling, heads whirring; the place was like a waterhole on the savannah where people took turns being prey and predator. Except for the boy. He had looked relaxed. Right until now. Johnny followed his gaze to the door at the back of the kitchen where Martha was emerging from the staffroom. She had put on her coat and was clearly on her way home. And Johnny saw the boy's pupils dilate. Studying other people's pupils was something an addict did almost automatically. Are they using? Are they high? Are they dangerous? In the same way he would watch what other people did with their hands. Hands that might steal from you or reach for a knife. Or, in threatening situations, instinctively cover and protect the place where someone kept their drugs or their money. And right now, the boy's hands were in his pockets. The same pocket he had put the earrings. Johnny wasn't stupid. Or, yes, he was, but not in every respect. Martha enters, boy's pupils dilate. The earrings. The chair scraped against the floor as the boy got up with a feverish look that was fixed on her.

Johnny cleared his throat. 'Stig . . .'

But it was too late, he had already turned his back on Johnny and started walking towards her.

At the same moment the front door opened and in came a man who immediately stood out. Short black leather jacket, close-cropped dark hair. Broad shoulders and a determined expression. With an irritated movement he pushed aside a resident frozen in a crouching junkie position who was in his way. He gestured to Martha who waved back. And Johnny saw now that the boy had noticed. How he stopped as if he had lost his momentum, while Martha continued towards the door. He saw the man stick his hand in the pocket of his leather jacket and turn out his elbow, so that she could slip her hand under his arm. Which she did. It was the practised movement of two people who have been together for a while. Then they disappeared outside in the windy and suddenly chilly evening.

The boy stood in the middle of the floor, stunned, as if he needed time to digest the information. Johnny saw every head in the room turn to size the boy up. He knew what they were thinking.

Prey.

Johnny was woken by the sound of crying.

And, for a moment, he thought about the ghost. The baby. That it was here.

But then he realised that the sound was coming from the top bunk. He turned over on his side. The bed started shaking. The crying turned into sobbing.

Johnny got up and stood in front of the bunk bed. He put his hand on the shoulder of the boy who was trembling like a leaf. Johnny switched on the reading lamp on the wall above him. The first thing he saw were bared teeth biting into the pillow.

'Does it hurt?' Johnny said it as a statement rather than a question.

A deathly pale, sweaty face with sunken eyes stared back at him.

'Heroin?' Johnny asked.

The face nodded.

'D'you want me to see if I can get you some?'

A shaking of the head.

'You know you're in the wrong place if you're trying to quit, don't you?' Johnny said.

Nodding.

'So what can I do for you?'

166

The boy moistened his lips with a white tongue. He whispered something.

'Eh?' Johnny said, leaning in. He could smell the boy's heavy, rotten breath. He could barely decipher the words. He straightened up and nodded.

'As you wish.'

Johnny went back to bed where he stared up at the underside of the mattress above him. It was covered with plastic to protect it against the residents' bodily fluids. He listened to the constant noise from the centre, the sound of the endlessly hunted, running footsteps in the corridor, swearing, thumping music, laughter, knocking on doors, desperate screams and agitated dealing taking place right outside their door. But none of it could drown out the quiet sobbing and the words the boy had whispered:

'Stop me if I try to get out.'

19

'SO YOU'RE WITH HOMICIDE NOW,' Fredrik said, smiling behind his sunglasses. The designer logo on the sidebar was so small that you needed Simon's eagle eyes to see it, but someone with greater brand awareness than Simon to know just how exclusive it was. Still, Simon presumed that the sunglasses must be expensive, in line with Fredrik's shirt, tie, manicure and haircut. But really, a light grey suit with brown shoes? Or maybe that passed for trendy these days.

'Yes,' Simon said and squinted. He had sat down with the wind and the sun to his back, but the sunbeams bounced off the glass surfaces of the newly constructed building across the canal. They were meeting at Simon's request, but it was Fredrik who had suggested the Japanese restaurant on Tjuvholmen; Tjuvholmen meant 'isle of thieves' and Simon wondered if it was pertinent to all the investment companies which were located there, including Fredrik's. 'And you're investing money for people who are so rich they no longer care what happens to it?'

Fredrik laughed. 'Something like that.'

The waiter had placed a small plate in front of each of them with what looked like a tiny jellyfish. Simon suspected that it might actually be a tiny jellyfish. It was probably everyday fare on Tjuvholmen; sushi had become the pizza of the upper-middle class.

'Do you ever miss the Serious Fraud Office?' Simon said, sipping water from his glass. It purported to be glacial water from Voss that had been sent to the US and then imported back to Norway, stripped of essential minerals that the body needed and which you could get for free in clean and tasty Norwegian tap water. It cost sixty kroner per bottle. Simon had given up trying to understand market forces, their psychology, and the jostling for power. But Fredrik hadn't. He understood. He played the game. Simon suspected he always had done. He had much in common with Kari; too well educated, too ambitious, and all too aware of his own value for the police to be able to keep him.

'I miss my colleagues and the excitement,' Fredrik said. 'But not the slow pace and the bureaucracy. Perhaps you quit for the same reason?'

He raised his glass too quickly to his lips for Simon to read his face to determine if he genuinely didn't know or was just pretending. After all, it was shortly after Fredrik had announced his departure to what many regarded as the dark side that the row over the money laundering case had erupted. Fredrik had even been one of the people working on the case. But perhaps he no longer had any police contacts.

'Something like that,' Simon muttered.

'Murder is more up your street,' Fredrik said and glanced with feigned discretion at his watch.

'Talking about my street,' Simon said, 'I wanted to meet because I need a loan. It's for my wife, she needs an eye operation. Else – do you remember her?'

Fredrik chewed his jellyfish and made a sound that could mean both yes and no.

Simon waited until he had finished.

'I'm sorry, Simon, we only invest our clients' money in blue-chip companies or in government-backed bonds, we never lend to the private market.'

'I'm aware of that, but I'm asking you because I can't go down the usual routes.'

Fredrik carefully dabbed the corners of his mouth and put the napkin on his plate. 'I'm sorry I can't help you. An eye operation? That sounds serious.'

The waiter arrived, took Fredrik's plate, saw that Simon's was untouched and looked quizzically at him. Simon gestured for him to take it away.

'You didn't like it?' Fredrik said and asked for the bill in a few words which might be Japanese.

'I don't know, but I'm generally sceptical when it comes to invertebrates. They slip down too easily, if you know what I mean. I don't like waste, but that particular animal looked as if it was still alive, so I'm hoping it might get a second chance in the aquarium.'

Fredrik laughed unnecessarily heartily at his joke; relieved that the second part of their conversation appeared to be over. He grabbed the bill the moment it arrived.

'Let me . . .' Simon began, but Fredrik had already slipped his credit card into the payment terminal the waiter had brought and was pressing the keypad.

'It was good to see you again and I'm sorry I wasn't able to help you,' Fredrik said when the waiter had disappeared and Simon could sense that the pressure on the seat of Fredrik's chair had already eased.

'Did you read about the Iversen killing yesterday?'

'Oh God, I did, yes.' Fredrik shook his head, took off his sunglasses and rubbed his eyes. 'Iver Iversen is one of our clients. A tragedy.'

'He was already a client of yours when you worked for the Serious Fraud Office, I believe.'

'Excuse me?'

'A suspect, I mean. It's a great shame that everyone with your qualifications quit. With people like you on the team we might have been able to bring the case to trial. The property business needs overhauling; we used to agree about that, don't you remember, Fredrik?'

Fredrik put on his sunglasses again. 'You always did gamble with high stakes, Simon.'

Simon nodded. So Fredrik did know why Simon had suddenly changed departments.

'Talking of gambling,' Simon said. 'I'm only a stupid cop without a degree in finance, but whenever I read Iversen's accounts, I always wondered how that company managed to stay afloat. It was hopeless at buying and selling property; most of the time it suffered considerable losses.'

'Yes, but it was always good at managing property.'

'Blessed be losses you can carry forward. Because of them Iversen has hardly paid any tax on his operating profits in the last few years.'

'Good heavens, you sound as if you're back with the Serious Fraud Office.'

'My password still gets me access to the old files. I stayed up last night reading them on my computer.'

'Did you? But there's nothing illegal about that, those are the tax rules.'

'Yes,' Simon said, resting his chin on his hand and looking up at the blue sky. 'And you would know; after all, you investigated Iversen. Perhaps Agnete Iversen was killed by an embittered tax collector.'

'What?'

Simon laughed briefly and got up. 'Just an old man winding you up. Thanks for lunch.'

'Simon?'

'Yes.'

'I don't want you to get your hopes up, but I'll ask around about your loan.'

'I appreciate that,' Simon said and buttoned up his jacket. 'Bye.'

He didn't need to turn round; he knew that Fredrik was watching him pensively as he walked away.

Lars Gilberg put down the newspaper he had found in the rubbish bin outside 7-Eleven that would serve as tonight's pillow. He saw that page after page was about the murder of this rich woman from the west side of Oslo. If the victim had been some poor sod who had died from a contaminated overdose down by the river or in Skippergata, he would barely have warranted a few lines. A hotshot from Kripos, a man called Bjørnstad, announced that every available resource would be deployed in the investigation. Oh, really? How about first catching the mass murderers who mixed arsenic and rat poison in the drugs they sold? Gilberg peered out from his shadow-land. The figure approaching him wore a hoodie and looked like one of the regular joggers who included the path along the river in their running route. But he had spotted Gilberg, was slowing down, and Lars Gilberg presumed him to be either a cop or a posh boy looking for speed. It wasn't until he was under the bridge and had pulled back his hood that Gilberg recognised the boy. He was sweaty and out of breath.

Gilberg got up from his groundsheet, eager, happy almost. 'Hello, lad. I've looked after your stuff, you know, it's still there.' He nodded towards the bushes.

'Thank you,' the boy said, squatting down and checking his pulse. 'But I was wondering if you could do me another favour.'

'Of course. Anything.'

'Thank you. Which dealers sell Superboy?'

Lars Gilberg closed his eyes. Dammit. 'Don't do it, lad. Not Superboy.'

'Why not?'

'Because I can name three people killed by that shit this summer alone.'

'Who sells the purest goods?'

'I don't know about purity. It's not my poison. But the dealer is easy, only one outlet in this town sells Superboy. The dealers always work in pairs. One has the drugs and the other takes the money. They hang out under Nybrua.'

'What do they look like?'

'It varies, but usually the money man is a stocky, acne-scarred guy with short hair. He's the boss, but he likes being on the street and handling the money himself. He's a suspicious bastard, doesn't trust his dealers.'

'Stocky and acne-scarred?'

'Yes, he's easy to recognise from his eyelids. It's like they hang down over his eyes and make him look sleepy. You get me?'

'Do you mean Kalle?'

'Y'know 'im?'

The boy nodded slowly.

'Then you know what happened to his eyelids?'

'What are his opening hours, do you know?' the boy asked.

'They're there from four o'clock to nine o'clock. I know this because the first customers start queuing half an hour before. And the last ones come racing, just before nine, like rats up a drainpipe, in case they miss him.'

The boy put his hood back up. 'Thanks, mate.'

'Lars. My name is Lars.'

'Thanks, Lars. Do you need anything? Money?'

Lars always needed money. He shook his head. 'What's your name?'

The boy shrugged. The what-do-you-want-me-to-be-called? shrug. Then he continued his run.

Martha was sitting in reception when he came up the stairs and continued straight past her.

'Stig!' she called out.

It took a moment too long before he stopped. Now that could be down to his generally impaired reflexes. Or that his name wasn't Stig. He was sweating; it looked as if he had been running. She hoped it wasn't away from trouble.

'I've got something for you,' she said. 'Wait!'

She picked up the box, told Maria she would be back in a couple of minutes and hurried after him. She touched his elbow lightly with her hand. 'Come on, we'll go up to yours and Johnny's.'

When they entered the room, they were met by an unexpected sight. The curtains were drawn so that the room lay bathed in light, there was no Johnny and the air was fresh because one of the windows had been opened – as much as the window lock permitted. The council had told them to install window locks in every room after several incidents where pedestrians on the pavement below had come close to being hit by the large, heavy objects which were regularly hurled from the centre's windows; radios, speakers, stereos and the occasional television. The centre's residents got through a lot of electrical goods, but it was organic material which had triggered the order. Due to the extensive social phobia rampant among the residents, they were often reluctant to use the communal toilets. So a few had been given permission to keep a bucket in their room which they emptied at regular – though sadly sometimes irregular – intervals. One of the irregulars had kept his bucket on the window-sill so that he could open the window and get rid of the worst smells. One day, a staff member had opened the door to the room and the draught had blown over the bucket. It was during the renovation of the new patisserie and as fate would have it a painter was on a ladder directly below the window. The painter had escaped without permanent injury, but Martha – who had been the first person to arrive at the scene and come to the assistance of the shocked man – knew that the incident had left him mentally scarred.

'Sit down,' she said, pointing to the chair. 'And take off your shoes.'

He did as he was told. She opened the box.

'I didn't want the others to see them,' she said and took out a pair of soft, black leather shoes. 'They were my father's,' she said, handing them to him. 'You take about the same size.'

He looked so surprised that she felt herself blushing.

'We can't send you to a job interview in trainers,' she added hastily.

She looked around the room while he put them on. She wasn't sure, but thought she could smell detergent. The cleaners hadn't been here today, as far as she knew. She walked up to a photograph attached to the wall with a drawing pin.

'Who is that?'

'My father,' he said

'Really? A police officer?'

'Yes. Look.'

She turned to him. He had got up and pressed first his right foot and then his left on the floor.

'And?'

'They're a perfect fit,' he smiled. 'Thank you so much, Martha.'

She jumped when he said her name. It wasn't that she wasn't used to hearing it, the residents used their first names all the time. Surnames, home addresses and the names of family members were, however, confidential; after all, the staff witnessed drug dealing every day. But there was something about the way he said it. Like a touch. Careful and innocent, but just as tangible. She realised it was inappropriate for her to be alone with him in the room; her initial assumption had been that Johnny would be here as well. She wondered where he could be; the only things that could make Johnny get out of bed were drugs, the toilet or food. In that order. And yet she stayed where she was.

'What kind of job are you looking for?' she asked. She was aware she sounded slightly breathless.

'Something in the judicial system,' he said gravely. There was something very sweet about this earnestness. Almost precocious.

'A bit like your father?'

'No, police officers work for the executive power. I want to work for the judicial power.'

She smiled. He was so different. Perhaps that was the reason she had been thinking about him, because he was nothing like the other addicts. And he was so very different from Anders as well. Where Anders always had steely control, this guy seemed open and vulnerable. Where Anders was suspicious and dismissive of people he had yet to know and possibly give his seal of approval to, Stig seemed friendly, kind, naive almost.

'I've got to go now,' she said.

'Yes,' he said, leaning against the wall. He had unzipped his hoodie. The T-shirt underneath was soaked in sweat and stuck to his body.

He was about to say something when her walkie-talkie crackled.

She raised it to her ear.

She had a visitor.

'What were you going to say?' she asked when she had acknowledged the message.

'It can wait,' the boy said and smiled.

It was the older police officer again.

He was waiting for her at reception.

'They let me in,' he said apologetically.

Martha looked reproachfully at Maria, who held up her hands in a what's-the-big-deal? gesture.

'Do you have somewhere we can . . . ?'

Martha took him into the meeting room, but didn't offer him coffee.

'Do you know what this is?' he asked, holding up his mobile phone so she could see the screen.

'A picture of some soil?'

'It's a shoeprint. That probably doesn't mean very much to you, but I've been wondering why I thought that shoeprint seemed so familiar. And then I realised it's because I've seen it at so many potential crime scenes. You know, places where we find dead bodies. Mostly as tracks in the snow at a container port, in a drug den, near a drug dealer in a backyard, in a World War II bunker doubling up as a shooting gallery. In short . . .'

'In short, places frequented by the type of people who live here.' Martha sighed.

'Exactly. Death is usually self-inflicted, but whatever the cause, this shoeprint keeps reappearing. Those blue army trainers have become the most common footwear for drug addicts and homeless people across all of Norway because the Salvation Army and Bymisjonen hand them out. And therefore they are completely useless as evidence, there are too many of them on the feet of people with criminal records.'

'So what are you doing here, Chief Inspector Kefas?'

'They no longer make these trainers and those in use wear out. But if you look carefully at the picture, you'll see that the shoeprint has a clear pattern, meaning these trainers are new. I checked with the Salvation Army and they told me that they sent their last batch of blue trainers to you in March of this year. So my question is simply: have you handed out any shoes like this since the spring? Size 8½.'

'The answer is yes, of course.'

'Who—'

'Lots.'

'Size—'

'Size 8½ is the most common shoe size for men in the Western world – also among drug users, as it happens. I'm not able or prepared to tell you anything more than that.' Martha looked at him with tightened lips.

Now the police officer sighed. 'I respect your loyalty to the residents. But we're not talking about a gram of speed here, this is a murder inquiry. I found this shoeprint where that woman up at Holmenkollåsen was shot and killed yesterday. Agnete Iversen.'

'Iversen?' Martha suddenly felt breathless again. How odd. But then again the therapist who had given her the diagnosis 'compassion fatigue' had told her to look out for signs of stress.

Chief Inspector Kefas tilted his head slightly to one side. 'Yes, Iversen. It's had a lot of press coverage. Shot on the doorstep of her home—'

'Yes, yes, I saw some headlines. But I never read such stories, we have enough upset in this job. If you know what I mean.'

'I do. Her name was Agnete Iversen. Forty-nine years old. Previously in business, now a housewife. Married with a twenty-year-old son. Chair of the local Women's Institute. A generous donor to the Norwegian Tourist Association. So she probably qualifies as a pillar of the community.'

Martha coughed. 'How can you be sure that the shoeprint belongs to the killer?'

'We can't. But we found a partial shoeprint with the victim's blood in the bedroom, and that shoeprint could match this one.'

Martha coughed again. She ought to get it checked out by a doctor.

'But suppose I could remember the name of anyone given size 8½ trainers, how can you know which ones are from the crime scene?'

'I'm not sure that we could, but it looks as if the killer stepped in the victim's blood and it got into the sole pattern. And if it's coagulated, there could still be blood traces left in the grooves.'

'I understand,' Martha said.

Chief Inspector Kefas waited.

She got up. 'But I'm afraid I'm no use to you. Of course I can check with the other staff members, see if they remember a size 8½.'

The police officer stayed where he was as if to give her a chance to change her mind. And tell him something. Then he too got up and handed her his card.

'Thank you, I appreciate that. Call me, day or night.'

Martha stayed in the meeting room after Chief Inspector Kefas had left. She bit her lower lip.

She had told him the truth. 8½. It was the most common shoe size for men.

'Closing time,' Kalle announced. It was nine o'clock and the sun was starting to set behind the buildings on the riverbank. He took the last hundred-krone notes and put them in his money belt. He had heard that in St Petersburg drug dealers carrying cash were robbed so often that the mafia had given them steel money belts that were welded around their waists. The belt had a thin slit into which you inserted the money and a code known only to the guy in the back office, so that dealers couldn't be tortured into revealing it to any robbers or be tempted to steal the cash themselves. The dealer had to sleep, eat, crap and screw with the money belt in place, but even so Kalle had given the option serious consideration. He was bored out of his wits standing here evening after evening.

'Please!' It was one of those emaciated junkie bitches, all skin and bone, skin stretched across her skull Holocaust-style.

'Tomorrow,' Kalle said and started to walk away.

'I have to have some!'

'We're all out,' he lied and signalled to Pelvis, his dealer, to walk on.

She started crying. Kalle felt no compassion, these people just had to learn that the shop shut at nine o'clock and that it was no good turning up at two minutes past. Of course he could have hung around till ten past, quarter past even, to sell to those who managed to scrape together the money at the last minute. But ultimately it was about getting the work/life balance right, knowing when he could go home. Nor would staying open for longer improve his profit margin as they had the monopoly on Superboy; she would be back when they opened tomorrow.

She grabbed his arm, but Kalle shrugged her off. She stumbled onto the grass and fell to her knees.

'It's been a good day,' Pelvis remarked as they walked briskly down the path. 'How much, do you think?'

'*What do you think?*' Kalle snapped at him. Even multiplying the number of bags by the price was beyond this moron. You just couldn't get the staff these days.

Before they crossed the bridge, he looked over his shoulder to check they weren't being followed. It was a habit he had acquired long ago, the result of his dearly bought experience of being a drug dealer carrying too much cash, a robbery victim who would never report anything to the police. Dearly bought experience acquired on a summer's day by the river when he hadn't been able to keep his eyes open and had nodded off on a bench with 300,000 kroner's worth of heroin he was going to sell for Nestor. When he woke up, the drugs were gone, obviously. Nestor had sought him out the next day and explained that the boss had been kind enough to give Kalle a choice. Both thumbs – because he had been so clumsy. Or both eyelids because he had fallen asleep on the job. Kalle had chosen the eyelids. Two men dressed in suits, one dark-haired and one blond, had pinned him down while Nestor pulled out his eyelids and sliced them off with his hideous, curved Arabic knife. Afterwards Nestor had – also on the boss's instructions – given Kalle money for a taxi to the hospital. Surgeons had explained that in order to give him new eyelids, they would need to graft skin from another area of his body and that he was lucky he wasn't Jewish and hadn't been circumcised. It turned out that the foreskin was the type of skin whose properties most closely resembled those of eyelids. All things considered, the operation had been a success and Kalle's standard answer to anyone who asked how he'd lost his eyelids was that he'd had an accident with some acid and that the new skin had been grafted from his thigh. Someone else's thigh, he explained, if the person asking was a woman in his bed, who demanded to see the scar. And that he was a quarter Jewish, in case she was wondering about that as well.

For a long time he had believed that his secret was safe, right until the guy who had taken over his job with Nestor had come over to him in a bar and asked in a loud voice if he didn't think it stank of dick curd when he rubbed his eyes in the morning. The guy and his friends had roared with laughter. Kalle had smashed a beer bottle against the bar and glassed him, pulling the bottle out and glassing him again and again until he was quite sure the guy had no eyes left to rub. The next day Nestor visited Kalle and told him that the boss had heard the news and that Kalle could have his old job back, seeing as it was now available and that he approved of his resourcefulness. Since that day Kalle never closed his eyes until he was absolutely certain that everything was under control. But all he could see now was the pleading woman on the grass and a solitary jogger with a hoodie.

'Two hundred grand?' Pelvis guessed.

Moron.

After walking through Oslo's eastern centre and the more dubious but character-building streets of Gamlebyen for fifteen minutes, they entered an abandoned factory area through an open gate. Tallying up shouldn't take them more than an hour. Apart from them there was only Enok and Syff, who sold speed by Elgen and Tollbugata, respectively. Afterwards they had to cut, mix and wrap new bags for tomorrow. Then he could finally go home to Vera. She had been sulking recently. The Barcelona trip he had promised her hadn't happened because he had been busy dealing all spring, so he had promised her a trip to Los Angeles this August instead. Unfortunately his criminal record had led to his visa application being turned down. Kalle knew that women like Vera weren't patient, they had options, so he had to screw her regularly and dangle trinkets in front of her greedy almond eyes to keep her. And that took time and energy. But also money, which meant more work. He was caught between a rock and a hard place.

They crossed an open area with oil-stained gravel, tall grass and two lorries with no tyres permanently parked on Leca blocks, and jumped up onto a loading ramp in front of a red-brick building. Kalle entered the four-digit code on the panel, heard the lock buzz and they opened the door. Drum and bass sounds pounded towards them. The council had converted the ground floor of the two-storey factory into rehearsal rooms for young bands. Kalle had hired a room on the first floor for a peppercorn rent under the pretext of running a band management and booking agency. They had yet to secure any band a single booking, but everyone knew these were difficult times for the arts.

Kalle and Pelvis walked down the corridor towards the lift while the front door slowly closed on stiff springs behind them. Through the noise Kalle thought for a moment that he could hear running footsteps on the gravel outside.

'Three hundred?' Pelvis volunteered.

Kalle shook his head and pressed the button for the lift.

Knut Schrøder laid down his guitar on top of the amplifier.

'Fag break,' he said and headed for the door.

He knew that his fellow band members were rolling their eyes at each other. Another fag break? They had a gig at the youth club in three days and it was a sad fact that they had to rehearse like maniacs so as not to sound completely crap. Knut thought the other band members were a bunch of choirboys: they didn't smoke, rarely drank alcohol and had never seen a joint let alone touched one. How could that ever be rock 'n' roll? He closed the door behind him and heard them start the song from the top without him. It didn't sound too bad, but was totally lacking in soul. Unlike him. He smiled at the thought while he passed the lift and the two empty rehearsal rooms along the corridor on his way to the exit.

It was exactly like the best bit in the Eagles DVD *Hell Freezes Over* – Knut's secret guilty pleasure – when the band rehearses with the Burbank Philharmonic Orchestra and the orchestra plays 'New York Minute' frowning with concentration and Don Henley turns to the camera, wrinkles up his nose and whispers: '. . . but they don't have the *blues* . . .'

Knut passed the rehearsal room whose door was always open because the lock was damaged and the hinges bent so that it was impossible to close it. He stopped. There was a man inside with his back to him. In the past vagrants looking for instruments or equipment that could readily be converted into cash constantly broke into the building, but that had stopped once the booking agency on the first floor had moved in and spent money on a new, solid front door with an entry-code lock.

'Hey, you!' Knut said.

The guy turned round. It was difficult to work out what he was.

A jogger? No. Yes, he was wearing a hoodie and tracksuit bottoms, but he wore smart, black leather shoes. Only vagrants dressed that badly. But Knut wasn't scared, why should he be? He was as tall as Joey Ramone and wore the same leather jacket. 'What are you doing here, man?'

The guy smiled. Which meant he couldn't be a member of a biker gang. 'Just a bit of clearing up.'

That sounded plausible. It was what happened to the communal rehearsal rooms; everything was trashed or stolen and no one ever took responsibility for keeping them clean. The window was still covered by sound-insulating sheets, but the only remaining instrument was a shabby bass drum where someone had painted 'The Young Hopeless' in Gothic lettering on the drumhead. On the floor among cigarette butts, broken guitar strings, a solitary drumstick and some duct tape, was a desk fan which the drummer had presumably used to stop himself from overheating. Plus a long jack cable which Knut could have checked to see if it was working, but which was bound to be faulty. Fair enough, jack cables were unreliable consumables, the future was wireless and his mother had promised Knut that she would sponsor a wireless system for his guitar if he quit smoking, an incident which had inspired him to write the song 'She Sure Drives a Hard Bargain'.

'Isn't it a bit late for a council worker to be still at it?' Knut said.

'We're thinking of rehearsing again.'

'We?'

'The Young Hopeless.'

'Ah, you're with them?'

'I used to be their drummer. I thought I saw the back of the other two guys when I came in, but they disappeared up in the lift.'

'No, they're with a band management and booking agency.'

'Oh? Could they be useful to us?'

'I don't think they're taking new clients. We knocked on their door and were told to fuck off.' Knut grinned, took a cigarette from the packet and stuck it between his lips. Perhaps the guy was a smoker and would have a fag outside with him. They could chat about music. Or kit.

'I'll go and check anyway,' the drummer said.

The guy looked more like a vocalist than a drummer. And it struck Knut that it might be a good idea if this guy were to talk to the booking people, he seemed to have something about him . . . some charisma. And if they opened the door to him, perhaps Knut himself could stop by later.

'I'll come with you to show you where it is.'

The guy looked reluctant. Then he nodded. 'Thank you.'

The big goods lift moved so slowly that Knut had enough time to explain in detail why the Mesa Boogie amplifier was awesome and delivered a proper rock sound.

They stepped out of the lift, Knut turned left and pointed to the blue metal door, the only door on the floor. The guy knocked. A few seconds later a small hatch at head height opened and a pair of bloodshot eyes appeared. Just like the time Knut had tried it.

'What do you want?'

The guy leaned closer to the hatch, probably in an attempt to see what was behind the man in the door.

'Would you consider booking gigs for the Young Hopeless? We're one of the bands that rehearse downstairs.'

'Fuck off and don't show your face here again. *Capisce?*'

The guy, however, remained close to the hatch and Knut could see his eyes dart from side to side.

'We're quite good. Do you like Depeche Mode?'

A voice rang out from somewhere behind the bloodshot eyes. 'Who is it, Pelvis?'

'Some band.'

'Get rid of them, for fuck's sake! And get back to work, I wanna be home by eleven.'

'You heard the boss.'

The hatch slammed shut.

Knut walked the four steps back to the lift and pressed the button. The doors opened reluctantly and he entered. But the guy had stayed put. He looked at the mirror the booking agency had put up at the top of the wall to the right when you exited the lift. It reflected their metal door, God only knew why. True, this wasn't Oslo's nicest neighbourhood, but for a booking agency they were remarkably paranoid. Perhaps they stored a lot of cash from gigs in their office? He had heard that well-known Norwegian bands were paid half a million for the biggest festival jobs. Another reason to keep rehearsing. If only he could get that wireless system. And a new band. With soul. Perhaps he and the new guy could join forces? The guy had finally returned to the lift, but was holding a hand in front of the sensors so the doors could not close. Then he withdrew his hand and studied the fluorescent lighting in the lift ceiling. On second thoughts, no. Knut had spent enough time working with psychos.

He went outside to smoke his cigarette while the guy returned to the rehearsal room to clear up. Knut was sitting on the flatbed of one of the rusted trucks when the guy came out.

'I reckon the others are late, but I can't get hold of them because my phone battery is dead,' he said, holding up a mobile that looked very new. 'So I'm off to get some cigarettes.'

'Have one of mine,' Knut said, holding out the packet. 'What kind of drums have you got? No, let me guess! You look old-school. Ludwig?'

The guy smiled. 'Thank you, that's kind of you. But I only smoke Marlboro.'

Knut shrugged. He respected people who were loyal to their

brand, be it drums or cigarettes. But *Marlboro*? That was like saying you would only ever drive a Toyota.

'Peace, man,' Knut said. 'Laters.'

'Thanks for your help.'

He watched the guy walk across the gravel towards the gate, before he turned round and came back.

'I've just remembered the code to the door is on my mobile,' he said with a slightly embarrassed smile. 'And . . .'

'It's gone dead. 666S. I thought of it myself. Do you know what it means?'

The guy nodded. 'It's the Arizona police code for suicide.'

Knut blinked several times. 'Is it?'

'Yep. The "S" stands for suicide. My dad taught me that.'

Knut saw the guy disappear out of the gate and into the light summer evening as a gust of wind caught the tall grass over by the gate and made it sway back and forth like a concert audience in response to some sentimental ballad. *Suicide.* Bloody hell, that was so much cooler than 666 Satan!

Pelle looked in the rear-view mirror and rubbed his bad foot. Everything was bad; business, his mood and the address which the customer in the back had just given him, the Ila Centre. So, for now, they were stationary in what was practically Pelle's regular spot in the cab rank in Gamlebyen.

'You mean the hostel?' Pelle asked.

'Yes. But now it's called . . . Yes, the hostel.'

'I don't drive anyone to the hostel without being paid up front. Sorry, but I've had some bad experiences.'

'Of course. I hadn't thought of that.'

Pelle watched as his customer or, more accurately, potential customer rummaged around his pocket. Pelle had been in his cab for thirteen hours straight, but it would be a few more hours before he would drive home to his flat in Schweigaards gate, park the cab, stagger up the stairs on the folding crutches he kept under the seat, collapse on his bed and fall asleep. Hopefully without dreaming. Though that depended on the dream. It could be heaven or hell, you never knew. The customer handed him a fifty-krone note and a handful of change.

'This is just over a hundred, it's not enough.'

'A hundred isn't enough?' said the now not so potential customer apparently with genuine surprise.

'Long time since you last took a cab?'

'You could say that. It's all I've got, but perhaps you could drive as far as that gets me?'

'Sure,' Pelle said, put the money in the glove compartment since the guy didn't look like he would want a receipt, and hit the accelerator.

Martha was alone in room 323.

She had sat in reception and watched first Stig then Johnny go out. Stig had been wearing the black shoes she had given him.

The centre's regulations allowed them to search a resident's room without warning or permission if they suspected them of keeping weapons. But the rules also stated that searches should normally be carried out by two staff members. Normally. How do you define normal? Martha looked at the chest of drawers. And then at the wardrobe.

She started with the chest of drawers.

It contained clothes. Just Johnny's clothes; she knew what clothes Stig owned.

She opened the door to the wardrobe.

The underwear she had given Stig lay neatly folded on one shelf. His coat was on a hanger. On the top shelf was the red sports bag she had seen him arrive with. She was reaching up to lift it down when she spotted the blue trainers at the bottom of the wardrobe. She let go of the bag, bent down and picked up the shoes. Took a deep breath. Held it. She was looking for coagulated blood. Then she turned them over.

She breathed a sigh of relief and felt her heart skip a beat.

The soles were completely clean. The pattern wasn't even stained.

'What are you doing?'

Martha spun round as her heart began beating wildly. She pressed her hand to her chest. 'Anders!' She bent double and laughed. 'You scared me half to death.'

'I've been waiting for you,' he pouted and stuffed his hands into the pockets of his leather jacket. 'It's almost nine thirty.'

'I'm sorry, I lost track of time. Someone said one of the residents might be keeping weapons in his room and it's our duty to check.' Martha was so flustered that the lie came effortlessly.

'Duty?' Anders snorted. 'Perhaps it's time you started thinking about what duty really means. Most people think of their family and home when they talk about duty, not working in a place like this.'

Martha sighed. 'Anders, please don't start . . .'

But she already knew that he wasn't going to give in, as usual it had taken him only seconds to get wound up. 'There's a job for you at my mother's gallery whenever you want it. And I agree with her. It would be much better for your personal development to mix with more stimulating people there than the losers in this place.'

'Anders!' Martha raised her voice, but knew that she was too tired, she didn't have the energy. So she walked up to him and put her hand on his arm. 'Don't call them losers. And I've told you before, your mother and her customers don't *need* me.'

Anders snatched back his arm. 'What people in this place *need* isn't you, but for the state to stop bailing them out. Those bloody junkies are Norway's pet project.'

'I'm not prepared to have this discussion again. Why don't you drive on without me and I'll take a taxi when I'm done?'

But Anders folded his arms across his chest and leaned against the door frame. 'So which discussion are you prepared to have, Martha? I've been trying to get you to set a date—'

'Not now.'

'Yes, now! My mother wants to plan her summer and—'

'Not now, I said.' She tried to push him aside, but he refused to budge. He stuck out his arm to block her path.

'What kind of answer is that? If they're paying for—'

Martha ducked under his arm, out into the corridor and started walking away.

'Hey!' She heard the door of the room slam shut and Anders's footsteps behind her. He grabbed her arm, spun her round and pulled her close. She recognised the expensive aftershave his mother had given him for Christmas, but which Martha couldn't stand. Her heart almost stopped when she saw the black emptiness in his eyes.

'Don't you dare walk away from me,' he snarled.

She had automatically raised a hand to shield her face and now she saw the shock in his face.

'What's this?' he whispered with steel in his voice. 'You think I'm going to hit you?'

'I . . .'

'Twice,' he hissed and she felt his hot breath on her face. 'Twice in nine years, Martha. And you treat me as if I was some bloody . . . some bloody wife-beater.'

'Anders, let go, you're—'

She heard a cough behind her. Anders released his hold on her arm, stared furiously over her shoulder and spat out the words:

'So, junkie, you want to get past or not?'

She turned round. It was him. Stig. He just stood there, waiting.

He moved his calm gaze from Anders to her. It asked a question. Which she answered with a nod; everything was fine.

He nodded and stepped past them. The two men glowered at each other as he passed. They were the same height, but Anders was broader, more muscular.

Martha watched Stig as he continued down the corridor.

Then her gaze returned to Anders. He had tilted his head and was glaring at her with this hostile expression which he exhibited more and more often, but which she had decided was caused by the frustration he experienced at not getting the recognition he felt he deserved at work.

'What the fuck was that?' he said.

He didn't used to swear, either.

'What?'

'It was like the two of you . . . communicated. Who is that guy?'

She exhaled. Relieved, almost. At least this was familiar territory. Jealousy. It hadn't changed since they were teenage sweethearts and she knew how to handle it. She put her hand on his shoulder.

'Anders, don't be so silly. Now come with me, we'll go and get my jacket and then we're going home. And we're not going to argue tonight, we're going to cook dinner.'

'Martha, I—'

'Shh,' she said, but knew she already had the upper hand. 'You cook dinner, while I take a shower. OK? And we're going to talk about the wedding tomorrow. Is that all right?'

She could see that he wanted to protest, but she placed her finger on his lips. The full lips which she had fallen for. She traced her finger downwards, stroking the dark, carefully trimmed stubble. Or was it his jealousy that first attracted her? She could no longer remember.

By the time they got into his car, he had calmed down. It was a BMW. He had bought the car against her will, thinking she would grow to like it once she had experienced how comfortable it was, especially for long drives. And how reliable it was. When he started the car, she caught a glimpse of Stig again. He came out of the entrance, quickly crossed the street and headed eastwards. The red sports bag was slung over his shoulder.

20

SIMON DROVE PAST THE PLAYING fields and turned into the street where they lived. He could see that his neighbour was barbecuing again. The loud, sun-baked and beer-soaked outbursts of laughter emphasised the summer silence in the neighbourhood. Most houses were empty and only a single car was parked along the road.

'And we're home,' Simon said and pulled up in front of their garage.

He didn't know why he said it. Else could surely see where they were.

'Thank you for taking me to the movies,' Else said and put her hand on his on top of the gearstick, as if he had walked her to her front door and was about to say goodnight and leave here there. I could never do that, Simon thought and smiled at her. He wondered how much of the film she had been able to see. Going to the cinema had been her idea. He had glanced furtively at her several times during the movie and seen that at least she had laughed in all the right places. But then again, Woody Allen's humour lay more in the dialogue than in slapstick. Never mind, they had had a lovely evening. Another lovely evening.

'But I bet you missed Mia Farrow,' she teased him.

He laughed. It was a private joke. The first film he had taken her to see had been *Rosemary's Baby*, Roman Polanski's disgustingly brilliant movie with Mia Farrow who gives birth to a child who turns out to be the devil's son. Else had been horrified and for a long time she had believed that it was Simon's way of letting her know that he didn't want children – especially when he insisted that they see it again. Not until later – after a fourth Woody Allen film with Mia Farrow – did she click that it was Farrow and not the spawn of the devil who so fascinated him.

As they walked from the car towards their front door, Simon saw a brief flash of light from the street. Like a revolving lighthouse beam. It was coming from the parked car.

'What was that?' Else asked.

'I don't know,' Simon said and unlocked the front door. 'Would you mind putting on some coffee? I'll be with you in a moment.'

Simon left her and crossed the street. He knew the car didn't belong to any of their neighbours. Or anyone living nearby. In Oslo limousines were associated mainly with embassies, the royal family or government ministers. He knew only one other person who drove around with tinted windows, plenty of leg room and his own driver. A driver who had just got out and was holding open the door to the back for Simon.

Simon bent down, but remained outside. The small man sitting inside had a pointy nose in his round, ruddy face of the type people described as 'jovial'. The blue blazer with the gold buttons – a favourite with 1980s Norwegian bankers, shipowners and crooners – had always made Simon wonder if it disguised a deeply anchored fantasy among Norwegian men to be the captain of a ship.

'Good evening, Chief Inspector Kefas,' said the small man in a bright, cheerful voice.

'What are you doing in my street, Nestor? Nobody here wants to buy your crap.'

'Now now. Always the dogged crime fighter, eh?'

'Give me a reason to arrest you and I will.'

'Unless it's against the law to help people in trouble, I don't think that will be necessary. Why don't you get in so we can talk without being disturbed, Kefas?'

'I fail to see why I'd want to do that.'

'So your eyesight is bad as well?'

Simon stared at Nestor. Short arms and a small, thick upper body. And yet the sleeves on his blazer were still so short that the golden cufflinks in the shape of the initials 'HN' peeked out. Hugo Nestor claimed to be Ukrainian, but according to the file they had on him, he was born and bred in Florø, came from a fishing family and his surname had originally been Hansen before he changed it. He had never spent time abroad apart from a brief and unfinished economics course in Lund, Sweden. God only knew where he had picked up that strange accent, but it certainly wasn't the Ukraine.

'I wonder if your young wife could see which actors were playing in the movie, Kefas. But then I guess she'd heard that Allen wasn't in it himself. That Jew has such a disgusting, chattering voice. Not that I have anything against Jews as individuals, I just think that Hitler was right about them as a race. The Slavs are the same. Even though I'm an East European, I have to admit that he had a point when he said that the Slavs can't lead themselves. On a racial level, I mean. And this Allen, isn't he a paedophile as well?'

The file also said that Hugo Nestor was Oslo's most important drugs and human trafficking operator. Never convicted, never charged, always suspected. He was too smart and too careful, the slippery eel.

'I don't know, Nestor. What I do know is that there's a rumour that your guys expedited the prison chaplain. Did he owe you money?'

Nestor smiled overbearingly. 'Isn't it beneath your dignity to listen to rumours, Kefas? You usually have a bit of class, in contrast to your colleagues. If you'd had more than rumours – such as a reliable witness willing to come to court and point the finger, for example – you'd already have made an arrest. Isn't that right?'

A slippery eel.

'Anyway, I want to offer you and your wife money. Enough money, say, for a very expensive eye operation.'

Simon gulped; he heard his voice croak when he replied: 'Did Fredrik tell you?'

'Your former colleague at the Serious Fraud Office? Let me put it this way, I've heard about your predicament. I presume that you went to him with your request in the hope it would reach ears such as mine. Isn't that right, Kefas?' He smiled. 'Anyway, I have a solution which I think would suit us both. So why don't you get in?'

Simon took hold of the door handle and saw Nestor automatically shuffle across the seat to make room for him. He concentrated on breathing calmly so that rage wouldn't make his voice quiver. 'Carry on talking, Nestor. Give me an excuse for arresting you, please.'

Nestor raised a questioning eyebrow. 'What excuse would that be, Chief Inspector Kefas?'

'Attempted bribery of a public servant.'

'Bribery?' Nestor laughed a brief, squealing laughter. 'Let's call it a business proposal, Kefas. You'll see that we can . . .'

Simon never heard the rest of the sentence as the limousine was clearly soundproof. He walked away without looking back, wishing he had slammed the car door even harder. He heard the car start and the tyres crunch against the gravel on the tarmac.

*   *   *

'You seem upset, darling,' Else said when he had sat down at the kitchen table next to his coffee cup. 'Who was it?'

'Someone who was lost,' Simon said. 'I told him where to go.'

Else shuffled over to him with the coffee pot. Simon stared out of the window. The street was deserted now. Suddenly a burning pain spread across the top of his thighs.

'Damn!'

He knocked the coffee pot out of her hands and it landed on the floor with a bang while he shouted: 'Bloody hell, woman, you've just poured boiling coffee all over me! Are you . . . are you . . .' One part of his brain knew what was coming and was trying to block the word, but it was like slamming the back door of Nestor's car: he didn't want to be there, he refused, he wanted to destroy, he would rather plunge the knife into himself. And into her.

'. . . blind?!'

The kitchen fell silent; all he could hear was the coffee-pot lid rolling across the linoleum floor and the bubbling of coffee seeping out of the pot. No! He hadn't mean it. He hadn't.

'I'm sorry. Else, I'm . . .'

He got up to embrace her, but she was already on her way to the sink. She turned on the cold tap and held a tea towel under it. 'Pull down your trousers, Simon, let me . . .'

He put his arms around her from behind. He pressed his forehead against her neck. He whispered: 'I'm sorry, so sorry. Please, forgive me? I . . . I just don't know what to do. I should be able to help you, but I . . . I can't, I don't know, I . . .'

He couldn't hear her crying yet, only feel that her body was trembling and how it spread to his. His throat thickened, he suppressed his own sobs and didn't know if he had managed it, only that they were both shaking.

'I'm the one who should say sorry,' she sobbed. 'You could be with someone better, someone who doesn't . . . scald you.'

'But there is no one better,' he whispered. 'All right? So you just go ahead and pour boiling coffee all over me, I won't ever let go. OK?'

And he knew that she knew that it was true. That he would do anything, suffer anything, sacrifice everything.

. . . it would reach ears such as mine . . .

But he hadn't been able to bring himself to do it.

He heard the neighbours' distant, ecstatic howls of laughter in the darkness while her tears flowed.

Kalle looked at the time. Twenty to eleven. It had been a good day; they had shifted more Superboy than they normally did over a whole weekend, so the cashing up and the preparation of new wraps had taken longer than usual. He took off the gauze mask they wore when they cut and mixed the drugs on the worktop in the plain, twenty-metre-square room which served as office, drug factory and bank. Obviously, the drug was cut before it reached him, but even so Superboy was still the purest drug he had come across in his career as a dealer. So pure that if they didn't don gauze masks, they would not only be high, but also dead from inhaling the particles which whirled up in the air when they cut and handled the pale brown powder. He put the masks in the safe in front of the piles of banknotes and bags of drugs. Should he called Vera and tell her he would be late? Or was it time he put his foot down, told her who was boss, who brought home the dough and who should be able to come and go without accounting for his movements all the bloody time?

Kalle told Pelvis to check the corridor. From the iron door to their office the lift was just a few metres away on the right. At the far end of the corridor was a door leading to a stairwell, but that door they had – against fire regulations – sealed with a chain so that it was permanently locked.

'Cassius, check the car park,' Kalle called out in English while he locked up the safe. It was a quiet office with no noise other than anything that travelled from the rehearsal rooms, but he liked shouting. Cassius was the biggest and fattest African in Oslo. His shapeless body was so huge it was impossible to know what was what, but if just ten per cent of him was muscle, it would be enough to stop most people.

'No cars, no people in the car park,' Cassius said as he peered out between the iron bars in the window.

'Corridor all clear,' said Pelvis, who was looking out of the hatch in the door.

Kalle turned the combination wheel. He savoured the smooth, oiled resistance, the soft clicking. He kept the combination in his head and only there, it wasn't written down anywhere, and there was no logic to it, no combination of birthdays or similar.

'Let's go,' he said and straightened up. 'Have your guns ready, both of you.'

They gave him a puzzled look.

Kalle hadn't said anything to them, but there had been something about the eyes he had seen staring through the hatch earlier. He knew that they had seen Kalle sitting at the table. OK, so it was just some guy from a crappy band looking for management, but there had been enough money and drugs on the table for any idiot who wanted to have a go. Hopefully, the guy had also noticed the two guns on the table which belonged to Cassius and Pelvis.

Kalle went over to the door. It could be locked from the inside, and only his key unlocked it. It meant that Kalle could lock in anyone who worked here if he himself had to go out. The bars in front of the window were solid. In short, no one who worked for Kalle could run off with the money or the drugs. Or let in uninvited guests.

Kalle looked through the hatch. Not because he'd forgotten that

Pelvis had just announced that the coast was clear, but because he automatically assumed that Pelvis would betray his boss by opening the door if someone was prepared to make it worth his while. Damn, Kalle would have done the same himself. He *had* done the same himself.

He couldn't see anyone through the hatch. He checked the mirror which he had mounted on the wall to make sure that no one could hide by pressing themselves against the door below the hatch. The dimly lit corridor was empty. He turned the key and held the door open for the other two. Pelvis walked out first, then Cassius and finally Kalle. He turned round to lock the door.

'What the . . . !' It was Pelvis.

Kalle turned back, and it wasn't until now that he could see what he had been unable to from the hatch due to the angle: that the lift doors were open. But he still couldn't see what was inside the lift as the light inside it was off. All he could see in the dim corridor light was something metallic on one side of the lift door. Duct tape covering the sensors. And broken glass on the floor.

'Watch out . . .'

But Pelvis had already taken the three steps to the open lift.

Kalle's brain registered the flame from the muzzle in the darkness of the lift before it received the signal about the bang.

Pelvis whirled around as if someone had slapped him. He stared at Kalle with a stunned expression. It looked as if he had been given a third eye in his cheekbone. Then his life left him and his body fell to the ground like a coat shrugged off by its owner.

'Cassius! Shoot for fuck's sake!'

In his panic, Kalle forgot that Cassius didn't speak Norwegian, but it clearly wasn't an issue, he had already aimed his pistol at the darkness inside the lift and fired. Kalle felt something strike his chest. He had never been at the wrong end of a pistol before, but now he knew why the people he had aimed his gun at had frozen in such a comical manner, as if they were filled with cement. The pain in his chest spread, he couldn't breathe, but he had to get away, there was air behind the bulletproof door, safety, a door he could lock. But his hand refused to obey, it couldn't get the key into the lock, it was like a dream, like moving underwater. Fortunately he was shielded by Cassius's vast body that kept shooting and shooting. Finally the key went in and Kalle turned it, flung the door open and hurled himself inside. The next bang had different acoustics and he reckoned that it must be coming from inside the lift. He spun round to slam the door shut, but it was pressing against Cassius, half of whose shoulder and an arm as thick as a thigh were trapped inside. Damn! He tried to push it away, but more of Cassius was trying to get into the office.

'Come on in then, you fat fuck!' Kalle hissed and opened the door.

The African poured in like rising bread dough, spreading his body mass over the threshold and the floor inside. Kalle stared down at his glassy expression. The eyes bulged like the eyes of a freshly caught deep-water fish, his mouth opened and closed.

'Cassius!'

The only reply he got was a wet smack when a big, pink bubble burst on the African's lips. Kalle pressed his legs against the wall in an attempt to move the black mountain out of the way so he could close the door again, but it was no use, so he bent down and tried to drag him inside instead. Too heavy. The pistol! Cassius had landed on top of his own arm. Kalle straddled the body, trying desperately to slip his hand under it, but for every roll of fat he passed there was another and still no pistol. He had his arm buried in fat up to his elbow when he heard footsteps outside. He knew what was about to happen, tried to get out of the way, but was too late, the door smacked into his head and he blacked out.

When Kalle opened his eyes, he was lying on his back staring up at a guy in a hoodie, wearing yellow washing-up gloves and pointing a pistol straight down at him. He turned his head, but saw no one else, only Cassius who lay with half his body inside the door. From this angle, Kalle could see the barrel of Cassius's pistol sticking out from under his stomach.

'What do you want?'

'I want you to open the safe. You have seven seconds.'

'Seven?'

'I started counting down before you woke up. Six.'

Kalle scrambled to his feet. He was woozy, but he made his way to the safe.

'Five.'

He turned the combination wheel.

'Four.'

One more digit and the safe would open and the money would be gone. Money he would personally have to replace, those were the rules.

'Three.'

He hesitated. What if he could get hold of Cassius's pistol?

'Two.'

Would the guy really shoot or was he just bluffing?

'One.'

The guy had killed two people without batting an eyelid, a third body wouldn't bother him.

'OK,' Kalle said, stepping aside. He couldn't bear to look at the piles of banknotes and bags of drugs.

'Put everything into this,' the guy ordered him and handed him a red sports bag.

Kalle did as he was told. Not slowly or quickly, he simply put the contents into the bag while his brain counted automatically. 200,000 kroner. 200,000 . . .

When he had finished, the guy told him to toss the bag on the floor in front of him. Again Kalle did as he was told. At that moment he realised that if he was going to get shot, it would be now. Here. The guy no longer needed him. Kalle took two steps towards Cassius. He had to go for the gun.

'If you don't do it, then I won't shoot you,' the guy said.

What the hell, was he a mind-reader?

'Put your hands on your head and walk out into the corridor.'

Kalle hesitated. Could this mean that he might let him live? He stepped over Cassius.

'Lean against the wall with your hands above your head.'

Kalle did what the guy said. He turned his head. Saw that the guy had already picked up Pelvis's pistol and was now squatting on his haunches with his hand under Cassius, but his eyes on Kalle. He managed to get hold of Cassius's gun as well.

'Take out the bullet in the wall over there, would you please?' said the guy and pointed, and Kalle realised where he had seen him before. By the river, it was the jogger. He must have followed them. Kalle looked up and saw the end of a mangled bullet stuck in the mortar. A fine spray of blood led from the wall to where it had come from: Pelvis's head. It hadn't travelled at great speed so Kalle could pick it out with his fingernails.

'Give it here,' said the guy, taking the bullet with his free hand. 'Now I want you to find my other bullet and the two empty shells. You have thirty seconds.'

'What if the other bullet is inside Cassius?'

'I don't think so. Twenty-nine.'

'Look at that mountain of fat, man!'

'Twenty-eight.'

Kalle threw himself on his knees and started looking. He cursed himself for not spending more money on stronger light bulbs.

At thirteen he had found four of Cassius's shells and one of the other guy's. At seven, he had found the other bullet which the guy had fired at them; it must have gone straight through Cassius and ricocheted off the metal door because the door had a small dent.

When the countdown was over, he still hadn't found the last shell.

He closed his eyes. Felt how one of the slightly too tight eyelids scraped his cornea while he prayed to God to live one more day. He heard the shot, but felt no pain. He opened his eyes and realised he was still crouching on all fours on the floor.

The guy lifted the barrel of Pelvis's gun from Cassius.

Christ, the guy had shot Cassius again with Pelvis's gun to be sure he was dead! And now he went over to Pelvis, held Cassius's gun in the same place where the first bullet had entered, adjusted the angle. And pulled the trigger.

'Fuck!' Kalle screamed and heard the terror in his own voice.

The guy put the others' two guns in the red sports bag and pointed at Kalle with his own. 'Come on. Into the lift.'

The lift. The broken glass. It had to be in the lift. He had to attack him in the lift.

They stepped inside and in the light from the corridor Kalle could see that there was more broken glass on the lift floor. He selected a longish piece which looked as if it would be perfect for the job. Once the doors shut it would be completely dark and all he would have to do was bend down, grab the shard and swing it in one flowing movement. He had to . . .

The doors closed. The guy stuck his gun into the lining of his trousers. Perfect! It would be like killing a chicken. It grew dark. Kalle bent down. His fingers found the shard of glass. He straightened up. Then found himself paralysed.

Kalle didn't know what kind of hold it was, only that he was immobilised, he couldn't even move a finger. He tried shaking himself loose, but it was like pulling at the wrong end of a knot, the grip tightened further and his neck and arms hurt like hell. It had to be some kind of martial art technique. The shard of glass slipped out of his hand. The lift started moving.

The doors opened again, they heard the never-ending thumping bass and the hold loosened. Kalle opened his mouth and drew breath. The gun was pointed at him again and indicated for him to move down the corridor.

Kalle was ordered into one of the empty rehearsal rooms where he was told to sit down on the floor with his back to the radiator. He sat without moving and stared at a bass drum with the name 'The Young Hopeless' scrawled across it while the guy tied him to the radiator with a long, black cable. There was no point in fighting back, his attacker didn't intend to kill him or he would be dead already. And the money and the drugs could be replaced. He would have to pay for them out of his own pocket, of course, but what was foremost in his mind was how to explain to Vera that there was unlikely to be another shopping trip to some cool city in the foreseeable future. The guy took two guitar strings from the floor, tied the thicker one around his head over the bridge of his nose and the thinner one around his chin. He must have tied them to the radiator behind him; Kalle could feel the metal of the thinner string dig into his skin and press against his lower gum.

'Move your head,' the guy said. He had to shout over the music coming from further down the corridor. Kalle tried to turn his head, but the guitar strings were too tight.

'Good.'

The guy put an electric fan on a chair, switched it on and aimed it at Kalle's face. Kalle closed his eyes against the current of air and felt his sweat dry on his skin. When he opened his eyes again, he could see that the guy had placed one of the unmixed kilo bags of Superboy on the chair in front of the fan and had pulled his hoodie up to cover his nose and mouth. What the hell was he doing? Then Kalle spotted the shard of glass.

It felt as if a cold hand was squeezing his heart.

He knew what was about to happen.

The guy swiped the sliver of glass. Kalle steeled himself. The tip of the glass hit the plastic bag, sliced it open and in the next second the air filled with white powder. It got it into Kalle's eyes, mouth and nose. He closed his mouth. But he had to cough. He closed his mouth again. Felt the bitter taste of the powder stick to his mucous membranes which started stinging and burning; the drug was already entering his bloodstream.

The photograph of Pelle and his wife was stuck to the dashboard on the left side, in between the steering wheel and the door. Pelle ran his finger over the smooth, greasy surface. He was back in his usual spot in Gamlebyen, but it was a waste of time, it was summer quiet and the trips which flashed up on the display screen departed from other destinations in town. Still, he could always hope. He saw a man leave through the gate to the old factory. He walked with a purpose and speed that indicated he had places to go to and wanted to flag down the only taxi at the cab rank before the light on the roof went out and it drove off. But then he suddenly stopped and leaned against the wall. Doubled up. He was standing right under a street light so Pelle could clearly see the stomach contents splash down on the tarmac. No way he was having him in his cab. The guy remained crouched and vomiting. Pelle had been there many times himself, he could taste bile in his mouth simply by looking. Then the guy wiped his mouth on the sleeve of his hoodie, straightened up, pulled the strap of the bag back up over his shoulder and continued towards Pelle. It wasn't until he was very close that Pelle realised that it was the same guy he had driven only an hour ago. The guy who hadn't had enough money to get to the hostel. And now he was indicating to Pelle that he wanted another trip. Pelle pressed the central locking button and opened the window a crack. Waited until the guy had come up to the side of the car and had tried to open the door in vain.

'Sorry, mate, I'm not going to take this fare.'

'Please?'

Pelle looked at him. Trails of tears down his cheeks. God only knew what had happened, but it wasn't his problem. True, the guy might have a hard-luck story to tell, but you didn't survive as a taxi driver in Oslo for long if you opened your door and let in other people's messes.

'Listen, I saw you throw up. If you throw up in the cab, it'll cost you a thousand kroner and me a lost day's income. Besides, last time you were in this cab, you were skint. So I'm going to pass, OK?'

Pelle rolled up the window and stared right ahead in the hope that the boy would move on without causing trouble, but got ready to drive away should it become necessary. Christ, how his foot hurt tonight. Out of the corner of his eye he saw the boy open his bag and take out something which he pressed against the window.

Pelle half turned his head. It was a thousand-krone note.

Pelle shook his head, but the guy stayed where he was, motionless. Waiting. Pelle wasn't really worried, the guy hadn't been trouble earlier this evening. On the contrary, rather than hassle Pelle to drive a bit further as most people short of cash would have done, he had thanked him when Pelle had stopped to let him out when the meter had reached the amount he had given him. Thanked him so sincerely that Pelle had felt guilty for not driving him all the way to the hostel – it would have only taken him another two minutes. Pelle sighed and pressed the button which unlocked the doors.

The guy slipped into the back seat. 'Thank you, thank you so much.'

'Fine. Where to?'

'First up to Berg, please. I'm just dropping something off, so I'd be grateful if you could wait. Then to the Ila Centre. I'll pay you up front, obviously.'

'No need,' Pelle said, starting the car. His wife was right, he was too good for this world.

PART THREE

21

IT WAS TEN O'CLOCK IN the morning and the sun had been shining on Waldemar Thranes gate for a long time when Martha parked her Golf convertible. She got out and walked with light footsteps past the patisserie to the entrance of the Ila Centre's cafe. She noticed some men – and even some women – glancing at her as she walked by. That in itself wasn't unusual, but today she seemed to attract extra attention. She attributed it to her extraordinarily high spirits, but couldn't think of any specific reason for them. She had argued with her future mother-in-law about the wedding date, with Grete – the manager of the hostel – about the allocations to the rota, and with Anders about practically everything. Perhaps she was in a good mood because it was her day off, because Anders had gone with his mother to their cabin for the weekend, and because she had all this sunshine to herself for two whole days.

When she entered the cafe, she saw all the paranoid heads look up. All except one. She smiled, waved as people called out to her and walked up to the two girls behind the counter. Handed one of them a key.

'You'll be fine. Just get through it. Remember, there are two of you.'

The girl nodded, but she looked pale.

Martha poured herself a cup of coffee. She stood with her back to the room. She knew that she had spoken a little more loudly than necessary. She turned round and smiled as if surprised when she met his gaze. Went over to the table where he sat alone. She held the cup up to her lips, talked over it.

'You're up early?'

He raised an eyebrow and she realised the seeming idiocy of her remark – it was past ten o'clock.

'Most people here tend to get up very late,' she added quickly.

'Yes, they do,' he smiled.

'Listen, I just wanted to apologise for what happened yesterday.'

'Yesterday?'

'Yes. Anders isn't usually like that, but sometimes . . . Whatever, he had no right to talk to you like that. Call you a junkie and . . . well, you know.'

Stig shook his head. 'You don't have to apologise, you didn't do anything wrong. Nor did your boyfriend, I *am* a junkie.'

'And I'm a lousy driver. That doesn't mean I let people say so to my face.'

He laughed. She saw how the laughter softened up his features, made him look even more boyish.

'And yet you still drive, I see.' He nodded towards the window. 'Your car?'

'Yes, I know it's a wreck, but I like the independence and freedom it gives me. Don't you?'

'I wouldn't know, I've never driven a car.'

'Never? Really?'

He shrugged.

'That's so sad,' she said.

'Sad?'

'Nothing beats driving a convertible with the hood down in the sunshine.'

'Even for a . . .'

'Yes, even for a junkie,' she laughed. 'Best trip you'll ever have, trust me.'

'Then I hope you'll take me for a drive some time.'

'Of course,' she said. 'How about now?'

She saw the mild surprise in his gaze. She had blurted out the offer on impulse. She knew the others were looking at them. So what? She could sit for hours with the other residents talking about their personal problems without anyone thinking anything of it; on the contrary, it was a part of her job. And today was her day off and she could spend it any way she liked, couldn't she?

'Sure,' Stig replied.

'I only have a few hours,' Martha said, aware of a slightly flustered quality to her voice. What she already having second thoughts?

'As long as I can have a go,' he said. 'At driving. It looks like fun.'

'I know a place. Come on.'

As they left, Martha could feel everyone's eyes on her.

Stig was concentrating so hard that she had to laugh. Crouching and gripping the steering wheel he drove painfully slowly in large circles around the car park in Økern which was deserted at the weekends.

'Good,' she said. 'Now try driving in figures of eight.'

He did as she said and revved the engine a little, but when the revs increased, he instinctively took his foot off.

'The police came by the other day,' Martha said. 'They wanted to know if we'd handed out any new trainers. It was because of the Iversen murder, if you've heard about that.'

'Yes, I've read about it,' he said.

She looked at him. She liked that he had been reading. Most of the residents never read a single word, didn't absorb any news, didn't know who the Prime Minister was or what 9/11 meant. But they could tell you to the nearest krone what speed cost anywhere, the purity of heroin and the percentages of active ingredients in any new pharmaceutical product.

'And talking of Iversen, wasn't that the name of the man who might be able to get you a job?'

'Yes. I went there, but he doesn't have anything now.'

'Oh, what a shame.'

'Yes, but I'm not going to give up, I have more names on my list.'

'Great! So you have a list?'

'Yes, I do.'

'Why don't we try changing gears?'

Two hours later they were racing down Mosseveien. She was driving. To one side the Oslo Fjord glittered in the sunshine. He had proved to be a quick learner. There had been some trying and failing with gear-changing and the clutch, but once they had resolved that, it was as if he simply programmed his brain to remember any action that had worked and repeated it, automated it. After three attempts at hill starts, he could do it without using the handbrake. And when he had understood the geometry of parallel parking, he mastered it with an almost irritating deftness.

'What's that?'

'Depeche Mode,' he said. 'Do you like it?'

She listened to the chanting, two-part vocals and the mechanical rhythm.

'Yes,' she said, turning up the volume of the CD player. 'It sounds very . . . English.'

'True. What else can you hear?'

214

'Hm. Cheerful dystopia. As if they don't take their own depression all that seriously, if you know what I mean.'

He laughed. 'I know what you mean.'

After some minutes on the motorway, she turned off towards Nesoddtangen peninsula. The roads grew narrower, the traffic lighter. She pulled over and stopped.

'Are you ready for the real thing?'

He nodded. 'Yes, I'm ready for the real thing.'

He had replied with a passion that made her suspect he was talking about more than just driving a car. They got out of the car and switched places. She watched him sit close to the steering wheel and look straight ahead, concentrating. He pushed the clutch down and put the car in gear. He pressed the accelerator carefully and tentatively.

'Mirror,' she said, while checking the rear view herself.

'All clear,' he said.

'Indicator.'

He flicked the indicator, muttered an 'on' and gently released the clutch.

Slowly they moved out onto the road. With the revs slightly too high.

'Handbrake,' she said and grabbed the stick between them to release it. She felt his hand come across to do the same, touch hers and flinch as if he had burned himself.

'Thank you,' he said.

They drove for ten minutes in total silence. They let a driver who was in a hurry overtake them. A trailer truck came towards them. She held her breath. She knew that on the narrow road, she would – even though she knew there was room for both of them – automatically brake and pull to the side. But Stig wasn't daunted by it. And the strange thing was that she trusted him to make the right call. The male brain's innate understanding of three dimensions. She saw

215

his hands resting calmly on the steering wheel. And she concluded that he lacked the very trait which she had in abundance; the tendency to doubt her own judgement. She could see from the fine, thick veins on the top of his hand how calmly his heart was pumping out blood. Blood to his fingertips. She saw his hands turn the steering wheel quickly, but not too far to the right, when the rush from the truck took hold of the car.

'Wow!' he laughed with excitement and looked at her. 'Did you feel that?'

'Yes,' she said. 'I felt that.'

She directed him to the tip of Nesodden and up a gravel track where they parked behind a row of low houses with small windows at the back and large windows overlooking the sea.

'Renovated holiday cottages from the 1950s,' Martha explained as she walked in front of him down the path through the tall grass. 'I grew up in one of them. And this was our secret sunspot . . .'

They had reached a rocky point. Below them lay the sea and they could hear the gleeful squealing of children splashing. A short distance away lay the quay with the shuttle ferry that sailed north to Oslo, which on a clear day looked as if it was only a few hundred metres away. The actual distance was five kilometres, but most people who worked in the capital preferred commuting by ferry rather than make the forty-five-kilometre trip around the fjord by car.

She sat down and inhaled the salty air.

'My parents and their friends used to call Nesodden "Little Berlin",' Martha said. 'Because of all the artists who settled here. It was cheaper to live in a draughty cottage than in Oslo. If the temperature fell too far below freezing, people would gather in the least cold house. Which was ours. They used to stay up and drink red wine until the morning because there weren't enough mattresses for everyone to sleep on. Then we would all have a big, communal breakfast.'

'Sounds nice.' Stig sat down next to her.

'Yes, it was. People here looked out for each other.'

'How idyllic.'

'I don't know about that. From time to time they would argue about money, criticise each other's art or sleep with each other's spouses. But the place was alive, it was exciting. My sister and I actually believed we lived in Berlin until my father showed me on the map where the real Berlin was. And explained to me that it was a long way away, more than a thousand kilometres. But that one day we would drive there. And we would visit the Brandenburg Gate and Charlottenburg Palace where my sister and I would be princesses.'

'Did you ever go there?'

'To the real Berlin?' Martha shook her head. 'My parents never had very much money. And they didn't live to be very old. I was eighteen when they died and I had to look after my sister. But I've always dreamt about Berlin. So much so that I'm no longer sure if it really exists.'

Stig nodded slowly, closed his eyes and lay down on his back in the grass.

She looked at him. 'Why don't we listen to some more of your music?'

He opened one eye. Squinted. 'Depeche Mode? The CD is in the CD player in the car.'

'Hand me your mobile,' she said.

He gave it to her and she started pressing buttons. Soon rhythmic breathing sounds were coming from the small speakers. Then a deadpan voice suggested taking them on a trip. Stig looked so shocked that she had to laugh.

'It's called Spotify,' she said, putting the mobile between them. 'You can stream music from the Web. Is all this news to you?'

'We weren't allowed mobiles in jail,' he said, eagerly picking up the mobile.

'In jail?'

'Yes, I've done time.'

'You were dealing?'

Stig shielded his eyes from the sun. 'That's right.'

She nodded. And smiled quickly. What had she, of all people, imagined? That he was a heroin addict *and* a law-abiding citizen? He had done what he had to do, just like everyone else.

She took the phone from him. Showed him the GPS function and how it could tell them where on the map they were and how to calculate the shortest driving route to any place in the world. She took a photo of him with the camera function, pressed the *record* button, held it up and asked him to say something.

'Today is a lovely day,' he said.

She stopped the recording and played it back to him.

'Is *that* my voice?' he asked, surprised and clearly embarrassed.

She pressed *stop* and played it again. The voice sounded constricted and tinny through the loudspeakers: 'Is *that* my voice?'

And she laughed when she saw the expression on his face. She laughed even harder when he snatched the phone from her, found the record button and said that now it was her turn, now she had to say something, no, she had to sing.

'No!' she protested. 'I'd rather you took my picture.'

He shook his head. 'Voices are better.'

'Why?'

He made a motion as if to tuck his hair behind his ear. The habitual gesture of someone who has had long hair for so long that he has forgotten it's been cut off, she thought.

'People can change the way they look. But voices stay the same.'

He looked across the sea and she followed his gaze. Saw nothing but the shimmering surface, some seagulls, rocks and sails in the distance.

'Some voices do,' she said. She was thinking of the baby. The whimpering on the walkie-talkie. That never changed.

'You like singing,' he said. 'But not in front of others.'

'What makes you say that?'

'Because you like music. But when I asked you to sing, you looked just as petrified as that girl in the cafe when you gave her the key.'

She jumped. Had he read her mind?

'What was she scared of?'

'Nothing,' Martha said. 'She and the other girl are supposed to shred and reorganise the files in the attic. Nobody likes going up there. So the staff take turns whenever a job needs doing.'

'What's wrong with the attic?'

Martha followed a seagull which hung suspended in the air, high above the sea, shifting only slightly from one side to the other. The wind up there must be much stronger than it was down here.

'Do you believe in ghosts?' she said quietly.

'No.'

'Me neither.' She leaned back on her elbows so that she couldn't see him without turning. 'The Ila Centre looks as if it's nineteenth century doesn't it? But it was actually built in the 1920s. To begin with it was just an ordinary boarding house.'

'The cast-iron letters on the front.'

'That's right, that's from back then. But during the war the Germans turned it into a home for unmarried mothers and their children. There are so many tragic stories from those years and they left their mark in the walls. One of the women who came to stay there had a baby boy and claimed it was a virgin birth – something girls would occasionally say when they found themselves in trouble in those days. The man everyone suspected was married and, of course, denied being the father. There were two rumours about him. The first that he was a member of the Resistance. The second that he was a German spy who had infiltrated the Resistance and that was why the Germans had given the woman a place at the home and not arrested the man. Anyway, one morning the suspected father was shot dead on a crowded tram in the centre of Oslo. The killer was never identified. The Resistance claimed they had liquidated a traitor, the Germans that they had caught a member of the Resistance. In order to convince anyone who had doubts, the Germans suspended the body from the top of Kavringen Lighthouse.'

She pointed across the sea.

'Sailors passing the lighthouse in the daytime could see the withered corpse which the seagulls had pecked at and those who passed at night could see the vast shadow it cast across the water. Until suddenly one day the body was gone. Some said that the Resistance had removed it. But from that day the woman started to lose her mind and claimed that the dead man was haunting her. That he came to her room at night, that he leaned over their baby's cot, and that when she screamed for him to get out, turned to her with black holes where his eyes used to be.'

Stig raised an eyebrow.

'This is how the story was told to me by Grete, the manager at the Ila Centre,' Martha said. 'Anyway, legend has it that the baby wouldn't stop crying, but whenever the women in the other rooms complained and told the woman to comfort her child, she replied that the child cried for both of them and would do so forever.' Martha paused. Her favourite part of the story was coming up. 'Rumour had it that the woman didn't know which side her child's father worked for, but to pay him back for denying paternity she had reported him as a member of the Resistance to the Germans *and* told the Resistance he was a spy.'

A sudden, cold gust of wind made Martha shudder and she sat up and hugged her knees.

'One morning the woman didn't come down for breakfast. They found her in the attic. She had hanged herself from the big cross-beam in the roof. You can see a pale stripe in the wood where she supposedly tied the rope.'

'And now she haunts the attic?'

'I don't know. All I know is that it's a difficult place to be. I don't believe in ghosts, but no one seems able to spend much time in that attic. It's as if you can sense evil. People get headaches, they feel pushed out of the room. And often they'll be new members of staff or contractors hired to do maintenance work, people who don't know the story. And, no, there isn't asbestos in the insulation or anything like that.'

She studied him, but he didn't display the sceptical expression or the small smile she had half expected. He just listened.

'But that's not all,' she went on. 'The baby.'

'Yes,' he said.

'Yes? Have you guessed it?'

'It was gone.'

She looked at him in amazement. 'How did you know?'

He shrugged. 'You told me to guess.'

'Some people think that the mother gave it to the Resistance the same night she hanged herself. Others that she killed the child and buried it in the back garden so that no one would take it from her. Anyway . . .' Martha took a deep breath. 'It was never found. And the strange thing is every now and then we hear a noise on our walkie-talkies, but we can't work out where it comes from. But we think it's . . .'

She thought he looked as if he had guessed that as well.

'A baby crying,' she said.

'A baby crying,' he repeated.

'Many people, especially new staff, get freaked out when they hear it, but Grete tells them that the walkie-talkies sometimes pick up signals from baby monitors in the neighbourhood.'

'But you don't think so?'

Martha hesitated. 'She might be right.'

'But?'

Another gust of wind. Dark clouds had appeared in the west. Martha was regretting not bringing a coat.

'I've been working at the Ila Centre for seven years. And when you said that voices never change . . .'

'Yes?'

'I swear it's the same baby.'

Stig nodded. He said nothing, didn't try to offer an explanation or a comment. He just nodded. She liked that.

'Do you know what those clouds mean?' he asked at last and got up.

'That it's going to rain and it's time we went home?'

'No,' he said. 'That we need to go swimming right now, so we'll have time to dry in the sun.'

'*Compassion fatigue*,' Martha said. She was lying on her back, looking up at the sky; she still had the taste of salt water in her mouth and she could feel the warm rock against her skin and through her wet underwear. 'It means that I've lost the ability to care. It's so unthinkable in the Norwegian care sector that we don't even have a Norwegian word for it.'

He made no reply. And that was fine, she wasn't really talking to him, he was just an excuse to think out loud.

'I guess it's a way of protecting yourself, detaching when it gets too much. Or maybe the well has run dry, perhaps I'm all out of love.' She thought about it. 'No, that's not true. I have plenty . . . just not . . .'

Martha saw a cloud shaped like Great Britain drift across the sky. Just before it passed the treetop above her head, it turned into a mammoth. In many ways it was like lying on her therapist's couch. He was one of those who still used a couch.

'Anders was the bravest and the nicest boy at school,' she said to the clouds. 'Captain of the school football team. Please don't ask me if he was head of the student council.'

She waited.

'Was he?'

'Yes.'

They both burst out laughing.

'Were you in love with him?'

'Very much. Still am. I'm in love with him. He's a good guy. There's more to him than just being nice and fit. I'm lucky to have Anders. What about you?'

'What about me?'

'How many girlfriends have you had?'

'None.'

'None?' She raised herself up on her elbows. 'Good-looking guy like you, I don't believe it.'

Stig had taken off his T-shirt. His skin was so pale in the sunshine that it almost blinded her. She noticed with some surprise that he had no fresh needle marks. She guessed they must be in his thighs or groin.

'Really?' she said.

'I did kiss some girls . . .' He caressed the old marks with his hand. 'But this was my only lover . . .'

Martha looked at the needle marks. She, too, wanted to run her fingers across them. Make them go away.

'When I first interviewed you, you said you'd quit,' she said. 'I won't tell Grete. Not for a while. But you know . . .'

'. . . that the centre is only for active users.'

She nodded. 'Do you think you'll be able to do it?'

'Pass my driving licence?'

They exchanged smiles.

'I'm clean today,' he said. 'Tomorrow is another day.'

The clouds were still a long way away, but she could hear a distant rumbling, a warning of what was to come. And it was as if the sun knew it too, and burned a little more brightly.

'Give me your phone,' she said.

Martha pressed 'record'. Then she sang the song her father used to play on his guitar to her mother. Usually when one of their countless summer parties was starting to wind down. He had sat right where they were sitting now with his battered guitar, strumming so quietly it was barely audible. The Leonard Cohen song about how he had always been her lover, that he would travel with her, follow her blindly, that he knows she trusts him because he has touched her perfect body with his mind.

She sang the lyrics in a small, fragile voice. It was always like that when she sang; she sounded much weaker and more vulnerable than she was. From time to time she wondered if she really was like that, and whether it was the other voice, the tougher voice she used to protect herself with, which wasn't her.

'Thank you,' he said when she had finished. 'That was really beautiful.'

She didn't wonder why it was embarrassing. She wondered why it wasn't more embarrassing.

'It's time we drove back.' She smiled and handed him the phone.

She should have known that trying to take down the old, rotting hood was asking for trouble but she wanted to feel the fresh air as they drove. It took them more than fifteen minutes of hard work, alternating practical thinking with brute force, but finally they got it down. And she knew that she would never get it up again, not without spare parts and Anders's help. When she got in the car, Stig showed her his phone. He had entered Berlin on the GPS.

'Your father was right,' he said. 'From little Berlin to big Berlin is 1,030 kilometres. Estimated driving time twelve hours and fifteen minutes.'

She drove. She drove fast as if there was something urgent they had to do. Or were trying to escape. She looked in the mirror. The white, towering clouds over the fjord reminded her of a bride. A bride marching purposefully and unstoppably towards them trailing a veil of rain.

The first heavy drops hit them when they were in dense traffic on Ring Road 3 and she realised immediately that the battle was lost.

'Exit here,' Stig said, pointing.

She did as he said, and suddenly they found themselves in a residential area.

'Take a right here,' Stig said.

The drops were falling more densely. 'Where are we?'

'Berg. Do you see that yellow house?'

'Yes.'

'I know the people who own it, it's empty. Stop outside that garage and I'll open the garage door.'

Five minutes later they were sitting in the car which was now parked between rusting tools, worn-down tyres and garden furniture draped in cobwebs while they watched the rain tip down outside the open garage door.

'It doesn't look like it's going to stop for a while,' Martha said. 'And I think the hood is a write-off.'

'I agree,' Stig said. 'How about a cup of coffee?'

'Where?'

'In the kitchen. I know where the key is.'

'But . . .'

'This is my house.'

She looked at him. She hadn't driven fast enough. She hadn't made it in time. Whatever it was, it was too late.

'OK,' she said.

22

SIMON ADJUSTED THE GAUZE MASK and studied the body. It reminded him of something.

'The council owns and runs this venue,' Kari said. 'They hire out rehearsal rooms to young bands for next to nothing. Better to sing about being a gangster than drive around the streets and actually be one.'

Simon remembered what it was. Jack Nicholson frozen to death in *The Shining*. He had watched it on his own. It was after her. And before Else. Perhaps it was the snow. The dead man looked as if he was lying in a snowdrift. A fine layer of heroin covered the body and most of the room. Around the dead man's mouth, nose and eyes the powder had come into contact with moisture and started to clump.

'A band that rehearses further down the corridor found him when they were going home,' Kari said.

The body had been discovered last night, but Simon hadn't been informed until he came to work earlier that morning that a total of three people had been found killed. And that Kripos was handling the case.

In other words, the Commissioner had asked Kripos for assistance – which was the same as giving them the case – without even consulting his own Homicide Squad first. The outcome might ultimately have been the same, but even so.

'His name is Kalle Farrisen,' Kari said.

She was reading aloud from the preliminary report. Simon had called the Commissioner and asked that it be sent to them. And requested immediate access to the crime scene. After all, it was still their turf.

'Simon,' the Commissioner had said, 'take a look at it, by all means, but don't get involved. You and I are too old for a pissing contest.'

'*You* might be too old,' Simon had replied.

'You heard me, Simon.'

Simon pondered it from time to time. There was no doubt which of them had had the greatest potential. Where had the road forked? When had it been decided who would occupy which chair? Who would be sitting in the high-backed chair in the Commissioner's office and who would be occupying the battered one in the Homicide Squad with his wings clipped? And that the best of them would end up in a chair in his study with a bullet from his own gun through his head.

'The guitar strings around his head are bottom E and G and manufactured by Ernie Ball. The jack-to-jack cable is made by Fender,' Kari read.

'And the fan and the radiator?'

'What?'

'Nothing. Go on.'

'The fan was switched on. The medical examiner's preliminary conclusion is that Kalle Farrisen suffocated.'

Simon studied the knot on the jack cable. 'It looks like Kalle was forced to inhale the drug which was blown into his face. Would you agree?'

'I would,' Kari said. 'He managed to hold his breath for a short while, but eventually he had to give in. The guitar strings prevented him from turning his head away. But he tried, that's why he has injuries from the thinner guitar string. The heroin ends up in his nose, stomach and lungs, it's absorbed into the bloodstream, he starts feeling drugged and carries on breathing. But more faintly now because the heroin is suppressing his respiration. And finally, he stops breathing altogether.'

'Classic case of death by overdose,' Simon said. 'Same thing happened to several of his customers.'

He pointed to the cable. 'And whoever tied this knot is left-handed.'

'We can't go on meeting like this.'

They turned round. Åsmund Bjørnstad was standing in the doorway with a wry smile and two people behind him who were holding a stretcher.

'We want to move the body now, so if you're done . . .'

'We've seen everything we wanted to,' Simon said, getting up laboriously. 'Would it be all right if we took a look around?'

'Of course,' the Kripos investigator said, still with this half-smile, gallantly showing them the way. Simon rolled his eyes at Kari in surprise, who in return raised her eyebrows as if to say he's changed his tune.

'Any witnesses?' Simon asked in the lift and looked at the broken glass.

'No,' Bjørnstad said. 'But the guitarist from the band who found the body says that there was a guy here earlier in the evening. He claimed to be playing in a band called the Young Hopeless, but we've checked and that band no longer exists.'

'What did he look like?'

'The witness says the guy wore a hoodie that covered his head. Lots of young people do these days.'

'So he was young?'

'The witness thought so. Somewhere between twenty and twenty-five.'

'What colour was his hoodie?'

Bjørnstad flipped open his notebook. 'Grey, I believe.'

The lift doors opened, they stepped out carefully and straddled cordons and flags set out by the CSOs. There were four people on this floor. Two living and two dead. Simon nodded briefly to one of the living. He had a bushy ginger beard and was crouching on all fours over a body, holding a torch the size of a fountain pen in his hand. The deceased had a large wound under one eye. A dark red halo of blood on the floor surrounded his head. At the top of the halo the blood spatter formed a pattern that resembled a tear-drop. Simon had once tried to explain to Else how a crime scene could be beautiful. He had tried once and never again.

Another and much bigger victim lay on the threshold with his upper body inside the door.

Simon's gaze automatically scanned the walls and found the bullet hole in the wall. He noticed the hatch in the door and the mirror up under the ceiling. Then he took a step backwards into the lift, raised his right arm and took aim. Changed his mind and raised his left arm instead. He had to take one step to the right to make the angle fit with the trajectory of a bullet through the head and – if the skull hadn't caused the bullet to change direction – into the bullet hole in the plaster. He closed his eyes. He had stood in the same position recently. On the steps outside the Iversen home. Aimed with his right hand. There he had also had to adjust his position to make the angle fit. Move one foot to just outside the flagstones. Onto the soft soil. The same soft soil which was around the bushes. But there hadn't been a matching shoeprint on the soil next to the flagstones.

'Shall we carry on the guided tour inside, ladies and gentlemen?'

Bjørnstad held the door open and waited until Kari and Simon had stepped over the body and entered. 'The council rented out this room to what they thought was a band booking and management agency.'

Simon peered inside the empty safe. 'What do you think happened?'

'Gang-related incident,' Bjørnstad said. 'They hit the factory around closing time. The first victim was shot while he lay on the floor – we've recovered the bullet from the floorboards. The second victim was shot as he lay across the threshold – there's a bullet in the floor there as well. They got the third man to open the safe. They took the money and the drugs, and then killed him downstairs to send a message to the competition about who's in charge now.'

'I see,' Simon said. 'And the shells?'

Bjørnstad laughed quickly. 'I know. Sherlock Holmes smells a connection with the Iversen murder.'

'No empty shells?'

Åsmund Bjørnstad looked from Simon to Kari and back to Simon. Then – with a magician's hey presto smile – he produced a plastic bag from his jacket pocket. He dangled it in front of Simon's face. It contained two empty shells.

'Sorry to bust your theory, old boy,' he said. 'Besides, the big bullet holes in the victims indicate a far bigger calibre than the one we found in Agnete Iversen. That concludes your guided tour. I hope you enjoyed it.'

'I just have three questions before we leave.'

'Go on then, Chief Inspector Kefas.'

'Where did you find the empty shells?'

'Next to the bodies.'

'Where were the victims' weapons?'

'They didn't have any. Final question?'

'Did the Commissioner tell you to be cooperative and give us the guided tour?'

Åsmund Bjørnstad laughed. 'Possibly through my boss in Kripos. We always do what our bosses tell us, don't we?'

'Yes,' Simon said. 'If we want to get ahead, then that's what we do. Thanks for the tour.'

Bjørnstad stayed behind in the room, but Kari followed Simon. She stopped behind him when Simon, rather than going straight into the lift, asked the bearded CSO to lend him his torch and went over to the bullet hole in the wall. Pointed the torch at it.

'Have you already removed the bullet, Nils?'

'That must be an old hole; we didn't find any bullets there,' Nils said while he examined the floor around the body with a simple magnifying glass.

Simon squatted down, moistened the tips of his fingers and pressed them against the floor right under the hole. He held up his fingers to Kari. She could see that tiny plaster particles had stuck to his skin.

'Thanks for the use of your torch,' Simon said and Nils looked up, nodded briefly and took the torch.

'What was that about?' Kari asked when the lift doors had closed in front of them.

'I need a moment to think, then I'll tell you,' Simon said.

Kari was annoyed. Not because she suspected her boss of being coy, but because she couldn't follow him. Not being able to keep up wasn't something she was used to. The doors opened and she stepped out. She turned round and looked quizzically at Simon, who was still inside the lift.

'May I borrow your marble, please?' he asked.

She sighed and stuck her hand into her pocket. Simon placed the small, yellow marble in the middle of the lift floor. It rolled at first slowly, then with increasing speed to the front of the lift where it disappeared down the gap between the inner and the outer doors.

'Oops,' Simon said. 'Let's go down to the basement and look for it.'

'It's not irreplaceable,' Kari said. 'I've got more at home.'

'I'm not talking about the marble.'

Kari hastened after him again, still two steps behind. At least. A thought occurred to her. The thought of another job she could have gone for and could be doing right now. Better pay, more independence. No eccentric bosses and foul-smelling bodies. But that time would come; for now it was a question of arming herself with patience.

They found the stairwell, the basement corridor and the lift door. In contrast to the floors above this was a simple metal door with a mottled glass pane. Across the door was a sign. LIFT CONTROL. KEEP OUT. Simon shook the door handle. Locked.

'Run back upstairs to the rehearsal rooms and see if you can find a cable,' Simon said.

'What kind of—'

'Anything,' he said and leaned against the wall.

She swallowed a protest and headed back to the stairs.

Two minutes later she was back with a jack-jack cable and watched while Simon unscrewed the plugs and stripped off the plastic around the wires. Then he bent the cable into a U-shape and slipped it in between the lift door and the frame at the height of the door handle. They heard a loud click, and a couple of sparks flew. He opened the door.

'Christ,' Kari said. 'Where did you learn that?'

'I was trouble when I was little,' Simon said, levering himself down to the bottom of the lift shaft which was half a metre lower than the basement floor. He looked up the lift shaft. 'If I hadn't become a police officer . . .'

'Isn't this a bit risky? Kari said, feeling a prickling on her scalp. 'What if the lift comes down?'

But Simon was already kneeling on all fours and sweeping the concrete floor with his hands.

'Do you need a little light down there?' she asked, hoping that he couldn't hear the tension in her voice.

'Always,' he laughed.

A tiny scream escaped Kari when she heard a small bang and saw the thick, oiled wires starting to move. But Simon quickly got to his feet, pressed his palms against the basement floor and pulled himself up into the corridor. 'Come,' he said.

She half ran after him up the stairs, through the exit door and across the gravelled area.

'Wait!' she said before he got into the car which they had parked between the two derelict trucks. Simon stopped and looked at her across the roof of the car.

'I know,' he said.

'What do you know?'

'That it's bloody irritating when your partner goes solo and doesn't tell you what's going on.'

'Exactly! So when will you—'

'But I'm not your partner, Kari Adel,' Simon said. 'I'm your boss and your mentor. It'll happen when it happens. Do you understand?'

She looked at him. Saw the breeze toss his comically thin hair to and fro across the shiny scalp. Saw the flint in his otherwise friendly gaze.

'Understood,' she said.

'Take these.' He opened one hand and threw something across the roof of the car. She cupped hands and caught both items. She looked at them. One was the yellow marble. The other was an empty shell.

'You can discover new things by changing your perspective and your location,' he said. 'You can compensate for any blind spots. Let's go.'

She got into the passenger seat, he started the car and drove

233

across the gravel to the gate. She kept her mouth shut. Waited. He stopped and looked for a long time and very carefully to the right and the left before he pulled out onto the road, like cautious, elderly male drivers are wont to do. Kari had always imagined it was because of lower testosterone levels. But it struck her now – almost as a new insight – that all rationality was built on experience.

'At least one shot was fired inside the lift,' he said and positioned himself behind a Volvo.

She still didn't say anything.

'And your objection is?'

'That it doesn't match the evidence,' Kari said. 'The only bullets were those that killed the victims and they were found right under them. The victims must have been lying on the floor when they were shot and that doesn't match the angle if they were shot from the lift.'

'No, and besides, there was a powder burn to the skin of the guy who was shot in the head, and burned cotton fibres in the shirt around the bullet wound on the other victim. Which suggests?'

'That they were shot at close range while they were lying down. It matches the empty shell cases that were found next to them and the bullets in the floor.'

'Right. But don't you find it weird that the two men collapse on the floor and then they're shot?'

'Perhaps they got so scared when they saw the gun that they panicked and tripped. Or they were ordered to lie down before they were executed.'

'Good thinking. But did you notice something about the blood around the body nearest the lift?'

'That there was a lot of it?'

'Yes.' He spoke with a drawl that told her this wasn't the end of it.

'The blood had flowed from the victim's head and formed a pool,' she said. 'It means that he wasn't moved after he was shot.'

'Yes, but at the edge of the pool, the blood was sprayed. As if it had splattered. In other words, the flowing blood covered parts of the area where it had first spattered from his head. And given the length and the range of the blood spurt, the victim must have been standing straight up when he was shot. That was why Nils was going over it with his magnifying glass – he couldn't get the blood evidence to match.'

'But you can?'

'Yes,' Simon said simply. 'The killer fired the first shot from inside the lift. It went through the victim's head and left the hole you saw in the wall. While the shell landed on the lift floor—'

'—rolled along the sloping floor, fell through the crack and down the lift shaft?'

'Yep.'

'But . . . the bullet in the floorboard . . .'

'The killer shot him again at close range.'

'The entry wound . . .'

'Our friend from Kripos thought the killer had used a bigger calibre bullet, but if he'd known more about ballistics, he would have noticed that the empty shells are from small calibre bullets. So the big entry wound is really two small, overlapping entry wounds which the killer tried to make look like one. That's why he took away the first bullet which made the hole in the wall.'

'So it wasn't an old bullet hole as the CSO thought,' Kari said. 'That's why there was fresh plaster dust on the floor right below.'

Simon smiled. She could see that he was pleased with her. And she realised to her surprise that it cheered her up.

'Look at the type description and the serial number on the shell case. It's a different kind of ammunition from what we found on the first floor. It means the shot the killer fired from the lift came from a different gun to the one he subsequently used on the victims.

I think ballistics will be able to prove that they came from the victims' own guns.'

'Their own?'

'This is more your area of expertise, Adel, but I find it hard to believe there would be three unarmed guys in a drug den. The killer took their guns with him so that we wouldn't discover he'd used them.'

'You're right.'

'The question,' Simon said, pulling in behind a tram, 'is of course why it matters so much to him that we don't find the first bullet and the empty shell.'

'Isn't it obvious? The imprint from the firing pin would give us the gun's serial number and the Gun Register would soon lead us to—'

'Wrong. Look at the back of the shell. No mark. He was using an older gun.'

'OK,' Kari said, reminding herself never to use the word 'obvious' again. 'Then I don't know what it is. But I have a strong feeling that you're about to tell me . . .'

'I am, Adel. The empty shell you're holding is the same type of ammo used to shoot Agnete Iversen.'

'I see. But are you saying . . . ?'

'I believe the killer tried to cover up that he also killed Agnete Iversen,' Simon said and stopped so abruptly for a yellow light that the car behind him sounded its horn. 'The reason he picked up the empty shell at Iversen's isn't as I thought at first because it had a mark from the firing pin. It was because he was already planning a second killing and doing as much as he could to minimise the risk that we would make the connection. I bet that the empty shell the killer took with him from the Iversen house was of the same series as the one you have here.'

'Same ammo type, but it's a very common one, isn't it?'

'Yes.'

'So what makes you so sure there's a connection?'

'I'm not sure,' Simon said, staring at the traffic light as if it were a bomb with a timer. 'But only ten per cent of the population is left-handed.'

She nodded. She tried her own reasoning. Gave up. Sighed. 'Pass, I give up again.'

'Kalle Farrisen was tied to the radiator by someone who is left-handed. Agnete Iversen was shot by someone who is left-handed.'

'I understand about the former. But the latter . . .'

'I should have worked it out much earlier. The angle from the doorway to the kitchen wall. If the bullet that killed Agnete Iversen was fired by a right-handed killer and from the spot I first believed, he would have had to stand on one side of the flagstone path and there would be prints in the soft soil from one of his shoes. The answer is of course that he had both feet on the flagstones because he was shooting with his left hand. Poor police work on my part.'

'Let me see if I've got this right,' Kari said, resting her chin on her palms. 'There is a connection between Agnete Iversen and the three victims here. And the killer has gone to great lengths to make sure we don't spot it because he's afraid it's that very connection which will identify him.'

'Good, Officer Adel. You've changed your perspective and location, and now you can see.'

Kari heard an angry hooting and opened her eyes again.

'The light's green,' she said.

23

IT WAS NO LONGER RAINING quite as hard, but Martha had pulled her jacket over her head as she watched while Stig retrieved the key and unlocked the basement door. The basement, like the garage, was filled with objects which told a family history; rucksacks, tent pegs, a pair of red down-at-heel boots which looked as if they had been used in some sort of sport, boxing, perhaps. A sledge. A manual lawnmower that had been replaced with a petrol-driven one in the garage. A big, rectangular chest freezer. Wide shelves with cordial bottles and jam jars joined together by cobwebs, and a nail with a key and a tag whose faded letters would once have told you what the key was for. Martha stopped at the row of skis, some of them still coated with the mud from an Easter skiing trip. One of the skis, the longest and the broadest, had split lengthways.

When they got inside the house, Martha realised immediately that no one had lived there for years. Perhaps it was the smell, the dust or maybe it was the invisible layer of time. And she had her theory confirmed when they entered the living room. She couldn't see a single object that had been manufactured in the last decade.

'I'll make some coffee,' Stig said and went into the adjacent kitchen.

Martha looked at the photographs on the mantelpiece.

A wedding photo. The likeness, especially to the bride, was striking.

Another photograph – probably taken a couple of years later – showed them with two other couples. Martha had a hunch that it was the men who linked the couples together, and not the women. It was to do with the way the men looked like each other. Their identical, almost posturing stances, the confident smiles, the way they took up space, like three friends – and alpha males – leisurely marking out their respective territory. Equals, she thought.

She went out into the kitchen. Stig was standing with his back to her, leaning towards the fridge.

'Did you find any coffee?' she asked.

He turned, quickly snatched a yellow Post-it note from the fridge door and stuffed it in his trouser pocket.

'Yes,' he said and opened the cupboard above the sink. He measured coffee into a filter, put water in the coffee-maker and switched it on with quick, familiar movements. He took off his jacket and hung it on the back of one of the kitchen chairs. Not the one closest to him, but the one closest to the window. His chair.

'You used to live here,' she declared.

He nodded.

'You look a lot like your mother.'

He smiled wryly. 'That's what people said.'

'Said?'

'My parents are no longer alive.'

'Do you miss them?'

She could see it in his face immediately. How this simple, almost commonplace question hit him like a wedge into an opening he had forgotten to seal. He blinked twice and opened and closed his mouth, as if the pain was so unexpected and so sudden that he had lost the power of speech. He nodded and turned to the coffee-maker, adjusting the pot as if it wasn't sitting on the hotplate properly.

'Your father looks very authoritarian in those photographs.'

'He was.'

'In a good way?'

He turned to her. 'Yes, in a good way. He took care of us.'

She nodded. She thought about her own father, who had been the opposite.

'And you needed looking after?'

'Yes.' He smiled quickly. 'I needed looking after.'

'What? You're thinking of something.'

He shrugged.

'What is it?' she said again.

'Oh, I saw you look at the broken ski.'

'What about it?'

He gazed absent-mindedly at the coffee which had started dripping into the pot. 'We used to visit my grandfather up in Lesjaskog every Easter. There was a ski-jumping hill there where my father held the record. My grandfather had held the previous record. I was fifteen years old and I had trained all winter so that I could set the new record. Only it was a late Easter that year, mild, and when we came up to my grandfather's there was hardly any snow left at the bottom of the hill which lay in the sun and twigs and rocks were sticking up. But still I had to try it.'

He glanced quickly upwards at Martha, who nodded to encourage him.

'My father knew how much I wanted to have a go, but he told me not to, it was too dangerous. So I just nodded and talked a boy from a neighbouring farm into being my witness and measuring the length. He helped me spread extra snow in the area where I was planning to land, and then I raced up to the top of the hill, put on the skis which my father had inherited from his father, and set off. The hill was unbelievably slippery, but I came off to a good start. In fact, much too good. I flew and I flew, I felt like an eagle, I didn't give a damn about anything because this was it, this was exactly what it all was about, nothing could be bigger than this.' Martha could see his eyes shine. 'I landed roughly four metres beyond the place where we had spread the snow. The skis cut right through the sludge and a sharp stone sliced open my right ski as if it was a banana split.'

'And what happened to you?'

'I snowploughed. I carved a furrow across the slush and well beyond it.'

Alarmed, Martha put her hand on her collarbone. 'Good God. Were you hurt?'

'Black and blue. And I got soaking wet. But I didn't break anything. And even if I had, I probably wouldn't have noticed because my only thought was, what will my father say? I've done something he told me not to. And I've ruined his ski.'

'And what did he say?'

'He didn't say much, he just asked me what I thought would be a suitable punishment.'

'And what did you say?'

'I told him to ground me for three days. But he said that as it was Easter, two days would have to do. After my father's death, my mother told me that while I was grounded, he got the boy from the farm to show him where I landed and tell him the whole story over and over. And that he had laughed until he cried every time. But my mother made him promise not to tell me, that it would simply encourage me to more madness. So instead he took the damaged ski home under the pretext of wanting to fix it. But my mother said that was nonsense, that it was his most precious keepsake.'

'Can I have a look at it again?'

He poured coffee for both of them and they took their cups with them down to the basement. She sat on the top of the chest freezer and watched him while he showed her the ski. A heavy, white ski made by Splitkein with six grooves on the underside. And she thought what a very strange day it had been. Sunshine and showers. The blinding sea and the dark, cold basement. A stranger she felt she had known all her life. So far away. So near. So right. So wrong . . .

'And were you right about the jump?' she asked. 'Was there really nothing bigger than that?'

He tilted his head pensively to one side. 'My first fix. That was bigger.'

She bumped her heels carefully against the chest freezer. Perhaps the chill was coming from there. And it struck her that the power to the freezer must be on – a tiny red lamp glowed between the handle and the keyhole in the freezer lock. Which seemed odd given that everything else in the house suggested it had been abandoned for a long time.

'Well, at least you set a new record,' she said.

He shook his head while he smiled.

'You didn't?'

'A jump is invalid if you fall, Martha,' he said and took a sip of his coffee.

And she thought that though it wasn't the first time she'd heard him say her name, it felt as if it was the first time she'd heard *anyone* say it.

'So you had to carry on jumping. Because boys measure themselves against their fathers and daughters against their mothers.'

'Do you think so?'

'All sons believe that one day they'll turn into their father, don't you think? That's why they're so disillusioned when their father's weaknesses are revealed; they see their own failings, their own

242

future defeats waiting for them. And sometimes the shock is so devastating that it makes them give up before they've even started.'

'Was it like that for you?'

Martha shrugged. 'My mother should never have stayed married to my father. But she chose to conform. I hurled it at her once when we argued about something she wouldn't let me to do, I don't even remember what it was. I screamed that it was unfair to deny me happiness just because she denied it to herself. I've never regretted saying anything that much in my whole life and I'll never forget her wounded look when she replied: 'Because I risk losing the one thing which brings me most happiness. You.'

Stig nodded and looked out of the basement window. 'Sometimes we're wrong when we think that we know the truth about our parents. Perhaps they weren't weak. Perhaps something happened to give you the wrong impression. What if they were strong? What if they were willing to leave behind a disgraced name, allow themselves to be stripped of all honour, take the blame, to save the ones they loved? And if they were that strong, perhaps you're strong, too.'

The trembling in his voice was almost imperceptible. Almost. Martha waited until he turned his gaze on her again before she asked:

'So what did he do?'

'Who?'

'Your father.'

She saw his Adam's apple slide up and down. Saw him blink more quickly. Press his lips together. She saw that he wanted to. Saw him watch the take-off point come closer. He could break the fall by throwing himself to the side.

'He signed a suicide note before they shot him,' Stig said. 'To save my mother and me.'

Martha felt dizzy while he continued to speak. She might have pushed him over the edge, but she was going down with him. And now there was no way back to the point where she could erase what she had learned. Deep down, had she known what she was doing all along? Had she wanted this wild floating, this free fall?

Stig and his mother had been to a wrestling tournament in Lillehammer that weekend. His father would normally have gone with them, but had said that he needed to say at home, that he had something important to do. Stig had won in his weight class and when they came home, had run to his father's study to tell him. His father had been sitting with his back to him and his head resting on the desk. At first Stig thought his father had fallen asleep while working. Then he saw the gun.

'I had only seen that gun once before. My father used to write his diary in his study, a diary bound in black leather with yellow pages. When I was little he used to say it was his confession. I used to think that to go to confession was just another word for writing, right up until I was eleven and my RS teacher told me that to confess is to tell someone your sins. When I came home from school that day, I crept into his study and found the desk key – I knew where he kept it. I wanted to know what my father's sins were. I unlocked . . .'

Martha took a breath as if she were the one telling the story.

'But the diary wasn't there. Instead I found an old-fashioned, black pistol. I locked the drawer, returned the key and sneaked out. And I felt ashamed. I had tried to spy on my own father, to expose him. I never told anyone and I never tried to find out where he kept his diary again. But when I stood behind my father in his study that weekend, it came back to me. It was my punishment for what I had done. I put my hand on his neck to wake him up. It wasn't just that he wasn't warm, it was the chill, a kind of hard, marble-cold death exuded from his body. And I knew that it was my fault. Then I saw the letter . . .'

Martha looked at the vein on his neck while he told her that he had read it. Seen his mother stand in the doorway. He told her how at first he was going to tear up the letter, pretend that it never existed. But he hadn't been able to do it. And when the police came, he had given it to them. And he could tell from looking at them that they wanted to shred it, too. The vein bulged as if he was an inexperienced singer. Or someone who isn't used to talking very much.

His mother had started taking the antidepressants her doctor prescribed. Then other pills on her own initiative. But like she used to say, nothing worked better or faster than alcohol. So she had started drinking. Vodka for breakfast, lunch and dinner. He had tried to take care of her, get her off the pills and booze. In order to do that he had had to quit wrestling and other after-school activities. His teachers had come to their door, rung the doorbell and asked why he, who used to get such fine grades, was skiving and he had thrown them out. His mother had deteriorated, becoming increasingly unbalanced and eventually suicidal. He was sixteen years old when he discovered a syringe among the pills while clearing up his mother's bedroom. He had known what it was. Or at least what it was for. He had plunged it into his own thigh and it had made everything better. The next day he had gone down to Plata and bought his first wrap. Six months later he had sold everything in the house that could easily be converted into cash and robbed his defenceless mother blind. He didn't care about anything, least of all himself, but he needed money to keep the pain at bay. Since he was under eighteen and couldn't be sent to adult prison, he had started paying for his habit by confessing to minor robberies and burglaries with which older criminals were charged. When he turned eighteen and such offers dried up and the pressure, the constant pressure to get money only grew worse, he had agreed to take the fall for two murders in return for being supplied with drugs while he was in prison.

'And now you've served your sentence?' she said.

He nodded. '*I* certainly have.'

She slipped off the chest freezer and went up to him. She wasn't thinking, it was too late for that. She reached out her hand and touched the vein in his neck. He looked at her with big, black pupils that almost filled the iris. Then she put her arms around his waist and he put his arms around her shoulders, like two dancers who couldn't decide which of them should lead. They stood like this for a while, then he pulled her close. He was burning up, he must have a fever. Or did she? She closed her eyes, felt his nose and lips against her hair.

'Let's go upstairs,' he whispered. 'I've got something for you.'

They went back to the kitchen. It had stopped raining outside. He took something from the pocket of his jacket which was hanging over the kitchen chair.

'These are for you.'

The earrings were so beautiful they initially left her speechless.

'Don't you like them?'

'They're gorgeous, Stig. But how did you . . . Did you steal them?'

He looked gravely at her without replying.

'I'm sorry, Stig.' Her thoughts were muddled and tears welled up in her eyes. 'I know you're not using any more, but I can see that the earrings used to belong to someone—'

'She's no longer alive,' Stig interrupted her. 'And something that beautiful should be worn by someone who is.'

Martha blinked in confusion. Then the penny dropped. 'They belonged . . . they were . . .' She looked up at him, half blinded by tears. 'Your mother's.'

She closed her eyes, felt his breath on her face. His hand on her cheek, throat, neck. Her own free hand which she placed on his side, wanting to push him away. Pull him closer. She knew they had long since kissed in their imagination. Hundreds of times, at least, since the first time they met. But it was different when their lips finally touched and an electric shock went through her. She kept her eyes closed, felt his lips, so soft, his hands gliding across the small of her back, his stubble, his smell and his taste. She wanted it, wanted all of it. But the touch also awakened her, tore her out of the lovely dream she had allowed herself to get lost in because there had been no consequences. Not until now.

'I can't,' she whispered in a trembling voice. 'I've got to go now, Stig.'

He released her and she quickly turned away. She opened the front door, but paused before she left.

'It was my fault, Stig. We can never meet again like this. Do you understand? Never.'

She closed the door behind her before she could hear his reply. The sun had forced its way through the layer of clouds and the steam rose from the glittering, black tarmac. She stepped out into the humid heat.

Through his binoculars Markus saw the woman hurry into the garage, start the old Golf they had arrived in and reverse out, still with the hood down. She drove so fast that he couldn't focus on her properly, but it looked as if she was crying.

Then he aimed the binoculars at the kitchen window again. Zoomed in. The man was standing there watching her. His hands were clenched, his jaw was tight and the veins bulged at his temples as if he was in pain. And the next moment Markus knew why. The son stretched out his arms, opened his hands and pressed them against the inside of the windowpane. Something gleamed in the sunlight. Earrings. They stuck to each palm and two thin streams of blood trickled down to his wrists.

24

THE OFFICE WAS IN TWILIGHT. Someone had turned off all the lights when they left, probably thinking they were the last ones there, and Simon had let it stay that way, the summer evenings were still light enough. Besides, he had a new keyboard with illuminated keys, so he hadn't even needed to turn on his reading lamp. Their floor of the office building alone consumed 250,000 kWh per year. If they could bring it down to 200,000, they would apparently save enough money to run two extra emergency vehicles.

He navigated his way around the Howell Clinic's website. The pictures from the eye clinic were nothing like most other American private hospitals, which resembled five-star hotels with smiling patients, ecstatic testimonies and surgeons who looked like film stars and airline pilots. This clinic displayed only a few photographs and sober information about staff qualifications, results, articles published in reputable journals and Nobel Prize nominations. And most important of all: the percentage of successful operations for the procedure Else needed. The figure was well above fifty – but not as high as he had hoped. On the other hand, it was low enough for him to believe it. There were no prices listed on the website.

But he hadn't forgotten what it was. It was high enough for him to believe it.

He sensed movement in the darkness. It was Kari.

'I tried calling you at home. Your wife said you were here.'

'Yes.'

'Why are you working so late?'

Simon shrugged. 'When you can't go home with good news, sometimes you put off going home for as long as you can.'

'What do you mean?'

Simon ignored her. 'What do you want?'

'I did as you said, turned over every stone, looked for every possible and impossible connection between the Iversen murder and the triple homicide. And I can't find a single thing.'

'You realise, of course, that that doesn't rule out that there *is* a connection,' Simon said and moved to another page on the website.

Kari pulled out a chair and sat down. 'Well, if there is, then I certainly can't find it. And I've had a very good look. And I've been thinking—'

'We like thinking.'

'Perhaps it's this simple: the burglar spotted two opportunities – the Iversen house and a location with drugs and money. And he had learned from his first robbery that you should always make people give you the code to their safe before you kill them.'

Simon looked up from his computer. 'A robber, who has already shot two people, squanders half a kilo of Superboy with a street value of half a million kroner to kill his third victim?'

'Bjørnstad thought it was gang-related, a way to send a message to the competition.'

'Gangs can send messages without spending half a million on postage, Officer Adel.'

Kari threw back her head and sighed. 'Agnete Iversen definitely isn't mixed up with drug dealing and the likes of Kalle Farrisen, I think we can be sure of that.'

'But there *is* a connection,' Simon insisted. 'What I don't understand is that now when we've uncovered what he's trying to hide, namely that there *is* a connection, we still can't identify what that connection is. If the connection really is that obscure, why go to all the trouble of hiding that it's the same killer?'

'Perhaps the cover-up isn't designed to confuse us,' Kari yawned.

She closed her mouth immediately when she saw Simon stare at her with wide eyes.

'Of course. You're right.'

'Am I?'

Simon got up. Then he sat down again. He slammed the desk with the palm of his hand. 'He's not worried that the police might work out his identity. This is about someone else.'

'He's scared that someone else will come after him?'

'Yes. Or perhaps he doesn't want to alert them to his presence. But at the same time . . .' Simon cupped his chin with his hand and swore under his breath.

'At the same time what . . . ?'

'It's more complicated than that. Because he's not hiding altogether. Killing Kalle in that manner *is* sending someone a message.' Simon kicked off irritably and the chair tilted back. They sat, not saying a word while the darkness grew denser around them without them noticing. Simon was the first to break the silence. 'I've been thinking that Kalle's life was ended in the same way as some of his customers. Respiratory failure following an overdose. As if the killer is some kind of avenging angel. Does that ring any bells?'

Kari shook her head. 'Only that Agnete Iversen probably wasn't executed according to the same logic; as far as I know she never shot anyone in the chest.'

Simon got up. Walked over to the window and stared down at

the street lights. A rumbling came from under the wheels of two skateboards. Two boys, both wearing hoodies, passed below him.

'Oh, I forgot,' Kari said. 'I did find one connection. Between Per Vollan and Kalle Farrisen.'

'Yes?'

'I spoke to one of my old CIs from the Drug Squad. He said he thought it was odd that two people who knew each other so well had died in such a short space of time.'

'Vollan knew Farrisen?'

'Yes. Well. Too well, according to my CI. And another thing. I've checked Kalle's file. He was questioned repeatedly in connection with a murder investigation some years ago, he was even remanded in custody. The victim was never identified.'

'Never?'

'All we know is that she was a young Asian girl. Dental analysis suggested she was sixteen years old. A witness saw a man inject her using a syringe in a backyard. The witness picked out Kalle in a line-up.'

'Aha.'

'But Kalle was released when someone else confessed.'

'Lucky guy.'

'Yes. Incidentally, the man who confessed to the murder is the same one who has just escaped from Staten Prison.'

Kari watched Simon's immobile figure in front of the window. She wondered if he had heard what she said; she was about to repeat it when his rough, comforting grandfatherly voice rang out:

'Kari?'

'Yes?'

'I want you to check out absolutely every aspect of Agnete Iversen's life. See if there is something that even looks like a gunshot anywhere near her. Anything – do you understand?'

'Sure. What do you have in mind?'

'I'm thinking . . .' the soothing quality of his voice had gone, 'that if . . . *if* . . . then . . .'

'Then what?'

'Then this has only just begun.'

25

MARKUS HAD SWITCHED OFF THE light in his bedroom. Watching others in the knowledge that they couldn't see you was a strange feeling. Even so, a jolt like an electric shock went through him every time the Son looked out of the window and right into Markus's binoculars. It was almost as if he knew someone was spying on him. The Son was in his parents' bedroom now, he sat on that pink blanket box which Markus knew was empty except for some duvet covers and sheets. The room with no curtains was lit up by a ceiling lamp with four light bulbs which made it easy to see inside. And since the yellow house lay on a lower level than Markus's own, and Markus was sitting on the top bunk of the bed which he had dragged over to the window, he could see what the Son was doing. Which wasn't much; he had been sitting there for a long time with his earphones plugged into his mobile, listening to something. It must be a good song because every three minutes he would press the phone again as if he couldn't get enough of it. And every time he would smile in the same place, even though he was probably feeling a little sad because of that girl. They had kissed and then she had rushed off as fast as she could. Poor guy. Markus wondered if he should go over and knock. Ask the Son if he fancied coming to their house for dinner. His mother would probably think it was nice. But the Son looked sad, so perhaps he didn't want company. There was always tomorrow. Markus would get up early, go over and ring the doorbell, bring him some warm bread rolls. Yes, that was what he was going to do. Markus yawned. And in his head he, too, played a song. No, not really a song, it was just a sentence. But it was going around his head on a loop. Ever since that thug from Tåsen had asked the Son if he was Markus's father. 'Might be.'

Might be. Wow!

Markus yawned again. It was bedtime. After all, he was getting up early tomorrow to heat bread rolls. But as he was about to lower the binoculars, something happened. The Son had got up. Markus pressed the binoculars to his eyes again. The Son had moved the rug and lifted up the loose floorboard. The hiding place. He was putting something in the hiding place. It was the red sports bag. He opened it. Took out a bag of white powder. Markus knew immediately what it was, he had seen bags like that on TV. Drugs. Suddenly the Son lifted his head. He looked as if he was listening out for something; he pricked up his ears like antelopes at the watering hole on *Animal Planet*. And now Markus could hear it, too. The distant sound of an engine. A car. There weren't many of them in his street this late at night during the summer holidays. The Son sat very still as if paralysed. Markus saw the headlights light up the tarmac. A big, black car, what they call an SUV, stopped below the street lamp between their houses. Two men got out. Markus studied them through his binoculars. They were both wearing black suits. *Men in Black*. The second was the best. But the smaller of them had blond hair and that was all wrong. The taller did have black curly hair just like Will Smith, but he had a massive bald patch and his skin was as white as chalk. Markus watched them straighten their suits as they looked at the yellow house. The balding man pointed to the window in the bedroom which was lit up and they quickly walked up to the gate. The Son would have some visitors at last!

Just like Markus, they jumped over the fence rather than going through the gate. And like him, they had realised that walking across the lawn made much less noise than taking the gravel path. Markus swung the binoculars towards the bedroom again. The Son had gone. He had probably seen them, too, and had gone downstairs to let in his guests. Markus aimed the binoculars at the front door where the two men had already walked up the steps. It was too dark for Markus to be able to see exactly what happened. But he heard something smash and then the door opened. Markus stopped breathing.

They . . . they had broken in. They were burglars!

Perhaps someone had told them that the house was empty. Whatever, he had to warn the Son – what if they were dangerous?! Markus jumped down from the bed. Should he wake his mother? Ring the police? And say what? That he was spying on his neighbour with his binoculars? And if they came to dust for fingerprints to find the burglars, they would find his, Markus's, fingerprints! And the Son's drugs so that he would go to prison as well. Markus stood in the middle of the floor; he had no idea what to do. Then he detected movement in the bedroom across the street. He held up his binoculars again. It was the men, they were in the bedroom. They were looking for something. In the wardrobe, under the bed. They . . . they had guns! Markus instinctively took a step backwards when the tall man with the curls came over to the window, checked that it was shut and stared out, right at Markus. The Son must have hidden himself, but where? He appeared to have put the bag with the drugs back in the hiding place, but it wasn't big enough for a person. Hah! They would never find the Son, he knew his house much better than they did, just like the Vietnamese soldiers knew the jungle much better than the Americans. He just had to be quiet as a mouse, just like Markus himself had been. The Son would be all right. He had to be all right! Dear God, please let him be all right.

Sylvester glanced around the bedroom and scratched the naked crescent between his dark curls. 'Dammit, Bo, he must have been here! I'm sure the light wasn't on in any of the windows yesterday.' He flopped down on the pink blanket box, stuck the gun in his shoulder holster and lit a cigarette.

The small blond man stood in the middle of the floor, still holding his gun. 'I've a hunch that he's here somewhere.'

Sylvester waved his cigarette. 'Relax, he's been and gone. I checked both loos and the other bedroom.'

The blond man shook his head. 'No, he's somewhere in this house.'

'Give over, Bo, he's not a ghost, just an amateur who's been lucky. Up until now.'

'Maybe you're right. But I'd never underestimate Ab Lofthus's son.'

'Am I supposed to know who that is?'

'Before your time, Sylvester. Ab Lofthus was the toughest cop in town, by a mile.'

'How would *you* know?'

'Because I met the guy, you moron. Back in the nineties me and Nestor were in the middle of a deal at Alnabru when Lofthus and another cop just happened to drive by. Lofthus knew straight away that they had stumbled on a drugs deal, but rather than call for backup, him and his partner tried to nick us. Ab Lofthus single-handedly beat up four of our guys before we managed to floor him. Which was no easy matter, let me tell you – the guy was a wrestler. We were gonna shoot him right there and then, but

Nestor chickened out, was scared that spilling cop blood would be bad for business. And while we were arguing about it, the guy was lying there screaming "Bring it on!" like that deluded knight in *Monty Python* – do you remember? They chop off his arms and legs, and still he won't accept that he's beaten.'

Bo laughed. Like you laugh at a treasured memory, Sylvester thought. The man was sick, he loved death and mutilation and would lie on his couch watching entire seasons of *Ridiculousness* on the Web because it consisted of footage of people properly hurting themselves, not just the funny home videos of people tripping over or spraining fingers, something the whole family could laugh at.

'I thought you said there were two of them,' Sylvester argued.

Bo snorted. 'His partner backed off immediately. Very happy to cooperate, fell on his knees and begged for mercy, you know the type.'

'Yep,' Sylvester said. 'A loser.'

'Nope,' Bo said. 'A winner. It's called emotional intelligence. And that guy's strategy took him further along than you would think. But enough of that. Let's check the house again.'

Sylvester shrugged and was almost out of the door when he realised that Bo hadn't followed him. He turned round and looked at his partner who was still standing in the same place, staring at the spot where Sylvester had just been sitting. At the lid of the blanket box. Bo raised a finger to his lips and pointed at the box. Sylvester took out his gun and flicked the safety catch aside. He felt his senses heighten; the light grew stronger, sounds intensified and his pulse throbbed in his neck. Without making any noise Bo shifted to the left of the blanket box so that Sylvester also had a clear line of fire. Sylvester closed both hands around the gun handle and moved closer. Bo signalled that he would open the lid. Sylvester nodded.

He held his breath as Bo – with his pistol aimed at the blanket box – placed the fingertips of his left hand under the edge of the lid. Waited a second, listened. And flipped open the lid.

Sylvester felt the resistance from the trigger against his forefinger.

'Damn!' Bo hissed.

Apart from the bed linen, the blanket box was empty.

Together Bo and Sylvester searched the other rooms, turning the lights on and off, but found nothing. Eventually they went back to the bedroom where everything was as they had left it.

'You were wrong,' Sylvester said, articulating the words slowly and clearly because he knew exactly how much they would anger Bo. 'He's gone.'

Bo rolled his shoulders as if his suit didn't fit him properly. 'If the boy has gone, but left the light on, it could mean that he's planning on coming back. And if we're ready and waiting when he does, it makes our job easier than if we have to force our way in.'

'Maybe,' Sylvester said. He could see where this was heading.

'Nestor wants us to get him asap. He can do a lot of damage, you know.'

'Yeah, right,' Sylvester scowled.

'So you stay here tonight in case he comes back.'

'Why do I always get the crappy jobs?'

'The answer starts with an S.'

Seniority. Sylvester heaved a sigh. He wished that someone would shoot Bo so that he would get a new partner. One with less seniority.

'I suggest you wait in the living room where you'll have a view of the front door and the basement door,' Bo said. 'We can't be sure this guy is as easy to end as that chaplain.'

'I heard you the first time,' Sylvester said.

Markus saw the two men leave the well-lit bedroom and shortly afterwards the small blond man left the house, got in the SUV and drove away. The Son was still in there somewhere, but where? Perhaps he had heard the car start and drive off, but did he know that one of the men was still in the house?

Markus aimed his binoculars at the dark windows, but he couldn't see anything. The Son could have sneaked out of the back of the house and got away, but Markus didn't think so; he had sat by the window listening out, he would have heard something.

Markus sensed movement and aimed the binoculars at the bedroom which was still the only room in the house with the light on. And saw that he was right.

The bed. It was moving. Or rather, the mattress was. It was pushed up and to the side. And there he was. He had hidden between the bed slats and the big, thick double mattress which Markus loved lying on. Just as well that the Son was so skinny; had he been as fat as Markus's mother feared that Markus would be one day, they would have seen him. Carefully the Son made his way to the loose floorboard, lifted it up and took something from the red sports bag. Markus zoomed in. He focused. And gasped.

Sylvester had positioned the armchair so that he could see the front door and the gate outside. The gate was lit up by a street light, but he would hear in plenty of time if anyone came; he knew that from the crunching of the gravel when Bo left.

It might turn out to be a long night so he needed to think of something that would help him stay awake. He checked the bookcase and found what he was looking for: the family photo album. He switched on a reading lamp and angled it away from the window so that the light couldn't be seen from the outside. He started flicking through the photographs. They looked like a happy family. So very different from his own. Perhaps this explained his obsession with other people's pictures. He liked looking at them and trying to imagine what it must be like. He knew that these family photos didn't tell the whole truth, obviously, but surely they told *a* truth. Sylvester paused at a picture of three people, possibly taken during the Easter holidays. Smiling and tanned, they were standing in front of a cairn. The woman was in the middle; Sylvester presumed from the other pictures that she was the mother. To her left the father, this Ab Lofthus. And to his right, a man with frameless glasses. 'The Troika and me on a trip. Photographer: The Diver' read the caption in feminine handwriting below. Sylvester looked up. Had he heard something? He looked towards the gate outside. No one there. And the sound hadn't come from the front door or the door to the basement. But something had changed, the density of the air, there was something substantial in the darkness. The darkness. He would always be a little scared of the dark, his dad had made sure of that. Sylvester concentrated on the photograph again. On how happy they looked. Everyone knew you shouldn't be scared of things that go bump in the night.

The noise sounded as if it had come from his dad's belt.

Sylvester stared at the picture.

It was now spattered with blood and had a hole which went straight through the album. Something white floated down and got caught in the blood. A feather? It had to come from the chair's upholstery. Sylvester thought he must be in shock because he felt no pain. Not yet. He looked at his gun which had slipped down on the floor and out of his reach. He waited for the next gunshot, but it didn't come. Perhaps the guy thought that he had killed him. In which case he had a chance as long as he played dead.

Sylvester closed his eyes, heard the boy come in and held his breath. Felt a hand on his chest searching his jacket, finding his wallet and driving licence and removing them. Two arms clasped him around his waist, dragged him out of the chair and eased him up onto his shoulder; then the boy started walking. He must be very strong.

He heard the sound of a door opening, a light being switched on, footsteps staggering down the staircase, and felt raw air. He was being carried down to the basement.

They were downstairs now. There was a noise of plastic seals loosening their grip. Then Sylvester fell, but his landing was much softer than he had feared. He sensed pressure in his ears and it grew darker. He opened his eyes. It was completely dark. He couldn't see anything, he was lying in some sort of box. The darkness is nothing to be afraid of. There are no monsters. He heard footsteps shuffle back and forth until they faded away. The basement door slammed shut. He was alone; the boy hadn't noticed anything amiss. Now it was a question of staying calm, not doing anything rash. Wait until the boy had gone to bed. Then he could make his getaway. Or call Bo and get him and his guys to pick him up and kill the boy. The strange thing was he still didn't feel much pain, only warm blood dripping down on his hand. But he was cold. Very cold. Sylvester tried moving his legs in order to twist himself into a position where he could reach his mobile, but was unable to, his legs must have fallen asleep. He managed to ease his hand inside his jacket pocket and pull out his phone. He pressed it and the display lit up the darkness.

Sylvester held his breath.

The monster was right in front of his face, staring at him with bulging eyes above an open mouth lined with tiny sharp teeth.

A codfish, probably. Wrapped in cling film. Around it lay several freezer bags, some boxes of Frionor seafood, chicken fillets, pork joints, berries. The glow from his phone was reflected in ice crystals in the snow-white walls that surrounded him. He was in a freezer.

Markus stared up at the house and counted the seconds.

He had opened the window, heard the bang coming from inside and seen a flash of light from the living room. Then everything had gone quiet again.

Markus was convinced that it was a gunshot, but who had done the shooting?

Dear God, please let it be the Son. Please don't let it be him who was shot.

Markus had counted to one hundred when he saw the door to the bedroom open. Thank you, God, thank you; it was him!

The Son returned the pistol to the sports bag, removed the loose floorboard and started loading plastic bags of white powder into the sports bag. When he was done, he slung the bag over his shoulder and left the room without switching off the light.

Shortly afterwards the front door slammed shut and Markus saw the Son march towards the gate. Stop, look left and right and then disappear down the street in the same direction Markus had first seen him come from.

Markus flung himself down on his back in the bed. Stared at the ceiling. He was alive! He shot baddies! Because . . . they had to be villains, didn't they? Of course they were. Markus was so excited he knew he wouldn't be able to sleep a wink tonight.

Sylvester heard the front door slam shut. The chest freezer was too well insulated for him to be able to hear much, but the door had been slammed so hard that he had felt the vibrations. At last. Of course his phone couldn't send or receive anything from a freezer in a basement, so after three attempts he had given up trying. Sylvester was starting to feel pain now while at the same time he was growing drowsy, but the cold kept him awake. He pressed his palms against the lid and pushed. Felt a small dart of panic when it didn't budge immediately. Pushed harder. It still didn't give. He remembered the sound of the plastic seals, how they had glued themselves together, it was just a question of a little more force. He pressed his hands against the lid, pushing as hard as he could. There was no movement. And that was when he realised. The boy had locked the freezer.

This time the panic wasn't just a prickling, it was a stranglehold.

Sylvester began to hyperventilate, but forced himself to block out his panic to prevent the dam from bursting, and letting the darkness, the real darkness, flood in. Think. Keep a lid on things and think clearly.

His legs. Why hadn't he thought of them before? He knew that his legs were much stronger than his arms. He could easily lift over two hundred kilos on the leg press, against barely seventy kilos on the bench press. And this was only a freezer lock, it was designed to prevent people from nicking meat and berries, not stop a big, desperate man who really wanted to get out. There was enough space between him and the lid so that if he bent his knees and pressed his feet against the lid . . .

But he was unable to bend his knees.

They quite simply refused to obey him. He had never had such a bad case of pins and needles before. He tried again. No response; it was as if they had been disconnected. He pinched his shin. He pinched his thigh. The dam started to crack. Think. No, don't think! Too late. The hole in the photo album, the blood. The bullet must have severed his spinal cord. That would explain the absence of pain. Sylvester touched his stomach. It was wet with blood. But it was like touching someone else's body.

He was paralysed; from the waist down. He bashed the lid with his fists, but it was no use, all that opened were the floodgates in his mind. The dam he had learned must never be opened. His dad had taught him that. But now the cracks appeared and Sylvester knew that he would die as in his nightmares. Locked up. Alone. In the darkness.

26

'THIS IS THE PERFECT SUNDAY morning,' Else announced as she looked out of the car window.

'Agreed,' Simon said, changing down through the gears and glancing at her. He wondered how much she took in, if she could see that Palace Gardens were especially green after yesterday's violent downpour. If she could even see that they were driving past Palace Gardens.

It was Else herself who had suggested that they visit the Chagall exhibition at Høvikodden and Simon had said that it was an excellent idea, only he just had to swing by an old colleague who lived in Skillebekk which was on the way to the art gallery.

There were plenty of parking spaces along Gamle Drammensveien. The old patrician houses and apartment blocks looked decidedly empty during the holidays. The occasional embassy flag stirred in the breeze.

'I won't be long,' Simon said. He got out and walked up to the door of the address he had found on the Net. The name he was looking for was listed at the top of a row of doorbells.

After ringing the bell twice, Simon was about to give up when he heard a woman's voice.

'Yes?'

'Is Fredrik there?'

'Eh . . . Who wants to know?'

'Simon Kefas.'

There was silence for a few seconds, but Simon could hear crackling as a hand was placed over the microphone on the intercom. Then she was back. 'He'll be down in moment.'

'OK.'

Simon waited. It was too early for normal people to be up and about, so the only ones he saw in the street were a couple his own age. They looked as if they were out on a Sunday walk. A walk whose starting point was also its destination. The man was wearing a tweed cap and nondescript khaki trousers. This was how you dressed when you grew old. Simon looked at his reflection in the glass pane in the carved oak front door. Tweed flat cap and sunglasses. Khaki trousers. Sunday uniform.

It was taking a while; he guessed he must have woken Fredrik up. Or his wife. Or whoever she was. Simon looked across to the car and saw that Else was looking straight at him. He waved. No reaction. The front door opened.

Fredrik appeared in jeans and a T-shirt. He had taken the time to shower – his wet, thick hair was combed back from his face.

'This is unexpected,' he said. 'What—'

'Why don't we go for a little walk?'

Fredrik looked at his heavy wristwatch. 'Listen, I'm—'

'Nestor and his drug-dealing underlings paid me a visit,' Simon said loud enough for the couple nearby to hear. 'But I'm happy to carry this on upstairs in the flat where your . . . wife is?'

Fredrik looked at Simon. Then he closed the door behind him.

They walked along the pavement. Fredrik's flip-flops slapped against the tarmac and cast an echo between the walls.

'He came to offer me that loan I had discussed with you, Fredrik. *Only* discussed with you.'

'I haven't spoken to anyone called Nestor.'

'You don't have to refer to him as "anyone called Nestor", we're both well aware that you know the name. You're free to lie about any other knowledge you have of him.'

Fredrik stopped. 'Come on, Simon. Getting you that loan from any of my clients was impossible. So I discussed your problem with a third party. That was what you expected me to do, wasn't it? Be honest?'

Simon made no reply.

Fredrik sighed. 'Listen, I was only trying to help. The worst that could happen was surely that you got an offer you couldn't refuse.'

'The worst that could happen is that now some scumbags think they've found a way to get to me. Finally, they're thinking. Because they never had anything on me before, Fredrik. On you, yes, but me, never.'

Fredrik leaned against the railings. 'Maybe that's your real problem, Simon. The reason you never had the career you should have had.'

'Because I wasn't for sale?'

Fredrik smiled. 'Your temper. Your lack of diplomacy. You even insult people who are trying to help you.'

Simon looked down at the old abandoned railway line below. From the days when Vestbanen was still in use. He didn't know why, but it made him both melancholic and excited to see that the cutting in the ground was still there. 'Have you read about the triple homicide in Gamlebyen?'

'Of course,' Fredrik said. 'The papers write about little else. Every member of Kripos has been drafted in, or so it would seem. Do you still get to play with them?'

'They prefer to keep the best toys to themselves as usual. Kalle Farrisen was one of the men killed. Do you recognise the name?'

'I can't say that I do. But if Homicide isn't allowed a look-in, why are you—'

'Because Farrisen was once suspected of having killed this girl.' Simon produced the picture he had printed out from the file and gave it to Fredrik. He watched him study the pale face with the Asian features. You didn't need to see the rest of her body to realise that she was dead.

'She was found in a backyard; it was made to look as if she had accidentally OD'd. Fifteen years old. Sixteen, perhaps. She had no papers, so we never found out who she was or where she was from. Or how she got into Norway. Possibly in a container on a ship from Vietnam. The only thing they did discover was that she was pregnant.'

'Yes, wait, I remember that case. I thought someone had confessed?'

'Yes. Late in the day and much to everyone's surprise. What I want to ask you is: was there any connection between Kalle Farrisen and your favourite client, Iversen?'

Fredrik shrugged and looked across the fjord. He shook his head. Simon followed his gaze towards the forest of masts on the yachts moored in the marina where the term 'yacht' these days meant something slightly smaller than a frigate.

'Did you know that the man who confessed to and was convicted of the murder of that girl has escaped from prison?'

Fredrik shook his head again.

'Enjoy your breakfast,' Simon said.

Simon was leaning against the curved cloakroom counter at the art gallery in Høvikodden. Everything was curved. Everything was neo-expressionist. Even the glass walls separating the rooms were curved and possibly neo-expressionist as well. He looked at Else. Else looked at Chagall. She seemed so small as she stood there. Smaller than Chagall's figures. Perhaps it was the curves, perhaps they created an Ames Room illusion.

'So you went to see this Fredrik just to ask him that one question?' asked Kari, who was standing next to him. She had come over twenty minutes after he had called her. 'And what you're saying is . . .'

'That I knew he would deny it,' Simon said. 'But I had to look at him to know if he was lying.'

'You are aware, despite certain TV series that claim the opposite, that it's extremely difficult to tell for certain if someone is lying?'

'Fredrik isn't just "someone". I've experience of listening to him lying, I recognise his "tell".'

'So Fredrik Ansgar is a notorious liar?'

'No. He lies out of necessity, not from predisposition or inclination.'

'Right. And how do you know that?'

'I didn't before we started working together on a big property investigation at the Serious Fraud Office.' He could see that Else was looking a little lost and he coughed loudly so that she could hear where he was. 'It was tricky to prove that Fredrik was lying,' Simon continued. 'He was the investigation's only expert accountant and it was difficult for us to verify everything he said. To begin with it was minor discrepancies and odd coincidences, but the sum total seemed a little too big just to be a coincidence. He failed to inform us of certain things or directly misinformed us. I was the only one who got suspicious. And in time I learned to tell when he was lying.'

'How?'

'It was very simple. His voice.'

'His voice?'

'Lying triggers emotions. Fredrik was good at lying with his choice of words, logic and body language. But his voice was the one emotional barometer he couldn't control. He couldn't strike quite the right natural tone, he had a lying inflection, which he himself could hear and he knew that it might give him away. When he was asked a direct question and had to give a straight answer, he couldn't trust his voice. So he started nodding or shaking his head by way of response.'

'And when you asked him if he knew of any connection between Kalle Farrisen and Iversen?'

'He just shrugged as if he didn't know.'

'So he was lying?'

'Yes. And he shook his head when I asked him if he knew that Sonny Lofthus had escaped from prison.'

'Isn't that a little simplistic?'

'Yes, but Fredrik is a simple man who just happens to know his times tables better than most people. Listen, this is what I want you to do. I want you to go through all of Sonny Lofthus's convictions. See if you can find out if there were any other suspects in each case.'

Kari Adel nodded. 'Great, I didn't have any plans for this weekend anyway.'

Simon smiled.

'That Serious Fraud Office case,' Kari said. 'What was it about?'

'Fraud,' Simon said. 'Tax avoidance, serious money, important names. As the case stood, it could bring down high-profile business people as well as politicians and it looked as if it could take us to Mr Big.'

'Who was?'

'The Twin.'

Kari shivered. 'That's a strange nickname, I must say.'

'Not as strange as the story behind it.'

'Do you know the Twin's real name?'

Simon shook his head. 'He goes by several names. So many that he's totally anonymous. When I started in the Serious Fraud Office, I was naive enough to think that the biggest fish would be the most noticeable. The truth is, of course, that someone's importance is inversely proportional to their visibility. The Twin eluded me yet again. Because of Fredrik's lies.'

'Do you think that Fredrik Ansgar could have been the mole?'

Simon shook his head vigorously. 'Fredrik wasn't even working for the police back when the mole started operating. I believe he was a minor player at that stage, but it's clear that he could have done a lot of damage if he had been allowed to rise up the ranks. So I stopped him.'

Kari's eyes widened. 'You shopped Fredrik Ansgar to the Commissioner?'

'No. I made him an offer. He could either go quietly or I would take what little I had on him to the top. It probably wasn't enough to warrant an investigation or a dismissal, but it would have clipped his wings, put his career on hold for a while. He agreed to leave.'

A vein bulged on Kari's forehead. 'You . . . you just let him go?'

'We got rid of a rotten apple without dragging the police force through the mud. Yes, I let him go.'

'You can't just let people like that walk away.'

He heard the outrage in her voice. Quite right.

'Fredrik is a small fish and, like I said, he would have got away with it. He couldn't even be bothered to pretend that it wasn't a good offer. In fact, he feels that he owes me a favour.'

Simon turned to her. He had intended to provoke her. And it had worked. But it seemed as if her outrage had already passed. Now she just looked like she had found yet another reason to quit the force at the earliest opportunity.

'What's the story behind the Twin's nickname?'

Simon shrugged. 'I believe he had an identical twin brother. When he was eleven years old, he dreamt two nights in a row that he killed this brother. He concluded that since they were identical twins, it was logical to assume that his brother had had the same dream. From then on it was simply a question of beating the other one to it.'

Kari looked at Simon. 'Beating the other one to it,' she repeated.

'Excuse me,' Simon said and rushed after Else who was about to walk into a glass wall.

Fidel Lae saw the car before he heard it. This was the thing about new cars, they hardly made any noise. If the wind was coming from the road, across the moor and towards the farm, he might hear the crunching of tyres against the gravel, gear-changing or high-revving as the car drove up the hills, but otherwise Fidel had to rely on his eyes for warning. Of cars, yes. People or animals were another matter – then he had the best alarm system in the world. Nine Dobermann pinschers in a cage. Seven bitches that had a litter every year, which sold for twelve grand – per puppy. They constituted his kennel's official business where dogs were delivered microchipped to buyers, insured against latent defects and their pedigree registered with the Norwegian Kennel Club.

The unofficial part of the kennel lay deeper into the woods.

Two bitches and one male. Not registered anywhere. Argentine mastiffs. The Dobermann pinschers were scared witless of them. Fifty-five kilos of aggression and loyalty covered in an albino-white short coat which explained why Fidel's dogs all had names with the word 'ghost' in them: the bitches were Ghost Machine and Holy Ghost, the male Ghostbuster. The buyers could call the puppies what the hell they like as long as they paid up. 120,000 kroner. The price reflected the rarity of the dog, its effective killer instinct and the fact that the breed was banned in Norway and in several other countries. As his customers weren't especially price-sensitive or concerned about Norwegian legislation, there was little to suggest that the price would go down. On the contrary. For that reason Fidel had moved the Argentine mastiff enclosure even further into the forest this year, so that their barking couldn't be heard on the farm.

The car was heading for the farm, the track led nowhere else, so Fidel walked quietly down to the gate which was always shut.

Not to prevent the Dobermanns from getting out, but to stop trespassers from getting in. And since everyone except his customers were trespassers, Fidel had a refurbished Mauser M98 to hand in a small shed backing onto the kennel near the gate. He kept fancier weapons in the main building, but he could always argue that he used the Mauser for elk hunting as elks did sometimes walk across the moor. Whenever the wind didn't blow from the direction of the enclosure with the Argentine ghosts, that is.

Fidel arrived at the gate at the same time as the car with a rental company's logo on the exterior. Fidel could tell from the crunching gears that the driver had little experience with this particular make of car; he also took his time switching off the headlights, the windscreen wipers and, finally, the engine.

'All right?' Fidel said, studying the guy who appeared from the car. Hoodie and brown shoes. A townie. Every now and then some of them did make their way here on their own and without having made an appointment. But it was rare. Fidel didn't advertise with directions on the Net like the other kennels. The guy came up to the gate which Fidel showed no sign of wanting to open.

'I'm looking for a dog.'

Fidel pushed the peak of his cap up on his forehead. 'Sorry, but you've made a wasted trip. I don't talk to potential owners of any of my dogs without getting references first. That's just how it is. A Dobermann pinscher isn't a cuddly family dog, it needs an owner who knows what he's taking on. Call me on Monday.'

'I'm not looking for a Dobermann,' the guy said and looked past Fidel. Past the farm and the cages for his nine legal bitches. To the forest behind. 'And my reference is Gustav Rover.' He held up a business card. Fidel peered at it. *Rover's Motorcycle Workshop*. Rover. Fidel had a good memory for names and people because he didn't see many of either. The motorcycle guy with the gold tooth. He had been here with Nestor to buy an Argentine mastiff.

'He said your dogs will keep an eye on the Belarus cleaners and make sure they don't do a runner.'

Fidel spend some time scratching a wart on his wrist. Then he opened the gate. This guy couldn't be police, they weren't allowed to entrap people by provoking crimes such as selling illegal dogs, it would sabotage their entire case. At least that was what his lawyer told him.

'Have you got . . . ?'

The guy nodded, stuck his hand in the pocket of his hoodie and pulled out a large wad of notes. Thousand-kroner notes.

Fidel opened the gun cabinet and took out the Mauser.

'I never go and see them without this,' he explained. 'If one of them were to get out . . .'

It took them ten minutes to walk to the enclosure.

During the last five they could hear furious and increasingly loud barking.

'They think they're about to be fed,' said Fidel, but didn't add: with you.

The manic dogs hurled themselves at the wire fence when the men came into view. Fidel felt the ground shake when they fell back. He knew exactly how deep the fence posts had been sunk, he only hoped it was deep enough. The imported German cages had metal floors, so that dogs like terriers, dachshunds and bloodhounds couldn't dig themselves out, and corrugated-iron roofs that kept them dry and prevented even the fittest ones from leaping over the fence.

'They're most dangerous when they're in a pack,' Fidel said. 'Then they follow the top dog, Ghostbuster. He's the biggest.'

The customer just nodded. He looked at the dogs. Fidel knew he must be scared. The open jaws with rows of glistening, gleaming teeth arranged on pale pink gums. Fuck, he was even scared himself. Only when he was with a single dog, preferably one of the bitches, could he be sure that he was the boss.

'With a puppy you must establish yourself as the top dog quickly and make sure it stays that way. Remember that kindness in the form of indulgence and forgiveness will be viewed as weakness. Undesirable behaviour must be punished, and that's your job. Do you understand?'

The customer turned to Fidel. There was something strangely remote in his smiling eyes when he repeated: 'Punishing undesirable behaviour is my job.'

'Good.'

'Why is that cage empty?' The customer pointed to an enclosure near the dogs.

'I used to have two males. If I had put them in the same cage, one of them would have ended up dead.'

Fidel took out a bunch of keys. 'Come and have a look at the puppies, they have their own cage over there—'

'Before you do that, tell me something . . .'

'Yes?'

'Is it desirable behaviour to let a dog bite a young girl in the face?'

Fidel stopped in his tracks. 'Eh?'

'Is it desirable behaviour to use dogs to bite off a girl's face when she tries to escape slavery, or should it be punished?'

'Listen, the dog is just acting on instinct and you can't blame it just because—'

'I'm not talking about the dog. The owners. Should they be punished, in your opinion?'

Fidel looked closely at his customer. Could he be a cop after all? 'Well, if such an accident did happen, then—'

'I doubt it was an accident. Afterwards, the owner cut the girl's throat and dumped her body in the forest.'

Fidel gripped the Mauser harder. 'I don't know anything about that.'

'But I do. The owner's name was Hugo Nestor.'

'Listen, do you want a dog or not?' Fidel raised the barrel of his rifle – which up until now had been pointing at the ground – a few inches.

'He bought the dog from you. He has bought several dogs from you. Because you sell dogs that can be used for such purposes.'

'What would you know about that?'

'A lot. For twelve years I sat in a cage listening to people tell me stories. Ever wondered what it's like to sit in a cage?'

'Listen—'

'You can try it now.'

Fidel didn't have time to get the rifle in place before the other man had locked him in a hold from behind and was pressing his arms so tightly against his body that the air left Fidel with a hiss. The kennel owner barely registered the frantic barking as he was picked up. The other man leaned back as he lifted Fidel and threw him in a large arc over his head. But when Fidel hit the ground neck and shoulders first, the guy threw himself so that he landed on top of Fidel. Fidel gasped for air as he struggled to free himself. But he stopped abruptly when he stared into the muzzle of a gun.

Four minutes later Fidel was staring at the retreating back of the man who looked as if he was walking on water as he crossed the moor in the fog. Fidel's fingers were gripping the meshed fence next to the big padlock. He was locked in the empty cage. In the next cage, Ghostbuster had lain down and was watching him lazily. The man had filled the bowl in Fidel's cage with water and left him four boxes of Raw dog food. And he had taken his mobile, his keys and his wallet. Fidel started to scream. And the white devils responded with howling and barking. From an enclosure built so deep into the forest that no one could hear or see them.

Fuck!

The man had gone. A strange silence descended. A bird screeched. Then Fidel heard the first drops of rain hit the corrugated-iron roof.

27

WHEN SIMON STEPPED OUT OF the lift and into Homicide's office at 8.08 on Monday morning, he had three things on his mind. That Else had been bathing her eyes in the en suite bathroom earlier, completely unaware that Simon had been watching her from the bedroom. That he had possibly given Kari too much work to do on a Sunday. And that he hated the office layout, especially after one of Else's friends who was an architect had told him that it was a myth that open-plan offices save floor space per employee, that noise issues meant that so many meeting rooms and buffer zones had to be created that any gain was eaten up by the additional expenditure.

He went over to Kari's desk.

'You're in early,' he said.

A rather bleary face looked up. 'Good morning to you too, Simon Kefas.'

'Thank you. Found anything?'

Kari leaned back in her chair. Even though she was yawning, Simon thought he detected a certain satisfaction behind her expression.

'First I looked for a connection between Iversen and Farrisen. Nothing. Then I looked up Sonny Lofthus's convictions and any other potential suspects. Lofthus was convicted of the murder of an unidentified, possibly Vietnamese girl who died from a drug overdose, and at first the police had suspected Kalle Farrisen. But Lofthus was also doing time for another killing. That of Oliver Jovic, a drug dealer, a Kosovo Serb who was trying to butt into the market when he was found in Stensparken with a glass bottle of Coke down his throat.'

Simon pulled a face. 'They slashed his throat?'

'No, that's not what I meant. A bottle of Coke had been rammed down his throat.'

'Down his throat?'

'The bottle neck first. Easier that way. Pushed right down so that the bottom presses against the back of the teeth.'

'How do you know . . . ?'

'I saw the photos. The Drug Squad thought it was a message to show potential competitors what would happen if you try to bite off more than you can chew in the coke market.' She looked up quickly at Simon and added: 'Coke bottle as in Coca-Cola.'

'Yes, thank you, I get it.'

'The police launched an investigation, but got nowhere. The case was never actually abandoned, but very little happened until Sonny Lofthus was arrested for the murder of the Asian girl. He confessed to murdering Jovic as well. In the interview records he states that he and Jovic had met in the park to settle a debt, that Lofthus didn't have enough money and that Jovic had threatened him with a gun. Lofthus had attacked him and floored him. I guess the police thought it sounded reasonable, given that Lofthus used to wrestle.'

'Hm.'

'The interesting thing is that the police lifted a fingerprint from the bottle.'

'And?'

'And it didn't belong to Lofthus.'

Simon nodded. 'And how did Lofthus explain that?'

'He said he'd found the empty bottle in a nearby bin. That junkies like him do this all the time to get the deposits on them back.'

'But?'

'Junkies don't collect recyclables. It would take too long to get together enough money for that day's fix. And the report stated that the fingerprint was a thumb and that it had been lifted from the bottom of the bottle.'

Simon could see where she was going with this, but didn't want to spoil it by beating her to it.

'I mean, who puts their thumb on the bottom of a bottle when they drink from it? If, however, you were forcing a bottle down someone's throat . . .'

'And you don't think the police considered that at the time?'

Kari shrugged. 'I don't think the police ever prioritise drug hits. They hadn't found a match for the thumbprint in the database. So when someone offers them a confession to a case they've had lying around for a while . . .'

'Then they say thank you very much, mark the case as solved and move on?'

'That's how you work, isn't it?'

Simon sighed. *You*. He had read in the newspapers that the police's reputation among the public was starting to rise after the last few years' scandals, but the force was only slightly more popular than the railways. *You*. He imagined she was thanking her lucky stars that she already had one foot out of this open-plan office.

'So Sonny Lofthus was convicted of two murders, but in both cases suspicion pointed to drug dealers. Are you saying that he's a professional scapegoat?'

'Wouldn't you?'

'Perhaps. But there still isn't anything that links him to either Farrisen or Agnete Iversen.'

'There is a third murder,' Kari said. 'Kjersti Morsand.'

'The shipping owner's wife,' Simon said, although his thoughts had now turned to coffee and the coffee machine. 'That's Buskerud Police's case.'

'That's correct. Had the top of her head sawn off. Sonny Lofthus was also suspected of that killing.'

'That can't be right, surely? He was banged up when it happened.'

'No, he was out on day release. He was in the area. They even found one of his hairs at the crime scene.'

'You're joking,' said Simon, instantly forgetting all about coffee. 'There would have been something about it in the papers. Notorious killer linked to crime scene – what could be more newsworthy than that?'

'The Buskerud officer who is heading the investigation has chosen not to make it public,' Kari said.

'Why not?'

'Ask him.'

Kari pointed and Simon noticed a tall, broad man walking towards them from the coffee machine with a mug in his hand. Despite the summer temperature he was wearing a thick woolly jumper.

'Henrik Westad,' the man said, holding out his hand. 'I'm an inspector with Buskerud Police. I'm leading the Kjersti Morsand investigation.'

'I asked Henrik to drive over here this morning for a chat,' Kari said.

'You drove all the way from Drammen in the morning rush hour?' Simon said, shaking the man's hand. 'We're very grateful.'

'*Before* the morning rush hour,' Westad said. 'We've been here since six thirty. I didn't think there was much more to be said about the investigation, but your colleague here is very thorough.'

He nodded to Kari and sat down in the chair opposite her.

'So why didn't you make it known that you had found a convicted killer's hair at the scene?' Simon said, looking enviously at the mug Westad was raising to his lips. 'It's as good as saying you've solved the case. The police don't normally hold back good news.'

'That's true,' Westad said. 'Especially when the owner of that hair had confessed to the killing the first time we interviewed him.'

'So what happened?'

'Leif happened.'

'Who's Leif?'

Westad nodded slowly. 'I could have issued a press release with what we had after the first interview, but something didn't add up. Something about the suspect's . . . attitude. So I waited. And the second time we interviewed him, he retracted his confession and claimed that he had an alibi. A guy called Leif who drove a blue Volvo with an "I ♥ Drammen" sticker, and who Lofthus for some reason thought had heart problems. So I checked with the Volvo dealers in Drammen and the Cardiology Unit at Buskerud Central Hospital.'

'Yes?'

'Leif Krognæss, aged fifty-three. He lives in Konnerud in Drammen and he immediately recognised the suspect from the photo I showed him. He had seen him at a lay-by on the old main road that runs parallel to Drammensveien. You know, one of those areas with picnic benches and tables where you can enjoy being outside. Leif Krognæss had gone for a little drive in the sunshine, but had pulled over and sat in the lay-by for several hours because he felt strangely exhausted. I don't believe it's popular with motorists, they prefer the new road, and besides there's a pond with midges. Anyway, on that day two men were sitting at another picnic table. They just sat there, without saying anything for hours as if they were waiting for something. Then one of the men glanced at his watch and said that it was time to go. As they passed Krognæss's table, the other man bent down, asked Krognæss what his name was and then told him to see a doctor, that there was something wrong with his heart. Then the first man pulled the second man away; Krognæss assumed that he must be a psychiatric patient on an outing, and they had driven off.'

'But he couldn't shake off the episode,' Kari said. 'So he went to see his doctor. Who discovered that he did indeed have heart trouble and had him admitted to hospital immediately. And that's why Leif Krognæss remembers a man he met only briefly at a lay-by on the old main road by the River Drammen.'

The River Drammen, Simon thought.

'Yep,' Westad said. 'Leif Krognæss said the guy saved his life. But that's not the point. The point is that the medical examiner's report states that Kjersti Morsand was killed at the very time the men were sitting in the lay-by.'

Simon nodded. 'And the strand of hair? You haven't checked how it could have ended up at the crime scene?'

Westad shrugged. 'Like I said, the suspect has an alibi.'

Simon was aware that Westad had yet to mention the boy's name. He cleared his throat. 'It could appear that the hair was planted. And if Sonny Lofthus was granted day release in order to make it look like he committed the murder, then one of the prison officers from Staten must be in on it. Is that why it's been hushed up?'

Henrik Westad pushed his mug across Kari's desk; perhaps the taste no longer appealed to him. 'I've been told to hush it up,' he said. 'Someone higher up has made it very clear to my boss to leave the matter alone until they've had a chance to have another look at it.'

'They want to double-check the facts before the scandal becomes public,' Kari said.

'Let's hope that's all it is,' Simon said quietly. 'So why are you talking to us if you've been told to keep quiet, Westad?'

Westad shrugged again. 'It's tough to be the only one who knows. And when Kari mentioned that she was working with Simon Kefas . . . Well, people say you have integrity.'

Simon looked at Westad. 'You know that's just another word for troublemaker, don't you?'

'Yes,' Westad said. 'I don't want any trouble. I just don't want to be the only one who knows.'

'Because it feel safer that way?'

Westad shrugged a third time. He no longer seemed quite so tall and broad when he was sitting down. And despite the jumper he looked like he was cold.

There was complete silence in the rectangular boardroom.

Hugo Nestor's attention was fixed on the chair at the head of the table.

The high-backed chair covered with white buffalo hide was facing away from them.

The man in the chair had demanded an explanation.

Nestor lifted his gaze to the painting on the wall above the chair. It depicted a crucifixion. Grotesque, bloody and excessive in rich detail. The man on the crucifix had two horns on his forehead and burning, red eyes. Apart from those details, the likeness was obvious. Rumour had it that the artist had painted the picture after the man in the high-backed chair had cut off two of his fingers because he owed him money. The bit about the fingers was true, Nestor had witnessed it himself. Rumour also had it that only twelve hours had passed between the artist exhibiting the painting in his gallery and the man in the chair removing it. That, along with the man's liver. That rumour wasn't true. It had taken eight hours, and they had taken his spleen.

As far as the buffalo hide was concerned, Nestor could neither confirm nor deny the story that the man in the chair had paid 13,500 dollars to hunt and kill a white buffalo, the most sacred animal for Lakota Sioux Indians, that he had shot it with a crossbow and when the animal had refused to die even after two arrows to its heart, the man in the chair had straddled the half-ton animal and used his thigh muscles to wring its neck. But Nestor saw no reason to doubt the story. The weight difference between the animal and the man was minimal.

Hugo Nestor shifted his eyes from the painting. There were three other people in the room apart from him and the man on the buffalo hide chair. Nestor rolled his shoulders and felt his shirt stick to his back under the suit jacket. He rarely sweated. Not only because he avoided the sun, poor-quality wool, exercise, lovemaking and other physical exertions, but because he – according to his doctor – had a fault in his inbuilt thermostat which would otherwise cause people to sweat. So even when he did exert himself, he never sweated, but he risked overheating. It was a genetic disposition which proved what he had always known: that his alleged parents weren't his real parents, that his dreams about lying in a cradle in a place that looked like photographs he had seen of Kiev in the 1970s were more than just dreams, they were his earliest childhood memories.

But he was sweating now. Even though he was the bearer of good news, he was sweating.

The man in the chair hadn't raged. Hadn't fumed about the money and drugs that had been stolen from Kalle Farrisen's office. Not screamed how was it possible that Sylvester had gone missing. Or roared why the hell hadn't they found that Lofthus boy yet. Despite everyone knowing what was at stake. There were four scenarios and three of them were bad. Bad scenario number one: Sonny killed Agnete Iversen, Kalle and Sylvester and he would continue to kill anyone they work with. Bad scenario number two: Sonny is arrested, confesses and reveals the names of the real killers in the murders he has served time for. Bad scenario number three: in the absence of the boy's confession, Yngve Morsand is arrested for his wife's murder, can't handle the pressure and tells the police what really happened.

When Morsand had first come to them and said that he wanted his unfaithful wife killed, Nestor had taken it to mean that he wanted to hire a hit man. But Morsand insisted on the pleasure of killing his wife himself, he just wanted them to arrange for someone else to take the fall since he, as the cuckolded husband, would automatically be the police's prime suspect. And at the right price everything is for sale. In this case, three million kroner. A reasonable hourly rate for a life sentence, Nestor had argued, and Morsand had agreed. Afterwards when Morsand had explained how he wanted to tie up the unfaithful bitch, put the saw to her forehead and look her in the eyes while he cut off her head, Nestor had felt the hairs on the back of his neck stand up in a mixture of horror and excitement. They had arranged everything with Arild Franck: the boy's day release, his geographical location, and sent him off with one of Franck's trusted, corrupt and well-paid prison officers, a hermit of a chubby chaser from Kaupang who spent his money on cocaine, paying off his debts and on hookers so fat and ugly, you would have thought the money would change hands in the opposite direction.

The fourth and only good scenario was very simple: find the boy and kill him. It should be straightforward. It should have been done long ago.

And yet the man spoke calmly in his deep, murmuring voice. And it was the voice that made Nestor sweat. From the tall white chair the voice had asked Nestor for an explanation. That was all. An explanation. Nestor cleared his throat, hoping that his voice wouldn't betray his terror, which was always present when he was in the same room as his boss.

'We went back to the house to look for Sylvester. All we found was an empty armchair with a bullet hole to the back. We've checked with our contact in Telenor's operations centre, but none of their base stations has picked up a signal from Sylvester's mobile since late last night. This means that either Lofthus destroyed his phone or his phone is somewhere with no coverage. In any case, I think there's a real risk that Sylvester is no longer alive.'

The chair at the head of the table turned slowly and the man came into view. The bulging body, muscles that strained all the seams of his suit, the high forehead, the old-fashioned moustache, the dense eyebrows over a deceptively sleepy gaze.

Hugo Nestor tried to meet that gaze. Nestor had killed women, men and children, he had looked them in the eye while he did it, without even blinking. Quite the opposite, he had studied them to see if he could see it – mortal fear, the certain knowledge of what was about to happen, any insight the dying might gain at the threshold to the hereafter. Like that Belarus girl whose throat he had cut when the others were unwilling. He had stared into her pleading eyes. It was as if he got off on a mixture of his own feelings, his rage at the others' and the woman's capitulation and weakness. Got off on the excitement of holding a life in his hands and deciding whether – and indeed when – he would carry out the act that would end it. He could extend her life by a second, and then another second. And another one. Or not. It was entirely up to him. And it struck him that this was the closest he would ever come to the sexual ecstasy which people spoke about, a union which for him was only associated with mild discomfort and an embarrassing attempt at coming across as a so-called normal person. He had read somewhere that one individual in every hundred was asexual. It made him an exception. But it didn't make him abnormal. On the contrary, he could concentrate on what really mattered, build his life, his reputation, enjoy the respect and fear of others without any distractions and the loss of energy that came from the sexual addiction other people were slaves to. Surely that was rational and – consequently – normal? He was a normal person who wasn't frightened of, but, rather, curious about death. And, in addition, he had good news for his boss. But Nestor managed to hold his boss's gaze for only five seconds before he had to look away. Because what he saw in it was colder and emptier than death and annihilation. It was perdition. The promise that you had a soul and that it would be taken from you.

'But we've got a tip-off about where the boy might be,' Nestor said.

The big man raised one of his distinctive eyebrows. 'Who from?'

'Coco. A drug dealer who lived at the Ila Centre until recently.'

'The psycho with the stiletto, yes?'

Nestor had never be able to establish exactly how his boss got his information. He was never seen in the streets. Nestor had never met anyone who claimed to have spoken to him, let alone seen him. And yet he knew everything and that was the way it had always been. In the day of the mole that was not surprising, then his boss would have had access to practically everything the police did. But after they had killed Ab Lofthus when he was about to expose him, the mole's activities appeared to have ceased. This was almost fifteen years ago now, and Nestor had accepted that he would probably never know the identity of the mole.

'He talked about a young guy at Ila who had so much money that he paid his room-mate's debt,' Nestor said in a carefully rehearsed tone of voice and with what he thought was an East Slavic 'r'. 'Twelve thousand kroner in cash.'

'No one at Ila ever pays off another junkie's debts,' said the Wolf, an older man who was responsible for the trafficking of girls.

'Quite,' Nestor said. 'But this young guy did – even though his room-mate accused him of stealing some earrings. So I thought—'

'You're thinking about the money in Kalle's safe?' the big man said. 'And the jewellery that was stolen at Iversen's, yes?'

'Yes. So I went to see Coco and showed him a picture of the guy. And he confirmed it was him, Sonny Lofthus. I even know his room number. 323. The question is now how we . . .' Nestor pressed his fingertips together and smacked his lips as if he could taste the synonyms for 'kill him'.

'We won't be able to get in,' the Wolf said. 'Or at least not without getting noticed. The gate is locked, there are receptionists and CCTV everywhere.'

'We could use one of the residents for the job,' said Voss, formerly head of a security company who had been sacked after being involved in the importation and dealing of anabolic steroids.

'We're not going to leave this to a junkie,' the Wolf said. 'Not only has Lofthus eluded our own – presumably competent – people, he would also appear to have killed one of them.'

'So what do we do?' Nestor said. 'Lie in wait for him outside the centre? Install a sniper in the building opposite? Set fire to the centre and jam the fire exits?'

'This isn't the time for jokes, Hugo,' Voss said.

'You ought to know that I never joke.' Nestor felt his face getting hot. Hot, but not sweaty. 'If we don't get him before the police—'

'Good idea.' The two words were spoken so quietly, they were barely audible. And yet they sounded like thunder in the room.

Silence followed.

'What is?' Nestor asked eventually.

'Not taking him before the police do,' said the big man.

Nestor looked around the room to make sure that he wasn't the only one who didn't understand before he asked: 'What do you mean?'

'Exactly what I said,' whispered the big man, smiling briefly and aiming his gaze at the only person in the room who had kept silent until now. 'You know what I mean, don't you?'

'I do,' the man replied. 'The boy will end up back at Staten Prison. Perhaps he'll take his own life – just like his father?'

'Good.'

'I'll tip off the police about where they can find the boy,' the man said, raising his chin and easing the skin of his neck away from the shirt collar of his green uniform.

'That won't be necessary. I'll deal with the police,' said the big man.

'You will?' Arild Franck said, sounding surprised.

The big man turned and addressed the whole table. 'What about this witness in Drammen?'

'He's in hospital, in Cardiology,' Hugo Nestor heard someone say while he himself stared at the painting.

'And what do we do about that?'

He stared.

'What we have to,' the bass voice replied.

He stared at the Twin hanging from the crucifix.

Hanging.

Martha sat in the attic.

Staring at the beam.

She had told her colleagues that she wanted to check the filing had been done properly. It was bound to be, she didn't care about that. She didn't care about anything these days. She was thinking about him, Stig, all the time and it was just as banal as it was tragic. She was in love. She had always believed she didn't have the capacity for strong emotions. She'd had crushes before, obviously, lots of them, but never like this. The other times there had been butterflies in her stomach, it had been an exciting game with heightened senses and flushed cheeks. But this was . . . a disease. Something had invaded her body and was controlling her every thought and action. She was love-struck. Struck down by an illness, or by malign fate. It was an apt expression. This was excessive. It was unwanted. It was tearing her apart.

The woman who had hanged herself up here in the attic – had it been the same with her? Had she, too, fallen in love with a man whom she knew, in her heart of hearts, was a wrong 'un? And had she, too, been so blinded by love that she had started debating right and wrong with herself, trying to carve out a new morality which was compatible with this wonderful disease? Or had she – like Martha – only found out when she was in much too deep? During breakfast Martha had returned to room 323. She had checked the trainers again. They smelled of detergent. Who washes the soles of a pair of practically brand-new trainers unless they have something to hide? And why had it filled her with such despair that she had gone up to the attic? Dear God, she didn't even want him.

She stared at the beam.

But she wouldn't do what the dead woman had done; report him. She couldn't. There had to be a reason, something she didn't know. He wasn't like that. In her job she had heard so many lies, excuses and versions of reality that ultimately she no longer believed that anyone was who they said they were. But one thing she did know: Stig was no cold-blooded killer.

She knew it because she was in love.

Martha buried her face in her hands. Felt the tears well up. Sat there, shaking in the silence. He had wanted to kiss her. She had wanted to kiss him. *Still* wanted to kiss him. Here, now, forever! Lose herself in this vast, wonderful, warm ocean of emotions. Take the drug, surrender, press the plunger, feel the high, be grateful and damned.

She heard sobbing. And felt the hairs stand up on her arm. Stared at the walkie-talkie. The tender whimpering of a baby.

She wanted to switch off the walkie-talkie, but she didn't. The crying sounded different this time. As if the child was scared and was calling out for her. But it was still the same child, always the same child. Her child. The lost child. Trapped in a vacuum, in a nothingness, trying to find its way home. And no one could or wanted to help it. No one dared. Because they didn't know what it was and people fear the unknown. Martha listened to the crying. It rose in pitch and intensity. Then she heard a loud crackling and a hysterical voice:

'Martha! Martha! Come in . . .'

Martha froze. What was that?

'Martha! They're raiding the centre! They're armed! For God's sake, where are you?'

Martha picked up the walkie-talkie and pressed the talk button. 'What's going on, Maria?' She released the button.

'They're dressed in black and wearing masks, they have shields and guns and there are so many of them! You have to come downstairs!'

Martha got up and ran out of the door. She heard her own feet clatter down the steps. Flung open the door leading to the corridor to the second floor. Saw a man dressed in black spin round and point a shotgun or possibly a machine gun at her. Saw three others standing in front of the door to room 323. Two of them were swinging a short battering ram between them.

'What—' Martha began, but broke off when the man with the machine gun stepped in front of her and raised a finger to what she presumed were his lips under the black balaclava. She stiffened for a second before she realised that the only thing stopping her was his idiotic weapon.

'I want to see a search warrant right now! You've no right to—'

There was a loud crash as the battering ram hit the door below the lock. The third man opened the door a fraction and tossed in something that looked like two hand grenades. Then the men turned away and covered their ears. Good God, were they . . . ? The flash of light from the doorway was so bright that all three police officers cast shadows in the already well-lit corridor, and the explosion was so loud that Martha's ears rang. Then they stormed into the room.

'Get back, miss!'

The words coming from the policeman in front of her were muffled. He appeared to be shouting. Martha just looked at him. Like the others he was wearing Delta Force's black uniform and bulletproof vest. Then she retreated back through the door, into the stairwell. Leaned against the wall. Checked her pockets. The card was still in her jacket pocket as if she had known all along that she would need it one day. She rang the number under the name.

'Yes?'

The voice is a strangely accurate temperature gauge. Simon Kefas's sounded tired and stressed, but lacking the excitement which a raid, a big arrest, should give it. From the acoustics she also deduced that he wasn't in the street outside or in any of the rooms at the Ila Centre, but in a big space, surrounded by other people.

'They're here,' she said. 'They're throwing grenades.'

'What are you talking about?'

'This is Martha Lian from the Ila Centre. There's an armed response unit here. We're being raided.'

In the pause which followed she heard a voice in the background make an announcement, a name, a call for a doctor to attend the post-op ward. The Chief Inspector was in a hospital.

'I'll be over right away,' he said.

Martha ended the call, opened the door and returned to the corridor. She could hear the crackling and hissing of police radios.

The police officer pointed his gun at her. 'Hey, what did I just tell you?!'

A metallic voice in his radio said: 'We're bringing him out now.'

'Go on, shoot me if you have to, but I'm in charge here, and I've yet to see a search warrant,' Martha declared and marched past him.

And then she saw them emerge from room 323. He was hand-cuffed and being led out by two police officers. He was almost naked, wearing only a pair of slightly too big, white underpants and he looked oddly vulnerable. Despite his muscular torso he seemed skinny, sunken, finished. A trickle of blood was dripping from one ear.

He looked up. Met her eyes.

Then they walked past her and out of sight.

It was over.

Martha breathed a sigh of relief.

Having knocked on the door twice, Betty took out the master key and let herself into the suite. As usual she took longer than neces-sary so that even if the guest was in his room, he would have time to avoid a potentially embarrassing situation. This was the policy at the Plaza Hotel: the staff shouldn't see or hear anything that shouldn't be seen or heard. But this wasn't Betty's policy. Quite the opposite. Her mother had always said that Betty's curiosity would get her into trouble one day. And, yes, it had done, and on more than one occasion. But as a receptionist it had also come in useful; no one else at the hotel had the same nose for con men as Betty. It had almost become her trademark, exposing people who intended to live, eat and dine at the hotel with no intention of paying their bills. And she was often proactive; Betty had never hidden her ambitions. During her last annual review, her boss had praised her for being vigilant, but discreet, and always putting the hotel's interests first. Said that she could go far, that reception was just a stepping stone for someone like her. The suite was one of the biggest in the hotel with a panoramic view of Oslo. It had a bar, a kitchenette, a bathroom and the separate bedroom had an en suite bathroom. She could hear the shower running in the en suite.

According to guest registration his name was Fidel Lae and

money was clearly no object. The suit she was bringing him was made by Tiger and had been bought in Bogstadveien earlier that day, sent to the tailor for alterations using their express service, and then delivered to the hotel by taxi. In the summer the hotel would usually employ a bellboy to take items to rooms, but this summer had been so quiet that the receptionists did it themselves. Betty had volunteered immediately. Not because she had any real grounds for suspicion. When she had checked him in, he had paid for two nights in advance and con men did *not* do that. But there was something about him that didn't ring true. He hadn't looked like the kind of guy who books the top-floor suite. More like someone who slept rough or would stay in a hostel for backpackers. He seemed so inexperienced and concentrated so hard during check-in as if he had never stayed in a hotel before, but had read about it in theory, and was now keen to get everything just right. Plus he had paid cash.

Betty opened the wardrobe and saw there was already a tie and two new shirts in there, also by Tiger and probably bought at the same shop. A pair of new, black shoes was on the floor. She read the name 'Vass' on the insole. She hung up the suit next to a long, soft suitcase with wheels. It was almost as tall as she was; she had seen cases like this before, they were used for transporting snowboards or surfboards. She was tempted to unzip it, but poked the suitcase instead. The fabric gave way. Empty – or at least there wasn't a snowboard inside. Next to the suitcase stood the only item in the wardrobe which didn't look new, a red sports bag with the words *Oslo Wrestling Club*.

She closed the doors to the wardrobe, walked over to the open bedroom door and called out towards the bathroom door: 'Mr Lae! Excuse me, Mr Lae!'

She heard the tap turn off and shortly afterwards a man appeared with swept-back wet hair and shaving foam all over his face.

'I've hung your suit in the wardrobe. I was told to pick up a letter, to be franked and posted?'

'Oh, yes. Thank you so much. Could you hang on a minute?'

Betty walked over to the living-room window, took in the view towards the new Opera House and the Oslo Fjord. The new high-rise buildings stood close together like pickets in a fence. Ekebergåsen. The Post Office building. The town hall. The rail tracks which came in from the whole country and merged together in a nerve bundle below her at Oslo Central Station. She noticed the driving licence on the large desk. It wasn't Lae's. Next to it lay a pair of scissors and a passport-sized photo of Lae wearing the prominent, square glasses with the black frames she had seen him with when she had checked him in. Further along the desk lay two identical and clearly new briefcases. The corner of a plastic bag stuck out from under the lid of one of them. She stared. Matt, but transparent plastic. With the traces of something white on the inside.

She took two steps back so that she could look into the bedroom. The door to the bathroom was open and she could see the back of the guest in front of the mirror. He had a towel wrapped around his waist and was concentrating hard on shaving. It meant that she had a short window of opportunity.

She tried opening the briefcase containing the plastic bag. It was locked.

She looked at the code lock. The small metal wheels showed 0999. She looked at the other briefcase. 1999. Did the two brief-cases have the same code? In which case 1999 looked like the code. A year. The year of someone's birth, perhaps. Or the Prince song. In which case it wouldn't be locked.

Betty heard the guest turn on the tap in the bathroom. He was splashing water on his face now. She knew she really shouldn't.

She lifted the lid of the second briefcase. And gasped.

The briefcase was stuffed full with bundles of banknotes.

Then she heard footsteps coming from the bedroom and quickly shut the lid, took three brisk steps and stopped at the door to the corridor with her heart pounding.

He came out from the bedroom and looked at her with a smile. But something about him had changed. Perhaps it was just that he was no longer wearing his glasses. Or it was the bloody piece of tissue over one eye. At that moment she realised what was different. He had shaved off his eyebrows, that was it. Who on earth *removes* their eyebrows? Apart from Bob Geldof in *The Wall*, of course. But he was mad. Or pretending to be mad. Was the man in front of her insane? No, mad people didn't have briefcases full of money, they only *thought* they did.

He opened the desk drawer, took out a brown envelope and handed it to Betty.

'Please would you make sure that goes in today's post?'

'I'm sure we can manage that,' she said, hoping he hadn't detected her trepidation.

'Thank you so much, Betty.'

She blinked twice. Of course – her name was on the hotel badge.

'Have a nice day, Mr Lae,' she smiled and put her hand on the door handle.

'Wait, Betty . . .'

She felt her smile congeal. He had seen her open the briefcase, he was about to—

'Perhaps it's . . . eh, customary to tip for such services?'

She breathed a sigh of relief. 'Not at all, Mr Lae.'

It wasn't until she was in the lift that she realised she was sweating profusely. Why could she never rein in her curiosity? Nor could she very well tell anyone that she had been riffling through a guest's property. Anyway, since when was it illegal to keep money in a briefcase? Especially if you worked for the police. Because that was what it said on the front of the brown envelope. *Police HQ, Grønlandsleiret 44. For the attention of Simon Kefas.*

Simon Kefas was standing inside room 323, looking around.

'So Delta raided the room?' he said. 'And took away the guy in the bottom bunk? Johnny – what was his name?'

'Puma,' Martha said. 'I called because I thought perhaps you had . . .'

'No, I had nothing to do with it. Who is Johnny's room-mate?'

'He calls himself Stig Berger.'

'Hm. And where is he now?'

'I don't know. No one does. The police have asked everyone here. Listen, if it's not you, then I want to know who ordered the raid.'

'I don't know,' Simon said, opening the wardrobe. 'Only the Commissioner can authorise a Delta deployment, check with him. Are these Stig Berger's clothes?'

'As far as I know.'

He had a hunch that she was lying, that she knew they belonged to him. He picked up the blue trainers at the bottom of the wardrobe. Size 8½. Put them back, closed the wardrobe and spotted the photo fixed to the wall next to the wardrobe. Any doubts he might have had until now evaporated.

'His name is Sonny Lofthus,' Simon said.

'What?'

'The other resident. His name is Sonny and this is a picture of his father, Ab Lofthus. His father was a police officer. His son became a killer. So far he has killed six people. You're welcome to complain to the Commissioner, but I think we can safely say that Delta's presence was justified.'

He saw how her face seemed to stiffen and the pupils contracted as if there was suddenly too much light. Staff here had seen a thing or two, but it was still a shock to learn that they had given shelter to a mass murderer.

He squatted down on his haunches, there was something under the bunk bed. He pulled it out.

'What is it?' she asked.

'A stun grenade,' he said, holding up the olive-green object which looked like the rubber grip on the handlebars of a bicycle. 'It produces a powerful flash of light and a bang of around 170 dB. It's not dangerous, but it leaves people so blind, deaf, dizzy and disorientated for a few seconds that Delta have time to do what they have to do. But they didn't pull the pin out of this one, so it never went off. That's how it is, people make mistakes under pressure. Don't you agree?'

He glanced at the trainers and then looked up at her. But when she returned his gaze, it was steady and firm. He saw nothing there.

'I have to get back to the hospital,' Simon said. 'Will you call me if he comes back again?'

'Are you all right?'

'Probably not,' Simon said. 'But the patient is my wife. She's going blind.'

He looked down at his hands. He was tempted to add: *just like me.*

28

HUGO NESTOR LOVED VERMONT. IT was one of the few restaurant-bar-nightclub combinations that had actually succeeded in all three areas. The clientele was made up of the rich and beautiful, the not-beautiful but rich, the not-rich but beautiful, a cross section of celebrities, semi-successful financiers and people who worked nights in the entertainment and nightlife industry. Plus successful criminals. It was at Vermont in the nineties that the Tveita Gang and people involved in money laundering, bank and post office robberies had bought methuselahs of Dom Perignon, and because Norwegian strippers at the time had lacked a certain finesse, had better ones flown in from Copenhagen for a quick lap dance in their private dining room. They had used drinking straws to blow cocaine directly into the various orifices of the strippers, and eventually into their own, while the waiters brought them oysters, Périgord truffles and foie gras from geese that had been treated much as they were treating themselves. In short, Vermont was a place with style and tradition. A place where Hugo Nestor and his people could sit every night at their cordoned-off table and watch the world outside go to hell. A place where you could do business, where bankers and financiers could mix with criminals without the cops who frequented Vermont reading too much into it.

Consequently the request from the man who had sat down at their table wasn't among the more unusual. He had come in, looked around and pushed his way through the crowds right over to them, but been stopped by Bo when he tried to straddle the red cordon that marked out their territory. After exchanging a few words, Bo had come over to Nestor and whispered into his ear: 'He wants an Asian girl. He says it's for a client who'll pay whatever it costs.'

Nestor tilted his head and sipped his champagne. There was a saying of the Twin's that he had made his own: *Money can buy you champagne.* 'Does he look like a cop to you?'

'No.'

'Me neither. Get him a chair.'

The guy was wearing a suit that looked expensive, a freshly ironed shirt and a tie. He had pale eyebrows above a pair of prominent, exclusive spectacles. No, correct that, *no* eyebrows.

'She has to be under twenty.'

'I don't know what you're talking about,' Nestor said. 'Why are you here?'

'My client is a friend of Iver Iversen.'

Hugo Nestor looked at him closely. He didn't have any eyelashes, either. Perhaps he had alopecia universalis like Hugo's brother – alleged brother – who didn't have a single body hair. In which case the hair on the guy's head had to be a wig.

'My client is in shipping. He'll pay you cash and in heroin that has come in by sea. You probably know better than I do what that means in terms of purity.'

Fewer stops. Fewer middlemen cutting the drugs.

'Let me call Iversen,' Nestor said.

The guy shook his head. 'My client demands total discretion, neither Iversen nor anyone else must know. If Iversen is dumb enough to tell his close friends what he gets up to, then that's his problem.'

And potentially ours, Nestor thought. Who was this guy? He didn't look like an errand boy. A protégé? A highly trusted family lawyer?

'I understand, of course, that a direct approach from a man you don't know requires extra assurances of a safe transaction. My client and I therefore suggest an advance to prove we're serious. What do you say?'

'I say 400,000,' Nestor said. 'It's just a figure I plucked out of the air, I still don't know what you're talking about.'

'Of course not,' the guy said. 'We can do that.'

'How soon?'

'I'm thinking tonight.'

'Tonight?'

'I'm only in town until tomorrow morning, then I fly back to London. The money is in my suite at the Plaza.'

Nestor exchanged looks with Bo. Then he drained the tall champagne flute in one gulp.

'I don't understand a word you're saying, mister. Unless you're trying to tell me that you're inviting us back for a drink in your suite.'

The guy flashed a smile. 'That's exactly what I'm saying.'

They searched the guy the moment they reached the car park. Bo held him while Nestor checked him for weapons and microphones. The guy let himself be frisked without resisting. He was clean.

Bo drove the limo to the Plaza and they walked from the multi-storey car park behind Spektrum to the towering glass prism that was the Plaza Hotel. They looked down at the city from the external lift and Nestor thought it was a metaphor – people down there grew smaller the higher he himself rose.

Bo took out his pistol as the guy opened the door to the suite. There was no obvious reason to expect an ambush; Nestor currently had no living enemies that he knew of. No unresolved disputes in the market and the police were free to arrest him if they wanted to, but they didn't have anything on him. And yet he sensed an unease which he couldn't quite pin down. He put it down to professional vigilance and decided not to drop his guard, something other people in the business could learn from. Nestor hadn't got to where he was without good reason.

The suite was fine. Amazing view, he'd give them that. The guy had set out two briefcases on the coffee table. While Bo checked the other rooms, the guy went behind the bar and started mixing drinks.

'Go ahead,' he said, extending his hand towards the briefcases.

Nestor sat down at the coffee table and opened the lid of first one, then the other. There was more than 400,000 kroner. There had to be.

And if the drugs in the other briefcase were as pure as the guy had suggested, there was more than enough to buy a small village of Asian girls.

'Do you mind if I turn on the TV?' Nestor asked, picking up the remote control.

'Be my guest,' the guy said; he was busy mixing drinks, something he didn't look comfortable doing, although at least he was slicing lemon for the three gin and tonics.

Nestor pressed the pay-TV button, flicked past the children and family movies to the porn channel and turned up the sound. He went over to the bar.

'She is sixteen years old and will be delivered to the car park at Ingierstrand Lido at midnight tomorrow. You'll pull up in the middle of the car park and stay in your car. One of my men will come over to you, get in the back and count the money. Then he'll leave with the money and someone else will bring the girl. Understood?'

The guy nodded.

What Nestor didn't mention, because it didn't need saying, was that the girl wouldn't be in the same car as the car that came to pick up the money. The money would have left the meeting place before the car with the girl arrived. Same principle as in a drug deal.

'And the money . . . ?'

'Another 400,000,' Nestor said.

'Fine.'

Bo entered from the bedroom and stopped to look at the screen. He appeared to enjoy it. Most people seemed to. Nestor only found porn useful because it offered a predictable and steady soundtrack of moaning that frustrated any possible bugging of the room.

'Ingierstrand Lido tomorrow at midnight,' Nestor repeated.

'Let's drink to it,' the guy said, holding out two glasses.

'Thanks, but I'm driving,' Bo said.

'Of course,' the guy laughed and slapped his head. 'Coke?'

Bo shrugged and the guy opened a can of Coke, poured it into a glass and cut another slice of lemon.

They toasted and sat down at the table. Nestor signalled to Bo who picked up the first bundle of banknotes from the briefcase and started counting out loud. He had brought a bag with him from the car into which he put the money. They never accepted the customer's bags, they might contain sensors that could trace where the money was taken. It wasn't until Nestor heard Bo miscount that he realised something was wrong. Only he didn't know what. He looked around. Had the walls changed colour? He looked down at his empty glass. Looked at Bo's empty glass. And the lawyer guy's glass.

'Why isn't there any lemon in yours?' Nestor asked. His voice sounded very far away. And the reply came from the same distant place.

'Citrus fruit intolerance.'

Bo had stopped counting; his head was slumped over the money.

'You've drugged us,' Nestor said and reached for the knife in his leg sheath. He had time to register that he was patting the wrong leg before he saw the base of the lamp coming towards him. Then everything went black.

Hugo Nestor had always loved music. And he didn't mean the kind of noise or childish series of notes which common people called music, but music for adults, thinking people. Richard Wagner. Chromatic scale. Twelve half-tones with frequency ratios based on the 12th root of 2. Clean, pure mathematics, harmony, German order. But the sound he was hearing now was the opposite of music. It was discordant, nothing related to anything else, it was chaos. When he had regained consciousness, he had realised he was in a car, in some sort of large bag. He had felt nauseous and dizzy; his hands and feet were tied together with something sharp that cut into his skin – plastic ties probably, he sometimes used them on the girls.

When the car had stopped, he had been lifted out and realised he must be inside a soft case with wheels. Half lying down, half standing upright, he had been pushed and dragged across a rugged terrain. He had heard whoever was pulling the suitcase pant and wheeze. Nestor had called out to him, made financial offers in return for his release, but had got no response.

The next sound he had heard was this unmusical, atonal hullabaloo which only rose in strength. And which he recognised the moment the suitcase was put down and he lay on his back, feeling the ground underneath him and knowing – because he had now worked out where he was – that the cold water seeping through the suitcase and then through his suit was marsh water. Dogs. The short, choppy barking of Argentine mastiffs.

What he didn't know was what it was all about. Who the guy was and why this was happening to him. Was it a turf war? Was the guy who had abducted him the same guy who had killed Kalle? But why go about it this way?

The suitcase was unzipped and Nestor squinted, blinded by the light from the torch pointing straight at his face.

A hand grabbed his neck and pulled him to his feet.

Nestor opened his eyes and saw a pistol gleam dully in the light. The dogs' barking had suddenly stopped.

'Who was the mole?' said the voice behind the torch.

'What?'

'Who was the mole? The police thought it was Ab Lofthus.'

Hugo Nestor narrowed his eyes against the light. 'I don't know. You might as well shoot me, I don't know.'

'Who does know?'

'No one. None of us. Perhaps someone in the police.'

The torch was lowered and Nestor saw that it was the lawyer guy. He had taken off his glasses.

'You need to be punished,' he said. 'Would you like to ease your conscience first?'

What was he talking about? He sounded like a priest. Was this about that chaplain they had killed? But he was only a corrupt paedophile – surely no one would want to avenge him?

'I've no regrets,' Nestor said. 'Just get it over with.'

He felt strangely calm. Perhaps it was a side effect of the drug. Or that he had thought it through enough times already, accepted that his life would probably end like this, with a bullet to the brain.

'Not even for that girl you allowed to get mauled before you cut her throat? With this knife . . . ?'

Nestor blinked as the torchlight bounced off the curved blade. His own Arabic knife.

'Don't . . .'

'Where do you keep the girls, Nestor?'

The girls? Was that what he wanted, to take over the trafficking? Nestor tried to concentrate. But it was difficult, his brain was foggy.

'Do you promise not to shoot me if I tell you?' he asked, even though he realised that a yes would have about as much credibility as the German mark did in 1923.

'Yes,' the guy said.

So why did Nestor still believe him? Why did he believe the promise that he wouldn't be shot from a guy who had done nothing but lie from the moment he appeared at Vermont? It had to be his crazy brain clinging to this last straw. Because there was nothing else, nothing but this foolish hope in a dog kennel in a forest at night: that the guy who had abducted him was telling the truth.

'Enerhauggata 96.'

'Thank you so much,' the guy said and stuck the pistol into the waistband of his trousers.

Thank you so much?

The guy had taken out his mobile and was entering some information from a yellow Post it note, a phone number, probably. The display lit up his face and it occurred to Nestor that he might be a priest after all. A priest who didn't lie. A contradiction in terms, obviously, but he was convinced that such priests existed, who weren't *aware* that they were lying. He carried on pressing keys. A text message. He sent it with a final push of the buttons. Then he slipped the mobile into his pocket and looked at Nestor.

'You've done a good deed, Nestor, there is a chance they might be rescued now,' he said. 'I thought you would want to know that before you . . .'

Before I what? Nestor gulped. The guy had promised not to kill him! Had . . . Wait. He had promised not to *shoot* him. The light from the torch was now pointing straight at the padlock to the enclosure. The guy inserted a key into the lock. Nestor could hear the dogs now. Not barking, only a barely audible, but harmonised bass. A muted growl that came from the pits of their stomachs and rose in volume, tone and pitch, hushed and controlled like Wagner's contrapuntal music. And no drugs could suppress his fear now. Fear that felt like being hosed down with icy water. If only the pressure could have washed him away, but this man was on the inside, inside him, hosing down the inside of his head and body. There was no escape. It was Hugo Nestor himself who was holding the hose.

Fidel Lae sat in the darkness, staring. He had stopped moving or making a sound. Only curled up in an attempt to keep warm and control his shaking. He recognised the two men's voices. One was the man who had appeared out of nowhere and locked him up more than twenty-four hours ago. Fidel had barely eaten any of the dog food, only drunk the water. And shivered with cold. Even on a summer night the chill eats its way into your body, petrifies it, chases you around. He had screamed for help until his throat felt raw and he had no voice left, until blood and not saliva moistened his throat and the water he had drunk offered no relief, but stung and burned like alcohol. When he heard the car, he had tried screaming again, but started sobbing when his voice made no sound; it merely grated like a rusty engine.

Then he could tell from the dogs that someone was approaching. He had hoped. And prayed. And finally seen the silhouette against the summer-night sky, seen that he was back. The man who had floated over the moor yesterday was now bent double as he dragged something along. A suitcase. With a living human being inside. A man who stood with his hands tied behind his back and his feet pressed so close together that he clearly had problems keeping his balance when he was put in front of the gate to the enclosure where Fidel was.

Hugo Nestor.

They were only four metres from Fidel's cage, and yet he couldn't hear what they were talking about. The man unlocked the padlock and put his hand on Nestor's head as if blessing him. He said something. Then he gave Nestor's head a little push. The plump man in the suit screamed briefly, then he fell backwards and hit the gate, which opened inwards. The dogs stirred. The man quickly pushed Nestor's feet inside and closed the gate. The dogs hesitated. Then Ghostbuster seemed to jerk and started moving. Fidel watched the white dogs as they pounced on Nestor. Their movements were so silent that he could clearly hear the chomping jaws, the sound of flesh being torn, the almost ecstatic growling and then Nestor's scream. A single, quivering, strangely pure note that rose towards the light Nordic sky where Fidel could see insects dance. Then the note was suddenly cut short and Fidel saw something else rise, it looked like a swarm coming towards him and he felt the spray of tiny warm droplets and knew what it was because he had himself cut the artery of a still living elk on a hunting trip. Fidel wiped his face with the sleeve of his jacket and looked away. He saw that the man outside the cage had also turned away. Saw his shoulders shake. As if he was crying.

29

'IT'S THE MIDDLE OF THE night,' the doctor said, rubbing his eyes. 'Why don't you go home and get some sleep, Kefas, and we'll do this tomorrow?'

'No,' Simon said.

'As you wish,' the doctor said, indicating to Simon to take a seat on one of the chairs along the wall of the bleak hospital corridor. When the doctor sat down next to him and paused before leaning towards him, Simon knew that it was bad news.

'Your wife doesn't have much time left. If she's to have any chance of a successful operation, she needs to have surgery in a matter of days.'

'And there's nothing you can do?'

The doctor sighed. 'Normally we don't advise patients to go abroad and subject themselves to expensive private treatment – especially when the outcome of surgery is relatively uncertain. But in this case . . .'

'You're saying I need to get her to the Howell Clinic now?'

'I'm not saying you have to do anything. Many blind people live a full life with their handicap.'

Simon nodded while his fingers stroked the stun grenade he still kept in his pocket. He tried to process the information, but it was as if his brain was trying to run away, seeking refuge by speculating if handicap wasn't a non-PC word. He supposed they called it 'differently abled' now. Or had that – like hostel – also become non-PC? Things changed so quickly that he couldn't keep up, and health and social care terminology seemed to go off faster than milk.

The doctor cleared his throat.

'I . . .' Simon began and heard his mobile crackle. He grabbed it, grateful for some time out. He didn't recognise the sender of the text message.

You'll find Nestor's prisoners in Enerhauggata 96. Hurry. The Son.

The Son.

Simon pressed a number.

'Listen, Simon,' the doctor said, 'I don't have time to—'

'That's all good,' Simon said and held up a hand to silence the doctor as he heard a sleepy voice answer the call: 'Falkeid.'

'Hi, Sivert, it's Simon Kefas. I want you to dispatch Delta to raid the following address: Enerhauggata 96. How fast can you get there?'

'It's the middle of the night.'

'That's not what I was asking.'

'Thirty-five minutes. Have you got authorisation from the Commissioner?'

'Pontius isn't available right now,' Simon lied. 'But relax, we've got grounds for the raid as far as the eye can see. Trafficking. And time is of the essence. Just do it, it'll be on my head.'

'I hope you know what you're doing, Simon.'

Simon hung up and looked at the doctor. 'Thank you, Doctor, I'll think about it. Now I've got to get back to work.'

Betty heard the mating noises as soon as they exited the lift on the top floor.

'Really.' Betty frowned.

'It's pay-TV,' said the security guard she had taken with her.

They had received complaints from the neighbouring rooms and, as a matter of policy, Betty had made a note in the night log at reception. '02.13 a.m. noise complaint about Suite 4.' She had called Suite 4, but got no reply. Then she had called security.

They ignored the 'Do Not Disturb' request hanging on the door handle and knocked hard. Waited. Knocked again. Betty shifted her weight from one foot to another.

'You look nervous,' the security guard said.

'I've a feeling that the guest is up to . . . something.'

'Something?'

'Drugs – what do I know?'

The security guard released the button on his cosh and straightened up while Betty slipped the master key into the lock. Opened the door.

'Mr Lae?'

The living room was empty. The mating noises were coming from a woman in a red leather corset with a white cross that was supposed to indicate she was a nurse. Betty grabbed the remote control from the coffee table and turned off the TV while the security guard entered the bedroom. The briefcases had gone. Betty noticed empty glasses and half a lemon on the bar counter. The lemon had dried out and its flesh had a strange brown colour. Betty opened the wardrobe. The suit, the large suitcase and the red sports bag were gone. It was the oldest trick in the hotel fraud book, hanging a 'Do Not Disturb' sign outside the door and turning on the TV so that it sounded as if the guest was still there. But Mr Lae had paid for the room in advance. And she had already checked that no charges from the restaurant or the bar had been made to the room.

'There's a guy in the bathroom.'

She turned to the security guard who was standing in the doorway to the bedroom.

She followed him inside.

The man lying on the bathroom floor looked like he was hugging the lavatory. A closer inspection revealed that he was tied to it with strips around his wrists. He was wearing a black suit, had blond hair and didn't look entirely sober. High on something. Or low. Heavy eyelids blinked sleepily at them.

'Cut me loose,' he said with an accent she couldn't place anywhere on the globe.

Betty nodded to the security guard who took out a Swiss army knife and cut the plastic strips.

'What happened?' she asked.

The man staggered to his feet. Swayed slightly in front of them. He struggled to focus his swimming eyes. 'We played some stupid game,' he mumbled. 'I'm going to go now . . .'

The security guard positioned himself in the doorway and blocked his path.

Betty looked around. Nothing had been damaged. The bill had been paid. All they had was a complaint about television noise. What they risked was trouble with the police, negative press coverage and a reputation for being a meeting place for unsavoury elements. Her boss had praised her for being discreet, for putting the hotel's interests first. Said that she could go far, that reception was only a stepping stone for someone like her.

'Let him go,' she said.

Lars Gilberg was woken up by a rustling from the bushes. He turned over. Saw the contours of a figure among the branches and leaves. Someone was trying to steal the boy's stuff. Lars wiggled out of the filthy sleeping bag and scrambled to his feet.

'Oi, you!'

The figure stopped. Turned round. The boy was transformed. It wasn't just the suit. It was something about his face, it looked swollen somehow.

'Thanks for looking after my stuff,' the boy said, nodding to the bag he had tucked under his arm.

'Hm,' Lars said and moved his head closer to see if that made it easier to spot the change. 'You're not in trouble, are you, lad?'

'Oh, yes, indeed I am,' the boy smiled. But there was something about his smile. Something pale. His lips were trembling. He looked as if he had been crying.

'Do you need help?'

'No, but thanks for asking.'

'Hm. I won't see you again, will I?'

'No, I don't think so. Live well, Lars.'

'I will. And you . . .' He took a step forward and placed a hand on the boy's shoulder. 'Live long. Promise me that?'

The boy nodded quickly. 'Check under your pillow,' he said.

Lars automatically looked at his bedding under the arch. And when he turned round again, he just had time to see the back of the boy before he was swallowed up by the darkness.

Lars returned to his sleeping bag. He spotted an envelope sticking out from under his pillow. He picked it up. 'To Lars' it said. He opened the envelope.

Lars Gilberg had never seen so much money in his entire life.

'Shouldn't Delta be here by now?' Kari asked, yawned and glanced at her watch.

'Yes,' Simon said and looked out. They had parked halfway up Enerhauggata and number 96 lay fifty metres in front of them, on the other side of the street. It was a white-painted, two-storey wooden house, one of those which had been reprieved when Enerhaugen's picturesque buildings were demolished in 1960 to make way for four tower blocks. The small house lay so still and peaceful in the summer night that Simon found it hard to imagine that people could be kept prisoner inside it.

'*We feel a dash of guilt,*' Simon said. '*But I think that glass and concrete are more suitable for people today.*'

'What?'

'I'm quoting the CEO of OBOS Building Society, in 1960.'

'Is that right?' Kari said and yawned again. Simon wondered if she hoped he would feel a dash of guilt for dragging her out of bed in the middle of the night. It could be argued that her presence wasn't strictly necessary for such a raid. 'Why isn't Delta here?' she asked again.

'I don't know,' Simon said, and at that moment the inside of the car was lit up by the display on his phone which lay between the seats. He looked at the number.

'But we soon will,' he said, slowly lifting the mobile to his ear. 'Yes?'

'It's me, Simon. No one is coming.'

Simon adjusted the rear-view mirror. A psychologist might be able to explain why Simon did that, but it had become an automatic response to the other man's voice. Simon focused on the mirror to see what was behind him.

'Why not?'

'Because the grounds for the raid haven't been properly justified, its necessity explained and you've made no attempt to go through the proper channels to authorise Delta.'

'You can authorise it, Pontius.'

'Yes. And I said no.'

Simon swore silently. 'Listen, it—'

'No, you listen to me. I've ordered Falkeid to stand down and told him and his men to go back to bed. Just what are you up to, Simon?'

'I have reason to believe that people are being held against their will at Enerhauggata 96. Honestly, Pontius, it—'

'Honesty is good, Simon. Remember that the next time you ring the head of Delta.'

'There was no time to explain. There *is* no time, dammit. You used to trust my judgement.'

'Your use of past tense is correct, Simon.'

'So you don't trust me now, is that it?'

'You gambled away all your money, remember? Including your wife's. What does that tell me about your judgement, in your opinion?'

Simon clenched his teeth. There had been a time when it wouldn't have been so easy to predict which one of them would win an argument or who would get the best grades, run the fastest or get the prettiest girl. The only certainty was that they would unite behind the third man in the troika. But he was dead now. And though he had been the best thinker and the strongest of the three, Pontius Parr had always had one advantage: he thought further than either of the other two.

'We'll do it early tomorrow morning,' the Commissioner said with the easy self-confidence which these days made people believe that Pontius Parr knew best. Including Pontius himself. 'If you've got a tip-off about suspected trafficking at the address then it won't disappear overnight. Go home and get some sleep now.'

Simon opened the car door and got out while indicating to Kari to stay where she was. He closed the door and walked a few metres down the road. He spoke quietly into the mobile.

'It can't wait. This is urgent, Pontius.'

'What makes you think that?'

'The tip-off.'

'And how did you come by it?'

'A text message from someone . . . anonymous. I'll go in on my own.'

'What? Don't even think about it! Stop, Simon. Do you hear me? Are you there?'

Simon looked at his mobile. Pressed it to his ear again. '*An assessment carried out by the officer at the scene*. Do you remember learning that, Pontius? Do you remember them teaching us that it always trumped orders from officers remote from the scene?'

'Simon! Oslo is in chaos as it is. The City Council and the media are on our backs over these killings. Don't jump off the deep end this time. Simon!'

Simon hung up, turned off his mobile and opened the boot of his car. Unlocked the gun box. Took out his shotgun, his pistol and some boxes of ammunition. Took out the two bulletproof vests lying loose in the boot and got into the car.

'We're going in,' he said, handing the shotgun and one vest to Kari.

She looked at him. 'Was that the Commissioner you were just talking to?'

'It was,' Simon said, checking that the cartridge clip on the Glock 17 pistol was full. Slotted it back into the handle. 'Pass me the handcuffs and the stun grenade in the glove compartment, would you?'

'You've got a stun grenade?'

'By-product of the raid at the Ila Centre.'

She handed Simon his Peerless handcuffs and the grenade. 'Has he given us permission to go in?'

'He has been informed,' Simon said, putting on the bulletproof vest.

Kari cocked the shotgun and loaded it with cartridges with swift, familiar movements.

'Grouse hunting since I was nine,' she said by way of explanation, having noticed Simon's look. 'But I prefer rifles. How do we do this?'

'On three,' Simon said.

'I mean, how do we approach—'

'Three,' Simon said and opened the car door.

The Bismarck Hotel was located in the centre of Oslo, that much was true. The small hotel lay in the middle of Kvadraturen where the city had been founded, at the point where the drugs market met the red-light district. And true to its location, it rented out rooms by the hour with towels that were stiff from boil washing. The rooms hadn't been redecorated since the hotel was taken over by its current owner sixteen years ago, but the beds had to be replaced every two years as a result of wear and tear.

So when Ola, who was the owner's son and had worked in reception since he was sixteen years old, looked up from his PC at 03.02 a.m. and saw a man standing in front of the counter, it was natural for Ola to assume that the man was in the wrong place. Not only was he wearing a nice suit and carrying two briefcases and a red sports bag, but he was without a female or male companion. The man, however, insisted on paying up front for a room for one week, and accepted the towel with an almost humble thank-you before he disappeared up to the second floor. Ola went back to reading *Aftenposten*'s web page about a wave of murders in Oslo, speculations as to whether a gang war had broken out and how it might be connected to the killer who had absconded from Staten. He studied the photo for a while. Then he clicked on another page.

Simon stopped in front of the steps leading to the house and gestured to Kari to have her weapon ready and watch the first-floor windows. Then he walked up the three steps and tapped a knuckle softly against the door. He whispered 'Police'. Looked at Kari to assure himself that she could testify that he had followed the correct, official procedure. Another tap. He whispered 'Police' again. Then he grabbed the barrel of his pistol and leaned to the side to smash the glass in the window next to the door. He had the stun grenade ready in his other hand. He had a plan. Of course he had a plan. Kind of. As they say, the element of surprise is everything. Putting all his eggs in one basket. He always had. And that, as the young psychologist had explained, was his disease. Research proved that people constantly exaggerated the likelihood of something improbable happening to them, such as dying in a plane crash, their child being raped or abducted on their way to school, or that the horse on which you bet your wife's savings would stay the distance for the first time in its racing career. The psychologist had said that there was something in Simon's subconscious that was stronger than common sense, that it was a matter of identifying and starting a dialogue with this sick, crazy tyrant who terrorised and ruined his life. That he had to ask himself if there was something more important in his life. More important than the tyrant. Something he loved more than gambling. And there was. It was Else. And he had done it. He had talked to the beast, tamed it. He hadn't relapsed once. Not until now.

He took a deep breath. He was about to bash the pistol against the glass when the door opened.

Simon spun round with the pistol in front of him, but he wasn't as quick as he once was. Not even close. He wouldn't have had a chance if the man in the doorway had been armed.

'Hello,' was all the man said.

'Good evening,' Simon said, trying to regain his composure. 'Police.'

'How can I help you?' The man opened the door fully. He was dressed. Tight jeans. T-shirt. Bare feet. Nowhere to conceal a pistol.

Simon stuffed the stun grenade into his pocket and held out his warrant card. 'I'll have to ask you to come outside and stand up against this wall. Now.'

The man calmly shrugged his shoulders and did as he was told.

'Apart from the girls, how many people are in the house?' Simon asked while a quick frisking confirmed that the man was unarmed.

'Girls? I'm the only one here. What do you want?'

'Show me where they are,' Simon said, handcuffed the man, shoved him in front of him and indicated to Kari to follow. The man said something.

'What?' Simon said.

'I'm telling your colleague that she's welcome to come in as well. I've got nothing to hide.'

Simon remained standing behind the man. Stared at his neck. Saw his skin twitch slightly, like on a nervous horse.

'Kari?' Simon called out.

'Yes?'

'I want you to stay outside. I'm going in alone.'

'OK.'

Simon put a hand on the man's shoulder. 'Start walking and no sudden movements, I've got my pistol against your back.'

'What are—'

'Accept that for the time being I regard you as a criminal and I might shoot you; you can always get an unreserved apology afterwards.'

Without further protest the man entered the hallway. Simon automatically looked out for any evidence of what to expect inside. Four pairs of shoes on the floor. The man didn't live alone. A plastic bowl of water and a rug by the door to the kitchen.

'What happened to your dog?' Simon asked.

'What dog?'

'Do you drink from that bowl?'

The man made no reply.

'Dogs tend to bark when strangers approach the house. So either it's a rubbish guard dog or—'

'It's at the kennel. Where are we going?'

Simon looked around. There were no bars on the windows, the front door had a single lock with a turnkey on the inside. They weren't being held here.

'The basement,' Simon said.

The man shrugged and continued down the hallway. And Simon knew that he had hit the jackpot when he saw the man unlock the door to the basement. The door had two locks.

Simon recognised the smell as soon as they walked down the stairs and it confirmed his suspicions. That people were being kept there. Lots of people. He gripped the pistol more tightly.

But no one was there.

'What do you use these for?' asked Simon as they passed some lock-ups, which were separated by steel mesh rather than walls.

'Not much,' the man said. 'The dog lives here. And I store mattresses, as you can see.'

The smell was even more pungent now. The girls must have been kept here until very recently. Dammit, they were too late. But surely they would be able to pull DNA from the mattresses. Though what did that prove? That someone had been in contact with a mattress which was now in a basement. It would be more unusual if they didn't find DNA on old mattresses. They had nothing. Only an unauthorised raid. Damn, damn.

Simon noticed a small trainer with no laces lying on the floor near a door.

'Where does that door lead to?'

'Only to the driveway.'

Only. He was trying to play down the significance of the door. Just like he had stressed how much he wanted Kari to come inside the house.

Simon opened it and found himself looking straight at the side of a white van parked on the tarmac that had been laid between this house and the fence to the neighbouring house.

'What do you use the van for?' Simon asked.

'I'm an electrician,' the man said.

Simon took a few steps back. Crouched down and picked up the trainer from the basement floor. Size 5, possibly. Smaller than Else's shoes. He stuck his hand inside. It was still warm. It could be no more than a few minutes since the owner had lost it. At that moment he heard a sound. Muffled, trapped, but unmistakable. A yelp. Simon stared at the van and was about to stand up again when he received a kick to his side and fell as he heard the man scream: 'Drive! Drive!'

Simon managed to roll over and aim his pistol at the man, but the man had already slumped to his knees and folded his hands behind his head in total surrender. The engine started, the revs so high that it squealed. Simon rolled over onto his other side and could now see heads in the front of the van; the girls had clearly been hiding in the back.

'Stop! Police!' Simon tried to get to his feet, but it hurt like hell, the guy must have broken one of his ribs. And before Simon could point his pistol, the van was in motion and out of his firing range. Dammit!

There was a bang followed by glass shattering.

The squeal of an engine falling silent.

'Stay where you are,' Simon said and groaned as he scrambled to his feet and staggered out of the door.

The van had come to a standstill. Loud screaming and frantic barking could be heard coming from the inside.

But it was the scene in front of the van which Simon took a mental photograph of for his scrapbook. Kari Adel in a long, black leather coat standing in the beam from the headlights of the van which was now relieved of its windscreen. The stock of the shotgun in her shoulder and an underhand grip on the still smoking barrel.

Simon walked up to the side of the van and slid open the door on the driver's side. 'Police!'

The man inside didn't respond, he just continued to stare straight ahead as if in shock, with blood dripping from his hairline. His lap was filled with broken glass. Simon ignored the pain in his side, dragged the man out and down on the ground. 'Nose to the tarmac and hands behind your head! Now!'

Then he walked round the van and subjected the equally apathetic passenger to the same treatment.

Simon and Kari walked up to the side door in the body of the van. They could hear the dog yelp and bark from the inside. Simon grabbed the door handle and Kari positioned herself right in front of it with the shotgun at the ready.

'It sounds big,' Simon said. 'Perhaps you should take another step back?'

She nodded and did as he had suggested. Then he slid the door open.

A white monster shot out of the van and flew right at Kari with its jaws snarling and open. It happened so quickly that she didn't have time to fire her weapon. The animal slammed into the ground in front of her and stayed there.

Simon stared at his own smoking pistol in astonishment.

'Thank you,' Kari said.

They turned back to the van. Terrified, wide-eyed faces stared out at them from inside it.

'Police,' Simon said. And added when he saw from the expressions that this might not be considered universally good news: 'Good police. We're on your side.'

Then he took out his mobile and rang a number. Put the mobile to his ear and looked up at Kari.

'Do you think you could call the station and ask them to dispatch a couple of patrol cars?'

'So who are you ringing then?'

'The press.'

30

DAWN WAS STARTING TO BREAK over Enerhaugen, but the press hadn't finished taking pictures and interviewing the girls who had been given woollen blankets and tea which Kari had made in the kitchen. Three of the reporters were crowding around Simon in an attempt to milk him for even more details.

'No, we don't know if there are more people behind this than those we arrested here tonight,' Simon repeated. 'And, yes, it's correct that we raided this address following an anonymous tip-off.'

'Did you really have to kill an innocent animal?' asked a female journalist, nodding towards the dead dog which Kari had covered with a blanket from the house.

'It attacked us,' Simon said.

'Attacked you?' She snorted. 'Two adults against one small dog? Surely you could have found a way to restrain it.'

'The loss of life is always sad,' Simon said and knew that he shouldn't, but couldn't help himself and continued, 'but given that the life expectancy of a dog is in inverse proportion to its size, you will – if you take a look under the blanket – realise that this dog didn't have long to live, anyway.'

Stalsberg, a senior crime reporter who was the first person Simon had called, grinned.

A police SUV had appeared over the hill and parked behind the patrol car, which – to Simon's irritation – still had its blue light flashing on its roof.

'But rather than ask me any more questions, I suggest that you speak to the boss himself.'

Simon nodded towards the SUV and the journalists turned round. The man who emerged from the car was tall and slender with thin hair swept back and rectangular, frameless glasses. He straightened up and looked astonished as the journalists raced towards him.

'Congratulations on the arrests, Commissioner Parr,' Stalsberg said. 'Would you like to comment on how it looks as if you're finally making progress with the trafficking problem? Would you call this a breakthrough?'

Simon folded his arms across his chest and met Pontius Parr's icy stare. The Commissioner nodded almost imperceptibly, then he looked at the reporter who had asked the question. 'It's certainly an important step in the police's fight against trafficking. Before this current incident we've stressed that this issue must be given priority, and this prioritising has – as you can see – borne fruit. So we would like to congratulate Chief Inspector Kefas and his colleagues.'

Parr grabbed Simon as he headed back to his car.

'What the hell do you think you're doing, Simon?'

It was one of the things Simon had never understood about his old friend; how his voice never changed character or pitch. He could be exhilarated or furious, but his voice stayed exactly the same.

'My job. Catching villains.' Simon stopped, stuffed a piece of *snus* under his upper lip and offered the tin to Parr, who rolled his eyes. It was an old joke of which Simon never tired; Parr had never used *snus* or smoked a cigarette in his life.

'I mean this performance,' Parr said. 'You defy a direct order not to enter and then you invite every member of the media to come here. Why?'

Simon shrugged. 'I thought we could do with some favourable press coverage for once. Incidentally, it's not everyone, only those who were working the night shift. And I'm delighted that we agree that the assessment of the officer at the scene should be the decisive factor. If we hadn't, I don't think we would have found these girls – they were about to be moved on.'

'What I'm wondering is how you knew about this place.'

'As I told you before, a text message.'

'From?'

'Anonymous. It's a pay-as-you-go phone.'

'Get the phone companies to trace it. Find whoever it is as soon as possible so we can interview them for more information. Because unless I'm very much mistaken, we won't get a word out of the people we arrested here.'

'Oh?'

'They're just small fry, Simon. They know that the big fish will eat them up unless they keep their mouths shut. And it's the big ones we want, isn't it?'

'Of course.'

'Good. Listen, Simon, you know me, and you know that I can be too certain of my own brilliance at times, and . . .'

'And?'

Parr cleared his throat. Rocked back and forth on his heels as if to take off. 'And your assessment of the situation here tonight was better than mine. Plain and simple. It won't be forgotten at your next review.'

'Thank you, Pontius, but I'll be retired long before my next review.'

'That's true,' Parr smiled. 'But you're a fine policeman, Simon, you always were.'

'That's also true,' Simon said.

'How's Else?'

'Good, thank you. Or . . .'

'Yes?'

Simon took a breath. 'Good enough. We'll talk about it some other time. Bed?'

Parr nodded. 'Bed.' He patted Simon on the shoulder, turned round and walked towards the SUV. Simon looked after him. Hooked his index finger and pulled out the *snus*. It didn't taste right.

31

IT WAS SEVEN IN THE morning when Simon got to work. He had managed two and a half hours' sleep, one and a half cups of coffee, and half a headache pill. Some people could survive on very little sleep. Simon wasn't one of them.

Kari, however, might be. She certainly looked surprisingly alert as she strode towards him.

'So?' Simon said, slumping down in his office chair and tearing open the brown envelope which had been waiting for him in his pigeonhole.

'Not one of the three people we arrested last night is saying anything,' Kari said. 'Not a single word, in fact. They even refused to state their names.'

'What nice boys. Do we know them?'

'Oh yes. Plain clothes recognised them. They have previous convictions, all three of them. Their lawyer turned up unannounced in the middle of night and interrupted our attempts to get anything out of them. A man called Einar Harnes. I managed to trace the mobile with the text message from this Son. The mobile belongs to a Fidel Lae. Owns a kennel. He's not answering his phone, but the signals to the base stations indicate it's at his farm. We've dispatched two patrol cars there.'

Simon realised why she – unlike him – didn't look as if she had just got straight out of bed. It was because she had never made it that far, she had worked right through the night.

'Then there's this Hugo Nestor you asked me to find . . . ?' she continued.

'Yes?'

'He's not at his home address, doesn't answer his phone, nor is he at his office address, but they could all be fake. All I have so far is a plain-clothes cop who says she saw Nestor at Vermont last night.'

'Hm. Do you think I have bad breath, Officer Adel?'

'Not that I've noticed, but then again we haven't—'

'So you wouldn't regard this as a hint?'

Simon held up three toothbrushes.

'They look used,' Kari said. 'How did you get them?'

'Good question,' Simon said, peering into the envelope. He pulled out a sheet of paper with the logo of the Plaza Hotel at the top. But there was no sender. Just a short handwritten message:

Check for DNA. S.

He handed the sheet to Kari and looked at the toothbrushes.

'Probably some weirdo,' Kari said. 'Forensics have more than enough to do with the killings to—'

'Take them straight up there,' Simon said.

'What?'

'It's him.'

'Who?'

'"S". It's Sonny.'

'How do you know—'

'Tell them it's urgent.'

Kari looked at him. Simon's phone started to ring.

'OK,' she said, and turned to leave.

She was standing outside the lift when Simon came over and stood next to her. He had put on his coat.

'You're coming with me first,' he said.

'Oh?'

'That was Åsmund Bjørnstad. They've found another body.'

A woodland bird hooted hollowly from somewhere in the spruce forest.

Åsmund Bjørnstad had been stripped of all traces of arrogance. He was pale. He had come straight out with it on the phone: 'We need help, Kefas.'

Simon was standing beside the Kripos inspector and Kari, staring through the mesh of a cage, at the remains of a body which they had temporarily identified on the basis of various credit cards as Hugo Nestor's. Confirmation would have to wait until they had checked his dental records. Simon could deduce from where he was standing and looking at the fillings in the exposed teeth that the deceased had actually seen a dentist. The two police officers from the dog patrol who had taken away the Argentine mastiffs had provided a simple explanation for the state of the body: 'The dogs were hungry. Somebody forgot to feed them.'

'Nestor was Kalle Farrisen's boss,' Simon said.

'I know,' Bjørnstad groaned. 'All hell will break loose once the press finds out.'

'How did you find Lae?'

'Two patrol cars down at the farm were following a phone signal,' Bjørnstad said.

'I sent them,' Kari said. 'We got an anonymous text message.'

'First they discovered Lae's phone,' Bjørnstad said. 'It was on top

328

of the gate as if someone had left it there to be traced and found. But they didn't find Lae when they searched the house. They were about to leave when one of the police dogs reacted and wanted to go inside the forest. And that's when they found . . . this.' He flung out his hands.

'And Lae?' Simon asked, nodding towards the shivering man huddling under a woollen blanket, sitting on a tree stump behind them.

'The killer threatened him with a gun, he says. Locked him in the adjacent cage, took his mobile and his wallet. Lae was locked up for thirty-six hours. He saw everything.'

'And what's he saying?'

'He's broken, poor man, he can't stop talking. Lae sold dogs illegally and Nestor was his client. But he's unable to give a proper description of the killer. Still, it's common for witnesses not to remember the faces of people who threatened their lives.'

'Oh, they remember them,' Simon said. 'They remember those faces for the rest of their lives. They just don't recall them the way we see them, that's why their descriptions are wrong. Wait here.'

Simon went over to the man. Sat down on another tree stump next to him.

'How did he look?' Simon asked.

'I've already given a description—'

'Like this?' Simon said, producing a photograph from his inside pocket and showing it to him. 'Try to imagine him without the beard and the long hair.'

The man stared at the picture for a long time. Then he nodded slowly. 'That look. He had that look in his eyes. As if he was innocent.'

'Sure?'

'Absolutely.'

'Thank you.'

'He kept saying that the whole time. Thank you. And he cried when the dogs killed Nestor.'

Simon put the picture back in his pocket. 'One last thing. You told the police that he threatened you with a gun. In which hand did he hold the gun?'

The man blinked a couple of times as if he hadn't thought about it until now. 'Left. He was left-handed.'

Simon got up and walked back to Bjørnstad and Kari. 'It's Sonny Lofthus.'

'Who?' Åsmund Bjørnstad asked.

Simon looked at the inspector for a long time. 'I thought it was you who turned up with Delta, trying to catch him at the Ila Centre?'

Bjørnstad shook his head.

'Anyway,' Simon said, taking out the picture again. 'We need to issue a description and a wanted person notice so that the public can help us. We need to get this photo to the news desks at NRK and TV2.'

'I doubt if anyone will recognise him on the strength of that picture.'

'How soon can we get them to broadcast it?'

'They'll make room for this story immediately, trust me,' Bjørnstad said.

'For the morning news bulletins in fifteen minutes, then,' Kari said, taking out her mobile and turning on the camera function. 'Hold the picture up and keep it still. Who do you know in NRK that we can send it to?'

Morgan Askøy was carefully picking at a small scab on the back of his hand when the bus driver suddenly slammed on the brakes and Morgan inadvertently ripped off the scab. A drop of blood appeared. Morgan quickly averted his eyes, he couldn't stand the sight of blood.

Morgan got off the bus at Staten Maximum Security Prison where he had been working for two months. He was walking at the back of a group of other prison officers when a guy in a prison officer uniform came up alongside him.

'Good morning.'

'Good morning,' Morgan replied automatically and looked over, but couldn't place him. Even so, the guy continued walking alongside him as if they knew each other. Or as if he wanted to get to know him.

'You don't work in A Wing,' the guy remarked. 'Or are you new?'

'B Wing,' Morgan said. 'Two months.'

'Ah, right.'

The guy was younger than the other uniform fetishists. Mostly it was the older officers who travelled to and from work in their uniform, as if they were somehow proud of it. As did Franck, the assistant governor, himself. Morgan would have felt like an idiot if he had to sit on the bus and have people staring at him and perhaps asking questions about where he worked. At Staten. In a prison. No way.

He looked at the ID card on the young man's uniform. Sørensen.

They passed the security booth side by side and Morgan nodded to the security guard inside.

When they approached the entrance, the guy took out his mobile and lagged slightly behind; perhaps he was sending a text.

The door had slammed shut behind the staff in front of them, so Morgan had to pull out his own key. He unlocked the door. 'Thank you so much,' said the Sørensen guy as he slipped in in front of him. Morgan followed, but turned off towards the lockers. He saw the guy join the rest of the staff as they poured into the lock towards the wings.

*　　*　　*

Betty kicked off her shoes and flopped down on her bed. What a night shift. She was exhausted and knew she wouldn't be able to sleep for a while, but she had to give it a try at least. And in order to do that, she first had to rid herself of the feeling that she should have reported the incident in Suite 4 to the police. After she and the security guard had searched the room to see if anything was damaged or missing, Betty had tidied up and was about to throw away the half lemon when she discovered a used, disposable syringe in the bin. Without any prompting her brain had put two and two together: the discoloured citrus flesh and the syringe. She had traced her fingers over the lemon peel and found several tiny holes. Squeezed a drop of lemon juice into her hand and saw that the juice was cloudy, as if it contained chalk. She touched the drop carefully with her tongue to taste it; besides the almost overpowering acidity, there was another bitter, medicinal note. She had to make a decision. Was there a law against guests having strangely tasting lemons in their possession? Or a disposable syringe? What if they happened to be diabetic or suffer from some other condition? Or play bizarre games with visitors in their room? So she had carried the contents of the bin down to reception and disposed of it. Written a brief entry in the log about the noise coming from Suite 4 and the man they found tied to the lavatory. A man who had himself dismissed the whole incident. What else could she do?

She turned on the wall-mounted TV while she undressed, went to the bathroom, took off her make-up and cleaned her teeth. She could hear the steady hum of voices from TV2's news channel. She tended to leave it on at low volume because it helped her fall asleep. Possibly because the news anchor's reassuring voice reminded her of her father's, a voice which could report on the downfall of continents, and yet she would still feel safe. But the TV alone was not enough any more. She had started taking sleeping pills. Not very strong ones, admittedly, but even so. Her doctor said she should consider asking to be let off night shifts to see if that might help. But no one got to the top by shirking, you had to pull your weight. Over the noise of the tap and her own foaming toothbrush she heard the voice say that police were looking for a person in connection with the killing of a man in a dog kennel last night, and that they linked this person to the murder of Agnete Iversen and the triple homicide in Gamlebyen.

Betty rinsed her mouth, turned off the tap and went back to the bedroom. Stopped in her tracks on the threshold. Stared at the photo of the wanted man on the TV.

It was him.

He had a beard and long hair, but Betty was trained to strip a face of disguises and masks, comparing faces with the photographs the Plaza and other international hotels kept on file of notorious hotel con men who were bound to show up at their reception sooner or later. And it was him. The man she had checked in, only without glasses, but with eyebrows.

She stared at her mobile which she had left on her bedside table.

Attentive, but discreet. Puts the hotel's interests first. Could go far.

She pressed her eyes shut again.

Her mother had been right. That damn curiosity of hers.

From his office window, Arild Franck watched the officers from the night shift leave through the gate. He made a mental note of anyone who turned up late for the morning shift. It irritated him. People who couldn't do their job irritated him. Like Kripos and the Homicide Squad. The police had been given a tip-off to raid the Ila Centre and even so Lofthus had eluded them. It just wasn't good enough. And now they were having to pay the price for the police's ineptitude. Hugo Nestor had been killed last night. In a kennel. It was unbelievable that one man, a junkie, could cause so much mayhem. The law-abiding citizen in Franck was equally outraged by this repeated example of police incompetence; at times he even felt frustrated that the police had never managed to catch him, a corrupt assistant prison governor. He had seen the suspicion in Simon Kefas's eyes, but Kefas didn't have the guts to go after him, the big coward, he had too much to lose. Simon Kefas was only brave when there was money at stake. That bloody money. What had Franck expected? That it would buy him a bust, a reputation as a pillar of the community? And once he had become hooked on money, it was like heroin and the numbers in the bank account became the end rather than the means because there was no longer any meaningful goal. And just like the junkie, he knew and understood it, and yet he was incapable of doing anything about it.

'An officer called Sørensen is on his way to see you,' said his secretary in the front room.

'Don't let him—'

'He walked right past me, said it would only take a minute.'

'Really?' Franck frowned. Was Sørensen reporting fit for duty before his sick leave had ended? Out of character for a Norwegian worker. He heard the door behind him open.

'So, Sørensen,' Arild Franck said without turning round. 'Did you forget to knock?'

'Sit down.'

Franck heard the door being locked and he turned towards the voice in surprise. He stopped moving when he saw the gun.

'If you make a single sound, I'll shoot you right through your forehead.'

When you point a gun at someone, that person will usually focus all their attention on the gun and it will take time before they look at the person behind the gun. But when the boy lifted his foot and nudged the chair so that it rolled across the floor to the assistant prison governor, Franck saw who it was. The Son had returned.

'You've changed,' Franck said. He meant to say it with greater authority, but his throat was dry and no particular sound came out of it.

The gun rose slightly higher and Franck immediately dropped down on the chair.

'Put your arms on the armrests,' the boy said. 'I'm going to press the button on your intercom and you're going to tell Ina to go to the baker's to get some pastries. Now.'

The boy pressed the button.

'Yes?' They heard Ina's obliging voice.

'Ina . . .' Franck's brain searched desperately for alternatives.

'Yes?'

'Go . . .' Franck's search ended abruptly when he saw the boy's finger tighten on the trigger. '. . . down to the baker's and get me some fresh pastries, would you? Now.'

'OK.'

'Thank you, Ina.'

The boy released the trigger, put the gun down, took a roll of duct tape from his jacket pocket, walked round to Franck's chair and started taping his forearms to the armrests. Then he wound the tape around his chest and the backrest of the chair, and around his feet, the seat post and the castor. Then he picked up the gun again. A strange thought crossed Franck's mind: that he ought to be more frightened than he was. The boy had killed Agnete Iversen, Kalle, Sylvester, Hugo Nestor. Didn't he realise that he was going to die? Perhaps the difference was that he was here in his safe office at Staten and it was the middle of the day. That he had seen this boy grow up in his own prison and – except for that one incident with Halden – he'd never shown any propensity or ability to use violence.

The boy went through Franck's pockets and took out his wallet and car key.

'Porsche Cayenne,' the boy read aloud from the car key. 'That's an expensive car for a civil servant, isn't it?'

'What do you want?'

'I want answers to three simple questions. If you tell me the truth, I'll let you live. If you don't, I'm afraid I'm going to have to kill you.' He said it in an almost regretful tone of voice.

'The first question is, what's the name and number of the account Nestor sent money to when he paid you?'

Franck thought about it. No one knew about the account, he could say anything he liked, invent an account because no one could contradict it. Franck opened his mouth, but the boy interrupted him.

'If I were you I would think before speaking.'

Franck stared at the muzzle of the gun. What did he mean? No one could confirm or deny the account's existence. No one except Nestor had ever transferred money into it. Franck blinked. Had the boy forced the information out of Nestor before he killed him? Was this a test?

'The account is in the name of a company,' Franck said. 'Dennis Limited, registered in the Cayman Islands.'

'And the account number?' The boy held up something that looked like a yellowing business card. Had he noted down the number that Nestor had given him on it? But if the boy was bluffing, so what? He wouldn't be able to withdraw the money even if Franck did give him the account number. Franck started reeling off the digits.

'Slow down,' the boy said, looking at the business card. 'And speak more clearly.'

Franck did as he was told.

'Then only two questions remain,' the boy said when he had finished. 'Who killed my father? And who was the mole who helped the Twin?'

Arild Franck blinked. His body knew it. It knew it now and was pouring sweat out of every pore. It understood it was time to be scared. The boy had put the gun down again, but he had produced a knife instead. Hugo Nestor's revolting, curved, deadly weapon.

Franck screamed.

'Now I understand,' Simon said as he slipped his phone into his jacket pocket and steered out of the tunnel and into the light over Bjørvika and the Oslo Fjord.

'Understand what?' Kari said.

'One of the night receptionists at the Plaza just called the police to say that the man who's wanted for questioning spent a night in one of their suites. Under the name Fidel Lae. And that another man was found chained to the lavatory in the suite after some guests made a complaint about noise. This other man simply left as soon as they freed him. The hotel has also checked cameras at the entrance and they show Lofthus entering with Hugo Nestor and the man who was later found in the suite.'

'You still haven't told me what it is you understand.'

'Oh, right. How the three men in Enerhauggata knew we were coming for them. According to the night log at the hotel, the hand-cuffed man left the Plaza just as we were in place outside the trafficking address. He called and warned everyone that Nestor had been kidnapped and they started evacuating every exposed position in case Nestor gave them up. They knew what had happened to Kalle, didn't they? But just as they were about to drive off with the girls in the van, they realised we were already there. So they decided to wait for us to leave. Or for us to enter the house, so they could drive away unnoticed.'

'You've given this quite a lot of thought, haven't you?' Kari said. 'How they could have known that we were coming.'

'Possibly,' Simon said, turning off towards Police HQ. 'But now I've worked it out.'

'You know how it could have happened,' Kari corrected him. 'Are you going to tell me what you're thinking about now?'

Simon shrugged. 'That we have to get Lofthus before he wreaks more havoc.'

'Funny sort of guy,' Morgan Askøy said to his older colleague as they walked down the broad corridor. The cell doors were wide open, ready for morning inspection. 'Sørensen, his name was. He just came up to me.'

'Can't have been him,' his colleague said. 'There's only one Sørensen in A Wing and he's on sick leave.'

'Oh, it was him. I saw his ID card on his uniform.'

'But I spoke to Sørensen a couple of days ago – he'd just been readmitted to hospital.'

'So he made a quick recovery.'

'How odd. He was in uniform, you say? Can't have been Sørensen, he hates the uniform; he always gets changed here and keeps it in his locker. That's how Lofthus managed to steal it.'

'The inmate who escaped?'

'Yes. Are you enjoying your job, Askøy?'

'Yes.'

'Good. Make sure you take time off in lieu, don't be tempted to do too much overtime.'

They walked another six steps before they both stopped in their tracks and stared at each other. Saw each other's wide-open eyes.

'What did that guy look like?' his colleague exclaimed.

'What did Lofthus look like?' Morgan exclaimed.

Franck exhaled through his nose. His scream was muffled by the boy's hand pressing against his mouth. The boy kicked off his shoe, pulled off his sock and stuffed it into Franck's mouth and covered it with duct tape.

The boy cut away enough of the tape on the right armrest so that Franck's fingers could hold the pen he handed him and raise it to the sheet lying at the very edge of the desk.

'Answer me.'

Franck wrote.

Don't know.

Then he let go of the pen.

He heard the rasping sound of duct tape being torn in half, smelled the glue on the adhesive side before it was placed over his nostrils and cut off the air. Franck's body was out of his control, jerking and arching in the chair. Twisting and squirming. Dancing for that bloody boy! The pressure inside his head rose, soon it would explode. He had prepared to die when he saw the boy press the tip of the pen against the taut tape across his nostril.

He pierced it and Arild Franck's left nostril inhaled air while the first warm tears rolled down his cheek.

The boy gave him back the pen. Franck concentrated.

Have mercy. I would give you the mole's name if I knew it.

The boy read it. Closed his eyes and pulled a face as if in agony. He tore off another piece of tape.

The telephone on the desk started ringing. Franck stared at it hopefully. The office extension lit up on the display. It was Goldsrud, the shift supervisor. But the boy ignored it and focused entirely on reattaching the tape over Franck's nostrils. And Franck felt the shaking that accompanied his own panic. It almost made him wonder whether he was crying or laughing.

'There's no reply from the governor,' Geir Goldsrud said and hung up. 'And Ina isn't there, either – she picks up if he doesn't. But before we disturb the governor, let's run through this one more time. You're saying that the man you saw called himself

Sørensen and that he looked like him . . .' Goldsrud pointed to the TV monitor where he had brought up a picture of Sonny Lofthus.

'It doesn't *look* like him!' Morgan insisted. 'It *is* him, I keep telling you.'

'Relax,' his older colleague said.

'Easy for you to say,' Morgan snorted. 'The guy is only wanted for six murders.'

'I'll call Ina on her mobile and if she doesn't know where her boss is, we'll start our own search. But I don't want any panic, understood?'

Morgan looked at his colleague and back at the shift supervisor. It looked as if there was a shorter route to panic there than in Morgan himself. Personally, he just felt excited. Really excited. A prisoner, breaking into Staten, how was that even possible?

'Ina?' Goldsrud practically screamed into the phone and Morgan could see the relief in his face. It was tempting to accuse the shift supervisor of trying to avoid responsibility, but it must surely be hell to be middle management, reporting to the assistant prison governor. 'We need to get hold of Franck at once! Where is he?'

Morgan saw relief give way to bewilderment and then horror. Goldsrud ended the call.

'What . . . ?' the older colleague began.

'She says he has a visitor in his office,' Goldsrud said, getting up and going over to the gun cabinets at the far end of the room. 'A man called Sørensen.'

'So what do we do now?' Morgan asked.

Goldsrud stuck the key in the lock, turned it and opened the gun cabinet. 'This,' he said.

Morgan counted twelve rifles.

'Dan and Harald, you're coming with me!' Goldsrud shouted

and Morgan could no longer detect any trace of bewilderment, horror or fear of responsibility in his voice. 'Now!'

Simon and Kari were standing by the lift in the atrium at Police HQ when his mobile rang.

It was the Institute of Forensic Medicine.

'We have the preliminary DNA results from your toothbrushes.'

'Great,' Simon said. 'And the score at half-time is?'

'I'd rather call it thirty seconds before the whistle goes. Probability is over ninety-five per cent.'

'For what?' Simon said and saw the lift doors open.

'That we've found a partial match in our DNA database to the saliva from two of the toothbrushes. What's interesting about the match is that it isn't to a known criminal or a police officer, it's to a murder victim. More specifically, it proves that whoever used the toothbrushes is closely related to the victim.'

'I was expecting that,' Simon said, getting into the lift. 'The toothbrushes come from the Iversen family. I noticed they were missing in the Iversen bathroom after the murder. It's a partial DNA match to Agnete Iversen, isn't it?'

Kari looked quickly at Simon, who held up a hand in triumph.

'No,' replied the voice from the Institute of Forensic Medicine. 'We haven't actually got Agnete Iversen's DNA uploaded to our system yet.'

'Oh? Then how—'

'This is an unidentified murder victim.'

'You can prove a relationship between two of the toothbrushes and an unidentified murder victim? Unidentified as in?'

'As in unidentified. A very young and very dead female.'

'How young?' Simon asked and stared at the lift doors which were starting to close.

'Younger than we usually get them.'

'Come again?'

'A four-month-old foetus.'

Simon's brain tried to process the information to the best of its ability. 'Agnete Iversen had a late abortion, is that it?'

'No.'

'It isn't? Then who is— Damn!' Simon closed his eyes and pressed his forehead against the lift wall.

'You got cut off?' Kari asked.

Simon nodded.

'We'll be out of this lift in a second,' she said.

The boy punctured the tape twice. Once under each nostril. And Arild Franck sucked new seconds of life into his lungs. All he wanted to do was to live. And it was the only instinct his body obeyed.

'So, do you want to give me a name?' the boy asked in a low voice.

Franck breathed hard; he wished he had broader nostrils, wider nasal passages for this sweet, delicious air. He listened out for sounds that would tell him help was on its way, his rescue, while he shook his head, trying to indicate with his dry tongue behind the sock, the lips behind the tape, that he didn't have a name, didn't know who the mole was, that he was pleading for mercy. To go free. To be forgiven.

And he froze when he saw the boy stop in front of him and raise the knife. Franck couldn't move, every limb was taped down. Everything . . . The knife came down. Nestor's hideous, curved knife. Franck's head strained against the headrest, every muscle tensed up and he screamed silently when he saw the blood spurt from his body.

32

'TWO,' GOLDSRUD WHISPERED.

The men stood with their weapons at the ready, listening to the silence behind the door to the assistant prison governor's office.

Morgan exhaled. Now, it was about to happen now. This was the moment where he might finally get to take part in something he had dreamt about ever since he was a little boy. He would catch someone. Perhaps even . . .

'Three,' Goldsrud whispered.

Then he swung the sledgehammer. It hit the lock on the door and splinters flew from the frame as Harald, the tallest of them, forced his way through the door. Morgan entered with a rifle held at chest height and took two steps to the left like Goldsrud had instructed him to. There was only one person in the room. Morgan stared at the man in the chair with blood on his chest, his throat and his chin. Christ, there was so much blood! Morgan felt his knees weakening as if some kind of drug had been injected into them. He mustn't! But there was so much blood! And the man in the chair was shaking, convulsing as if he were being electrocuted. And his eyes stared at them, frantic, bulging as if he were a deep-sea fish.

Goldsrud took two steps forward and ripped the tape off the man's mouth.

'Where are you hurt, boss?'

The man opened his mouth wide, but no sound came out. Goldsrud stuck in two fingers and pulled out a black sock. Saliva poured from the man's mouth and Morgan recognised the voice of assistant prison governor Arild Franck as he screamed: 'Go after him! Don't let him get away!'

'We need to find out where he's injured and stop the—' Goldsrud was about to rip open his boss's shirt, but Franck yelled: 'Lock the bloody doors, he's going to get away! He has my car key! And my uniform cap!'

'Calm down, boss,' Goldsrud said as he cut the tape off one armrest. 'He's trapped; he won't get past the fingerprint sensors.'

Franck glared at him furiously and held up his now free hand. 'Oh yes, he will!'

Morgan stumbled backwards and had to lean against the wall for support. He tried, but failed to avert his eyes from the blood pouring from the place where the assistant prison governor Arild Franck should have had a forefinger.

Kari followed Simon out of the lift and down the corridor to the open-plan office.

'So,' she said, trying to digest the information. 'Three tooth-brushes were sent to you by post with a note from someone called "S" who said they ought to be checked for DNA?'

'Yes,' Simon said as he pressed the buttons on his phone.

'And two of the toothbrushes had DNA material that proves a family relationship to an unborn child? An unborn child who is registered as a murder victim?'

Simon nodded while holding a finger to his lips to indicate that he had re-established the connection. When he spoke, it was in a loud and clear voice and he had set the phone to loudspeaker mode.

'It's Kefas again. Who was the child, how did it die, and what was the family relationship?'

He held up his mobile between them so Kari could listen in.

'We don't know who the mother or the baby was, all we know is that the mother died – or was killed – by an overdose in the centre of Oslo. In the register she's just down as "unidentified".'

'We know about the case,' Simon said, swearing silently to himself. 'Asian, probably Vietnamese. And probably a victim of trafficking.'

'That's your department, Kefas. The baby, or the foetus, died because its mother died.'

'I understand. And who is the father?'

'The red toothbrush.'

'The . . . red one?'

'Yes.'

'Thank you,' Simon said and ended the call.

Kari went over to the coffee machine to fetch coffee for them both. When she came back, Simon was on another call which she guessed from his soft voice to be with Else. When he hung up, he had on this expression which some people over a certain age suddenly display for a few seconds, as if something has passed them by, as if they have the potential to crumble into dust on the spot. Kari had been about to ask how things were, but decided to let it lie.

'So . . .' Simon said, trying to sound cheerful. 'Who do we think is the daddy? Iver Senior or Junior?'

'We don't think,' Kari said. 'We know.'

Simon looked at her for a moment in surprise. Saw her slowly shake her head. Then he narrowed his eyes, bowed his head and ran his hand across it as if to smooth what little hair he had left.

'Of course,' he said quietly. 'Two toothbrushes. I must be getting old.'

'I'll go check to see what we have on Iver,' Kari said.

When she had gone, Simon turned on his computer and opened his mailbox.

Someone had sent him a sound file. Sent it from a mobile, it would appear.

No one ever sent him sound files.

He opened the file and pressed *play*.

Morgan looked at the incandescent assistant prison governor who was standing in the middle of the control room. He had wrapped gauze around the stump on his hand, but had dismissed the medical orderly's urgent requests to lie down.

'So you raised the barrier and just let the killer drive straight out?!' Franck thundered.

'He was driving your car,' the guard said, wiping sweat off his forehead. 'He was wearing your uniform cap.'

'But it wasn't me!' Franck roared.

Morgan didn't know if it was because Franck had high blood pressure, but the red, nauseating substance was seeping through the white gauze and Morgan was starting to feel faint again.

One of the telephones next to the monitors rang. Goldsrud picked it up and listened.

'They've found the finger,' he said, covering the mouthpiece with his hand. 'We'll drive you up to Ullevål Hospital for surgery, so they can—'

'Where?' Franck interrupted him. 'Where did they find it?'

'In plain sight on the dashboard of your Porsche. It was double-parked down in Grønland.'

'Find him! Find him!'

Tor Jonasson hung from the strap attached to the bar in the metro train. Mumbled an apology as he bumped into one of the other

346

sleepy morning commuters. He had to sell five mobile phones today. That was his target. And when he stood – or hopefully sat – on the train later this afternoon, he would know if he had succeeded. And that would bring him . . . happiness. Maybe.

Tor sighed.

He looked at the uniformed man standing with his back to him. Music was coming from the earphones he was wearing. The cable went to his hand which was holding a mobile that bore the tiny label of the shop where Tor worked on the back. Tor changed position so that he could study the man in profile. Tried to get a good look at him. Wasn't he the guy who wanted to buy batteries for that museum piece? The Discman. Tor had been intrigued enough to look it up on the Net. They had made Discmans up until 2000, when a Walkman that was compatible with MP3 had been invented. Tor stood so close behind him that he could hear the sound from the earphones over the carriage's rattling steel wheels, but it disappeared when the train went round a bend and the carriage creaked.

It had sounded like a lone female voice. But he had recognised the tune:

'*That you've always been her lover* . . .' Leonard Cohen.

Simon stared at the sound file icon in disbelief. It had taken him only a few seconds to play it. He pressed *play* again.

There was no doubt, it was the voice he had initially thought it was. But he didn't understand what it was about.

'What are you doing? Picking your lottery numbers?'

Simon turned round. Sissel Thou was doing her morning round and emptying the waste-paper bins.

'Something like that,' Simon said and pressed the *stop* button while she grabbed the bin from under his desk and tipped it into the trolley.

'You're throwing your money away, Simon, the lottery is for the lucky ones.'

'And you don't think that's us?' Simon said as he stared at the computer screen.

'Look at the world we've created,' she said.

Simon leaned back in his chair and rubbed his eyes. 'Sissel?'

'Yes?'

'A young woman was murdered and now it turns out she was pregnant. But I don't think the killer was scared of her, I think he was scared of her baby.'

'Uh-huh.'

Silence.

'Is that a question, Simon?'

Simon leaned his head against the neck rest. 'If you knew you were carrying the devil's son, would you still give birth to him, Sissel?'

'We've had this conversation before, Simon.'

'I know, but what did you say?'

She gave him a reproachful look. 'I said that nature sadly doesn't give the poor mother any choice, Simon. Or the father, for that matter.'

'I thought Mr Thou abandoned you?'

'I'm talking about you, Simon.'

Simon closed his eyes again. He nodded slowly. 'So we're slaves to love. And who we're given to love, that's a lottery too. Is that what you're saying?'

'It's brutal, but that's how it is,' Sissel declared.

'And the gods laugh,' Simon said.

'Probably, but meanwhile someone has to clear up the mess down here.'

Simon heard her footsteps fade away. Then he forwarded the sound file from his computer to his mobile, went to the Gents, entered one of the cubicles and played the recording again.

After playing it twice he finally understood what the numbers meant.

PART FOUR

33

SIMON AND KARI WALKED THROUGH the sunshine across the slightly too big, slightly too exposed, and slightly too summer-quiet Rådhusplassen.

'Fidel Lae's description helped us find the rental car,' Kari said. 'It had been returned, but fortunately it hadn't been cleaned yet. Forensics found mud stains that match the mud on the track leading to the dog kennel. And here was I thinking mud was just mud.'

'Every type has its own unique blend of minerals,' Simon said. 'Rented under what name?'

'Sylvester Trondsen.'

'Who's he?'

'A thirty-three-year-old man on unemployment benefit. Couldn't find him at his registered address. He has two convictions for assault. Our officers linked him to Nestor.'

'OK.' Simon stopped in front of an entrance between two boutiques. The door was tall and wide and signalled solidity and gravity. He pressed one of the buttons for the third floor. 'Anything else?'

'One of the residents at the Ila Centre told officers that it looked as if the new guy in room 323 and the deputy manager were getting along well.'

'Martha Lian?'

'They were seen leaving the centre in a car the other day.'

'Iversen Property,' said a voice through the holes in the brass plate over the doorbells.

'I want you to wait in reception while I talk to Iversen,' Simon said as they rode up in the lift.

'Why?'

'Because I might break a few rules and I would prefer not to drag you into it.'

'But—'

'I'm sorry, but that was actually an order, just so you know.'

Kari rolled her eyes, but said nothing.

'Iver,' the young man introduced himself as he came to meet them in reception. He shook hands firmly first with Simon, then with Kari. 'You're here to see my father.'

Something about the boy told Simon that he would normally be smiling and easy-going, that he didn't have experience of the pain and grief which Simon could read in the eyes under the floppy fringe. He guessed that was why the boy seemed so lost and confused.

'This way.' His father must have told him they were police officers and presumed, as did the father, that their visit related to the investigation into his mother's murder.

The office had views of Vestbanen and Oslo Fjord. Next to the door was a glass display cabinet with a detailed model of a skyscraper shaped like a Coca-Cola bottle.

The father looked like an older replica of the son. Same heavy fringe, smooth, healthy skin, a sunny but subdued gaze in his eyes. Tall, with good posture, firm chin, a man who looked you straight in the eye, friendly, but with a boyish, playful challenge. There was something assured, West Oslo-solid about these types, Simon thought, as if they had all been cast in the same mould; resistance fighters, polar explorers, the crew of the *Kon-Tiki*, police commissioners.

Iver Senior asked Simon to take a seat and sat down himself behind a desk below an old black-and-white photo of an apartment block, which was definitely Oslo at the turn of the nineteenth century, but which Simon couldn't momentarily place.

Simon waited until Iver Junior had left the office and then he came straight to the point.

'Twelve years ago a girl was found dead in a backyard in Kvadraturen in Oslo. This is what she looked like when she was found.'

Simon put the photo on Iversen's desk and watched the property investor's face carefully when he saw the picture. Not much of a reaction.

'A boy by the name of Sonny Lofthus confessed to the killing,' Simon said.

'I see.' Still no reaction.

'The girl was pregnant when she was found.'

Now there was a reaction. Flared nostrils, expanding pupils.

Simon waited a couple of seconds before launching the second stage of the attack.

'DNA evidence from toothbrushes in your home proves that someone in your household was the father of the unborn baby.'

A thickening of the artery in his neck, a change in facial colour, uncontrolled blinking.

'The red toothbrush is yours, Iversen, isn't it?'

'How . . . how did you . . . ?'

Simon smiled quickly and looked down at his hands. 'I, too, have a junior, she's waiting in reception. Only her brain is a bit quicker than mine. She was the first to draw the simple, logical conclusion that when the DNA on only two of three toothbrushes in the Iversen family shows a family relationship to the foetus, then the son in the house can't be the father. Then all three members of the family would be related to the foetus. So it had to be the only other male. You.'

Iver Iversen's healthy skin colour paled before disappearing altogether.

'You'll probably find the same thing happening to you when you get to be as old as me,' Simon said to comfort him. 'Their minds are so much quicker than ours, these youngsters.'

'But . . .'

'That's the thing about DNA. It doesn't leave much room for buts . . .'

Iversen opened his mouth while at the same time routinely forcing it into a half-smile. It was at this point in an awkward conversation that he would obviously normally provide what was known as comic relief, a disarming remark. Yes, that was it, something that made it feel less dangerous. But nothing came. There was nothing there.

'Now this old slowcoach . . .' in front of him Simon tapped his forehead with his finger, '. . . takes a little longer, but gets a little further. And the first thing he thought is that a married man like you has the most obvious motive in the world for getting rid of a pregnant and potentially troublesome woman. Wouldn't you agree?'

Iversen made no reply, but felt his Adam's apple reply on his behalf.

'The police released a photo of the woman to the newspapers asking if anyone knew her identity. And when her lover and the father of her child stayed as silent as the grave, didn't even provide the police with an anonymous tip-off, that makes it extra suspicious. Wouldn't you agree?'

'I didn't know . . .' he began, but stopped. Already regretting it. And then regretted having made it so plain that he regretted it.

'You didn't know that she was pregnant?' the police officer asked.

'No!' Iversen said, folding his arms across his chest. 'I mean, I knew . . . I know nothing about this. I'd like to call my lawyer now.'

'You clearly know something. But actually I believe you when you say you don't know everything. I think your wife, Agnete, was the one who knew everything. What do you think?'

Kefas. Chief Inspector, wasn't that how he had introduced himself? Iver Iversen reached for the telephone.

'What I think is that you have no proof and that this meeting is over, Mr Kefas.'

'You're right about the former, but wrong about the latter. This meeting isn't over because you ought to know what bridges you'll be burning by picking up that phone, Iversen. The police have no evidence against your wife, but the man who shot her clearly does.'

'And how is that possible?'

'Because he has been a scapegoat and father confessor for criminals in this town for twelve years. He knows everything.' Kefas leaned forward in his chair and jabbed the desk with his finger with every word. 'He knows that Kalle Farrisen killed the girl and that Agnete Iversen paid him to do it. He knows this because he went to prison for the murder. The fact that he hasn't come after you yet is the only reason I believe you might be innocent. Go ahead, pick up the phone and we'll play this by the book. That is to say, arrest you as an accessory to murder, tell the media everything we know about you and the girl, explain to your business associates that you'll be away for a while, tell your son that . . . well, what do you want us to tell your son?'

What to tell his son. Simon waited. Let it sink in. It was important for what was coming next. Let it take root. Give Iversen time to understand the magnitude, the consequences. Open himself up to alternatives which just two minutes ago would have been completely out of the question. Like Simon himself had had to do. And it had driven him here, to this.

Simon saw Iversen's hand flop and heard a wobbly, croaky voice: 'What do you want?'

Simon straightened up in the chair. 'You tell me everything now. If I believe you, then it's possible that not very much needs to happen. After all, Agnete has already been punished.'

'Punished?!' The widower's eyes blazed, but the fire was extinguished when it met Simon's icy stare.

'Fine. Agnete and I, we . . . didn't have much of a marriage. Not in that way. An associate had some girls. Asian. That's how I met Mai. She . . . had something, something I needed. Not youth or innocence and all that, but a . . . loneliness in which I recognised myself.'

'She was a prisoner, Iversen. She had been abducted from her home and her family.'

The property investor shrugged. 'I know, but I paid for her freedom. I gave her a flat where we met. It was just her and me. Then one day she told me she hadn't had her period for months. That she might be pregnant. I said she had to get rid of it, but she refused. I didn't know what to do. So I asked Agnete . . .'

'You asked your wife?'

Iversen held up a dismissive hand. 'Yes, of course. Agnete was a grown-up. She didn't mind others taking over duties she would rather not undertake herself. To be frank, I think she preferred women to men.'

'But she gave you a son?'

'They take their duties very seriously in her family and she was a good mother.'

'A family that is also the biggest private property owner in Oslo, with a perfect image and a family name so untarnished that an Asian bastard would quite simply be unthinkable.'

'Yes, Agnete was old-fashioned. And I went to her because ultimately she was in charge.'

'Because this company is built on her money,' Simon said. 'So Agnete decided to get rid of the problem. All of the problem.'

'I wouldn't know anything about that,' Iversen said.

'No, because you didn't ask. You left it to her to contact people who could do the job for you. And they in turn had to buy themselves a scapegoat when a witness told the police that they had seen someone inject the girl in that backyard. The tracks had to be covered and you paid.'

Iversen shrugged again. 'I haven't killed anyone, I'm just keeping my end of our deal by telling you what happened. The question is, are you going to keep yours?'

'The question,' Simon said, 'is how a woman like your wife found a piece of lowlife like Kalle Farrisen.'

'I've never heard of Kalle Farrisen.'

'No,' Simon said, folding his hands in front of him. 'But you know who the Twin is.'

A moment of perfect silence descended on the room. It was as if even the traffic outside held its breath.

'I beg your pardon?' Iversen said at last.

'I worked for the Serious Fraud Office for many years,' Simon said. 'Iversen Property did business with the Twin. You helped him launder money from his drugs and trafficking activities and in return he provided you with fictitious, tax-saving losses to the tune of hundreds of millions of kroner.'

Iver Iversen shook his head. 'I'm afraid I know nothing about any Twin.'

'Apart from you being afraid, that's a lie,' Simon said. 'I have evidence that the two of you worked together.'

'Do you now?' Iversen said and pressed his fingertips together. 'Then why didn't the Serious Fraud Office ever bring a case against me?'

'Because when I worked for the Serious Fraud Office I was leaned

357

on from the inside,' Simon said. 'But I know that the Twin used his blood money to buy commercial property from you and sell it back to you later at a much higher price. Or at least that's what the paperwork said. He would appear to have made a profit which allowed him to deposit his drugs money in the bank without the tax authorities asking questions about how he came by it. And it provided you with an apparent loss which you could offset against future profits and thus avoid contributing to society. A win–win situation.'

'An interesting theory,' Iversen said, shrugging. 'I've told you everything I know. Is there anything else?'

'Yes. I want to meet the Twin.'

Iversen heaved a sigh. 'I've just told you I don't know any Twin.'

Simon seemed to nod quietly to himself. 'Do you know something? We heard that so often at the Serious Fraud Squad that people started doubting if the Twin even existed, they thought he was just a myth.'

'It sounds to me as if he might just be that, Kefas.'

Simon rose. 'It's all good with me. But myths don't control the drugs and sex trafficking market in an entire city, year in, year out, Iversen. Myths don't liquidate pregnant women at the request of their business partners.' He leaned forward, planted both palms on the desk and exhaled so that Iversen got a taste of his old man's breath. 'Men don't get so terrified that they're willing to dive off a cliff because of a myth. I know he exists.'

Simon pushed himself up to standing and headed for the door while he waved his mobile phone. 'I'm calling a press conference the moment I get into the lift, so perhaps now is a good time for that father–son chat.'

'Wait!'

Simon stopped in front of the door without turning round.

'I'll . . . I'll see what I can do.'

Simon took out his card and put it on top of the glass display cabinet with the Coca-Cola skyscraper.

'You and he have until six o'clock.'

'Inside Staten?' Simon repeated as they went down in the lift. 'Lofthus attacked Franck in his own office?'

Kari nodded. 'That's all I know for now. What did Iversen say?'

Simon shrugged. 'Nothing. Not surprisingly, he insisted on speaking to his lawyer first. We'll have to talk to him tomorrow.'

Arild Franck sat on the edge of the bed waiting to be taken into surgery. He was dressed in one of the hospital's pale blue gowns and had an ID bracelet around his wrist. He had felt no pain for the first hour, but it was starting to hurt now and that measly little injection the anaesthetist had given him was doing no good at all. He had been promised a proper injection which they claimed would numb his entire arm right before the operation. A surgeon special-ising in hands had stopped by and told him in detail what micro-surgery was capable of these days, that the severed finger had arrived at the hospital, that the cut was nice and clean, and that once the finger was reunited with its rightful owner, the nerves would surely reattach so he would be able to use his finger for both 'this and that' in a few months. His attempt at humour was probably well intended, but Franck wasn't in a joking mood. So he had interrupted the surgeon and asked how long he would need to reattach the finger and when he could return to work. And when the surgeon had said that the operation itself would take several hours, Franck had – to the surgeon's amazement – looked at the clock and sworn softly, but audibly.

The door opened and Franck lifted his head. He hoped it was the anaesthetist because it wasn't just his finger that was throbbing furiously now, it was his head and all of his body.

But it wasn't anyone in white or green, it was a tall, slim man in a grey suit.

'Pontius?' Franck said.

'Hello, Arild. I just wanted to see how you were doing.'

Franck narrowed one eye. As if it made it easier for him to work out the real reason for the Commissioner's visit. Parr sat down on the bed beside him. Nodded towards his bandaged hand.

'Does it hurt?'

'It'll be fine. Tell me you're looking for him?'

The Commissioner shrugged. 'Lofthus has vanished into thin air. But we'll find him. Have you any idea what he wanted?'

'Wanted?' Franck snorted. 'Who knows what he wants? He's clearly on some sort of deranged crusade here.'

'Quite,' Parr said. 'So the real question is when and where he will strike next. Did he give you any indication?'

'Indication?' Franck groaned and bent his elbow gently. 'Like what?'

'You must have talked about something.'

'He talked. I was gagged. He wanted to know who the mole was.'

'Yes, I saw.'

'You *saw?*'

'From the papers in your office. Or at least those that weren't covered in blood.'

'*You* were in my office?'

'This is a top-priority case, Arild. The man is a serial killer. It's bad enough that the press is after us, but now the politicians are starting to interfere as well. From now on I'm going to be hands-on.'

Franck shrugged his shoulders. 'OK.'

'I have a question—'

'I'm about to go into surgery and it hurts like hell, Pontius. Can't it wait?'

360

'No. Sonny Lofthus was interviewed in connection with the murder of Kjersti Morsand, but denied any involvement. Did anyone tell him that her husband was our prime suspect before we found Lofthus's hair at the crime scene? Or that we had evidence to suggest Yngve Morsand killed her?'

'How would I know? What do you mean?'

'Oh, I was just wondering.' Parr put his hand on Franck's shoulder and Franck felt the pain shoot down to his hand. 'You just concentrate on your surgery.'

'Thank you, but there isn't really a lot to think about.'

'No,' Parr said, taking off his rectangular glasses. 'I don't suppose there is.' He started polishing them with an absent-minded expression. 'All you do is lie there while someone else does all the work.'

'Yes,' Franck said.

'While someone else puts you back together. Makes you whole again.'

Franck gulped.

'So,' Parr said, putting his glasses back on. 'Did you tell him who the mole was?'

'You mean, did I tell him it was his own father? *Ab Lofthus, he confessed.* If I had written that down on a piece of paper, that boy would have cut off my head.'

'What did you tell him, Arild?'

'Nothing! What could I have told him?'

'That's exactly what I've been wondering. I've been wondering what made the boy so sure that you had information that he was willing to break into your prison to get hold of it.'

'The boy's insane, Pontius. Sooner or later every drug addict turns psychotic, you know that. The mole? Dear God, that story disappeared along with Ab Lofthus.'

'So what did you tell him?'

'What do you mean?'

'He only severed one of your fingers. Everyone else was killed. You were spared, you must have given him something. Don't forget I know you, Arild.'

The door opened and two smiling hospital workers dressed in green entered. 'Ready to roll?' one of them smiled.

Parr straightened his glasses. 'You haven't got the guts, Arild.'

Simon walked down the street, bowing his head against the sea air that was sweeping in from the fjord, passing over Aker Brygge and Munkedamsveien before it was narrowed by the buildings and then accelerated up Ruseløkkveien. He stopped outside the church which had been squeezed in between two apartment blocks. St Paul's Church was more modest than its namesakes in other capitals. A Catholic Church in a Protestant country. It was facing the wrong way, westerly, and had just a hint of a church tower at the front. Only three steps led to the entrance. But it was always open. He knew that because he had been here before, late one evening in the middle of a crisis, and had hesitated before walking up those three steps. It had been right after he had lost everything, before he had found his salvation in Else.

Simon climbed the steps, pushed down the copper handle, opened the heavy door and entered. He wanted to close the door quickly behind him, but the stiff springs resisted. Had they been just as stiff that time? He didn't remember, he had been too drunk. He let go of the door which shut behind him, one centimetre at a time. But he remembered the smell. Foreign. Exotic. An atmosphere of spirituality. Magic and mysticism, fortune-teller and travelling circus. Else liked Catholicism, not so much the ethics as the aesthetics, and had explained to him how everything in the church building, even the most basic elements such as bricks, mortar and stained-glass windows, was endowed with a religious symbolism that bordered on the comical. And yet this simple symbolism possessed a gravitas, a subtext, a historical context and the faith of so many thinking people that it was impossible to dismiss. The narrow, white-washed and plainly decorated room containing rows of pews that led up to a single altar with Jesus hanging on the cross. A symbol of victory in defeat. Up against the wall on the left-hand side, halfway towards the altar, was the confessional box. It had two compartments, one had a black curtain in front of the opening, like a photo booth. When he came here that night, he hadn't known which of the two cubicles was intended for the confessing sinner before his alcohol-clouded brain had deduced that if the priest shouldn't be able to see the sinners, the priest must be in the photo booth. So he had staggered inside the curtainless cubicle and started talking to the perforated wooden board separating them. Confessed his sins. In an unnecessarily loud voice. Simultaneously hoping and dreading that there was someone on the other side, or that someone, anyone, would hear him and do the necessary. Offer him forgiveness. Or condemn him. Anything but this suffocating vacuum where he was alone with himself and his mistakes. Nothing had happened. And the next morning he had woken up without the usual headache – which was strange – and realised that life would continue as if nothing had happened, that ultimately no one cared. It was the last time he had set foot inside a church.

Martha Lian was standing near the altar with a brusquely gesticu-lating woman in an elegant suit and the type of short hairstyle which some older women think makes them look younger. The woman was pointing and explaining, and Simon caught words such as 'flowers', 'ceremony', 'Anders' and 'guests'. He had almost reached them when Martha Lian turned to face him. The first thing that struck him was how different she looked since the last time. How empty. Alone. And how miserable.

'Hi,' she said in a dull voice.

The other woman stopped talking.

'I'm sorry for intruding,' Simon said. 'At the Ila Centre, they said I would find you here. I hope I'm not interrupting something important.'

'Oh no, it's—'

'Yes, we're actually planning my son and Martha's wedding right now. So if it could wait, Mr . . . ?'

'Kefas,' Simon said. 'And, no, it can't wait. I'm a police officer.'

The woman looked at Martha with raised eyebrows. 'That's exactly what I mean when I say that you're living in a world that's all too real, darling.'

'Which you'll be spared from having to take part in, Mrs . . . ?'

'I beg your pardon?'

'Miss Lian and I will discuss this in private. Duty of confidentiality, and all that.'

The woman marched off on hard heels, and Simon and Martha sat down on the front pew.

'You were seen driving off in a car with Sonny Lofthus,' Simon said. 'Why didn't you tell me?'

'He wanted to learn to drive,' Martha said. 'I took him to a car park where we could practise.'

'He's wanted all over Norway now.'

'I saw it on TV.'

'Did he say or did you see him do anything that could suggest where he might be now? And I want you to think about this very carefully before you reply.'

Martha looked as if she thought very carefully indeed before she shook her head.

'No? Anything about his plans for the future?'

'He wanted to learn to drive.'

Simon sighed and smoothed his hair. 'You understand that you risk being charged as an accessory if you help him or hide information from us?'

'Why would I do that?'

Simon looked at her without saying anything. She was getting married shortly. So why did she look so unhappy?

'OK, OK,' he said and got up.

She stayed where she was and looked down at her lap.

'Just one thing,' she said.

'Yes?'

'Do you think he's the crazed killer everyone says he is?'

Simon shifted his weight from one foot to the other. 'No,' he said.

'No?'

'He's not crazy. He's punishing people. He's on a kind of vendetta.'

'What is he trying to avenge?'

'I think it's about his father who was a police officer; after he died, people said he was corrupt.'

'You say he punishes people . . .' She lowered her voice. 'Does he punish justly?'

Simon shrugged. 'I don't know. But he makes allowances.'

'Allowances?'

'He confronted the assistant prison governor in his office. That was audacious and it would have been much easier for him and a lot less risky if he had sought Franck out at his home.'

'But?'

'But it would have brought Franck's wife and child into the firing line.'

'Innocent bystanders. He doesn't want the innocent to get hurt.'

Simon nodded slowly. He saw something happen in her eyes. A spark. A hope. Was it really that simple? Was she in love? Simon straightened his back. Looked up at the altarpiece which showed the Saviour on the cross. Closed his eyes. Opened them again. To hell with it. To hell with it all.

'Do you know what his father, Ab, used to say?' he said, hoisting up his trousers. 'He said that the age of mercy is over and that the day of judgement has arrived. But as the Messiah is running late, we have to do his job for him. He alone can punish them, Martha. Oslo Police is corrupt, they're protecting the crooks. I think Sonny is doing this because he feels he owes it to his father, that this is what his father died for. Justice. The kind of justice which is above the law.'

He watched the older woman by the confessional box where she was discussing something with a priest in a low voice.

'And what about you?' Martha said.

'Me? I am the law. So I have to catch Sonny. That's just the way it is.'

'And that woman, Agnete Iversen, what crime did she commit?'

'I can't tell you anything about her.'

'I read that her jewellery was stolen.'

'Did you?'

'Did that include a pair of pearl earrings?'

'I don't know. Is it important?'

She shook her head. 'No,' she said. 'It isn't. I was trying to think of anything that might help you.'

'Thank you,' Simon said and buttoned his jacket. The hard heels were approaching. 'You have other things on your mind, I can see.'

Martha quickly glanced up at him.

'I'll talk to you later, Martha.'

As Simon left the church, his mobile rang. He looked at the display. The area code told him the call was coming from Drammen.

'Kefas.'

'It's Henrik Westad.'

The police officer who was investigating the murder of the shipping owner's wife.

'I'm at the Cardiology Unit at Buskerud Central Hospital.'

Simon could guess what was coming next.

'Leif Krognæss, our witness with heart trouble. They thought he was out of danger, but . . .'

'He died suddenly,' Simon said, sighed and pinched the bridge of his nose with his thumb and forefinger. 'He was alone in the ward when it happened. The post-mortem won't find any abnormalities. And you're calling me because you don't want to be the only one who can't sleep tonight.'

Westad didn't reply.

Simon put the mobile in his pocket. The wind was rising and he looked up at the sky above the roofs. He couldn't see it yet, but he could tell from his headache. A low pressure system was heading his way.

The motorbike in front of Rover was about to rise from the dead. It was a Harley-Davidson Heritage Softail, the 1989 model, with a huge front wheel, Rover's favourite. When he got it, it had been a dilapidated 1340cc wreck whose owner had treated it without the love, patience and understanding which an HD – in contrast to its more pliable Japanese cousins – demanded. Rover had replaced the crank bearing, the big-end bearing, the piston rings and reseated the valves, and very little of the original was left as the bike was transformed into a 1700cc with 119 b.h.p. to the rear wheel, which used to have only 43. Rover was wiping oil off the forearm with a tattoo of a cathedral when he noticed a change in the light. His first thought was that it was clouding over like the weather forecast had promised. But when he looked up, he noticed a shadow and a silhouette in the doorway to his workshop.

'Yes?' Rover called out and continued to rub oil off his arm.

The man started walking towards him. Silently. Like a predator. Rover knew that the nearest weapon was too far away for him to be able to reach it in time. And that was how it should be. He was done with that way of life. It was bullshit when people said it was hard not to fall back into your bad old ways once you were out of prison; it was just a question of willpower. It was that simple. If you wanted to, you could do it. But if your intention was merely an illusion, wishful thinking, just something to dress yourself up in, then you would be back in the gutter on day two.

The man was now so close that Rover could make out his facial features. But surely that was . . .

'Hello, Rover.'

It was him.

He held up a yellowing business card saying 'Rover's Motorcycle Workshop'.

'The address was right. You said you could get me an Uzi.'

Rover was now wiping his hands while he stared at him. He had read the newspapers. Seen the picture on TV. But what he was staring at now wasn't the boy from the cell at Staten, it was his own future. The future as he had imagined it.

'You took out Nestor,' Rover said, pulling the rag between his fingers.

The boy made no reply.

Rover shook his head. 'That means it's not just the police who are looking for you, but the Twin as well.'

'I know I'm trouble,' the boy said. 'I'll leave immediately if that's what you want.'

Forgiveness. Hope. A clean break. A second chance. Most people blew it, they continued making the same stupid mistakes their whole lives, they could always find an excuse to screw things up. They didn't know it themselves, or they pretended not to, but they had lost before they had even started. Because they didn't really want to succeed. But Rover wanted to. It wasn't that that was going to bring him down. He was stronger now. Wiser. But that said: if you're going to walk with your head held high, there's always a chance of falling flat on your face.

'Why don't we close the garage door?' Rover said. 'It looks like rain.'

34

THE RAIN WAS LASHING THE windscreen when Simon took the key out of the ignition and prepared to sprint from the car park to the hospital building. He spotted a blond figure in a coat right in front of his car. It was raining so hard that the raindrops bounced off the bonnet and the man's outline was blurred. The door to the driver's side was opened and another, dark-haired man asked him to come with them. Simon looked at the clock on the dashboard. 4 p.m. It was two hours before the deadline.

The two men drove him to Aker Brygge, a seafront development with shops, offices, some of the city's most expensive flats and around fifty cafes and bars. They walked along the promenade by the water and saw the ferry from Nesoddtangen dock as they turned into one of the many alleyways; they carried on walking until they reached a small iron staircase that led down to a door with a porthole that presumably evoked associations with seafood. Next to the door was a small sign saying 'Nautilus Restaurant' in unusually discreet letters. One of the men held the door open and they entered a narrow hallway where they shook the rain off their coats and hung them up in the unmanned cloakroom. There wasn't a soul to be seen and the first thought that crossed Simon's mind was that this was a perfect location for money laundering. Not too big, but with a rent and a position that made profitability plausible, but whose profits would never be questioned, as profits on which taxes are paid rarely are.

Simon was wet. When he wiggled his toes inside his shoes, they made tiny squelching sounds. But that wasn't the real reason he was cold.

The dining room was divided in half by a large, rectangular aquarium which also supplied the only source of illumination. At the table in front of it and with his back to the aquarium sat a huge figure.

He was the reason Simon was cold.

He had never seen him in the flesh before, but he didn't doubt for a second who it was.

The Twin.

The man seemed to fill the entire room. Simon didn't know if this was simply due to his physical size and obvious presence or the trappings of power and wealth, of this man's ability to control so many destinies. Or whether all the legends that surrounded his persona made him even bigger: the baggage of death, meaningless cruelty and destruction.

The man made an almost imperceptible gesture towards the chair which had been pulled out in front of him. Simon sat down.

'Simon Kefas,' the man said, stroking his chin with his forefinger.

Large men often had surprisingly high-pitched voices.

Not the Twin.

The rumbling bass of his voice raised ripples in the glass of water in front of Simon.

'I know what you want, Kefas.' The muscles swelled under the suit which looked as if it might burst at the seams at any moment.

370

'And what's that?'

'Money for Else's eye operation.'

Simon gulped at the sound of the name of his beloved in this man's mouth.

'The question is, what have you got to sell, yes?'

Simon took out his mobile, opened the mailbox, put the phone on the table and pressed *play*. The voice on the sound file he had received sounded tinny: '. . . what's the name and number of the account Nestor sent money to when he paid you? If I were you I would think before speaking.' A pause, then another voice: 'The account is in the name of a company. Dennis Limited, registered in the Cayman Islands.' 'And the account number?' Another pause. 'Eight, three, zero.' 'Slow down. And speak more clearly.' 'Eight. Three. Zero. Eight . . .'

Simon pressed stop. 'I presume you know who was answering the questions.'

The huge man responded with a tiny gesture that could mean anything. 'Is that what you're selling?'

'This recording was sent to me from a Hotmail address which I haven't been able to or indeed tried to trace. Because I'm currently the only person who knows about the sound file. Evidence that the prison gov—'

'Assistant prison governor.'

'—of Staten admits to having a secret account into which he has received money from Hugo Nestor. I checked the account number and the information is correct.'

'And how is this of value to me?'

'What is valuable to you is that I don't take this to my colleagues and you lose an important ally.' Simon cleared his throat. '*Yet* another important ally.'

The huge man shrugged. 'Assistant prison governors can be replaced. And, in any case, it looks as if Franck has served his purpose. What more have you got, Kefas?'

Simon stuck out his lower lip. 'I've evidence that you have laundered money through Iversen's property business. And DNA evidence linking Iver Iversen Senior to a Vietnamese girl, whom you trafficked into the country, murdered and made Sonny Lofthus take the fall for.'

The large man stroked his throat with two fingers. 'I'm listening. Go on.'

'If I get the money for the eye operation, I can make sure that neither of these cases will be investigated.'

'How much money are we talking about?'

'Two million kroner.'

'You could have blackmailed Iversen directly for that amount. So why are you really here?'

'Because I want more than money.'

'And what is that?'

'I want you to stop looking for the boy.'

'Lofthus's son? Why would I do that?'

'Because Ab Lofthus was a friend.'

The big man looked at Simon for a while. Then he leaned back in his chair and tapped the aquarium glass with his finger.

'It looks like a regular aquarium, yes? But do you know what the grey fish that looks like a sprat costs, Kefas? No, you don't, because I don't want the Serious Fraud Office to know that some collectors are willing to pay millions of kroner for it. It isn't especially impressive or attractive, but it's incredibly rare. So its price is determined by the value it has to the individual; the highest bidder.'

Simon shifted in his chair.

'The point is,' the big man said, 'I want the Lofthus boy. He's a rare fish and has greater value to me than to any other buyer. Because he has killed my people and stolen my money. Do you think I could have ruled this city for twenty years if I let people get away with stuff like that? He has turned himself into a fish I simply have to have. I'm sorry, Kefas. We'll give you the money, but the boy is mine.'

'All the boy wants is the mole who betrayed his father, then he'll go away.'

'And, as far as I'm concerned, he can have the mole, I've no use for him or her any more, the mole stopped operating twelve years ago. But even I never knew the mole's identity. We exchanged money and information anonymously, and that was fine by me, I got what I paid for. And so will you, Kefas. Your wife's eyesight, yes?'

'As you wish,' Simon said and got up. 'If you go after the boy, I'll get the money some other way.'

The big man heaved a sigh. 'I think you've misunderstood our negotiation, Kefas.'

Simon saw that the blond man had also risen.

'As an experienced gambler you ought to know that you should always check your cards carefully *before* you decide to play,' the big man said. 'Afterwards, it's too late, yes?'

Simon felt the blond man put his hand on his shoulder. He resisted the urge to push it away. He sat down again. The big man leaned across the table. He smelled of lavender.

'Iversen told me about the DNA samples you came to him about. And now there's this sound recording. That means you're in touch with the boy, am I right? So now you will lead us to him. Him and whatever he stole from us.'

'And if I say no?'

The big man heaved another sigh. 'What is it we all fear when we grow old, Kefas? Dying alone, yes? The real reason you're doing everything you can to restore your wife's sight is that you want her to look at you when you die. Because we tell ourselves it makes dying a little less lonely, yes? Well, imagine a deathbed even more lonely than one with a blind, but living wife present . . .'

'What?'

'Bo, show him.'

The blond man held up his mobile to Simon. Showed him a picture. He recognised the hospital ward. The bed. The sleeping woman in the bed.

'The interesting thing isn't that we know where she is right now,' the big man said. 'But that we found her, yes? In less than one hour after Iversen contacted us. And that means we'll be able to find her again, no matter where you hide her.'

Simon leapt out of the chair, his right hand shot towards the big man's throat, but it ended up in a fist that caught it as easily as if it had been a butterfly. And that now closed quietly around Simon's fingers.

'You have to decide what you value the most, Kefas. The woman you share your life with or this stray dog you've adopted.'

Simon swallowed. He tried to ignore the pain, the sound of his knuckle joints grinding against each other, but knew the tears of pain were giving him away. He blinked once. Twice. He felt a hot tear roll down his cheek.

'She needs to travel to the US within the next two days,' he whispered. 'I must have the money in cash on her departure.'

The Twin released his hold and Simon felt dizzy when the blood rushed back and exacerbated the pain.

'She'll be on a plane the moment you hand over the boy and the stolen goods,' the big man said.

The blond man escorted Simon out. It had stopped raining, but the air still felt clammy and heavy.

'What are you going to do to him?' Simon asked.

'You don't want to know,' said the blond man and smiled. 'But it was nice doing business with you.'

The door was closed and locked behind Simon.

He left the alley. Darkness was falling. Simon started to run.

* * *

374

Martha sat looking over the roast beef and the tall wine glasses, at the heads on the other side of the table, at the family pictures on the console table in front of the window, at the rain-sodden apple trees in the garden, up at the sky and into the approaching darkness.

Anders's speech was beautiful. No doubt about it, she could imagine one of the old aunts wiping away a tear.

'Martha and I have decided on a winter wedding,' he said. 'Because we know that our love can melt all ice, that our friends' hearts can warm any function room and that your – our family's – care, wisdom and guidance will be all the light we need on our dark winter path. And, of course, there is another reason . . .' Anders grabbed the wine glass and turned to Martha, who only just managed to tear herself away from the evening sky and return his smile. 'We simply can't wait until summer!'

Happy laughter and applause filled the room.

Anders seized her hand with his free one. He squeezed it hard, smiled, his fine eyes sparkling like the sea, and she knew he was aware of the impression he'd made. Then he bent down as if overcome by the occasion and kissed her quickly on the lips. The table erupted. He raised his glass.

'To us!'

Then he sat down. He caught her eye and flashed her an almost private smile. The smile which told the twelve dinner guests that he and Martha shared something special, something that belonged only to them. But just because Anders was playing to the gallery didn't meant it wasn't true. They *did* have something that belonged only to them. Something solid. They had been a couple for so long that it was easy to forget all the good days and the nice things they had done together. And they had worked through the bad times and come out stronger for it. She cared about Anders, she really did. Of course she did, otherwise why would she have agreed to marry him?

His smile stiffened slightly. It was telling her that she could try to show a little more enthusiasm, work with him here now that they had gathered their families to tell them their wedding plans. Her future mother-in-law had asked to make the announcement and Martha hadn't had the energy to protest. And now she got up and tapped her glass. It was as if someone had flicked a switch marked 'silence'. Not just because the guests were eagerly awaiting what she had to say, but because no one wanted to be skewered by the mother of the groom's withering stare.

'And we're so very thrilled that Martha has decided that the wedding ceremony will take place in St Paul's Church.'

Martha barely managed to stop herself from spluttering. *She* had decided?

'As you're aware, we're a Catholic family. And even though the average level of education and income is higher among Protestants than Catholics in many other countries, that isn't the case in Norway. In Norway we Catholics make up the elite. So, Martha, welcome to the A-team.'

Martha acknowledged the joke which she knew perfectly well wasn't a joke at all. She heard her future mother-in-law's voice continue, but she drifted off again. Because she had to get away. Escape to that other place.

'What are you thinking about, Martha?'

She felt Anders's lips against her hair and earlobe. She managed a smile because she was close to laughing. Laughing as she imagined getting up and telling him and the other guests that what she was thinking about was lying in the arms of a killer in the sun on a rock while a thunderstorm headed across the fjord towards them. But that didn't mean that she didn't love Anders. She had said yes. She had said yes because she loved him.

35

'DO YOU REMEMBER THE FIRST time we met?' Simon asked as he stroked Else's hand on the duvet. The two other patients in the ward were asleep behind their curtains.

'No,' she smiled and he imagined those strangely shiny, pure blue eyes of hers sparkle under the bandage. 'But you do. Go on then, tell me again.'

Instead of just smiling back, Simon chuckled quietly so that she could hear it.

'You were working in a florist's in Grønland. And I came in to buy flowers.'

'A wreath,' she said. 'You came to buy a wreath.'

'You were so beautiful that I made sure we chatted for much longer than was necessary. Even though you were far too young for me. But as we spoke, I grew young myself. And the next day I stopped by to buy roses.'

'You bought lilies.'

'Yes, of course. I wanted you to think they were for a friend. But the third time I bought roses.'

'And the fourth.'

'My flat was so full of flowers, I could barely breathe.'

'They were all for you.'

'They were all for *you*. I was merely looking after them for you. Then I asked you out. I've never been so scared in all my life.'

'You looked so nervous that I couldn't bear to say no.'

'That trick works every time.'

'No,' she laughed. 'You were nervous. But I was attracted by your sad eyes. A life lived. The melancholy of insight. That's irresistible to a young woman, you know.'

'You've always said it was my athletic body and that I'm a good listener.'

'No, I haven't!' Else laughed even louder and Simon laughed with her. Relieved that she couldn't see him now.

'You bought a wreath the first time,' she said quietly. 'You wrote a card and you looked at it for a while, then you threw it in the bin and wrote another one. After you'd gone, I picked the card out of the bin and read it. And it said "To the love of my life". That was what got my attention.'

'Oh? Wouldn't you rather have a man who thought he had yet to meet the love of his life?'

'I wanted a man who was capable of loving, *really* loving.'

He nodded. Over the years they had repeated this story to each other so often that the lines were rehearsed, as were their reactions and the apparent spontaneity. They had once sworn to tell each other everything, absolutely everything, and after they had done that, after they had tested how much truth the other could tolerate, their stories had become the walls and the roof that held their home together.

She squeezed his hand. 'And you were, Simon. You knew how to love.'

'Because you fixed me.'

'You fixed yourself. *You* decided to quit gambling, not me.'

'You were the medicine, Else. Without you . . .' Simon took a deep breath and hoped she couldn't hear the trembling in his voice because he didn't have the energy to go there now, not tonight. Didn't want to repeat the story about his gambling addiction and debts which he ultimately dragged her into. He had done the unforgivable, mortgaged their house behind her back. And lost. And she had forgiven him. She hadn't been angry or moved out or let him suffer the consequences or given him any kind of ultimatum. All she had done was to stroke his cheek and say that she forgave him. And he had cried like a child and at that moment his shame had extinguished the craving after the pulsating life in the intersection between hope and fear, where everything is at stake and can be won or lost in an instant, where thoughts of the catastrophic, final defeat are almost – almost – as tantalising as the thought of victory. It was true, he had quit that day. And he had never gambled since, hadn't bet as much as a beer, and it had been his salvation. It had been their salvation. That and their promise to tell each other absolutely everything. To know that he had the capacity for self-control and the courage to be totally honest with another person had done something to him, had restored him as a man and a human being, yes, even caused him to grow more than if he had never been at the mercy of his vices. Perhaps that explained why in his later years as a police officer he had gone from seeing every criminal as notorious and incorrigible to being willing to give everyone a second chance – in stark contrast to what his wide experience told him.

'We're like Charlie Chaplin and the flower girl,' Else said. 'If you play the movie backwards.'

Simon swallowed. The blind flower girl who thinks the tramp is a rich gentleman. Simon couldn't remember how, only that the tramp helps her get her sight back, but that afterwards he never reveals his identity because he is convinced that she wouldn't want him if she saw who he really was. And then, when she finds out, she loves him all the same.

'I'll go and stretch my legs,' he said, getting up.

There was no one else in the corridor. For a while he looked at the sign on the wall depicting a mobile with a red line across it. Then he took out his mobile and found the phone number. Some people think that if you send an email from a mobile via a Hotmail address on the Internet, the police won't be able to trace the phone number it was sent from. Wrong. It had been easy to find. It felt as if his heart was in his throat, as if it was beating behind his collarbone. There was no reason why he would pick up the phone.

'Yes?'

His voice. Alien, but yet so strangely familiar, like an echo from a distant, no, a near past. The Son. Simon had to cough twice before his vocal cords would make a sound.

'I have to meet you, Sonny.'

'That would have been nice . . .'

There wasn't a hint of irony in his voice.

'. . . but I'm not planning on being around for very long.'

Here? In Oslo, in Norway? Or here on Earth?

'What are you going to do?' Simon asked.

'I think you know what.'

'You're going to find and punish all the people responsible. The people you served time for. The people who killed your father. And then you want to find the mole.'

'I don't have very much time.'

'But I can help you.'

'That's very kind of you, Simon, but the best thing you can do to help me is carry on doing what you've been doing so far.'

'Oh? And what is that?'

'Not try to stop me.'

A pause followed. Simon listened out for any background noises that might reveal where the boy was. He heard a low, rhythmic pounding and sporadic shouting and screaming.

'I think we want the same thing, Simon.'

Simon gulped. 'Do you remember me?'

'I have to go now.'

'Your father and I . . .'

But the line had already gone dead.

'Thank you for coming.'

'Don't mention it, mate,' Pelle said, glancing up at the boy in the rear-view mirror. 'A taxi driver's meter runs less than thirty per cent of his working day so it's nice, both for me and my business, that you called. Where are you off to tonight, mister?'

'Ullern.'

The boy had asked him for his card the last time Pelle drove him. Passengers tended to do that from time to time if they were satisfied, but they never called. It was too easy to get a cab by flagging one down in the street. So Pelle had no idea why the boy specifically wanted him to drive all the way from Gamlebyen to Kvadraturen to pick him up outside the dubious Bismarck Hotel.

The boy was wearing a smart suit and Pelle hadn't recognised him at first. Something was different. He carried the same red sports bag plus a briefcase. A sharp jangle of metal had come from the bag as the boy dumped it on the back seat.

'You look happy in that photograph,' the boy said. 'You and your wife?'

'Oh, that one,' Pelle said and felt himself blushing. No one had ever commented on the picture before. He had stuck it low down on the left-hand side of the steering wheel, so that customers wouldn't be able to see it. But he was touched that the boy could see from the picture that they were happy. That *she* was happy. He hadn't selected the best picture of them, but the one where she looked happiest.

'I think she's cooking rissoles tonight,' he said. 'Later we might go for a walk in Kampen Park. The breeze up there will be very welcome on a hot day like this.'

'That sounds nice,' the boy said. 'You're lucky to have found a woman to share your life with.'

'Indeed I am,' Pelle said and looked up in the rear-view mirror. 'You couldn't be more right.'

Pelle usually made sure the customer did the talking. He liked it, getting a snippet of someone's life for the brief duration of a cab ride. Children and marriage. Jobs and mortgages. Sneak a peek at the trials and tribulations of family life for a short while. Not having to bring up the topics he knew so many taxi drivers enjoyed discussing. But a strange intimacy had grown between them; in fact, he quite simply enjoyed talking to this young man.

'How about you?' Pelle asked. 'Found yourself a girlfriend yet?'

The boy smiled as he shook his head.

'No? No one who revs up the old engine?'

The boy nodded.

'Yeah? Good for you, mate. And her.'

The boy's head movements changed direction.

'No? Don't tell me she doesn't fancy you? I admit you didn't look like much of a catch when you were throwing up against the wall, but today, in that suit and everything . . .'

'Thanks,' the boy said. 'But I'm afraid I can't have her.'

'Why not? Have you told her you love her?'

'No. Should you do that?'

'All the time, several times a day. Think of it as oxygen, you never stop needing it. I love you, I love you. Try it, then you'll see what I mean.'

There was silence in the back for a while. Then he heard a cough.

'How . . . how do you know if someone loves you, Pelle?'

'You just know. It's the sum total of all the little things you can never really put your finger on. Love surrounds you like steam in the shower. You can't see the individual drops, but you get warm. And wet. And clean.' Pelle laughed, embarrassed and almost a little proud at his own words.

'And you continue to bathe in her love and tell her that you love her every day?'

Pelle got the feeling that the boy's questions weren't spontaneous, that it was a subject he had intended to ask Pelle about because of the picture of him and his wife, that the boy must have spotted it on one of the other two rides they had taken.

'Absolutely,' Pelle said and felt as if something was stuck in his throat, a crumb or something. He coughed hard and turned on the radio.

The drive to Ullern took fifteen minutes. The boy gave Pelle an address in one of the roads which swung up towards Ullernåsen between gigantic wooden structures that looked more like fortifications than family homes. The tarmac had already dried after the rainfall earlier that day.

'Pull over here for a moment, would you, please?'

'But the gate is over there.'

'This is fine.'

Pelle pulled up along the kerb. The property was surrounded by a tall white wall with broken glass on the top. The vast, two-storey brick house lay at the top of a large garden. Music was coming from the terrace in front of the house and the light was on in every window. Floodlights in the garden. Two massive, broad-shouldered men in black suits were standing in front of the gate, one with a big white dog on a leash.

'Are you going to a party?' Pelle asked and massaged his bad foot. Now and then, the cramp came back like someone had thrown it at him.

The boy shook his head. 'I don't think I'm invited.'

'Do you know the people who live here?'

'No, I got the address when I was in prison. The Twin. Ever heard of him?'

'No,' Pelle said. 'But seeing as you don't know him, I can tell you that it ain't right for one person to have so much. Look at that house! This is Norway, not the US or Saudi Arabia. We're just a freezing cold bit of rock up here in the north, but we always had one thing that the other countries didn't have. A certain equality. A certain fairness. But now we're busy wrecking it for ourselves.'

They heard dogs barking in the garden.

'I think you're a wise man, Pelle.'

'Oh, I'm not sure about that. Why were you inside?'

'To find peace.'

Pelle studied the boy's face in the mirror. It was as if he had seen it somewhere else, and not just here in his cab.

'Let's get out of here,' the boy said.

When Pelle looked out of the windscreen again, he saw that the man with the white dog was coming towards them. Both of them had their eyes fixed on the car and had so much muscle packed inside their bodies that they waddled.

'Right,' Pelle said, flicking on the indicator. 'Where to?'

'Did you get to say goodbye to her?'

'What?'

'Your wife.'

Pelle blinked. Watched the man and the dog getting closer. The question had hit him like a punch to the stomach. He looked at the boy in the mirror again. Where had he seen him before? He heard growling. The dog must be getting ready to attack. He had driven the boy before, it was that simple, that had to be the reason. The memory of a memory. Like she was now.

'No,' Pelle said, shaking his head.

'An accident?'

Pelle swallowed. 'Yes. A car crash.'

'Did she know that you loved her?'

Pelle opened his mouth, but realised he wouldn't be able to say anything, so all he did was nod.

'I'm sorry she was taken from you, Pelle.'

He felt the boy's hand on his shoulder. And it was as if heat exuded from it and spread to his chest, stomach, arms and legs.

'We should probably get going now, Pelle.'

It wasn't until then that Pelle realised he had closed his eyes, and when he opened them again the man and the dog had come up alongside the car. Pelle revved the engine and released the clutch. He heard the dog barking furiously after them.

'Where are we off to?'

'To visit a man who is guilty of murder,' the boy said, pulling the red sports bag closer. 'But first we have to drop something off.'

'Who to?'

The boy smiled a strange, wistful smile. 'To someone whose picture I'd like to have on my dashboard.'

Martha was standing at the kitchen counter, pouring the coffee from the pot into a Thermos flask. She tried to shut out her future mother-in-law's voice. She tried to focus on what the guests were talking about in the dining room. But it was impossible, her voice was so insistent, so *demanding*.

'Anders is a sensitive boy, you understand. He's much more sensitive than you. You're the strong one. That's why you have to take charge and . . .'

A car pulled up and stopped in front of the gate. A taxi. A man in an elegant suit got out; he was carrying a briefcase.

She thought her heart would stop. It was him.

He opened the gate and started walking up the short gravel path to the front door.

'Excuse me,' Martha said, and slammed down the coffee pot in the sink with a bang and tried to look as if she wasn't rushing out of the kitchen.

It was a distance of only a few metres and yet she was breathless when she flung open the door before he had time to ring the bell.

'We have company,' she hissed, pulling the door behind her. 'And the police are looking for you. What do you want?'

He looked at her with those damned clear green eyes. He had shaved off his eyebrows.

'I want to ask for forgiveness,' he said. Quietly, calmly. 'And then I want to give you this. It's for the centre.'

'What is it?' she asked and looked at the briefcase he was holding out to her.

'For that building work you can't afford. Or some of it, at any rate . . .'

'No!' She glanced over her shoulder and lowered her voice. 'What's wrong with you? Do you really think I want your blood money. You kill people. The earrings you tried to give me . . .' Martha swallowed, shook her head fiercely and felt tiny, angry tears flow. 'They belonged . . . to a woman you *murdered*!'

'But—'

'Go away!'

He nodded. Took a step down, backwards. 'Why didn't you tell the police about me?'

'Who says I haven't?'

'Why haven't you, Martha?'

She shifted her weight from one foot to the other. Heard a chair scrape across the dining-room floor. 'Because I wanted to hear you tell me why you killed those people, perhaps?'

'Would it make a difference if I did?'

'I don't know. Would it?'

He shrugged. 'If you want to call the police, I'll be at my parents' house tonight. After that I'll disappear.'

'Why are you telling me this?'

'Because I want you to come with me. Because I love you.'

She blinked. What did he just say?

'I love you,' he repeated slowly and looked as if he was tasting his own words in surprise.

'My God,' she groaned in despair. 'You're mad!'

'I'm going now.' He turned towards the taxi which was waiting with its engine idling.

'Wait! Where will you go?'

He made a half-turn and smiled wryly. 'Someone told me about a great city in Europe. It's a long way to drive on your own, but . . .' He looked as if he wanted to say something more and she waited. And waited, and prayed that he would say it. She didn't know what it was, only that if he said the right thing, said the magic word, then it would set her free. But it was him who had to do it, *he* had to know what it was.

But he bowed quickly to her, turned round and started walking towards the gate.

Martha was tempted to call out after him, but what would she say? It was madness. A crazy infatuation. Something which didn't exist, which *couldn't* exist in the real world. Reality was in there, in the dining room behind her. She turned and went back inside. And looked straight into Anders's furious face.

'Move.'

'Anders, don't . . .'

He pushed her over, tore open the door and stormed out.

Martha got back on her feet and followed him out to the path in time to see Anders grab hold of Sonny and lash out at the back of his head. But Sonny must have heard Anders coming because he ducked, spun round in a kind of pirouette and wrapped his arms around Anders. Anders howled: 'I'm going to kill you!' and tried to free himself, but his arms were locked and he was helpless. Then, just as suddenly, Sonny let Anders go. At first Anders stared with astonishment at the man standing in front of him with his arms hanging passively by his sides. Then Anders raised his hand to strike. And punched him. He raised his fist ready for another blow. Landed it. It didn't make much noise. A dead, thudding smack of knuckles against flesh and bone.

'Anders,' Martha screamed. 'Anders, stop it!'

On the fourth punch the skin on the boy's cheekbone burst. On the fifth he sank to his knees.

The door on the driver's side of the taxi opened and the taxi driver made to get out, but the boy held up a hand to signal for him to keep out of it.

'You cowardly bastard!' Anders screamed. 'Stay the hell away from my fiancée!'

The boy raised his head as if to offer Anders a better angle, turning his undamaged cheek. Anders kicked him. The boy's head was thrown backwards and he collapsed onto his knees and flung out his arms like a football player skidding across the pitch in triumph.

The sharp sole of Anders's shoe must have caught Sonny's forehead because blood started pouring from a long cut right below the hairline. As Sonny's shoulders brushed the gravel and his jacket fell open, Martha saw Anders freeze in the run-up to another kick. Saw him stare at Sonny's belt and see what she saw. A pistol. A shiny pistol, whose barrel was buried in the trouser lining; it had been there all along, but Sonny hadn't touched it.

She put her hand on Anders's shoulder and he jumped as if she had just woken him up.

'Go inside,' she ordered him. 'Now!'

He blinked at her in confusion. Then he did as he was told. Walked past her up to the steps where the other guests had now gathered.

'Go inside!' Martha called out to them. 'He's a resident from the Ila Centre, I'll deal with it. All of you, go inside!'

Martha squatted down next to Sonny. Blood was pouring from his forehead and down the bridge of his nose. He was breathing through his mouth.

An insistent, demanding voice came from the steps: 'But is that really necessary, Martha darling? After all, you'll be leaving that place now that you and Anders are—'

Martha closed her eyes and steeled herself. 'And that goes for you, too. Shut up and get inside now!'

When she opened her eyes again, she could see that he was smiling. And then he whispered with bloody lips, so quietly that she had to bend down to hear him:

'He's right, Martha. You *really* can feel how love washes you clean.'

Then he got up, swayed for a moment before he staggered out of the gate and into the taxi.

'Wait!' she shouted and grabbed the briefcase which was still lying on the gravel path.

But the taxi was already driving down the road towards the darkness at the end of the residential area.

36

IVER IVERSEN BOUNCED ON HIS heels and twirled the stem of his empty Martini glass. He watched the guests gathered in clusters on the whitewashed terrace and in the living room inside. It was the size of a ballroom and furnished with the taste of someone who didn't have to live in it. 'Interior designers with unlimited budgets and limited talent,' as Agnete would have said. The men were wearing dinner jackets as the invitation had requested. The women were clearly outnumbered, but those who were there stood out even more. Blindingly beautiful, tantalisingly young and representing an interesting ethnic mix. High-slit dresses, naked backs and deep cleavages. Elegant, exotic and imported. True beauty is always rare. Iver Iversen wouldn't have batted an eyelid if someone had led a snow leopard through the room.

'It looks like every single financier in Oslo is here.'

'Only those who aren't particularly fastidious,' Fredrik Ansgar said, adjusting his bow tie and sipping his gin and tonic. 'Or are away at their holiday homes.'

Wrong, Iver Iversen thought. If they do business with the Twin, they'll have made the trip into town. They wouldn't dare do otherwise.

The Twin. He looked at the huge man standing by the piano. He could have been the model for the ideal worker on Soviet propaganda posters or the sculptures in Vigeland Park. Everything about him was solid, solid and chiselled: his head, arms, hands, calves. High forehead, solid chin, full lips. The person talking to him was heavily built and over 1.8 metres tall, but looked like a dwarf next to the Twin. Iver thought he vaguely recognised him. He had a patch over one eye. Probably some mogul he'd seen in the newspapers.

Iversen grabbed himself another Martini from the tray being carried by one of the waiters who orbited the room. He knew that he shouldn't, that he was already drunk. But he didn't give a toss, after all he was a grieving widower. Still, he knew drinking was exactly what he shouldn't be doing. He might end up saying something he would later regret.

'Do you know how the Twin got his name?'

'I've heard the story, yes,' Fredrik Ansgar said.

'I heard that his brother drowned, but that it was an accident.'

'An accident? In a bucket of water?'

Fredrik laughed and his gaze followed a dark-skinned beauty who glided past.

'Look,' Iver said. 'There's even a bishop here. I wonder how he got caught in the Twin's net.'

'Yes, it's an impressive gathering. Is it true he also has a prison governor in his pocket?'

'Let me put it like this, it doesn't stop there.'

'The police?'

Iver said nothing.

'How high up?'

'You're young, Fredrik, and even though you're on the inside, you're not yet in so deep that you don't have the option of retreat. But the more you know, the more trapped you are, believe me. If I had the chance to do things differently . . .'

'And what about Sonny Lofthus? And Simon Kefas? Will they be taken care of?'

'Oh yes,' Iver said, staring at a small, nimble girl sitting alone at the bar. Thai? Vietnamese? So young, pretty and dolled up. So instructed. So terrified and unprotected. Just like Mai. He almost felt sorry for Simon Kefas. He, too, was trapped. He had sold his soul for his love of a younger woman and, like Iver, he would come to know humiliation. At least Iver hoped that Simon would have time to feel it before the Twin did what was necessary and beat Simon Kefas to it. A lake in Østmarka? Perhaps Kefas and Lofthus would get a lake each.

Iver Iversen closed his eyes and thought about Agnete. He felt like hurling the Martini glass at the wall, but instead he drained it in one gulp.

'Telenor's operations centre, police assistance.'

'Good evening, this is Chief Inspector Simon Kefas.'

'I can tell from the number you're calling from. And that you're somewhere in Ullevål Hospital.'

'Impressive. However, I want you to trace a different number.'

'Have you got a warrant?'

'This is an urgent matter.'

'Fine. I'll report it tomorrow and you'll have to take it up with the public prosecutor then. Name and number?'

'All I have is the number.'

'And what would you like?'

'The location where the mobile is now.'

'We can only give you an approximate location. And if the mobile isn't in use, it can take time before our base stations pick up its signal. It happens automatically once every hour.'

'I'll call the number now so you get a signal.'

'So this isn't about someone who can't know that their phone is being traced?'

'I've been calling the number several times in the last hour and there's been no response so far.'

'Fine. Give me the number, ring it, and I'll tell you what we find out.'

Pelle stopped the taxi on the deserted gravel track. To his left the landscape sloped down towards the river that shimmered in the moonlight. A narrow bridge led from the gravel track back to the main road by which they had come. To his right a field of wheat whispered and swayed below the black clouds that raced across the sky which looked like a photographic negative in the light summer night.

Further down the road, within the forest in front of them, lay their destination: a large house surrounded by a white picket fence.

'I should be taking you to casualty instead so they could patch you up,' Pelle said.

'I'll be fine,' the boy said and placed a large-denomination bank-note on the armrest between the front seats. 'And thank you for the handkerchief.'

Pelle looked up at him the rear-view mirror. The boy had tied the handkerchief around his forehead. It was soaked in blood.

'Come on. I won't charge you. There's bound to be a casualty department somewhere in Drammen.'

'I might go tomorrow,' the boy said, clutching the red sports bag. 'I need to pay this man a visit first.'

'Is that safe? I thought you said he'd killed someone?' Pelle looked in the direction of the garage which was built into the house. So much space and yet no separate garage. The owner was probably a fan of American architecture. Pelle's grandmother had lived in a village of Norwegians who had once lived in America or had families living there now, where the most fundamentalist converts to their adopted country hadn't just had a house with a porch, a Stars and

Stripes on the flagpole and an American automobile in the garage, but also 110 volt electrical installations so they could plug in their jukeboxes, toasters and fridges which they had bought in Texas or inherited from a grandfather in Bay Ridge, Brooklyn.

'He's not going to kill anyone tonight,' the boy said.

'Even so,' Pelle said. 'Sure you don't want me to wait? It's half an hour back to Oslo and another taxi will cost you shedloads because it'll have to make the journey out here first. I'll stop the meter—'

'I really appreciate that, Pelle, but it's probably best for both of us if you're not a witness to anything. Do you understand?'

'No.'

'Good.'

The boy got out of the car. He looked at Pelle. Pelle shrugged and drove off; he heard the gravel crunch under the tyres while he followed the boy in his mirror. Saw him standing there. Then suddenly he was gone, swallowed up by the darkness in the woods.

Pelle stopped the car. He continued to stare at the mirror. The boy was gone. Just like his wife.

It was so difficult to grasp. That people who had been around, furnished your life, could simply evaporate and you never saw them again. Except in dreams. The good dreams. Because he never saw her in his nightmare. In the nightmare he saw only the road and the headlights of the oncoming car. In the nightmare he, Pelle Granerud, once a promising rally driver, didn't have time to react, didn't manage to carry out the simple manoeuvre needed to avoid a drunk driver on the wrong side of the road. Instead of doing the things he did every single day in training on the motor-racing circuit, he froze. Because he knew that he might lose the only thing he couldn't bear to lose. Not his own life, but that of his family: the two people who were his life. The two people he had just picked up from the hospital, they were his new life. Which started now.

He was a father. He got to be a father for just three days. And when he woke up, he was back in the same hospital. First they told him about the injuries to his legs. It was a misunderstanding, there had been a change of shift and the incoming staff didn't know that his wife and child had been killed in the accident. It was two hours before he found out. He was allergic to morphine, an inherited condition probably, and he had lain in unbearable agony screaming her name day after day. But she didn't come. And hour by hour, day by day, little by little he began to understand, that he would never, ever see her again. So he carried on screaming her name. Just to hear it. They hadn't had time to decide on a name for the baby. And it suddenly dawned on Pelle that it wasn't until tonight, when the boy had put his hand on his shoulder, that the pain disappeared completely.

Pelle could see the outline of a man in the white house. He was sitting behind a large, curtainless panorama window. The living room was lit up as if the man was on show. As if he was waiting for someone.

Iver could see that the big man was bringing the guest he had been talking to by the piano over to him and Fredrik.

'It's you he wants to talk to, not me,' Fredrik whispered and slipped away, having set his sights on something Russian over by the bar.

Iver gulped. How many years had he and the big man done business together, been in the same boat, shared upturns and the very occasional downturn, such as when the shock waves of the global financial crisis sloshed gently against the Norwegian coast? And yet he still tensed up, almost petrified, when the big man approached. People said that he could lift his own body weight on the bench press. And not just once, but ten reps in a row. But it was one thing for his physical presence to be so intimidating,

395

another for you to know that absolutely everything you said, every word, the slightest change in pitch, also – or indeed, especially – anything you didn't intend, he would catch. In addition to what your body language, facial colour and the movement of your pupils revealed, of course.

'So, Iver.' The low-frequency, rumbling voice. 'How are you doing? Agnete. Terrible business, yes?'

'It certainly is,' Iver said, looking around for a waiter.

'I want you to meet a friend of mine – the two of you have something in common. You have both been widowed recently . . .'

The man with the eyepatch extended his hand.

'. . . by the same killer,' said the big man.

'Yngve Morsand,' the man introduced himself and squeezed Iver's hand. 'I'm sorry for your loss.'

'Likewise,' Iver Iversen said. So that was why he thought the man looked familiar. It was the shipping owner, the husband of the woman who had been practically decapitated. Yngve Morsand had been the police's prime suspect for a while until they had found DNA at the crime scene. From Sonny Lofthus.

'Yngve lives just outside Drammen,' the big man said. 'And tonight we've borrowed his house.'

'Oh?'

'We're using it as a trap. We're going to catch the guy who killed Agnete, Iver.'

'The Twin says there's a good chance Sonny Lofthus will make an attempt on my life there tonight,' Yngve Morsand laughed and looked around for something. 'I've put money on it that he won't. Would you tell your waiters to get me something stronger than a Martini, Twin?'

'It's Sonny Lofthus's next obvious move,' the big man said. 'Luckily he's sufficiently systematic and predictable, so I think I'll be taking your money.' The big man grinned broadly. White teeth below his moustache, eyes like two slits in the fleshy face. He placed a gigantic hand on the shipowner's back. 'And I'd prefer it if you didn't call me that, Yngve.'

The shipowner looked up at him jokingly. 'You mean Twi— Aaah.' His mouth opened and his face contorted into a baffled, frozen grimace. Iver saw the big man's fingers release their grip around Morsand's neck and the shipowner bent forward to cough.

'So I think we're agreed on that, yes?' The big man raised his hand towards the bar and snapped his fingers. 'Drinks.'

Martha stuck her spoon diffidently into the cloudberry cream pudding while she ignored the words being hurled at her from every angle of the table. *Has this person assaulted you before? Is he dangerous? If he's a resident, surely you'll have to see him again, good God! What if the guy reports Anders to the police for his defence of her? Everyone knows how unpredictable these drug addicts are. But then again, he was probably high and won't be able to remember a thing.* An uncle thought he had looked like the man on TV who was wanted for murder. *What's his name – is he foreign? What is it, Martha, why don't you say anything? Surely you can guess why, she has a duty of confidentiality.*

'I'm eating my pudding,' Martha said. 'It's good, you should try some. I think I'll get some more.'

Anders came up behind her in the kitchen.

'I heard him,' he hissed. '*I love you?* That was the guy from the corridor at Ila. The one you were talking to. What's going on between the two of you?'

'Anders, don't . . .'

'Have you slept with him?'

'Stop it!'

'He definitely has a guilty conscience. If he didn't, he would have pulled his gun on me. What was he doing here – had he come to shoot me? I'm calling the police—'

'To tell them how you attacked and kicked a man in the head without provocation?'

'And who would tell them I wasn't being provoked? You?'

'Or the taxi driver.'

'*You?*' He grabbed her arm and laughed. 'Yes, you would, wouldn't you? You would take his side against your own fiancé. You fucking wh—'

She tore herself loose. A dessert plate hit the floor and smashed. The dining room fell completely silent.

Martha marched out into the hall, grabbed her coat and headed for the door. Stopped. Paused for a second. Then she turned round and marched into the dining room. She grabbed a spoon, white from cloudberry cream pudding, and tapped it against a greasy glass. She looked up and realised that last action had been superfluous, she already had everyone's attention.

'Dear friends and family,' she said. 'I wanted to add that Anders was right. We just can't wait until summer . . .'

Simon swore. He had parked in the middle of Kvadraturen and was studying a map of the area. Telenor's police assistance service had told him that the phone was here. The mobile Sonny Lofthus had used to text him. And which Simon now knew was a pay-as-you-go phone registered to a Helge Sørensen. It made sense, he had used the ID card of the same prison officer earlier.

But where could he be?

The coordinates covered only a few streets, but those streets were Oslo's most densely populated. Shops, offices, hotels, flats. Simon jumped when there was a knock on the side window. He looked up and saw a harshly made-up, chubby girl in hot pants whose breasts were squeezed into some kind of corset. He shook his head, she pulled an ugly face at him and walked off. Simon had forgotten that this was the city's busiest red-light district and that a single man in a parked car in these streets was inevitably regarded as a punter. A blow job in the car, ten minutes at the Bismarck Hotel or possibly up against the wall of Akershus Fortress. He had once been that man. It wasn't something he was proud of, but once upon a time he had been willing to pay for a crumb of human contact and a voice saying 'I love you'. The latter had fallen under the category of 'special services' and cost two hundred kroner extra.

He called the number again and watched the people walking up and down the pavements, hoping that one of them would reach for their phone and thus give themselves away. He sighed and ended the call. Looked at his watch. At least he knew that the phone was in the area, and that ought to indicate that Sonny was staying put and wasn't up to anything devilish tonight.

So why did Simon have the feeling that something wasn't right?

Bo sat in the unfamiliar living room, looking out of the large panorama window. He sat in front of a bright light which was aimed at the window so that anyone watching him from the outside would see only his silhouette and not his features. Hopefully Sonny Lofthus didn't have too clear an idea of Yngve Morsand's build. Bo was thinking that this was exactly how Sylvester had been sitting when he had left him in Lofthus's house. Good, stupid, loyal, loud Sylvester. And that that fucker had killed him. How he had done that, they would probably never know. Because there would never be an interrogation, a torture session where Bo could exact his revenge, savour it like he would a glass of retsina with its taste of resin. Some people couldn't stand it, but to Bo it represented the taste of his childhood, the island of Telendos, friends, a gently rocking boat in the bottom of which he would lie and look at the always blue Greek sky and hear the waves and the wind sing a duet together. He heard a click in his right ear.

'A car stopped down the road and then turned round.'

'Did anyone get out?' Bo asked. The earpiece, the cable and the microphone were so discreet that they wouldn't show up in the backlight from the outside.

'We didn't have time to see, but the car is driving away now. Perhaps it was lost.'

'OK. Everyone get ready.'

Bo adjusted his bulletproof vest. Lofthus wouldn't have time to fire any shots, but he preferred to take precautions. He had placed two men in the garden to grab Lofthus when he came through the gate or over the fence, and one in the corridor behind the unlocked front door. All other means of access to the house were closed and locked. They had been here since five o'clock in the afternoon, they were tired and the night had barely begun, but thoughts about Sylvester would keep him awake. The thought of getting that bastard. Lure him out here. If not tonight, then tomorrow, or the next night. From time to time Bo considered how strange it was that the big man – who possessed so little humanity himself – had such an insight into people. Their urges, weaknesses and motivations, how they reacted to pressure and fear and how he, with enough infor-mation about their temperament, proclivities and intelligence, could predict their next move with astonishing – or as the big man himself used to say: disappointing – accuracy. Sadly the big man had given orders that the boy must be killed immediately and not taken pris-oner so his death would be swift and far too free from pain.

Bo shifted in the chair when he heard a sound. And even before he had turned round, a thought crossed his mind. That he didn't have the big man's ability to predict what this guy would do next. Not when he left Sylvester in the yellow house, and not now.

The boy had a bloody handkerchief tied around his head and was standing in a side doorway, the one that led from the living room and straight into the garage.

How the hell had he got in that way, when they had locked the garage? He must have come from behind, from the forest. Picking a locked garage door was surely one of the first things a clever junkie would have learned. But this wasn't Bo's most pressing problem. His most pressing problem was that the boy was holding something which had an unfortunate resemblance to an Uzi, the Israeli machine gun that spits out nine x 19mm bullets faster than your average execution squad.

'You're not Yngve Morsand,' Sonny Lofthus said. 'Where is he?'

'He's here,' Bo said, turning his head to the microphone.

'Where?'

'He's here,' Bo repeated, a little louder this time. 'In the living room.'

Sonny Lofthus looked around as he walked towards Bo with the machine gun raised and his finger on the trigger. The clip appear to hold thirty-six bullets. He stopped. Had he spotted the earpiece and the cable from the microphone?

'You're talking to someone,' the boy said and had time to take a step backwards before the door to the hallway was flung open and Stan burst in with a pistol. Bo reached for his own Ruger as he heard the dry, crackling cough from the Uzi and a cascade of glass when the window behind him shattered. White stuffing spilled from the upholstered furniture and splinters flew from the parquet flooring. The guy splattered bullets generously with no particular target in mind. But it didn't matter, an Uzi will always outgun two pistols. Bo and Stan took shelter behind the nearest sofa. It fell silent. Bo was lying on his back clutching his pistol with both hands in case the guy's face appeared above the edge of the sofa.

'Stan!' he shouted. 'Take him out!'

No reply.

'Stan!'

'You do it!' Stan screamed from behind the sofa by the other wall. 'He's got a fucking Uzi, for fuck's sake!'

There was a click in Bo's earpiece: 'What's going on, boss?'

At the same moment Bo heard the sound of a car starting up and revving the engine loudly. Morsand had taken his stately Mercedes 280CE Coupe 1982 model to the Twin's party in Oslo, but his wife's run-around car – a cute little Honda Civic – was still there. Now that Morsand had killed her, he no longer had a wife who could run around in it, but the key must have been left in the ignition. It was probably what they did with wives and cars out here in the countryside, share them. He heard voices from his men outside.

'He's trying to get away!'

'Someone is opening the garage door.'

Bo heard a grating sound when the Honda was put into gear. And a groan when the engine choked. Was the guy a total amateur? He couldn't shoot and he couldn't drive.

'Get him!'

The car was started a second time.

'We heard something about an Uzi . . .'

'It's the Uzi or the Twin, *your choice!*'

Bo scrambled to his feet and ran to the shattered window in time to see the car jump out of the garage. Nubbe and Evgeni had positioned themselves in front of the gate. Nubbe was firing away with his Beretta, bullet after bullet. Evgeni had a Remington 870 with the barrel sawn off at the clip raised to his cheek. He jerked as he pulled the trigger. Bo saw the windscreen explode, but the car continued to accelerate, the front bumper hitting Evgeni right above the knees, flipping him up, and Bo saw him somersault in the air before the windscreen-less Civic swallowed him like a killer whale gulps down a seal. The Civic took out the gate and a section of the fence, drove straight across the narrow gravel path and into the wheat field on the other side. And, without slowing down, it ploughed on, screeching in first gear, as it carved a path through the golden sheaves bathed in moonlight, turned in a wide curve before returning to the gravel path further down. The engine howled even louder – the driver was obviously pushing down the clutch without taking his foot off the accelerator. Then he got the car into second gear, the engine came close to cutting out again, but it recovered and the car continued down the gravel path where, because the driver hadn't managed to switch on the headlights, it soon disappeared in the darkness.

'To the car!' Bo shouted. 'We have to catch him before he gets to town!'

Pelle stared after the Honda in disbelief. He had heard the shots and seen in his rear-view mirror how the car had burst out through the gate, sending pieces of white picket fence flying. Seen the car plough its way across the field planted with heavily subsidised agricultural produce before it had rejoined the track and continued its dubious journey. The boy was no experienced driver, that was for sure, but Pelle had breathed a sigh of relief when in the moon- light he could make out the bloodstained handkerchief above the wheel behind the shattered windscreen. At least the boy was still alive.

He heard shouting coming from the house.

The sound of guns being loaded in the quiet summer night.

A car starting.

Pelle had no idea who they were. The boy had told him – whether it was true or false – that the man inside the house was a killer. A man, perhaps a drunk driver who had killed, and was now out of prison again. Pelle didn't know. All he knew was that after months and years where he had made sure to spend most hours of the day and night behind the wheel of his cab, he was back there again. The place where he could react or freeze. Change the orbit of the stars – or not. A young man who couldn't get the girl he wanted.

He ran a finger over the photo beside the steering wheel. Then he put the car in gear and drove after the Honda. Drove down the hills and out onto the narrow bridge. Up on the ridge he could see a pair of headlights cut through the darkness. He accelerated, gained speed, turned the steering wheel slightly to the right, grabbed the handbrake, pressing and releasing the pedals quickly and musically like a church organist as he forced the steering wheel hard to the left. The rear of the car moved as expected as he executed the handbrake turn. And when the car stopped it was perfectly positioned diagonally across the bridge. Pelle nodded contentedly to himself; he hadn't lost his touch. Then he turned off the ignition, put the car into first gear, shuffled across to the passenger side and got out of the car. Checked that there was a gap of a maximum twenty centimetres between the side wall of the bridge and the car on both sides. Locked all the doors with a simple key click and started walking towards the main road. He thought about her, all the time he thought about her. If only she could see him now. See that he was walking. He felt almost no pain in his foot, he was barely limping. Perhaps the doctors had been right. Perhaps it was time to ditch the crutches.

37

IT WAS TWO O'CLOCK IN the morning and the summer night
was at its darkest.

From the deserted viewpoint in the forest clearing above Oslo, Simon
could see the fjord shimmer dully beneath the large yellow moon.

'Well?'

Simon pulled his coat more tightly around him as if he was cold.
'I used to bring the first girl I was in love with to this very spot.
Just to look at the view. To make out. You know . . .'

He saw Kari shift her weight.

'We had nowhere else to go. And many years later when Else
and I got together, I would bring her here, too. Even though we
had a flat and a double bed. It felt so . . . romantic and innocent.
It was like being just as much in love as the first time.'

'Simon . . .'

Simon turned round and viewed the scene again. The police cars
with the flashing blue lights, the cordons and the blue Honda
Civic with the broken windscreen and a dead man lying at an
unnatural angle, to put it mildly, in the passenger seat. There were
many police officers here. Too many. Panic many.

For once the medical examiner had beaten him to a crime scene and he surmised that the victim had broken both legs in a vehicle collision, been flung over the hood and into the car where he had broken his neck when he collided with the seat. However, the medical examiner had thought it was odd that the victim had sustained no facial injuries after his encounter with the windscreen, until Simon had picked a shot out of the seat upholstery. Simon had also requested an analysis of the blood found on the driver's seat, as the pattern didn't match the cuts to the victim's legs.

'So he specifically *asked* us to attend?' Simon said, nodding towards Åsmund Bjørnstad, who was standing near a CSO and waving his hands as he spoke.

'Yes,' Kari said. 'Because the car is registered to Kjersti Morsand, who is one of Lofthus's victims, he wanted to—'

'Suspected.'

'I beg your pardon?'

'Lofthus is merely suspected of killing Kjersti Morsand. Has anyone talked to Yngve Morsand?'

'He says he doesn't know anything; he's staying at a hotel in Oslo tonight, and the last time he saw the car it was in his garage. Police in Drammen say it looks as if there's been a shooting at his house. Unfortunately the nearest neighbour is a long way away, so there are no witnesses.'

Åsmund Bjørnstad walked up to them. 'We now know who the guy in the passenger seat is. Evgeni Zubov. A known offender. And police in Drammen say there are nine x 19mm Luger bullets in the floorboards of the house, spread in a fan formation.'

'An Uzi?' Simon said, raising an eyebrow.

'What do you think I should say to the press?' Åsmund said, gesticulating with a thumb over his shoulder. The first reporters were already hanging around the police tape by the road.

'The usual,' Simon said. 'Tell them something, but don't give them anything.'

Bjørnstad heaved a sigh. 'They won't leave us alone. When are we meant to get time to work? I hate them.'

'They have a job to do as well,' Simon said.

'The papers are turning him into a celebrity, did you know that?' Kari said as they watched the young inspector walk towards a sea of flashlights.

'Well, he's a talented investigator,' Simon said.

'Not Bjørnstad. Sonny Lofthus.'

Simon turned to her in surprise. 'Are they?'

'They call him a modern-day terrorist. They say he has declared war on organised crime and capitalism. That he's ridding society of parasites.'

'But he's a criminal himself.'

'It only makes the story even more juicy. Don't you ever read the papers?'

'No.'

'And you don't answer your phone, either. I've tried calling you.'

'I've been busy.'

'Busy? Oslo has been turned upside down by these murders, and you're not in the office and you're not in the field. You're supposed to be my boss, Simon.'

'Message received and understood. What was it?'

Kari took a deep breath. 'I've been thinking: Lofthus is one of very few adults in this country who doesn't have a bank account, a credit card or a registered address. But we know that he has enough cash from the Kalle Farrisen murder to stay in a hotel.'

'He paid cash at the Plaza.'

'Precisely. So I checked the hotels. Out of the 20,000 guests who stay in hotels in Oslo every night, on average only six hundred pay cash.'

Simon stared at her. 'Can you find out how many of those six hundred are staying in Kvadraturen?'

'Er, yes. Here's the list of the hotels.' She took a printout from her jacket pocket. 'Why?'

Simon took the printout with one hand while putting on his reading glasses with the other, unfolded the sheets and skimmed them. Looked at the addresses. One hotel. Two. Three. Six. And several of them with guests who had paid cash, especially the cheap ones. There were still too many names. And he guessed that some of the cheapest ones weren't even listed. Simon suddenly stopped reading.

Cheap.

The woman who had tapped on his window. A lovers' meeting in the car, at Akershus Fortress or . . . at the Bismarck. The hotel of choice for Oslo's prostitutes. Right in the middle of Kvadraturen.

'I asked you why.'

'Keep following up that lead, I have to go.' Simon started walking towards the car.

'Wait!' Kari called out and blocked his path. 'Don't you dare run off now. What's going on?'

'Going on?'

'You're on some sort of mission here. It's not on.' Kari brushed some strands of hair away from her face.

Simon could see it now; she was exhausted as well.

'I don't know what this is about,' she said. 'If you want to save the day, be a hero in the twilight of your career, prove Bjørnstad and Kripos wrong. But it's unacceptable, Simon. This case is too big to be a pissing contest for a bunch of overgrown boys.'

Simon looked at her for a long time. And, finally, he nodded slowly. 'You might be right. But my motives are not what you think.'

'Then tell me what they are.'

'I can't, Kari. You'll just have to trust me.'

'When we went to see Iversen, you said I had to wait outside because you were thinking of breaking the rules. I don't want to break the rules, Simon. I just want to do my job. So if you don't tell me what this is about . . .' Her voice was quivering. Definitely tired, Simon thought. '. . . then I'll have to go to someone higher up and tell them what's going on.'

Simon shook his head. 'Don't do it, Kari.'

'And why not?'

'Because,' Simon said, found her gaze and fixed it. 'The mole is still there. Give me twenty-four hours. Please.'

Simon didn't wait for her reply. It wouldn't make any difference. He walked past her and towards his car. He felt her eyes on his back.

On his way down the hills from Holmenkollåsen Simon played the soundtrack from the short phone conversation with Sonny. The rhythmic pounding. The exaggerated moaning. The thin walls in the Bismarck Hotel. How could he have failed to recognise that sound?

Simon looked down at the boy behind the reception counter who was studying his warrant card. So many years had passed and yet nothing had changed at the Bismarck. Apart from the boy; he hadn't sat there back then. And that was all right with him.

'Yes, I can see you're a police officer, but I don't really have a guestbook I can show you.'

'He looks like this,' Simon said, putting the photograph on the counter.

The boy studied it. He hesitated.

'The alternative is that we raid the building and shut the whole place down,' Simon said. 'What do you think your father would say if you got his brothel closed down?'

The family resemblance hadn't deceived him, he had been right.

'He's on the second floor. Room 216. You walk—'

'I'll find it. Give me a key.'

Again, the boy looked reluctant. Then he opened the drawer, removed a key from a big bundle and handed it to Simon. 'But we don't want any trouble.'

Simon walked past the lift and took the steps two at a time. He listened out as he walked down the corridor. It was quiet now. Outside room 216 he took out his Glock. Placed his finger on the two-part double-action trigger. Inserted the key as noiselessly as he could into the lock and turned it. Positioned himself at the side of the door with the pistol in his right hand and opened it with his left hand. Counted to four and stuck his head out and back in one quick movement. He exhaled.

It was dark inside, the curtains were closed, but it was light enough for Simon to have caught a glimpse of the bed.

It was made up and empty.

He went inside to check the bathroom. A toothbrush and some toothpaste.

He went back to the bedroom, didn't turn on the light, but sat down in the redundant chair near the wall. Took out his phone and pressed some buttons. A beeping began somewhere in the room. Simon opened the wardrobe. On top of a briefcase a mobile was glowing at him with his own number shown in the display.

Simon pressed *end call* and sank back in the chair.

The boy had deliberately left his phone behind so that he couldn't be traced. But he probably hadn't expected anyone to find it in a densely populated area such as this. Simon listened out into the darkness. Listened to a clock counting down.

Markus was still awake when he saw the Son coming down the road.

Markus had had the yellow house under surveillance ever since that other person had arrived some hours ago; he hadn't even changed into his pyjamas, he didn't want to miss a thing.

He recognised the Son from the way he moved as he walked in the middle of the quiet, night-time street and the street lights swept over him as he passed underneath them. He seemed tired, perhaps he had walked far, because he was staggering. Markus found him in his binoculars. He was wearing a suit, clutching his side and had a red handkerchief tied around his forehead. Was that blood on his face? Never mind, he must warn him. Markus opened his bedroom door carefully, tiptoed down the stairs, put on his shoes and ran down to the gate across the patchy, worn grass.

The Son noticed him and stopped right in front of the gate to his own house.

'Hello, Markus. Shouldn't you be in bed?'

His voice was calm and soft. He looked like he had been in the wars, but he spoke as if he was telling him a bedtime story. Markus decided he too would speak with a voice like that when he grew up and had stopped being scared.

'Are you hurt?'

'Someone bumped into me when I was driving,' the Son smiled. 'It's nothing.'

'There's someone in your house.'

'Oh?' the Son said, turning to the shiny black windows. 'Good guys or bad guys?'

Markus gulped. He had seen the photo on TV. But he had also heard his mother say that there was nothing to be scared of, that he only hurt bad people. And on Twitter several people were praising him, tweeting that the police should just let baddies kill baddies, that it was like using predators for pest control.

'Neither, I think.'

'Oh?'

*   *   *

Martha woke up when someone entered the room.

She had been dreaming. Dreaming about the woman in the attic. About the baby. That she saw the baby, that it was alive, that it had been there the whole time, trapped in the basement where it had been crying and crying while it waited to be let out. And now it was out. It was here.

'Martha?'

His voice, his lovely, calm voice sounded incredulous.

She turned over in the bed and looked at him.

'You said I could come,' she said. 'There was no one to let me in, but I knew where the key was, so . . .'

'You came.'

She nodded. 'I took this room, I hope it's OK.'

He just nodded and sat down on the edge of the bed.

'The mattress was on the floor,' she said and stretched. 'By the way, a book fell through the slats as I was putting the mattress back on the bed. I put it on the table over there.'

'OK?'

'What was the mattress doing—'

'I was hiding under it,' he said without taking his eyes off her. 'When I crawled out, I just eased it down on the floor and left it. What have you got there?'

He raised the hand with which he had been clutching his side and touched one of her ears. She didn't reply. She let him feel the earring. A gust of wind moved the curtains she had put up after finding them in the blanket box. A beam of moonlight crept in, caught his hand and face. She froze.

'It's not as bad as it looks,' he said.

'No, not the cut to your forehead. But you're bleeding somewhere else. Where?'

He pulled his jacket to one side and showed her. The right side of his shirt was soaked with blood.

'What was it?'

'A bullet. It just nipped me and went straight through. Completely harmless, it's just a little blood, it'll soon—'

'Shh,' she said and kicked off the duvet, took his hand and led him to the bathroom. Ignoring the fact that he could see her in her underwear while she searched through the medicine cabinet. Found some twelve-year-old disinfectant, two rolls of bandages, some cotton wool and a pair of small scissors. She made him strip from the waist up.

'As you can see it's just a dent in my spare tyre,' he smiled.

She had seen worse. She had seen better. She cleaned his injuries and taped cotton wool over the holes where the projectile had entered and exited. Then she wrapped a bandage around his waist. When she untied the handkerchief around his forehead, fresh blood started trickling from underneath the scab immediately.

'Did your mother have a sewing kit anywhere?'

'I don't need—'

'I said shh.'

It took four minutes and four stitches to sew the broken skin together.

'I saw the briefcase in the passage,' he said while she rolled several layers of gauze around his head.

'That's not my money. And the council has allocated us enough funds for the renovation work, so thanks but no thanks.' She taped the edges in place and stroked his cheek. 'There, that ought to—'

He kissed her. Right on the lips. Then he let go of her.

'I love you.'

Then he kissed her again.

'I don't believe you,' she said.

'You don't believe I love you?'

'I don't believe you've kissed other girls. You're a lousy kisser.'

The laughter made his eyes sparkle. 'It's been a long time. Remind me, please?'

'Don't worry about getting it right. Just let it happen. Kiss me lazily.'

'Lazily?'

'Like a soft, sleepy snake. Like this.'

She cradled his head gently between her hands and raised her lips to his. And it struck her how strangely natural it felt, as if they were two children playing an exciting but innocent game. And he trusted her. Like she trusted him.

'Do you see?' she whispered. 'More lips, less tongue.'

'More clutch, less gas?'

She giggled. 'Exactly. Let's go to bed.'

'What will happen there?'

'We'll just have to see. How's your side? Will it be all right?'

'All right for what?'

'Don't play the innocent with me.'

He kissed her again. 'Are you sure?' he whispered.

'No. So if we wait too long . . .'

'Let's go to bed.'

Rover got up and straightened his back with a groan. In his excitement he had failed to notice that his back had seized up; it was like when he made love to Janne, who stopped by from time to time to 'see what he was up to'. He had tried explaining that tinkering with the motorbike and tinkering with her had many similarities. That you could keep going in the same fixed position without being aware of aching muscles or time passing. But when you were done, then it was payback time. She had enjoyed the comparison. That was so like her.

Rover wiped his hands. The job was complete. The last thing he had done was attach a new exhaust pipe to the Harley-Davidson. It was like crossing the 't' and dotting the 'i'. Like when the piano tuner plays a piano he has just tuned. Just for the sheer fun of it. You could produce an extra 20 b.h.p. simply from modifying the exhaust pipe and the air filter, but everyone knew that the exhaust pipe was mainly about the sound. Getting it to produce that lovely, burring, juicy bass which didn't sound like anything else Rover had ever heard. Of course he could turn the key right away in order to listen to the music of the engine to confirm everything he already knew. Or he could save it for tomorrow morning, like a present to himself. Janne always said that you should never postpone your pleasures, that there was no guarantee that you would live another day. He guessed that was Janne being Janne.

Rover wiped the oil off his fingers with the rag and went to the back room to wash his hands. Looked at himself in the mirror. The oil smears on his face that looked like warpaint and the gold tooth. As usual he noticed how other needs announced themselves now that he was done; food, drink, rest. It was a great feeling. But there was also the strange emptiness that followed such an achievement. A 'Now what?' A 'What's the point of it all?' He chased the thoughts away. Looked at the warm water pouring from the tap. Then he stopped. Turned off the water. A sound had come from outside the garage. Janne? Now?

'I love you too,' Martha said.

At one point he had stopped – both of them panting, sweating, flushed – dried the sweat between her breasts with the sheet which she had pulled off the mattress, and said that they might find them here, that it was dangerous. And she had replied that she didn't scare easily once she had made up her mind. And that incidentally – if they really had to talk – she loved him.

'I love you.'

Then they carried on.

*   *   *

'It's one thing for you to stop supplying me with weapons,' the man said as he peeled the thin glove off his hand. It was the biggest hand Rover had ever seen. 'It's another when you start supplying my enemy, yes?'

Rover didn't struggle. He was being held by two men; a third was standing next to the big man, aiming a pistol at Rover's forehead. A pistol Rover knew only too well because he had modified it himself.

'Giving that boy an Uzi is like telling me to go to hell. Was that what you wanted? To send me to hell?'

Rover could have replied. Said that given what he already knew about the Twin, he guessed that was where he had come from in the first place.

But he didn't. He wanted to live. Just for a few more seconds.

He looked at the motorbike behind the big man.

Janne had been right. He should have started it. Closed his eyes and listened. He should have stopped to smell the flowers. It's such an obvious truth, it's so hackneyed and yet so impossible to comprehend until you stand at the threshold and you realise how banal it really is: that the only guarantee you have in life is that you're going to die.

The man put his gloves down on the worktop. They looked like used condoms. 'Now let me see . . .' he said, glancing around at the tools mounted on the walls. He pointed a finger at them as he chanted in a low voice: 'Eeny, meeny, miney . . .'

38

DAWN WAS STARTING TO BREAK.

Martha lay close to Sonny with her feet entwined in his. Heard the change to the steady sleeping rhythm in his breathing. But his eyes were still shut. She caressed his stomach and saw a small smile on his lips.

'Good morning, lover boy,' she whispered.

He grinned from ear to ear, but pulled a face as he tried to turn over to look at her.

'Does it hurt?'

'Only my side,' he winced.

'The bleeding has stopped, I checked a couple of times last night.'

'What? You took liberties with me while I was asleep?' He kissed her on the forehead.

'I thought you took a few liberties of your own, Mr Lofthus.'

'It was my first time, remember,' he said. 'I don't know the meaning of liberties.'

'You're a very good liar,' she said.

He laughed.

'I've been thinking,' she said.

'Yes?'

'Let's leave. Let's leave right now.'

He didn't reply, but she sensed his body stiffen. And she felt the tears come, suddenly and violently as if a dam had burst. He rolled over and held her.

He waited until her crying had subsided.

'What did you tell them?' he asked.

'I said that Anders and I couldn't wait until summer,' she sniffed. 'That we were going to end this right now. Or at least I was. And then I left. I went outside. Ran down to the high street. Hailed a cab. I saw him come running after me with that bloody mother of his at his heels.' She laughed out loud, then she started crying again. 'I'm sorry,' she sobbed. 'I'm so . . . so stupid! Dear God, what am I doing here?'

'You love me,' he whispered into her hair. 'That's what you're doing here.'

'And what? What kind of person loves a man who kills people, who is doing everything he can to get himself killed, and who eventually will be. Do you know what they call you on the Internet? The Buddha with the Sword. They've interviewed former inmates who portray you as some kind of saint. But do you know something?' She dried her tears. 'I think you're just as mortal as everyone else I've seen come and go at the Ila Centre.'

'We'll go away.'

'Then we have to do it now.'

'There are two more to go, Martha.'

She shook her head, the tears began to flow again and she hammered her fists into his chest with impotent rage. 'It's too late – don't you understand? Everyone is looking for you, *everyone*.'

'Only two more left. The man who decided that my father must be killed and made it look as if he was the mole. And the mole. Then we'll leave.'

'*Only* two left? You *only* have to kill another two people and then we can escape? Is it that easy for you?'

'No, Martha. It isn't easy for me. None of them were easy. And it's not true what they say, that it gets easier. But I have to do it, there's no other way.'

'Do you really think you'll survive?'

'No.'

'No?'

'No.'

'No! But in God's name, then why are you talking about—'

'Because you can only plan to survive.'

She fell silent.

He stroked her forehead, her cheek and her throat. And then he started talking. Quietly and slowly, as if he had to be sure that every word he chose was the right one.

She listened. He told her about his childhood. About his father. About his death and about everything that had happened since.

She listened and understood. Listened and didn't understand.

A ray of sunshine had crept in between the curtains by the time he had finished.

'Listen to yourself,' she whispered. 'You know this is insane, don't you?'

'Yes,' he said. 'But it's the only thing I can do.'

'The only thing you can do is kill a lot of people?'

He took a deep breath. 'All I ever wanted was to be like my father. When I read that suicide note, he disappeared. And so did I. But then – in prison – when I heard the true story of how he gave his life for me and my mother, I was born again.'

'Born again to do . . . this?'

'I wish there was another way.'

'But why? To fill your father's shoes? Because the son must . . .' She narrowed her eyes, forcing out the last tears. Promising herself that they would be the last. '. . . finish what his father couldn't?'

'He did what he had to do. I'm doing what I have to do. He died for us. When I'm done with this, I'm done. I promise you. Everything will be all right.'

She looked at him for a long time. 'I need to think,' she said at last. 'You go back to sleep.'

He slept while she lay awake. It wasn't until the birds started singing outside that she, too, fell asleep. And she was sure of it now.

She was crazy.

She had been so from the moment she saw him.

But she hadn't realised that she was just as mad as him until she let herself into the yellow house, found Agnete Iversen's earrings on the kitchen counter and put them on.

Martha was woken by the sound of children playing in the street outside. Cries of joy. Small running feet. She thought of how innocence walks hand-in-hand with ignorance. How insight never clarifies, only complicates. He slept so peacefully next to her that for a moment she thought he was already dead. She stroked his cheek. He muttered something, but didn't wake up. How could a hunted man sleep so soundly? The sleep of the just. It was said to be good.

She slipped out of bed, got dressed and went down to the kitchen. She found some coffee, but nothing else. The freezer she had been sitting on in the basement, perhaps he had a frozen pizza or something. She walked down the basement steps and grabbed the freezer handle. It was locked. She looked around. Her eyes fell on the nail in the wall and the key with the illegible tag. She took the key and inserted it in the lock. Turned it. *Voilà.* She flipped open the lid, leaned in and felt the chill against her chest and throat, then she let out a short scream and dropped the lid. Turned round and sank down with her back pressed against the freezer.

She remained on her haunches, breathing hard through her nose. Tried to blink away the sight of the body that had been staring up at her with an open, white mouth and ice crystals on the eyelashes. Her pulse was so fast that she felt faint. She listened to her heart. And to the voices. There were two of them.

One of them screamed in her ear that she was mad, that he was mad, a killer, that she had to run up the stairs and get out of the house now!

The other told her that this body was simply a physical manifestation of something she already knew and had accepted. Yes, he had killed people. People who deserved to die.

The screaming voice ordered her to stand up. It drowned out the voice telling her that this was the panic she would inevitably have to experience at some point. She had made a choice last night, hadn't she?

No, she hadn't.

She knew it now. That the choice of whether to jump down the hole and follow the rabbit, take the step into his world, or to stay here in the normal world, was being made here and now. This was her last chance to walk away. The next few seconds were the most important in her life. Her last chance to . . .

She got up. She was still dizzy, but she knew she could run fast. He would never catch her. She inhaled oxygen into her lungs and the blood transported it to her brain. She leaned against the freezer lid, saw her own reflection in the glossy surface. Saw the earrings.

I love him. That's why I'm doing this.

Then she opened the lid again.

The body had bled over most of the food. The design on the Frionor boxes seemed rather dated. They must be at least twelve years old, that sounded about right.

She concentrated on her breathing, on her thoughts, forcing away anything that wasn't helpful. If they were going to eat, she had to go to a shop. She would ask one of the children where the nearest supermarket was. Yes, that was what she was going to do. Eggs and bacon. Fresh bread. Strawberries. Yogurt.

She closed the lid. Pressed her eyes shut. She thought she was going to cry again. But instead she started laughing. The hysterical laughter of a person in free fall down the rabbit hole, she thought. Then she opened her eyes and walked towards the stairs. At the top of the stairs, she realised she was humming a tune.

That you've always been her lover and you want to travel with her.
Mad.

. . . And you want to travel blind and you know that she will trust you.

Mad, mad.

. . . for you've touched her perfect body with your mind.

Markus was playing Super Mario Brothers by the open window when he heard a door slam outside. He looked out. It was the pretty lady. Or at least she was pretty today. She walked from the yellow house and down to the gate. Markus remembered how the Son had lit up when he'd told him that she was the one he had seen enter the house. Not that Markus understood much about such things, but he had an inkling that the Son was in love with her.

The woman went over to the little girls who were playing with skipping ropes and asked them a question. They pointed and she smiled, called out something to them and walked quickly in the direction they had indicated. Markus was about to return to his game when he noticed that the curtains in the bedroom were open. He grabbed his binoculars.

It was the Son. He was standing by the window with his eyes closed and his hand resting on his side, on a bandage. He was naked and smiling. He looked happy. Like Markus on Christmas Eve, just before he unwrapped his presents. No, change that, the next day, when he woke up and remembered the presents he had been given the night before.

The Son took a towel from the cupboard, opened the door and was about to close it when he stopped. He looked to the side, down at the table. Grabbed something lying there. Markus zoomed in.

It was a book. Bound in black leather. The Son opened the book and began reading it. Then he dropped the towel. Sat down on the bed and carried on reading. He sat like this for several minutes. Markus saw his facial expression change and his body stiffen, freeze in a kind of crippled position.

Then he suddenly got up and hurled the book at the wall.

He grabbed the table lamp and subjected it to the same treatment.

He clutched his side, howled and slumped on the bed. Bowed his head, forcing it down with his hands which he had folded behind his neck. He sat with his body shaking as if he was having a fit.

Markus could see that something terrible had happened, but he didn't know what. He wanted to run over there, say or do something to comfort him. He knew how. He would often cheer his mother up. Talk to her, remind her of the nice things they had done together, did she remember them? There weren't many to choose between, only the same three or four events, so she always did. She would smile a kind of wistful smile and ruffle his hair. And then things would get better. But he hadn't done any nice things with the Son. And perhaps the Son preferred to be alone, something Markus could relate to, he was like that himself. When his mother wanted to comfort him because someone had upset him, he would just get irritated; it was as if her kindness weakened him, validated the bullies who called him a sissy.

But the Son was no crybaby.

Or was he?

He had just got up and turned to the window; he was crying. His eyes were red and his cheeks streaked with tears.

What if Markus had been wrong, what if the Son was just like him? Weak, cowardly, someone who fled, ran away to hide, scared of getting a beating? No, no, he wasn't like that, not the Son! He was big and strong and brave and he helped those who weren't or who had yet to become strong.

The Son picked up the book, sat down and started writing.

After a while he tore a page out of the book, scrunched it up and threw it in the waste-paper basket by the door. Started on another page. Not for so long this time. He pulled out the page and read what he had written. And then he closed his eyes and pressed the paper to his lips.

Martha put down the carrier bags of groceries on the kitchen worktop. Wiped the sweat from her brow. The shop had been further away than she had expected and she had practically run all the way back. She rinsed the box with strawberries under the tap, picked out the two biggest, juiciest berries and took the bouquet of buttercups she had picked along the roadside with her. Again she felt the sweet sting at the memory of his burning skin under the duvet. The heroin addict who got high from her touch. Because he was her drug now. Hooked after the first fix. She was lost and she loved it!

She sensed it on the stairs as soon as she saw the open bedroom door. Something was wrong. It was far too quiet.

The bed was empty. The lamp lay broken on the floor. His clothes were gone. Under the shards from the lamp she saw the black book she had found under the bed slats.

She called out his name even though she knew there would be no reply. The gate had been open when she came back and she was quite sure she'd closed it when she left. They had come for him, like he'd said. He had clearly struggled, but to no avail. She had left him asleep, she had failed to take care of him, she hadn't . . .

She turned round and spotted the note on the pillow. The paper was yellow and looked like it had been torn from the notebook. It was written with an old pen lying next to the pillow. Her initial reaction was that it must have been his father's pen. And before she had even read the words, she thought that history was repeating itself. Then she read the note, dropped the flowers and clasped her hand to her mouth, an automatic gesture to hide the ugly way the mouth contorted when the tears welled up.

Dear Martha

Forgive me, but I'm going to disappear now. I love you forever.

Sonny

39

MARKUS WAS SITTING ON THE bed in the yellow house.

After the woman had rushed off, only twenty minutes after the Son had left in a hurry, Markus had waited ten minutes before he realised that they weren't coming back.

Then he had crossed the road. The key to the house had been put back in its regular place.

The bed had been made and the shards from the lamp placed in the waste-paper basket. He found the scrunched-up piece of paper under the shards.

The words were written in a neat, almost feminine hand.

Dear Martha

My father once told me how he watched a man drown. He had been on patrol, it was the middle of the night and a boy had rung from the harbour at Kongen. The boy's father had fallen into the sea while they were mooring their boat. He couldn't swim and was clinging to the gunwale, but the son wasn't able to pull his father back on board. By the time the patrol car arrived, the boy's father had given up, let go and gone under. Several minutes had already passed and my father called for divers as the boy sobbed desperately. And while they waited, the man suddenly surfaced, his pale face gasping for air. The son let out a cry of joy. Then the father went under again. My father jumped into the water to rescue him, but it was too dark. When my father resurfaced, he looked straight into the still beaming face of the boy who thought that now everything was OK, his father was alive and the police were here. And my father told me how he had seen the heart torn out of the boy's chest when he realised that God had merely been toying with him by letting him think he was going to give back the father he had taken from him. My father said that if there was a God, then he was a cruel God. Now I think I understand what he meant, because I have finally found my father's diary. Perhaps he wanted us to know. Or maybe he was just cruel. Otherwise why keep a diary, but hide it in such an obvious place as under the mattress?

You have your whole life ahead of you, Martha. I think you can do something good with it. I can't do the same. Forgive me, but I m going to disappear now.

I love you forever.

Sonny

Markus looked at the table. There was the book which the Son had been reading.

Black leather cover, yellowing pages. He flicked through it.

He realised immediately that it was a diary even though there weren't entries written for each day. In some places there were months between the entries. Sometimes there would just be a date and a couple of sentences. For example, it said that 'the troika' would eventually break up, that something had come between them. A week later that Helene was pregnant and that they had bought their own house. But how hard it was to survive on just a policeman's salary, what a shame it was that both his and Helene's parents came from such reduced circumstances that they couldn't help them. Later on how happy he was that Sonny had started wrestling. Then a page about how the bank had raised interest rates, how they quite simply couldn't pay the mortgage, how he had to do something before the house was repossessed. Think of something. That he had promised Helene it would be OK. Fortunately, the boy didn't seem to have noticed that anything was troubling his parents.

19 March
Sonny says he wants to follow in my footsteps and become a police officer. Helene says that he is obsessed with me, that he worships me. I said it's all right for a son to do that and that I was no different. Sonny is a good boy, perhaps too good, it's a tough world, but a boy like him will always be a blessing to his father.

Some pages followed which Markus didn't quite understand. Words such as 'imminent personal bankruptcy' and 'sell my soul to the devil'. And the name 'the Twin'.

Markus turned to the next page.

4 August
Today at the station they talked about the mole again, saying the Twin must have a plant in the force. How strange that people, even police officers, have so little imagination. It's always one killer, one traitor. Don't they realise the genius of being two? That one will always have an alibi when the other is active, that in this way we'll both be completely above suspicion on so many occasions that we'll automatically be

eliminated as potential suspects? Yes, it's a good set-up. It's perfect. We're corrupt, thoroughly rotten police officers who have betrayed everything we believe in for a few measly pieces of silver. We've turned a blind eye to drug dealing, human trafficking, even murder. Nothing matters any more. Is there a way back? Is there any chance of confession, penitence and forgiveness without me ruining everything and everyone around me? I don't know. All I know is that I have to get out.

Markus yawned. Reading always made him sleepy, especially when there were so many words he didn't understand. He flicked ahead several pages.

15 September

I wonder how long we can carry on without the Twin finding out who we are. We communicate via Hotmail addresses from our separate, stolen computers which we've 'borrowed' from the evidence room, but it isn't failsafe. On the other hand, if he had wanted to, he could have arranged surveillance of the places where we make our drops. When I picked up the envelope which was taped to the underside of the bench at Broker's Restaurant in Bogstadveien the week before last, I was sure I had been spotted. A guy at the bar scowled at me, anyone could see he was a criminal. And I was right about him. He came over and told me that I had nicked him for handling stolen property ten years ago. Said it was the best thing that could have happened to him, that he had stopped keeping bad company and was now running a fish farm with his brother. Then he shook my hand and left. One story with a happy ending. The envelope also contained a letter in which the Twin wrote that he wants me – so clearly he doesn't know that there are two of us – to advance in the police force, get a top job where I can be more useful; both to him and to me. Access to sensitive information, more money. He wrote that he could help me advance, pull strings. I laughed out loud. The guy must be completely mad, a guy like that doesn't stop until he has achieved world domination. He is someone who doesn't stop, but has to be stopped. I showed the letter to Z. I don't know why, but he didn't laugh.

Markus could hear his mother calling him. He imagined that she had a job for him to do. He hated it when she did that, flung open a window and yelled his name across the neighbourhood as if he were a dog or something. He turned another page.

6 October

Something has happened. Z says he thinks we ought to quit while we're ahead, get out while the going is good. And the Twin hasn't replied to my email for several days. That's never happened before. Have the two of them been talking? I don't know if they have, but I do know that this isn't something we can just walk away from. I know that T2 no longer trusts me. For the same reason, I no longer trust him. We have shown each other our true faces.

7 October

Last night it was suddenly clear to me: the Twin only needs one of us and that's exactly what he'll get – one. The other will be the jilted lover, a bitter witness who must be eliminated. And Z has already realised this. So now it's urgent, I have to get him before he gets me. I've asked Helene if she could go with Sonny to the wrestling competition tomorrow as I have things to do. I have asked Z if we can meet at the medieval ruins in Maridalen at midnight, that we have things to discuss.

He sounded a little surprised that I wanted to meet in such a deserted place and so late, but said that it was fine.

8 October

It's quiet. I have loaded the pistol. It feels strange to know that I'm about to take a man's life. I keep asking myself what led me here. Did I do it for my family? Or for myself? Or was it the temptation to achieve something my parents couldn't, a position in society, the life I've seen handed to undeserving idiots on a plate? Am I resourceful and brave – or weak and spineless? Am I a bad person? I've asked myself this question: if my son had been in my shoes, would I want him to do what I have done? And that, of course, made the answer very obvious.

I'm going up to Maridalen soon, then we'll have to see if I come back a changed man. A killer.

I know it sounds strange, but sometimes I pray that someone will find this diary. That's human nature, I guess.

There was nothing more. Markus flicked through the blank pages and to the final ones which had been torn out. Then he put the diary back on the bedside table and walked quietly down the stairs while he heard his mother's voice call out his name over and over.

40

BETTY ENTERED THE CROWDED PHARMACY, tore off a numbered ticket where it said 'Prescriptions', and found a vacant chair along the wall among customers who were staring into space or, despite the sign prohibiting their use, pressing keys on their mobiles. She had convinced her doctor to write a prescription for stronger sleeping pills.

'These are hard-core benzodiazepines and only for short-term use,' he had said and repeated what she already knew; that their use created a vicious cycle which could lead to dependency and which didn't get to the root of the problem. Betty had replied that the root of the problem was that she couldn't sleep. Especially not after she had realised that she had been alone in a room with the country's most wanted killer. A man who had shot a woman in her own home in Holmenkollåsen. And today the newspaper said that he was also suspected of the murder of a shipowner's wife, that he had entered a house apparently chosen at random outside Drammen and nearly sawn off the top of her head. In the last few days Betty had wandered around like a zombie, half awake, half asleep, hallucinating. She saw his face everywhere, not just in the newspapers and on the TV, but on advertisements, on the tram, in reflections in shop windows. He was the postman, her neighbour, the waiter.

And now she saw him in here, too.

He was standing by the counter wearing a white turban or perhaps it was just a bandage around his head. He had put down a pile of disposable syringes and hypodermic needles on the counter and paid cash. The grainy pictures in the newspapers weren't terribly helpful, but Betty noticed that the woman on the chair next to her whispered something to her companion while she pointed at the man, so perhaps she had also recognised him. But when the man with the turban turned round and walked towards the exit, his body twisting to one side, Betty realised that she was seeing things again.

The ashen, withdrawn and stony face looked nothing like the face she had seen in Suite 4.

Kari leaned forward to read the numbers while she drove slowly past the large houses. She had made up her mind after a sleepless night. Sam – whom she had also kept awake – had said that Kari shouldn't take a job she didn't intend to stay in so seriously. It was true, of course, but ultimately Kari liked order. And this could affect her future, it could close doors to her. So she had reached the decision to make a direct approach.

She stopped the car. This was the right number.

She wondered if she should drive through the open gate and up to the house, but decided to park in the street. She walked up the steep tarmac drive. A sprinkler was whistling in the garden; apart from that it was completely quiet.

She climbed the steps and rang the bell. Heard fierce barking coming from the other side. She waited. No one came. She turned round and was about to walk down the steps, and there he was. The sun reflected in his rectangular spectacles. He must have come from behind the house and the garage; he must have moved quickly and quietly.

'Yes?'

He had his hands behind his back.

'I'm Officer Kari Adel. I'd like to talk to you about something.'

'And what might that be?' He stuck his hands behind the belt at the back as if to hoist up the beige chinos or pull out his shirt, after all it was a very hot summer's day. Or to stick a gun behind his belt and pull his shirt over it so it wouldn't show.

'Simon Kefas.'

'I see. And why have you come directly to me?'

Kari rolled her head from side to side. 'Simon led me to believe that I risked leaks if I took the traditional route. He still believes there's a mole in our ranks.'

'Does he now?'

'And that's why I thought it was best to come straight to the top. To you, Commissioner.'

'Well, well,' Pontius Parr said, rubbing his narrow chin. 'Then we'd better go inside, Officer Adel.'

A happy Airedale terrier jumped up at Kari in the hall.

'Willoch! We've talked about this . . .'

The dog dropped down on all fours and limited itself to licking Kari's hand while its tail went like a propeller. As they walked into the living room, Kari explained that she had been told that the Commissioner was working from home today.

'I'm skiving,' Parr smiled and extended his hand towards a large, inviting sofa covered with scatter cushions. 'I was meant to start my summer holiday this week, but with this killer on the loose . . .' He sighed and dropped down on one of the matching armchairs. 'So what's this about Simon?'

Kari cleared her throat. She had planned what she had to say with all sorts of reservations and assurances that she hadn't come to tell tales, only ensure the quality of their work. But now, as she sat here with Parr who seemed so relaxed and welcoming, who had even admitted that he was skiving, it felt more natural to get straight to the point.

'Simon is on a mission of his own,' she said.

The Commissioner raised an eyebrow. 'Go on.'

'We're investigating the case in parallel with Kripos, we're not working *with* them, and now he's stopped working with me as well. That's fine, but the problem is that he appears to have some sort of agenda. And I don't want to go down with him if he's doing something illegal. He's asked me to stay out of certain situations and stated quite plainly that he doesn't intend to play by the rules.'

'I see. And when was this?'

Kari gave him a brief summary of the meeting with Iver Iversen.

'Hmmmm,' Parr said, hanging on the 'm' forever. 'That's not good. I know Simon, and I wish I could say that this doesn't sound anything like him. But it does, unfortunately. What do you think his agenda is?'

'He wants to catch Sonny Lofthus single-handedly.'

Parr rested his chin between his thumb and forefinger. 'I see. Who else knows about this?'

'No one. I came straight here.'

'Good. Promise me that you won't mention it to anyone else. This is a delicate matter, as I'm sure you'll appreciate. Everyone's eyes are on the police right now and we can't afford to have individual officers behaving unprofessionally.'

'Of course, I understand.'

'Leave it with me. We'll never mention your involvement. This meeting never happened. It may sound dramatic, but in this way, you won't risk being labelled a snitch by your colleagues. Such names tend to stick.'

Tend to stick. She hadn't thought about that. Kari swallowed and nodded quickly. 'Thank you so much.'

'Not at all. Thank *you*, Adel. You've done the right thing. Now go back to work and carry on as if nothing's happened, as they say.' The Commissioner stood up. 'I have to get back to doing nothing, I'm supposed to be working from home.'

Kari got up, happy and relieved that this had proved to be far more pain-free than she'd hoped.

Parr stopped in the doorway. 'Where is Simon now?'

'I don't know, he just walked away from the crime scene where we found the car and the body last night, and no one has seen him since.'

'Hm. So you've no idea?'

'The last thing I did was give him a list of hotels where Lofthus might be staying.'

'Based on what?'

'That he pays cash. Hardly anyone does these days.'

'Clever. Good luck.'

'Thank you.'

Kari walked down the steps and was level with the sprinkler when she heard footsteps behind her. It was Parr.

'Just one more thing,' he said. 'Based on what I'm hearing, I understand there's a possibility that it might be you yourself who'll finally track down Lofthus for us.'

'Yes,' Kari said and knew it sounded as conceited as she had intended.

'If that were to happen, then remember that he's armed and dangerous. That you'll be treated sympathetically if you or several of your colleagues are forced to defend yourselves.'

Kari brushed aside the usual stray hairs. 'Just what exactly does that mean?'

'Just that the threshold for an armed response to stop this killer is low. Remember, he's already tortured one public servant.'

Kari could feel the wind blow a fine spray of water. 'Very well,' she said.

'I'll have a word with the head of Kripos,' Parr said. 'It might be an idea for you and Åsmund Bjørnstad to work together as a team on this investigation. I do believe you have the same understanding of the situation.'

Simon stared into the mirror. The years were passing. The hours were passing. He wasn't the man he had been fifteen years ago. He wasn't even the man he was seventy-two hours ago. Once he had believed he was invincible. Once he had believed he was scum. He had come to the conclusion that he was neither, that he was a human being of flesh and blood, with the potential to do the right thing. Or let himself be ruled by his basest instincts.

But did that mean that he, or anyone, had free will? Wouldn't we all, given the same mathematical equation, the same odds, the same probability of what paid off, make the same choices over and over? People claimed that you could change your values, a woman might come into your life, you might grow wiser and reach a new appreciation of what really mattered. Yes, but only because those other things had become important, all that had happened was that the numbers in the equation had changed, you still solved it in the same way. You would then have made those new choices over and over. Determined by the composition of chemical substances in your brain, available information, survival instinct, sexual urges, mortal fear, learned morality and herd instinct. We don't punish people because they are evil, but because they make bad choices, choices that are bad for the herd. Morality isn't heaven-sent or eternal, just a set of rules that benefit the herd. And those who are incapable of following the rules, the accepted pattern of behaviour, will never be able to conform because they have no free will; it's an illusion. Like the rest of us, lawbreakers just do what they do.

That is why they must be eliminated to ensure they don't procreate and so infect the herd with their negative behaviour genes.

Simon Kefas thought that what he was looking at in the mirror was a robot. Complex and complicated and filled with possibilities. But a robot all the same.

So what did the boy want to avenge? What did he hope to achieve? Save a world that didn't want to be saved? Exterminate all the things we won't admit we need? Because who can bear to live in a world without crime, without the idiotic rebellion of the stupid, without the irrational ones who bring about movement, change? Without the hope of a better – or a worse – world. This hellish restlessness, the shark's need for constant movement to get oxygen.

'This moment is fine. Let us stay as we are. Just like this.' Only it never happened.

Simon heard footsteps. He checked that his pistol's safety catch was off.

The key was turned in the lock.

The footsteps sounded quick. Someone was in a hurry. He counted the seconds without taking his eyes off his face in the mirror over the sink in the bathroom. The boy, having seen that everything was exactly as when he left the room, would relax and drop his guard. He might come in here, but by then he would have put down any weapons. Simon kept counting.

On twenty he opened the door and stepped out, holding his pistol.

The boy was sitting on the bed.

He had a bandage around his head. In front of him on the floor lay the briefcase from the wardrobe. It was opened and filled with bags of white powder which Simon recognised instantly. The boy had cut a hole in one of them. In his left hand he held a teaspoon with white powder, in the other a lit lighter. On the bed lay a pile of disposable syringes and a sheet of hypodermic needles.

'Who shoots first?' the boy asked.

41

SIMON SAT DOWN IN THE chair opposite him. Watched him hold the lighter under the teaspoon.

'How did you find me?'

'Your phone,' Simon said, without taking his eyes off the flame. 'And the background noises. Hookers at work. You know who I am?'

'Simon Kefas,' the boy said. 'I recognise you from the photographs.' The powder started to dissolve. Tiny bubbles rose to the surface. 'I won't resist arrest. I was going to turn myself in later today, anyway.'

'Oh? Why? Is your crusade over so soon?'

'There is no crusade,' the boy said, putting down the teaspoon with care. Simon knew this was to allow the liquid heroin to cool. 'There is only blind faith, those of us who still believe what we were taught as children. Until the day we discover that the world isn't like that. That we're trash. We're all rubbish.'

Simon put the gun in the palm of his hand and looked at it. 'I'm not taking you to the police station, Sonny. I'm taking you to the Twin. You, the drugs and the money you stole from him.'

The boy looked up at him as he tore the wrapper off a syringe. 'Fine. It's all the same to me. He's going to kill me?'

'Yes.'

'Taking out the trash. Just let me shoot up first.' He put a ball of cotton wool in the spoon, pushed the needle through it and pulled up the plunger. 'I don't know these drugs, they might not be pure,' he said, as if to explain the cotton-wool filtering.

Then he looked up at Simon to see if he appreciated the irony.

'Heroin from Kalle Farrisen's stash,' Simon said. 'You've had it all this time without being tempted to sample it?'

The boy laughed harshly, briefly.

'I put that badly,' Simon said. 'Delete "tempted". But you've managed to resist. How?'

The boy shrugged.

'I know a thing or two about addicts,' Simon said. 'The list of things that makes us quit isn't long. Either we've found Jesus, a girl, our own children or the man with the scythe. In my case it was a girl. And in yours?'

The boy said nothing.

'Your father?'

The boy simply probed Simon with his eyes as if he had discovered something.

Simon shook his head. 'You two are so alike. It's even clearer to me now than in the photos.'

'They always said that he and I were nothing like each other.'

'Not you and your father. You and your mother. You have her eyes. She used to get up at the crack of dawn, before the rest of us, and have breakfast before she rushed off to work. Sometimes I would get up early just to see her sit there, before she got ready to go out, tired, but with these amazing, beautiful eyes.'

The boy sat completely still now.

Simon kept turning the pistol over as if he was looking for something. 'We were four people who had nothing, who shared a flat in Oslo, it was cheaper that way. Three boys who went to the

Police College plus your mother. The three boys called themselves "the troika" and they were best mates. They were your father, me and Pontius Parr. Your mother had looked in the paper for a place to stay and taken our spare room. I think all three of us fell in love with her the moment we saw her.' Simon smiled. 'We circled each other, courting her in secret. And we were three handsome guys, I don't think she quite knew which one of us to pick.'

'I didn't know that,' the boy said. 'But I know she picked the wrong one.'

'Yes,' Simon said. 'She picked me.'

Simon looked up from his gun. Met Sonny's gaze.

'Your mother was the love of my life, Sonny. I nearly went completely under when she left me and started seeing your father. Especially when it turned out soon afterwards that she was pregnant. The two of them moved out, bought the house in Berg. She was pregnant, he was still at the Police College, they didn't have a pot to piss in. But interest rates were low and in those years the banks were throwing money at you.'

Sonny hadn't blinked once. Simon cleared his throat.

'It was around that time I started gambling in earnest. I was already in debt when I started betting on the horses. High stakes. There was something liberating about standing at the edge of the abyss and knowing that whatever happened it would take me away from where I was. Up or down, it almost didn't matter. At that time your father and I had drifted apart. I don't suppose I could bear his happiness. He and Pontius had become close buddies, the troika had dissolved. I made up some excuse when he asked me to be your godfather, but I sneaked into the back of the church when you were christened. You were the only baby who didn't cry. You just looked up calmly and smiled at the new, slightly nervous vicar as if you were christening him and not the other way round. I went right out and put 13,000 kroner on a horse called Sonny.'

'And?'

'You owe me 13,000 kroner.'

The boy smiled. 'Why are you telling me all this?'

'Because from time to time I've wondered if things had to be like that. If I could have chosen differently. If Ab could have. If you could have. Einstein said that the definition of insanity is doing the same thing over and over thinking you'll get a different outcome. But what if there was something else, divine inspiration, which could make us choose differently next time?'

The boy tied a rubber tube around his upper arm. 'You sound like a believer, Simon Kefas.'

'I don't know, I'm only asking. What I do know is that your father's intentions were good, no matter how harshly you judge him. He wanted to make a better life not just for himself, but for the three of you. Love was his downfall. And now you judge yourself just as harshly because you think you're his copy. But you're not your father. Just because he failed morally doesn't mean that you will. A son's responsibility isn't to be like his father, but to be better than him.'

The boy sank his teeth into the end of the rubber tube. 'Perhaps, but why does it matter now?' he said out of the corner of his mouth, pulling his head back so that the tube tightened and the veins on his forearm stood out. He held the syringe in an underhand grip with his thumb on the top of the plunger and the needle resting against the inside of his middle finger. Like a Chinese table-tennis player, Simon thought. He held the syringe with his right hand, even though he was left-handed, but Simon knew that junkies had to learn to shoot up with both hands.

'It matters because it's your turn to choose now, Sonny. Do you insert that needle? Or do you help me get the Twin? And the real mole?'

A drop glistened at the tip of the needle. From the street came the sound of traffic and laughter, from the neighbouring room quiet pillow talk. The calm summer pulse of the city.

'I'll set up a meeting where both the Twin and the mole will be present. But I can't do it unless you're alive, you're the bait.'

The boy didn't appear to have heard him, he had bowed his head and was practically curling around the syringe, getting ready for the high. Simon braced himself. And was surprised when he heard the boy's voice:

'Who is he, the mole?'

Simon felt a pain in his chest and realised that he had forgotten to breathe.

'You'll find out if you turn up, not before. I know what you're going through, Sonny. But there is always a point where things can no longer be put off, where you can't be weak one more day and promise yourself that tomorrow, tomorrow you will start that other life.'

Sonny shook his head. 'There won't be another life.'

Simon stared at the syringe. And that was when he realised. It was an overdose.

'Do you want to die without knowing, Sonny?'

The boy raised his gaze from the syringe and up to Simon.

'Look where knowing has got me, Kefas.'

'Is this it?' Åsmund Bjørnstad asked as he leaned across the steering wheel. He read the sign above the entrance. 'The Bismarck Hotel?'

'Yes,' Kari said and undid her seat belt.

'And you're sure this is where he is?'

'Simon wanted to know which hotels in Kvadraturen had guests paying cash. I guessed that he must know something, so I called the six hotels and sent them pictures of Sonny Lofthus.'

'And got a hit with the Bismarck?'

'The receptionist confirmed that the man in the picture is staying in room 216. He also said that a police officer had already been there and had accessed the room. That the hotel had done a deal with the police officer which he expected us to honour.'

'Simon Kefas?'

'I'm afraid so.'

'All right, we'd better get going.' Åsmund Bjørnstad picked up the police radio and pressed the talk button. 'Delta, come in.'

The loudspeaker crackled. 'Delta here. Over.'

'I give you permission to enter. It's room 216.'

'Received. We're going in. Over and out.'

Bjørnstad put down the police radio.

'What are their orders?' Kari said, sensing how tight her shirt felt.

'To prioritise their own safety, shoot to kill if necessary. Where are you going?'

'To get some fresh air.'

Kari crossed the street. In front of her ran police officers dressed in black and holding MP5 machine guns; some went into the hotel's reception, some into the yard where the back stairs and the fire exit were located. She walked through reception and was halfway up the stairs when she heard the crash of a door being smashed in and the dull bang of stun grenades. She continued up the stairs and along the corridor and heard the crackling of police radios: 'The area is cleared and secured.'

She turned into the room.

Four police officers: one in the bathroom, three in the bedroom. All wardrobes and windows opened. No one else. No possessions left behind. The guest had checked out.

Markus was sitting on his haunches, looking for frogs in the grass when he saw the Son come out of the yellow house and walk towards him. The afternoon sun hung so low over the roof that when the Son stopped in front of Markus, it looked as if it was shining out of his head. He was smiling, and Markus was pleased that he no longer looked as miserable as he had earlier that day.

'It was nice meeting you, Markus.'

'Are you going now?'

'Yes, I have to.'

'Why do you always have to go?' he burst out before he could stop himself.

The Son squatted down as well and put his hand on Markus's shoulder. 'I remember your father, Markus.'

'You do?' Markus said, sounding unconvinced.

'Yes. And no matter what your mother might say or think, he was always nice to me. Once he chased away a huge bull elk that had strayed from the forest and come into the neighbourhood.'

'He did?'

'Single-handedly.'

Then Markus saw a strange sight. Behind the Son's head, in the open bedroom window in the yellow house, the thin white curtains billowed out. Even though there was no wind at all. The Son got up, ruffled Markus's hair and started walking down the road. Swinging a briefcase as he whistled. Something caught Markus's eye, and he turned towards the house again. The curtains were on fire. And now he saw that the other windows were also open. All of them.

A bull elk, Markus thought. My father chased away a bull elk.

The house made a noise as if it was sucking in air. The sound took on rumbling undertones and then singing overtones that gained strength and turned into menacing, triumphant music. And how they jumped and twirled behind the black windows now, the yellow ballerinas already celebrating the downfall, Judgement Day.

Simon put the car in neutral and let the engine idle.

Further down the street, outside his house, was another car. A new, blue Ford Mondeo. Tinted windows at the back. An identical model had been parked outside the Eye Unit at the hospital. It could be a coincidence, of course, but he knew that Oslo Police had purchased eight Ford Mondeos last year. With tinted windows at the back so that you couldn't see the flashing blue light that was kept behind the rear headrest.

Simon grabbed the mobile lying on the passenger seat.

The call was answered before the phone had rung twice.

'What do you want?'

'Hello, Pontius. It must be very frustrating for you that my phone keeps moving.'

'Stop this lunacy now, Simon, and I promise you it won't have consequences.'

'None at all?'

'Not if you call it off now. Do we have a deal?'

'You always wanted to do deals, Pontius. Well, I've got a deal for you. Turn up at a restaurant tomorrow morning.'

'What's on the menu?'

'A couple of criminals whose arrest will be a feather in your cap.'

'Be more specific?'

'No. But I will give you an address and a time if you promise to bring only one person. My colleague, Kari Adel.'

There was silence for a moment.

'Are you trying to set me up, Simon?'

'Have I ever? Remember, you stand to win a great deal. Or more accurately: you have a lot to lose if you let these people get away.'

'Do I have your word that we're not walking into an ambush?'

'Yes. Do you think I would let anything happen to Kari?'

Pause.

'No. No, you never had that in you, Simon.'

'I guess that's why I never made it to Commissioner.'

'Very funny. When and where?'

'Seven fifteen. Aker Brygge, number 86. See you there.'

Simon opened the side window, tossed out the phone and saw it disappear over a neighbouring fence. In the distance he could hear the sound of fire engines.

Then he put the car in gear and revved the engine.

He drove westwards. At Smestad he took the exit to Holmenkollåsen. Zigzagged up to the viewpoint that had always given him a sense of perspective.

The Honda had been removed by now and the CSOs had finished their work.

After all, it was no longer a crime scene.

Not for a murder, anyway.

Simon parked the car so that he had a view of the fjord and the sunset.

As it started to grow dark, Oslo began to look more and more like a dying fire with glowing red and yellow embers. Simon pulled up the collar on his coat and reclined the seat. He had to try to get some sleep. Tomorrow was a big day.

The biggest of them all.

If luck was on their side.

'Try this one,' Martha said, handing the young man a jacket.

He was relatively new, she had only seen him here once before. Twenty years old, possibly, but he would be lucky if he lived to see twenty-five. Or at least that was the general opinion of the others in reception at the Ila Centre.

'Great, it suits you!' she smiled. 'Try wearing it with these, perhaps?' She handed him a pair of jeans, barely worn. She became aware that someone was standing behind her and turned round. He must have entered through the cafe, perhaps he had been standing in the doorway to the clothing storeroom, watching her for a while. The suit and the bandage around his head were enough to get him noticed, but Martha didn't even see them.

All she saw was his intense, hungry gaze.

Everything she didn't want. Everything she wanted.

Lars Gilberg turned over in his brand-new sleeping bag. The shop assistant in the outdoor store had looked sceptically at the thousand-krone note before accepting it and handing him the miraculous sleeping bag.

Gilberg blinked. 'You're back,' he declared. 'Jesus, you turned Hindu?' His voice echoed sharply under the arches of the bridge.

'Perhaps,' the boy smiled and squatted down beside him. 'I need a place to sleep tonight.'

'Be my guest. Though you look as if you could afford a hotel.'

'They'll find me there.'

'There's plenty of room here and no surveillance.'

'Can I borrow some of your newspapers, please? I mean, if you've read them, that is.'

Gilberg chuckled. 'You can borrow my trusty old snoozie – I use it as a mattress now.' He pulled the old, dilapidated and filthy sleeping bag out from underneath him. 'Know what? You take the new one and I'll sleep in the old one tonight. There's a little too much of me in the old one, know what I mean?'

'Are you sure?'

'Yes, old snoozie is missing me.'

'Thank you so much, Lars.'

Lars Gilberg just smiled in return.

And when he lay down, he felt a pleasant warmth that didn't come from the sleeping bag. It came from inside him.

It sounded as if the corridors heaved a collective sigh when all the cell doors at Staten were simultaneously locked for the night.

Johannes Halden sat down on his bed. It made no difference what he did. Sitting, lying or standing, the pain was the same. And he knew that it wouldn't go away, but would only grow worse with each passing day. His disease was visible now. The cancer in his lungs had been joined by a tumour the size of a golf ball in his groin.

Arild Franck had been true to his word. As a punishment for helping the boy escape, Johannes would be eaten up by cancer in his cell without medical attention or pain relief. It was possible that Franck might send him to the sickbay when he felt that Halden had suffered long enough and could die at any moment, simply to avoid having to register a death in a cell in his annual report.

It was very quiet. Camera-monitored and quiet. In the old days prison officers would do rounds after lockdown and hearing their footsteps had been comforting. One of the officers at Ullersmo Prison, Håvelsmo, an older, religious man, used to sing on his rounds. Old hymns in a deep baritone. It was the best lullaby a long-term prisoner could get, even the most psychotic ones stopped screaming when they heard Håvelsmo walk down the corridors. Johannes wished that Håvelsmo was here now. He wished that the boy was here now. But he wasn't complaining. The boy had given him what he wanted. Forgiveness. And a lullaby on top of that.

He held the syringe up to the light.

The lullaby.

The boy had told him that he'd got it in a Bible from the prison chaplain, the late Per Vollan – may his tormented soul find peace – and that this was the purest heroin available in Oslo. Then he had shown him how to inject it when the time came.

Johannes put the needle on top of a thick blue vein in his arm. He took a trembling breath.

So this was all there was, this was his life. A life which could have been so different if he hadn't said yes to smuggling the two sacks from Songkhla Port. Strange. Would he have said yes today?

No. But the man he once was had said yes. Over and over again. So it could be no other way.

He pressed the needle against the skin, shuddered slightly when he saw the skin yield and the needle slide in. Then he pressed the plunger down. Evenly and calmly. It was important to empty the syringe completely.

The first thing that happened was that the pain went away. As if by magic.

Then the second thing happened.

And he finally understood what the others had been talking about. The high. The free fall. The embrace. Could it really be that simple, that all this time it had only been one needle prick away? Had she only been one needle prick away? Because she was here now, in her silk dress, with her shiny black hair, her almond eyes. And her tender voice that whispered the difficult English words with soft cherry lips. Johannes Halden closed his eyes and collapsed on the bed.

Her kiss.

It was all he had ever wanted.

Markus stared at the TV.

They were talking about all the people who had been killed in the last few weeks, it was on the TV and the radio all the time. His mum had told him not to watch it so much, it would only give him nightmares. But he didn't have nightmares any more. And now he was on the telly and Markus had recognised him. He was sitting at a table covered with microphones answering questions and Markus remembered him because of his frameless glasses. Markus didn't know what any of it meant or how it all went together. All he knew was that the man wouldn't have to come over to turn on the heating in the yellow house now that it had burned down.

PART FIVE

42

AT 6.35 A.M., BEATRICE JONASEN, receptionist at Tomte & Øhre Solicitors, strangled a yawn while she tried to remember what film the woman in the trench coat in front of her reminded her of. Something with Audrey Hepburn. *Breakfast at Tiffany's?* The woman also wore a silk scarf and sunglasses that gave her a sixties look. She placed a bag on the counter, said it was for Jan Øhre as arranged, and left.

Half an hour later the sun bounced off the windows of Oslo town hall's red-brick facade, the first ferries docked at Aker Brygge and commuters from Nesoddtangen, Son and Drøbak poured ashore on their way to work. It was going to be another cloudless day, but there was a crispness in the air, a hint that not even this summer would last forever. Two men walked side by side along the prom-enade between the piers, passing restaurants with chairs still upside down on tables, clothes shops that wouldn't open for another couple of hours and street vendors unpacking and preparing for the last onslaught on the capital's tourists. The younger of the two men was wearing an elegant, but crumpled and stained, grey suit. The older wore a checked jacket bought in a sale at Dressmann and trousers that matched it only in terms of price. They wore identical sunglasses bought at a petrol station twenty minutes earlier, and were carrying identical briefcases.

The two men turned into a deserted alleyway. Fifty metres into it they walked down a narrow iron staircase to the modest door of a restaurant which, judging by the discreet sign, appeared to serve fish and seafood. The older man tried the door, but found it was locked. He knocked. A face, distorted as if in a funfair mirror, appeared on the other side of the porthole in the door. The lips moved and the words sounded as if they came from underwater: 'Hold up your hands where I can see them.'

They did as he said and the door was opened.

The man was blond and stocky. The pair looked down at the pistol he was pointing at them.

'Nice to see you again,' said the older man in the checked jacket and pushed his sunglasses up on his forehead.

'Come in,' the blond man said.

They entered and two men in black suits immediately started patting them down while the blond man leaned casually against the cloakroom counter, but without ever lowering his pistol.

A pistol was taken from the older man's shoulder holster and handed to the blond man.

'This one's clean,' said the other man in the black suit, nodding towards the young man. 'But he has some bandage thing round his waist.'

The blond man stared at the young man. 'So you're, like, the Buddha with the Sword, yeah? The Angel from Hell, eh?' The young man said nothing. The blond man spat on the floor in front of his shiny, black Vass shoes. 'Good nickname – looks like someone stitched a fucking crucifix on your forehead.'

'And on yours.'

The blond man frowned. 'What the fuck do you mean, Buddha?'

'Can't you feel it?'

454

The blond man took a step forward and raised himself up on his toes so that their noses almost touched.

'Now now,' the older man said.

'Shut up, grandad,' the blond man said, pulling aside the young man's jacket and shirt. His fingers slowly probed the bandage around his waist.

'Here?' he asked when his hand had reached the young man's side.

Two beads of sweat appeared on the young man's forehead above his sunglasses. The blond man prodded the bandage. The young man opened his mouth, but no sound came out.

The blond man snarled. 'Yep, here it is.' He dug his fingers in, squeezed the flesh and pulled.

A hoarse rattling came from the young man.

'Bo, he's waiting,' one of the others reminded him.

'Yeah, yeah,' the blond man said softly without taking his eyes off the young man who was gasping for air. The blond man pressed harder. A single tear rolled down the pale cheek under the young man's sunglasses.

'Greetings from Sylvester and Evgeni,' the blond man whispered. Then he released his grip and turned to the others.

'Take their briefcases and bring them in.'

The new arrivals handed over their briefcases and entered the dining room.

The older man instinctively slowed down.

The silhouette of a man, a big man, was outlined against the green light from the aquarium where colourful fish darted back and forth and a crystal sparkled on a large white stone with long grasses that waved in the current from the bubbles. Lobsters with wired claws lay on the bottom.

'Like I promised you . . .' the older man whispered. 'Here he is.'

'But where's the mole?' the young man said.

'Trust me, he'll be here.'

'Chief Inspector Simon Kefas,' the big man thundered. 'And Sonny Lofthus. I've been waiting a long time for this. Sit down.'

The young man moved more stiffly than the older as they stepped forward and took their seats opposite the big man.

Another man slipped in silently through the swing door to the kitchen. Broad-shouldered and with a bull neck like the other three. 'They came alone,' he said and positioned himself with the rest of the welcoming committee so that they formed a semicircle behind the two newcomers.

'Too bright for you in here, is it?' said the big man, addressing the young man who was still wearing his sunglasses.

'I can see everything I want to see, thank you,' the young man replied in a deadpan voice.

'Good answer – I wish I had your young, fresh eyes.' The big man pointed to his own eyes. 'Did you know that the eyes' sensitivity to light is reduced by thirty per cent before you've even turned fifty? Viewed like that life is a journey towards the darkness, not the light, yes? No pun intended as far as your wife is concerned, Chief Inspector Kefas. That's why we have to learn to navigate life without being able to see as soon as we can. We must acquire the mole's ability to use our other senses to see what obstacles and threats lie ahead of us, yes?'

He flung his arms out. It was like watching a JCB with two buckets.

'Or you could, of course, buy yourself a mole to see for you. The problem with moles is that they tend to stay underground, so they're easy to lose. That's how I lost mine. No idea what happened to him. And I understand that you've been looking for him as well, yes?'

The young man shrugged.

'Let me guess. Kefas talked you into coming here by promising you the mole, yes?'

The older man cleared his throat. 'Sonny is here of his own

volition because he wants to make peace. He thinks he has avenged his father. And that the parties should now go their separate ways. In order to show that he's serious, he's prepared to give back the money and the drugs he took. In return, the hunt for him will be called off. Could we have the briefcases, please?'

The big man nodded to the blond man who put the two brief-cases on the table. The older man reached for one of the briefcases, but the blond man pushed his hand away.

'As you wish,' said the older man, holding up his palms. 'I just wanted to show you that Mr Lofthus has brought you a third of the drugs and a third of the money for now. You'll get the rest when he has your promise of a truce and gets to walk out of here alive.'

Kari switched off the ignition in the car. Looked up at the neon sign of the former shipyard where red letters spelled out A-k-e-r B-r-y-g-g-e. People were flowing out from the ferry which had just arrived.

'Is it really safe for the Commissioner to meet with criminals without backup?'

'Like a friend of mine used to say,' Pontius Parr replied, checking his pistol before he put it back in the shoulder holster, '*no risk, no reward.*'

'That sounds like Simon,' Kari said and looked at the clock at the top of the town hall tower. 7.10.

'Correct,' Parr said. 'And do you know something, Adel? I have a feeling today will earn us many plaudits. I want you to accompany me to the press conference afterwards. The Commissioner and the young female officer.' He smacked his lips as if he was tasting something. 'Yes, I think that will go down well.' He opened the passenger door and got out.

Kari almost had to run along the promenade to keep up with him.

*   *   *

'Well?' the older man said. 'Do we have a deal? You get back what was taken from you and Lofthus gets safe passage so he can leave the country.'

'And you get a small commission for brokering the deal, yes?' The big man smiled.

'Exactly.'

'Mm.' The big man looked at Simon as if searching for something he couldn't find. 'Bo, open the briefcases.'

Bo stepped forward and tried to open the first one. 'It's locked, boss.'

'1,' the young man said in a soft, almost whispering voice, '9-9-9.'

Bo rotated the metal cylinders. Flipped up the lid. Swivelled the briefcase around to his boss.

'There we are,' the big man said, holding up one of the white bags. 'A third. And where is the rest?'

'In a secret location,' the older man said.

'Of course it is. And the code to the briefcase with the money?'

'The same,' the young man said.

'1999. The year your father passed away, yes?'

The young man said nothing.

'OK?' said the older man, forcing a smile and clapping his hands. 'Can we go now?'

'I thought we would eat together,' the big man said. 'You like lobster, don't you?'

No reactions.

He sighed. 'Frankly, I don't like lobster, either. But do you know something? I still eat it. Why? Because it's expected of a man in my position.' The suit jacket pulled back from his mighty chest as he threw his arms out. 'Lobster, caviar, champagne. Ferraris with missing spare parts, ex-models demanding divorce settlements. The loneliness on the yacht, the heat of the Seychelles. We do a lot of things we don't really want to, yes? But it's necessary to keep up the motivation. Not mine, but the motivation of the people who work for me. They need to see these symbols of success – of what I have achieved, of what they can achieve, if they do their job, yes?'

The big man stuck a cigarette in between his fleshy lips. The cigarette looked strangely small against his big head. 'But, of course, these status symbols are also there to remind potential rivals and opponents of my power. It's the same with violence and brutality. I don't like it. But sometimes it's necessary to maintain motivation. Incentivise people to pay me what they owe me. Induce them not to work against me . . .' He lit the cigarette with a pistol lighter. 'For example, there was a man who used to modify weapons for me. He retired. I accept that a man would rather fix motorbikes than make guns. What I can't accept is that he then gives an Uzi to someone he knows has already killed several of my men.'

The big man tapped the aquarium glass.

The young and the older man's gaze followed his finger. The young man jumped in his chair. The older man just stared.

The white stone with the undulating grass growing from it. It wasn't a stone. And the reflection didn't come from a crystal. But from a gold tooth.

'Now some people might think decapitating a man is excessive, but if you want to instil loyalty in your staff, sometimes you have to go the extra mile. I'm sure you'll agree with me, Chief Inspector.'

'I beg your pardon?' the older man said.

The big man tilted his head and studied him. 'Trouble hearing, Chief Inspector?'

The older man shifted his gaze from the aquarium back to the big man. 'Old age, I'm afraid. So if you could speak up, that would be helpful.'

The Twin laughed in surprise. 'Speak up?' He took a drag of his cigarette and looked across to the blond man.

'Did you check them for wires?'

'Yes, boss. We also checked the restaurant.'

'Then you're going deaf, Kefas. What's going to happen to you and your wife when . . . what's the saying? The blind will be leading the deaf?'

He looked around with his eyebrows raised and the four men immediately burst out laughing.

'They laugh because they're scared of me,' the big man said, addressing the young man. 'Are you scared, boy?'

The young man said nothing.

The older man glanced at his watch.

Kari glanced at her watch. 7.14. Parr had stressed that they had to be on time.

'This is it,' Parr said, pointing to the name at the front. He went up to the door of the restaurant and held it open for Kari.

It was dark and quiet in the cloakroom, but she could hear a voice coming from a room further down the corridor.

Parr took his pistol out of the shoulder holster and signalled to Kari to do the same. She knew stories were going around the station about her performance with the shotgun at Enerhaugen, so she had explained to the Commissioner that she, despite the evidence, was a novice in armed raids. But he had responded that Simon had insisted that she – and only she – should accompany him and added that in nine out of ten cases it was enough to show your warrant card. And in ninety-nine out of a hundred cases enough to show it along with a weapon. Even so, Kari's heart was pounding wildly as they moved swiftly down the corridor.

The voice fell quiet as they entered the dining room.

'Police!' Parr said, aiming the pistol at the people sitting at the only occupied table. Kari had taken two steps to the side and had the bigger of the two men in her sights. For one moment it was completely quiet except for Johnny Cash's voice and 'Give My Love to Rose' pouring out of a small speaker on the wall between the buffet and the stuffed head of a long-horned ox. A steak restaurant serving breakfast. The two men at the table, both wearing pale grey suits, looked at them in surprise. Kari realised that they weren't the only customers in the bright room after all; at a table by the window overlooking the seafront, an elderly couple looked like they were having a simultaneous heart attack. We must be in the wrong place, Kari thought. This couldn't possibly be the restaurant Simon wanted them to go to. Then the smaller of the two men dabbed his mouth with his napkin and spoke.

'Thank you for coming here in person, Commissioner. I can assure you that neither of us is armed or has evil intentions.'

'Who are you?' Parr thundered.

'My name is Jan Øhre, I'm a lawyer and I represent this gentleman, Iver Iversen Senior.' He extended his hand towards the taller man and Kari immediately recognised the likeness to Iversen Junior.

'What are you doing here?'

'The same as you, I presume.'

'Really? I was told there were criminals on the menu.'

'And that's a promise we intend to keep, Parr.'

'Well,' the big man said, 'you *should* be scared.'

He nodded to the blond man who pulled a slim, long-bladed knife from his belt, took a step forward, put his arm around the young man's forehead and pressed the knife against his throat.

'Do you really think I care about you stealing a bit of loose change from me, Lofthus? Forget the money and the drugs. I've promised Bo that he gets to cut you into little pieces, and I regard the lost drugs and the money as a good investment. A good investment in motivation, yes? There are several ways we can do this, of course, but you'll suffer a less painful death if you tell us what you did with Sylvester so that we can give him a Christian burial. So, what's it to be?'

The young man gulped, but said nothing.

The big man banged the table with his fist so the glasses jumped. 'Are you deaf as well?'

'Perhaps he is,' said the blond man whose face was right by the young man's ear sticking up under the arm he had wrapped around him. 'Buddha here is wearing earplugs.'

The others laughed.

The big man shook his head in despair while he scrolled his way to the code on the other briefcase.

'He's yours, Bo, cut him up.' There was a ping when the big man opened the briefcase, but the men were too focused on Bo's knife to notice the small metal pin falling from the inside of the briefcase and bouncing across the stone floor.

'Your tiny, clever mother is right about a lot of things, but wrong as far as you're concerned,' Simon said. 'She never should have let the devil's child suck her tits.'

'What the h—' the big man began. His men turned round. In the briefcase, next to a pistol and an Uzi, lay an olive-green object that looked like a handlebar grip of a bicycle.

The big man looked up again, just in time to see the older man flip down the sunglasses from his forehead.

'It's correct that I agreed with Chief Inspector Simon Kefas to meet you here with my client,' Jan Øhre said, having shown Pontius Parr ID to prove that he was indeed a lawyer. 'Didn't he tell you?'

'No,' Pontius Parr said. Kari could see the confusion and anger in Parr's face. Øhre exchanged glances with his client. 'Am I to take it that you don't know about our deal, either?'

'What deal?'

'Our plea bargain for a reduced sentence.'

Parr shook his head. 'All Simon Kefas told me was that I would have a couple of criminals handed to me on a plate. So what's this about?'

Øhre was about to reply when Iver Iversen leaned over and whispered something in his ear. Øhre nodded and Iversen sat back in his chair again and closed his eyes. Kari studied him. He looked broken, she thought. Beaten, resigned.

Øhre cleared his throat. 'Chief Inspector Kefas believes he has some . . . eh, evidence against my client and his late wife. It concerns a number of property transactions with a party by the name of Levi Thou. Perhaps better known by his nickname, the Twin.'

Thou, Kari thought. Not a common name, and yet she had heard it recently. Someone she had said hello to. Someone at the police station.

'Kefas also claims to have evidence of an alleged hit which he believes Agnete Iversen ordered. Kefas said that out of consideration for Iversen's son, he would refrain from presenting proof of the latter, and as far as the property transactions are concerned my client will be given a reduced sentence in return for a guilty plea and for giving evidence against Thou in a subsequent trial.'

Pontius Parr took off his rectangular glasses and polished them with his handkerchief. Kari was surprised at how childishly blue his eyes were.

'It sounds like an deal we can honour.'

'Good,' Øhre said, opened the briefcase that was lying on the chair next to him, took out an envelope and pushed it across the table to Parr.

'Here is a printout of all property transactions undertaken to launder money for Levi Thou. Iversen is also prepared to testify against Fredrik Ansgar, formerly of the Serious Fraud Office, who made sure that no one ever investigated the transactions.'

Parr took the envelope. Squeezed it.

'There's something else inside,' he said.

'A memory stick. It contains a sound file which Kefas sent to my client from a mobile, and which he requested should also be handed over to you.'

'Do you know what's on it?'

Øhre and Iversen exchanged looks again. Iversen cleared his throat.

'It's a recording of someone. Chief Inspector Kefas said that you would know who it was.'

'I brought along a computer in case you wanted to listen to it straight away,' Øhre added.

The open briefcase. The weapons. The olive-green grenade.

Chief Inspector Simon Kefas had time to press his eyes shut and cover his ears. There was a flash of light that felt like fire breathing on his face and a bang like a punch to the stomach.

Then he opened his eyes, lunged forward, grabbed the pistol from the briefcase and turned round. The blond man was frozen, as if he had just stared straight into the eyes of Medusa. He still had his arm around Sonny's head and the knife in his hand. And Simon saw it now, Sonny had been right: the guy really did have a cross on his forehead. A cross-hairs sight. Simon pulled the trigger and saw the hole the bullet made below the blond fringe. As the man fell, Sonny grabbed the Uzi.

Simon had explained to him that they would have a maximum of two seconds before the temporary paralysis would lift. They had sat in the hotel room at the Bismarck and practised this very moment, seizing the weapons and discharging them. They hadn't been able to predict the sequence of events in detail, obviously, and right up until the point where the Twin opened the briefcase, triggering the stun grenade, Simon had been sure that it would all go to hell. But when he saw Sonny pull the trigger and pirouette on one foot, he knew that the Twin wouldn't go home happy after this day at work. The bullets spat from the stuttering weapon that never made it past the first syllable. Two of the Twin's men were already down, and the third had managed to stick his hand inside his jacket when the spray of bullets drew a dotted line across his chest. He remained standing for a moment before his knees received the message that he was dead, and by then Simon had already turned to the Twin. And stared in astonishment at the empty chair. How could such a big man move so—

He spotted him at the end of the aquarium, right by the swing door to the kitchen.

He took aim and pressed the trigger three times in quick succession. He saw the Twin's jacket twitch and then the glass in the aquarium cracked. For a moment it looked as if the water might retain its rectangular shape, held together by habit or unseen forces, before it came crashing towards them like a green wall. Simon tried to leap aside, but he was too slow. He crunched a lobster underfoot as he took a step, felt his knee buckle and fell his full length in the deluge. When he looked up again, he couldn't see the Twin, only the flapping kitchen door.

'Are you OK?' Sonny asked as he offered to help Simon back on his feet.

'Never been better,' Simon groaned and knocked aside Sonny's hand. 'But if the Twin gets away now, he'll be gone for good.'

Simon ran to the kitchen door, kicked it open and entered holding the pistol in front of him. The harsh smell of a commercial kitchen. His gaze quickly scanned the brushed metal worktops and cookers, rows of pots, ladles and palette knives hanging from the low ceiling and obstructing his view. Simon squatted down to look for shadows or movement.

'The floor,' Sonny said.

Simon looked down. Red stains on the blue-grey tiles. His eyes hadn't deceived him, one of his bullets had found its target.

He heard the distant sound of a door slamming.

'Come on.'

The blood trail led them out of the kitchen, along a dark corridor where Simon tore off his sunglasses, up a staircase and down another corridor, which ended in a metal door. A door that would have made the very noise they had just heard. Even so, Simon checked all the side doors on their way down the corridor and looked inside. Nine out of ten men fleeing from two men and an Uzi would always take the shortest and most obvious way out, but the Twin was the tenth man. Always cold, always rational and calculating. The type who survives a shipwreck. He might simply have slammed the door in order to misdirect them.

'We're losing him,' Sonny said.

'Calm down,' Simon said and opened the last side door. Nothing.

And the bloodstains were now unequivocal. The Twin was behind the metal door.

'Ready?' Simon asked.

Sonny nodded and positioned himself with the Uzi aimed right at the door.

Simon pressed his back against the wall beside the door, lowered the handle and pushed open the metal door.

He saw Sonny get hit. By the sunlight.

Simon stepped outside. He felt the wind on his face. 'Damn . . .'

They were looking out at an empty street that lay bathed in morning sunshine. The street was Ruseløkkveien which intersected Munkedamsveien and disappeared upwards in the direction of the Palace Gardens. No cars, no people.

And no Twin.

43

'THE BLOOD STOPS HERE,' SIMON said, pointing at the tarmac. The Twin must have realised he was leaving a trail of blood and managed to stop it from dripping on the ground. The type that survives a shipwreck.

He stared up at the deserted Ruseløkkveien. Let his gaze sweep past St Paul's Church, past the small bridge where the road bent and disappeared out of sight. He looked left and right across Munkedamsveien. Nothing.

'Bloody he—' Sonny slapped his thigh with the Uzi in frustration.

'If he'd stayed on the road, we would have been in time to see him,' Simon said. 'He must have gone in somewhere.'

'Where?'

'I don't know.'

'Perhaps he had a car out here.'

'Perhaps. Hey!' Simon pointed at the ground between Sonny's shoes. 'Look, there's another bloodstain. What if—'

Sonny shook his head and opened his jacket. The side of the clean shirt Simon had given him was red.

Simon swore silently. 'That bastard managed to reopen the wound?'

Sonny shrugged.

Simon let his gaze wander upwards again. There was no street parking. No shops were open. Only closed gates leading to backyards. Where could he have gone? Look at it from another perspective, Simon thought. Compensate for the blind spots. Let in . . . He shifted his gaze. His pupils reacted to something. A sharp flash of sunlight bouncing off a small piece of moving glass. Or metal. Brass.

'Come on,' Sonny said. 'We'll try the restaurant again, perhaps he—'

'No,' Simon said in a low voice. A brass door handle. A closer that makes the door shut slowly behind you. A place that is always open. 'I can see him.'

'You can?'

'The church door up there, do you see it?'

Sonny stared. 'No.'

'It's still shutting. He's inside the church. Come on.'

Simon ran. He put one foot in front of the other and took off. It was a simple action, something he had done since he was a boy. He had run and run, every year a little faster. And then, every year a little more slowly. Neither his knees nor his breathing worked together like they used to. Simon managed to keep up with Sonny for the first twenty metres, then the boy took off. He was at least fifty metres ahead when Simon saw him leap up the three steps, throw open the heavy door and disappear inside.

Simon slowed down. Waited for the bang. The staccato, almost childish sound that gunshots acquired when you heard them through a wall. It didn't come.

He walked up the steps. Pulled open the heavy door and entered.

The smell. The silence. The weight of so many thinking people's faith.

The pews were empty, but candles were lit on the altar and Simon remembered that morning mass would start in half an hour. The candles flickered over the lost Saviour on the cross. Then he heard

468

the whispering, chanting voice and turned to the left.

Sonny was sitting in the open cubicle of the confessional with the Uzi aimed at the perforated wooden board separating it from the other cubicle whose black curtain almost covered the board opening. There was only a tiny crack between the curtain and the board, but through it Simon could see a hand. And on the stone floor, from underneath the curtain, a pool of blood was slowly spreading.

Simon crept closer; he caught Sonny's whispering:

'All earthly and heavenly gods have mercy on you and forgive your sins. You will die, but the soul of the penitent sinner shall be led to Paradise. Amen.'

Silence followed.

Simon watched Sonny tighten his finger around the trigger.

Simon put his gun back in the shoulder holster. He wasn't going to do anything, not a damn thing. The boy's verdict would be pronounced and executed. His own judgement would come later.

'Yes, we killed your father.' The Twin's voice sounded feeble behind the curtain. 'We had to. The mole had told me that your father was planning to kill him. Are you listening?'

Sonny didn't reply. Simon held his breath.

'He was going to do it that very night, in the medieval ruins in Maridalen,' the Twin continued. 'The mole said that the police were on to him, that it was only a question of time before he was exposed. So he wanted us to make the killing look like a suicide. Give the impression that your father was the mole, so that the police would call off the search. I agreed to it. I had to protect my mole, yes?'

Simon saw Sonny moisten his lips: 'And who is he, this mole?'

'I don't know. I swear. We only ever communicated by email.'

'Then you won't ever know.' Sonny raised the Uzi again, curled his finger around the trigger. 'Are you ready?'

'Wait! You don't have to kill me, Sonny, I'll bleed to death in here anyway. All I ask is that I get to say goodbye to my loved ones before I die. I let your father write a note telling you and your mother that he loved you. Please, show this sinner the same mercy?'

Simon could see Sonny's chest heave and sink. The muscles rippled along his jaw line.

'Don't,' Simon called out. 'Don't give it to him, Sonny. He—'

Sonny turned to him. There was gentleness in his eyes. Helene's gentleness. He had already lowered the Uzi. 'Simon, all he's asking is—'

Simon saw movement in the gap in the curtain, the hand being raised. A gold-plated pistol lighter. And Simon knew immediately that there wasn't enough time. Not enough time to warn Sonny and for him to react, not enough time to pull out his own gun from the shoulder holster, not enough time to give Else what she deserved. He was standing on the railings of the bridge across the Aker and the river was raging under him.

So Simon dived.

He dived out of life and into the wonderful, spinning roulette wheel. It didn't take intelligence or courage, only the folly of a doomed man who is willing to gamble a future he doesn't value highly, who knows he has less to lose than others. He dived into the open cubicle between the son and the perforated wooden board. He heard the bang. Felt the bite, the paralysing sting of ice or heat tearing his body in two, connections being severed.

And then came another sound. The Uzi. Simon's head was on the floor in the cubicle and he felt wooden splinters from the board rain down on his face. He heard a scream; he lifted his head and saw the Twin stagger out of the confessional and stumble between the pews, saw the bullets nip at the back of his suit like a swarm of angry bees. Empty shells from the Uzi – still red hot – cascaded onto Simon, scorching his forehead. The Twin knocked over pews, sank down on his knees, but he kept moving. He was refusing to die. It wasn't natural. Many years ago, when Simon had learned that the mother of one of Norway's most wanted men was working inside the police station as a cleaner and had sought her out, that had been the first thing she had said: that Levi wasn't natural. She was his mother and she loved him, obviously, but he had terrified her from the moment he was born, and not just because of his size.

And she told him about that time when her young but already gigantic son had come to work with her because there was no one at home to look after him, and he had stared at his reflection in a bucket of water on the cleaning trolley and said that there was someone in there, someone who looked just like him. Sissel had suggested that perhaps they could play together and gone to empty the waste-paper baskets. When she came back Levi had stuck his head in the bucket and was desperately kicking his legs in the air. His shoulders had become lodged inside the bucket so that she had to use all her strength to pull him out. He had been soaking wet and his face had gone all blue. But instead of crying like most children would have done, he had laughed. And said that the Twin had been bad, had tried to kill him. From that moment on she had wondered where he had come from and she hadn't felt free until the day he moved out.

The Twin.

Two holes appeared right above the fat folds between his broad neck and mighty back and the movements abruptly stopped.

Of course, Simon thought. A perfectly normal only child.

And he knew that the big man was dead even before he tottered forward and his forehead hit the stone floor with a thud.

Simon closed his eyes.

'Simon, where . . . ?'

'My chest,' Simon said and coughed. He could tell from the consistency on his skin that it was blood.

'I'll get you an ambulance.'

Simon opened his eyes. He looked down at himself. Saw the deep red stain spread on his shirt front.

'I won't make it, don't bother.'

'Yes, you will—'

'Listen.' Sonny had taken out his mobile, but Simon covered it with his hand. 'I know a little too much about gunshot wounds, all right?'

Sonny put his hand on Simon's chest.

'It's no good,' Simon said. 'You run along now. You're free, you've done what you had to do.'

'No, I haven't.'

'Run for my sake,' Simon said, grabbing the boy's hand. It felt so warm and familiar, as if it were his own. 'Your job is done now.'

'Lie still.'

'I said the mole would be there today, and he was. And now he's dead. So run.'

'The ambulance will be here soon.'

'Why won't you listen—'

'If you'd just stop talking—'

'It was me, Sonny.' Simon looked up into the boy's clear, mild eyes. 'I was the mole.'

Simon waited for the boy's pupils to expand in shock, for black to displace the bright green iris. But it didn't happen. And he understood.

'You knew, Sonny.' Simon tried to swallow, but had to cough again. 'You knew it was me. How?'

Sonny wiped the blood from Simon's mouth with his shirtsleeve. 'Arild Franck.'

'Franck?'

'After I cut off his finger, he started talking.'

'Talking? He knew nothing about me. No one knew that Ab and I were the moles, Sonny, no one.'

'No, but Franck told me what he *did* know. That the mole had a code name.'

'He told you that?'

'Yes. The code name was the Diver.'

'The Diver, yes. That was the name I used when I contacted the Twin. Back then one person used to call me that, you see. Just one person. So how did you know . . . ?'

Sonny took something out of his jacket pocket. Held it up in front of Simon. It was a photograph. It had dried specks of blood on it and showed two men and a woman by a cairn, all three of them young and laughing.

'When I was a boy I'd often look through our photo album and that was where I saw this picture taken in the mountains. And I asked my mother who he was, this mysterious photographer with the exciting nickname, the Diver. And she told me. That it was Simon, the third of three best friends. That she had nicknamed him the Diver, because he dived in where no one else dared.'

'So you put two and two—'

'Franck didn't know there were two moles. But what he did tell me made everything add up. That my father was about to expose you. So you killed him before he could do it.'

Simon blinked, but the darkness continued to creep in from the outer edges of his field of vision. Even so, he could see more clearly than ever. 'So you decided to kill me. That was why you contacted me. You wanted to be sure that I would find you. You were just waiting for me.'

'Yes,' Sonny said. 'Right until I found the diary and understood that my father was in on it. That there were two of you. Two traitors.'

'Then your world fell apart and you abandoned your mission. There was no longer any reason to kill.'

Sonny nodded.

'So what made you change your mind?'

Sonny looked at him for a long time. 'Something you said. That a son's responsibility isn't to be like his father, but to be . . .'

'. . . better than him.' Simon could hear police sirens in the distance. He felt Sonny's hand on his forehead. 'So be that, Sonny. Be better than your father.'

'Simon?'

'Yes?'

'You're dying. Is there anything you want?'

'I want to give her the gift of sight.'

'And forgiveness, do you want that?'

Simon closed his eyes again, hard, and shook his head. 'I can't . . . I don't deserve it.'

'None of us does. To err is human, to forgive is divine.'

'But I'm nothing to you, I'm a stranger who took away the people you loved.'

'You are someone, you're the Diver, who was always with them, but you weren't in the picture.' The boy lifted up Simon's jacket and slipped the photograph into his inside pocket. 'Take it with you on your journey, they're your friends.'

Simon closed his eyes. He thought: That's all right with me.

The son's words echoed in the space of the empty church:

'All earthly and heavenly gods have mercy on you and forgive your sins . . .'

Simon looked at a drop of blood that had just dripped from inside the boy's jacket and onto the church floor. He moved a finger down to the drop's golden-red surface. Saw how the blood seemed to stick to his fingertip; he raised the finger to his lips and closed his eyes. Stared into the foaming, white waterfall. The water. An icy embrace. Silence, solitude. And peace. And this time he wouldn't resurface.

In the silence that followed the second playing of the recording, Kari could hear birds chirping undisturbed outside the half-open window at the far end of the steak restaurant.

The Commissioner stared at the laptop in disbelief.

474

'Yes?' Øhre asked.

'Yes,' Parr said.

The lawyer pulled out the memory stick and handed it to Parr. 'Did you recognise that voice?'

'Yes,' Parr said. 'His name is Arild Franck, and he's the man who really runs Staten Maximum Security Prison. Adel, check if that account he mentions in the Cayman Islands really exists, will you? If what he says is true, we're facing a huge scandal.'

'I'm sorry to hear that,' Øhre said.

'Not at all,' Parr said. 'I've had my suspicions for years. We were recently given information by a courageous police officer in Drammen which suggested that Lofthus was granted day release from Staten so that he could take the fall for the Morsand murder. We've been keeping this to ourselves until we were sure we had a solid case before we went after Franck, but with this we ought to have more than enough ammunition. One last thing before we go . . .'

'Yes?'

'Did Chief Inspector Kefas say why he wanted you to meet with us, rather than meet you himself?'

Iversen exchanged glances with Øhre before he shrugged. 'He said he was busy with other things. And that you were the only two colleagues he trusted one hundred per cent.'

'I understand,' Parr said and got up to leave.

'There is one more thing . . .' Øhre said and picked up his phone. 'My client mentioned my name to Chief Inspector Kefas who contacted me to ask if I could organise transport and the payment for an eye operation he has arranged at the Howell Clinic in Baltimore tomorrow. I said I would. And I have a message from our receptionist who informs me that a woman arrived at our office an hour ago and handed over a red sports bag. The bag contains a considerable amount of cash. I just want to know if this is something the police would like to follow up?'

Kari was aware that the birdsong outside the window had stopped and been replaced by distant sirens. Several of them. Police cars.

Parr cleared his throat. 'I don't see how this information could be relevant to the police. And since the person who made the request must now be regarded as your client, then you have, as far as I'm concerned, attorney–client privilege and you would be unable to give me any more information were I to ask.'

'Excellent. Then we have the same understanding of the situation,' Øhre said and closed his briefcase.

Kari felt her mobile vibrate in her pocket, got up quickly, stepped away from the table and took out the phone. The marble came out with the phone and hit the wooden floor with a soft thud.

'Adel.'

She stared at the marble which seemed to hesitate, not knowing whether to move or stay where it was. But after a little quivering, it wobbled unsteadily in a southern direction.

'Thank you,' Kari said and put the phone back in her pocket. She turned to Parr who was about to get up. 'There are four dead bodies at a fish restaurant called Nautilus.'

Parr blinked four times behind his glasses and Kari wondered whether it was some kind of compulsive reaction, to blink once for every new body on his patch.

'Where is that?'

'Here.'

'Here?'

'Here on Aker Brygge. It's just a couple of hundred metres away.' Kari's eyes had found the marble again.

'Let's go.'

She wanted to run over and pick up the marble.

'What are you waiting for, Adel? Come on!'

The marble had acquired a steady course and was gaining speed; if she didn't make up her mind quickly, she would lose it.

'OK,' she said and rushed after Parr. The police sirens were louder now, the noise rose and sank, cut through the air like a scythe.

They ran outside, out into the white sunshine, into a morning full of promise, into the blue city. They kept running and the morning rush of people parted in front of them. Faces flickered in and out of Kari's field of vision. And something at the back of her brain reacted to one of them. Sunglasses and a pale grey suit. Parr was aiming for the alleyway where they had seen several uniformed police officers hurry inside. Kari stopped, turned round and saw the back of the grey suit board the ferry to Nesoddtangen which was about to sail. Then she turned back and ran on.

Martha had put down the hood of the convertible and was leaning her head against the neck rest. She looked at a seagull hovering in the wind between the blue sky and the blue fjord. Balancing the forces, its own and the external ones, as it scouted for food. Her breathing was deep and steady, but her heart was pounding because the ferry was about to dock. Not many people sailed from Oslo to Nesoddtangen this early in the morning, so he wouldn't be difficult to spot. If he had pulled it off. *If.* She muttered the prayer she had repeated ever since leaving Tomte & Øhre one and a half hours ago. He hadn't been on the previous ferry thirty minutes ago, but she had told herself that would have been too much to hope for. But if he wasn't on this one . . . Yes, then what? She had no plan B. Hadn't wanted one.

The passengers appeared. Yes, she was right, they weren't many, people tended to travel *into* the city in the morning, not out. She took off her tortoiseshell sunglasses. Her heart skipped a beat when she saw the pale grey suit. But it wasn't him.

Her heart sank.

Then another grey suit appeared.

He was stooping slightly as if he had taken in water and was listing.

She felt her heart swell in her chest and force sobs up her throat. Perhaps it was just the slanted morning light on his pale grey suit, but he looked as if he was glowing.

'Thank you,' she whispered. 'Thank you, thank you.'

She looked in the rear-view mirror, dried her tears and straightened her headscarf. Then she waved. And he waved back.

And as he walked up the hill to where she was parked, a thought occurred to her: that it was too good to be true. That she was looking at a mirage, a ghost, that he was dead, shot, that right now he was hanging from a lighthouse, crucified, and that she was looking at his soul.

He got into the car with great care and took off his sunglasses. He was pale. And she could tell from his red eyes that he had been crying. Then he flung his arms around her and pulled her close. At first she thought it must be her before she realised that the trembling was coming from his body.

'How—?'

'Fine,' he said, without letting go of her. 'Everything went fine.'

They sat in silence, clinging together like two people whose only fixed point is the other. She wanted to ask questions, but not now. There would be plenty of time for that later.

'Now what?' she whispered.

'Now,' he said, gently releasing her and sitting upright with a low groan. 'Now it starts. That's a big suitcase.' He nodded to the back seat.

'Only the bare essentials,' she smiled, pushed the CD into the CD player and handed him the mobile. 'I'll drive the first stretch. Will you be map reader?'

He looked at the display on the mobile as the flat, robotic voice started chanting: '*Your own . . . personal . . .*'

'1,030 kilometres,' he said. 'Estimated driving time twelve hours and fifty-one minutes.'

EPILOGUE

THE SNOWFLAKES SEEMED TO RISE from a colourless, bottom-less sky and stick to a roof of tarmac, pavement, cars and houses.

Kari was bending down on the steps and had just laced up her ankle boots so she got an upside-down view of the street between her legs. Simon had been right. You saw things differently when you changed your perspective and location. All blind spots could be compensated for. It had taken her time to realise it. To realise that Simon Kefas had been right about so many things. Not every-thing. But to an irritatingly high degree.

She straightened up.

'Have a great day, darling,' said the girl in the doorway and gave Kari a kiss on the lips.

'You too.'

'Sanding down floors probably isn't compatible with having a *great* day. But I'll try. When will you be home?'

'Dinner time, unless something happens.'

'Fine, though it looks as if something just did.'

Kari turned in the direction Sam was pointing. The car that had pulled up outside the gate was familiar and the face above the lowered side window even more so.

'What's up, Åsmund?' Sam called out.

'I'm sorry to interrupt your DIY, but I need to borrow your lady,' the inspector called back to her. 'Something's happened.'

Kari looked at Sam who slapped the back pocket of her jeans. Kari had hung up her skirt and suit jacket in the wardrobe back in the autumn and, for some reason, there they had stayed.

'Off you go and serve the public, girl.'

As they drove east on the E18, Kari stared at the snow-covered landscape. Thought about how the first snow always marked a dividing line, hiding everything that had been there before and changing the world you looked at. The months that followed the shootings at Aker Brygge and the Catholic church had been chaotic. Criticism had, not unexpectedly, been levelled at the police, charges of brutality and one man's insane mission. But, even so, Simon had been given a hero's funeral, he was the people's policeman, someone who had fought the city's criminals, laid down his life in the service of justice. As Commissioner Parr had said in his eulogy the public was prepared to overlook the fact that he hadn't followed the rule book down to the last detail. Or Norwegian law, for that matter. Parr could afford a certain moral flexibility given that he himself had pushed the boundaries of Norwegian tax legislation by placing some of his own money in anonymous trusts registered to the Cayman Islands. Kari had confronted Parr at the wake because her investigation into who paid the utility bills for Lofthus's house had led eventually her to him. And Parr had confessed to it on the spot, adding only that no laws had been broken and that his motive had been purely altruistic; to ease his own conscience for not taking care of Sonny and his mother after Ab's suicide. Parr said that it hadn't been cheap, but it meant that the boy would have a habitable house to live in once he had finished serving his sentence.

After a while people also began to accept that the Buddha with the Sword had vanished without a trace. His crusade appeared to have ended with the death of Levi Thou, also known as the Twin.

Else's sight was much better now. She had told Kari, who visited her some weeks after the funeral, that the operation in the US had been eighty per cent successful. That almost nothing was perfect. Not life, not people, not Simon. Only love.

'He never forgot her. Helene. She was the love of his life.' It had still been summer and they had sat on recliners in Else's garden in Disen, drinking port and watching the sun go down. And Kari had realised that Else had made a decision to share this with her. 'He told me that the two others who courted her, Ab and Pontius, were nicer, stronger, cleverer. But that he was the one who saw her as she really was. That was the strange thing about Simon. He saw people, he saw their angels and demons. While at the same time he fought his own demon, of course. Simon was a gambling addict.'

'He told me.'

'He and Helene started seeing each other, but his gambling debt made their lives chaotic. It didn't last long, but Simon felt he was dragging her down with him when Ab Lofthus came along and saved her from him. Ab and Helene moved out. Simon was heart-broken. And shortly afterwards he learned that she was pregnant. He gambled like a maniac, lost everything and was on the verge of the abyss. Then he sought out the devil and offered him the only thing he had left. His soul.'

'He went to the Twin?'

'Yes. Simon was one of the few people who knew who the Twin was and how to contact him. But the Twin never knew who Simon and Ab were, the information they gave him was delivered either through telephone calls or by letters. In time via the computer.'

The hum of traffic from Trondheimsveien and Sinsenkrysset reached them in the silence that followed.

'Simon and I told each other everything, but it was difficult for him to talk about this. How he had sold his soul. He believed that deep down he *desired* the shame, the degradation, the self-loathing, that it numbed the other pain. That it was a form of mental self-harm.'

She smoothed her dress. She looked so fragile and yet so strong as she sat there, Kari thought.

'But the worst for Simon was what he did to Ab. He hated Ab because he took from him the only thing that had ever had any value to him. He dragged Ab with him down into the abyss. Ab and Helene were deep in debt when the banking crisis came and interest rates shot up; only one thing could save them from home-lessness and that was quick money. So after Simon had struck a deal with the Twin, he went straight to Ab and made him an offer for his soul. At first Ab refused and threatened to report Simon to their boss. Then Simon used Ab's Achilles heel. His son. He said that this was how the real world was, and that his son would pay the price for his father's pride and grow up poor. Simon said that had been the worst thing, to watch Ab being eaten up, lose his soul. But also that it had made him feel less lonely. Right until the Twin wanted his mole to rise up the ranks in the police force, and then there was no longer room for two.'

'Why are you telling me this, Else?'

'Because he asked me to. He thought you ought to know before you made your choice.'

'He asked you to do it? Did he know that he was going to . . . ?'

'I don't know, Kari. He just said that he saw so much of himself in you. He wanted you to learn from his mistakes as a police officer.'

'But he knew I wasn't going to stay in the police force.'

'Aren't you?' The rays of sunlight gleamed dully in the port as Else raised her glass to her lips, sipping it carefully before putting it down again.

'When Simon realised that Ab Lofthus was willing to kill him to take the only spot with the Twin, he contacted the Twin and said he had to eliminate Ab, that Ab was on to both of them, that it was urgent. He said that he and Ab were like identical twins who had the same nightmare, which was that each was trying to kill the other. So he beat Ab to it. Simon killed his best friend.'

Kari swallowed. Fighting the tears. 'But he repented,' she whispered.

'Yes, he repented. He stopped being the mole. He could have continued. But then Helene died. Simon had reached the end of the road, he had lost everything there was to lose. So there was no longer anything to be scared of. And he spent the rest of his life doing penance. Making amends. And he was merciless in hunting down those who were corrupt, like he had once been, and that doesn't earn you many friends in the police force. He grew lonely. But he never felt sorry for himself, he thought loneliness was what he deserved. I remember him saying that self-loathing is the kind of hatred you feel every morning when you wake up and look at yourself in the mirror.'

'You saved him, didn't you?'

'He called me his angel. But it wasn't my love for him that saved him. Completely the opposite of what so-called wise men say, I'll argue that being loved never saved anyone. It was his love of me that did it. He saved himself.'

'By loving you back.'

'Amen.'

They sat outside until midnight, when Kari left.

On the way out, in the hallway, Else had shown her the photograph. Three people in front of a cairn.

'Simon had this on him when he died. There she is, Helene.'

'I saw a photo of her in the yellow house before it burned down. I told Simon that she looked like a singer or an actress.'

'Mia Farrow. He took me to see *Rosemary's Baby*, just so he could look at her. Even though he claimed he couldn't see the likeness.'

The photograph moved Kari strangely. It was something about their smiles. The optimism. The *faith*.

'You and Simon never talked about having children?'

She shook her head. 'He was scared.'

'Of what?'

'That his own vices would be passed down. The addiction gene. The destructive risk-taking. The lack of boundaries. The black moods. I guess he feared it might be the devil's child. I used to tease him and say he must have an illegitimate child somewhere and that was why he was scared.'

Kari had nodded. *Rosemary's Baby*. She had remembered the little old lady who cleaned at the police station and whose name had eventually come back to her.

Then Kari had said goodbye to Else and gone out into the summer night where first a mild breeze, and then time, had picked her up and whirled her away until she sat here, in a car, looking out at the virgin snow and thinking how it transformed the whole landscape. How often things turned out differently from what you had planned. She and Sam were already trying for a baby. To her own amazement, she had declined not only an interesting job offer from the Justice Department, but also a job with a huge salary with an insurance company.

It wasn't until they had left Oslo and driven across the small bridge and up the gravel path, that she asked Åsmund what had happened.

'Drammen Police called and asked us to assist them,' Åsmund said. 'The victim is a shipowner. Yngve Morsand.'

'Good God, it's the husband.'

'Yes.'

'Murder? Suicide?'

'I don't know the details.'

They parked behind the police cars, walked through the gate in the picket fence and up to the front door of the big house. They were met by an inspector from Buskerud Police. He hugged Kari and introduced himself to Bjørnstad as Henrik Westad.

'Could it be a suicide?' Kari asked on the way in.

'What makes you say that?' Westad said.

'Grief at the loss of his wife,' Kari answered. 'Because people suspected him of killing her, or that he actually did kill her and couldn't live with it.'

'It's possible . . .' Westad said as he ushered them into the living room.

The CSOs were practically crawling all over the man in the chair. Like white maggots, Kari thought.

'. . . but I doubt it,' Westad completed his sentence.

Kari and Bjørnstad stared at the body.

'Bloody hell,' Bjørnstad said in a low voice to Kari. 'Do you think that . . . he . . .?'

Kari thought about the hard-boiled egg she had had for breakfast. Or perhaps she was already pregnant; maybe that could explain why she felt so sick? She pushed the thought aside and concentrated on the body. It had one wide-open eye, a black patch over the other, and over the eyelid there was a jagged edge where the top of the head had been sawn off.

Jo Nesbo is a musician, songwriter, economist and prize-winning author. *The Bat*, his first crime novel, was published in Norway in 1997 and was an instant hit. His bestselling Harry Hole series has been a huge success in the UK and across the world, while his standalone crime novel, *Headhunters*, was made into an award-winning film.

www.jo-nesbo.co.uk

Charlotte Barslund is a translator of Scandinavian plays and novels. Her translation of *Calling Out For You* by Karin Fossum was nominated for the Crime Writers' Association Gold Dagger award, while her translation of *I Curse the River of Time* by Per Petterson was shortlisted for the *Independent* Foreign Fiction award.